DATE DUE

JY 9 '97			
FE 10 '98			
*			

OTHERSYDE

BOOKS BY J. MICHAEL STRACZYNSKI

OtherSyde
Demon Night
Tales from the New Twilight Zone
It's Getting Dark (1991)
The Complete Book of Scriptwriting

J. MICHAEL STRACZYNSKI

OTHERSYDE

DUTTON   NEW YORK

DUTTON

Published by the Penguin Group
Penguin Books USA Inc., 375 Hudson Street, New York, New York 10014 U.S.A.
Penguin Books Ltd, 27 Wrights Lane, London W8 5TZ, England
Penguin Books Australia Ltd, Ringwood, Victoria, Australia
Penguin Books Canada Ltd, 2801 John Street, Markham, Ontario, Canada L3R 1B4
Penguin Books (N.Z.) Ltd, 182–190 Wairau Road, Auckland 10, New Zealand

Penguin Books Ltd, Registered Offices:
Harmondsworth, Middlesex, England

First published by Dutton,
an imprint of
New American Library,
A Division of Penguin Books, USA, Inc.

First printing, June, 1990
1 3 5 7 9 10 8 6 4 2

Library of Congress Cataloging-in-Publication Data

Straczynski, J. Michael, 1954–
OtherSyde / J. Michael Straczynski. — 1st ed.
p.   cm.
ISBN 0-525-24873-0
I. Title.
PS3569.T6758085   1990
813'.54—dc20   89-26055
                                                  CIP
Printed in the United States of America
Set in Weiss
Designed by Steven N. Stathakis

Publisher's Note: This novel is a work of fiction. Names, characters, places, and incidents either are the product of the author's imagination or are used fictitiously, and any resemblance to actual persons, living or dead, events, or locales is entirely coincidental.

If we accept for a moment that we are most truly defined as individuals during the years just prior to entering the world as adults, then it should come as no surprise that this book deals with that period of time—and a great many other things, some of them dangerous and many-toothed. Given this subject matter, therefore, it is only proper that this novel is dedicated to

The Class and Faculty of Chula Vista High School
Class of '72

In particular: to teachers Jo Ann Massie and Rochelle Terry, who first taught me to hear the music. Also to teachers Dennis Renfro, John Head, Valerie Russel, and even Leonard Hummelman.

To those fellow students who welcomed me and made the experience what it could, and should be . . . as well as to those who made the experience what it should *not* have been.

Nothing is ever forgotten.

Finally, to the crowd at Fifth and E Streets, the wounded and the lost, who made it out alive or with at least some part of their souls intact. The pain goes on, but so does the work, and I guess it all balances out.

And with a nod to Lennox High School, Los Angeles, California, attended prior to CVHS, for one very nervous year.

J. MICHAEL STRACZYNSKI
Los Angeles, California
January 1, 1990

ACKNOWLEDGMENTS

No book comes into existence in a vacuum. As in a marathon, there are those who stand ready beside the long road, offering a word or a suggestion or a cup of Gatorade to keep you going. Without them and their kind, no book would ever be written, no tale told. Theirs are the unseen faces that do not appear on dust jackets or talk shows, and no awards have yet been devised to recognize and honor their contribution. All an author has to offer in return for services rendered is gratitude, and a few words in this space, too often passed over in the rush to begin the adventure.

So if the story pleases you, return here and note the names. They share responsibility. And blame.

Richard Marek, first and foremost, who commissioned and believed in this book; Henry Morrison, Candy Monteiro, and Fredda Rose, Demon Agents, who on my behalf have endured madness and contracts with stoic silence; Harlan and Susan Ellison, for kindnesses and friendship and support, who regularly showed up at my doorstep with pastries and magic in equal supply to fuel the writing; Mark Orwoll, who was there in the beginning, through the terrible years of false starts, and who perhaps most truly understands what all this means; Kathy Selbert, who read and encouraged through the dark times when the words seemed not to come; Larry DiTillio, whom I am honored to call my closest friend; and finally, most especially, Kathryn Drennan, who has illuminated my existence, never allowing me the self-indulgent luxury of doubt.

Thank you all.

jms

PROLOGUE

Now there was a day when the sons of God came to present themselves before the Lord, and Satan came also among them.

And the Lord said unto Satan, Whence comest thou? Then Satan answered the Lord and said, From going to and fro in the earth, and from walking up and down in it.

The Book of Job, 1:6-7

Tony Soznick steadied his hand long enough to put down his coffee and slide into the booth. He was better now than earlier, but he was still shaking. He wondered if the kid working the cash register had noticed. *Probably figures me for some drunk coming in for a doughnut between binges.*

He sighed, and tried to remember the taste of alcohol. It slipped away from him, and all he came up with was the memory of bile. But at least it was a *memory*, and he was grateful for that much.

God, how he needed a drink.

But it wouldn't let him, would it?

Slowly, methodically, he emptied his pockets onto the plastic table, counting change and stray bills, looking for hotel stubs, plane, train, or bus tickets, anything that would tell him where he'd been the last two months.

He'd have thought he would be used to it by now. But every time it happened, the terrifying sense of dislocation was just as strong as the time before.

Two months ago, he'd gone to sleep in his one-room flat on Sixteenth Street in Chicago. It had been ice cold for that time of year. That much he remembered. He'd pulled the thin sheets around him, and looked out through the window at the blinking red sign that flashed LIVE! DANCING! NUDE GIRLS! He found its rhythmic, constant presence reassuring; whenever he woke up it would be there, welcoming him, and each night it would be there to lull him to sleep. So he'd been looking out the window, and it was there for him as always, until something—

That was where it always broke down. As before, there was a sense of movement, of *something* in the dark. (Or was it only in his mind? Where *did* the darkness live? And where did it hide during the in-between times?) The only thing he remembered was squinting into the night as the familiar neon light grew indistinct. He tried to hold on to it, but it slipped away like quicksilver and the darkness fell upon him, as it always did.

And then he woke up.

And it was hot.

And it was two months later.

And now he was in Los Angeles, in the doughnut shop behind the hotel where he'd found himself in a different set of clothes, wearing a beard he'd grown during the intervening time, without any memory of how he got here, or where he'd been, or . . .

Say it.

. . .what he'd done.

He picked up the coffee. It was still hot enough to sear his throat going down, but he drank it anyway. He finished half the cup and set it down, wondering idly if he should get a doughnut to go with it. But he wasn't hungry, which meant he must have eaten recently. That was good. He remembered the time he'd awakened in Miami so malnourished he could barely move. The doctor had said it looked as if he hadn't eaten in nearly a week. He wondered what was even now digesting in his stomach. Hamburgers? Pot pie? Perhaps a choice cut of steak from one of the more fashionable restaurants in Beverly Hills?

He started to giggle, cut the impulse off at the source.

Get on with it, he thought. You know the routine.

He finished the inventory. Three hundred and twenty-five dollars, mostly in singles, some twenties, one fifty and one hundred dollar bill. He looked at the hundred dollar bill for a long time; something about it made him nervous. Where could he have gotten such a thing? How?

He found a bunch of quarters in a back pocket, along with a hotel room key. FOUR ACES INN, RENO, NEVADA, the tag said, which meant he had taken an overland route this time, no planes. He wondered if he'd had any luck at the slots.

His shirt pocket had a scrap of paper on which something had been scrawled in his handwriting, but he couldn't make sense of it. He stuffed it back into his pocket in case it might become clear later.

That was all of it, the complete extent of his possessions, and the only clues he had to the missing two months. He sometimes thought that it was for the best that he *didn't* know where he'd been during those interludes—the six months between when he'd gone to sleep in San Francisco and awakened in New Orleans, the three weeks between Philadelphia and Maine, the nine weeks between Boulder and Cleveland . . .

What if he *were* to figure it out? What if he were to go back, retrace his steps? What would he find? What terrible things might he have done, never remembering having done them?

That was the greatest terror: the fear that he might have done something . . . *bad* during those missing weeks and months, a fear only marginally balanced by his hope that in fact he had done nothing more than sleep on park benches and under freeways. After all, if he *had* done anything . . . anything *bad*, wouldn't the police be after him? Wouldn't he be in jail by now?

But he wasn't about to go to the police and try to find out. He remembered what had happened last time he'd tried. He'd gone to sleep the night before he was to go to the police, and awakened five weeks later in Butte, Montana, in the middle of the worst storm they'd had in years, wearing only thin slacks and a sweater.

It wasn't going to let him off that easily.

He stuffed the money back into his pockets, and slid out of the booth, glancing through the window of the doughnut shop across to a telephone pole. There it was, plastered on the splintered wood face— a sign covered top to bottom in fine, tiny handwriting. He knew, even from here, that the words would be written with almost painfully precise lettering, that the lines would slant down and to the right, and that none of the words would make sense.

Knew it because it was the same sign he'd seen on telephone poles and walls and bus stops in Butte, and Boulder, and Cleveland, and San Francisco, and all the rest.

And because there were at least five hundred more up in his hotel room.

He tossed the empty Styrofoam cup on his way out of the dough-nut shop, and walked across the street to the office supply store. He would need glue, lots of it, and a staple gun.

It was time to get to work.

BOOK ONE
THE ARRIVAL

For now should I have lain still and been quiet, I should have slept: then had I been at rest, with Kings and counsellors of the earth, which built desolate places for themselves.

The Book of Job, 3:13-14

1

"It'll be just fine, dear; you'll see."

Chris Martino *hmmmmed* absently at the voice from the other room, counting down the seconds until he would have to leave for the school bus. It was a game he played. Somehow, counting the seconds made the time seem to pass more slowly. But today there was something cruel, even relentless in the way the seconds flashed by on his digital watch, a present from his recent sixteenth birthday. It had been one of several surprises that day. *Happy birthday, kid—now pack your bags, we're moving to California!*

Some present.

From his mother's bedroom came the sound of dresser drawers and closet doors being opened and slammed shut in a rush. It was appropriate that they would begin their new lives—he at Lennox High, she at the office where she had been hired as a legal secretary—on the same day.

"Chris?" she called. "Better get ready. Have you got everything? Pens? Paper? Notebook?"

"Yeah, Mom," he called back, not bothering to check. He had gone over his supplies last night, in detail. Making the adjustment from Matawan, New Jersey, to Los Angeles may have left him mentally unprepared, but by god he would have sharp pencils! "All set."

Still, he was thankful that he had lucked into the Lennox school district rather than Inglewood High. It was a matter of only a couple of city blocks, but the distance made all the difference. He'd heard that the gangs were a lot rougher in Inglewood.

The door opened behind him, and his mother stepped out, wearing a robe over her dress and pulling pins from her hair. Though she didn't have to leave for another half-hour, she believed in being dressed well in advance. Mom was big on being prepared. The smell of perfume wafted through the door with her, a little strong. He hoped it wouldn't cling to his clothes.

Dressed up, he supposed she could be considered pretty. Some of the other kids back in Matawan had called her a real fox, which he kind of resented—after all, this was his *mother* they were talking about.

Pretty or not, though, she had better keep her perfume far away. Oh lord, if the other kids got a whiff of it on him—

"Well, sport," she said, smiling, "it's time!"

He nodded, seeing the reflection of her statement in the final tick of his watch. *It's time.* Wasn't that what they said to convicted murderers on Death Row?

With a peck on the cheek and the traditional chuck on the chin (he'd have to talk to her about that one of these days), he headed outside and down to the corner. After a few minutes, a dirty-yellow bus shuddered to a halt at the corner where he'd been told it would stop. Its doors belched open like dragon jaws, swallowing him and the two other waiting kids—sophomores, he guessed, and therefore beneath notice—then snapped shut behind them.

He found an empty seat and levered himself into it, hoping not to attract attention. Back home—back in Matawan—a new kid was always noticed, especially if he showed up mid-semester, like now. But no one even glanced at him. Maybe people in California came and went with such frequency that strangers were the rule rather than the exception.

So had his efforts *not* to attract attention actually caused him to stand out? He glanced around at the other occupants of the bus. Across the aisle, a pair of kids were punching each other in the shoulder to see who could take it the longest, someone else was listening to a radio, and a bunch more in back were laughing about something. He could smell grass, but couldn't see who had it. Then he found the source—a big kid, maybe a senior. He held the joint cupped in one hand, out of sight, then brought the cigarette up and took a drag in a move that was at once furtive and arrogant. It seemed to say, I know this stuff is illegal, but in another year it'll be a misdemeanor at best, therefore it's not worth the hassle to stop me, therefore go fuck yourself.

Abruptly, Chris realized that he was meeting the older kid's gaze.

Ohmygod I was staring . . .

"What're you staring at, shithead?" the older, heavier boy said.

"Nothing," Chris said, quickly turning his attention out through the window, to where a line of palm trees whizzed past. He felt like kicking himself. He hadn't even gotten to school yet, and already he'd antagonized somebody. He shut his eyes, feeling the familiar embarrassment, then opened them again.

More palm trees.

When they'd first arrived in Los Angeles, he couldn't get enough of the high, thin trees that seemed to grow everywhere, lining both major boulevards and tiny residential streets.

Right now, he hated the very sight of them.

2

Chris glanced at the index of classes he'd been sent earlier by the school, feeling helpless and confused. Home Room was in Room 638. Back in Matawan that would have meant the sixth floor, but here, the school was spread out, and none of the buildings were over two stories tall. He counted seven long, flat, off-green buildings in addition to the gymnasium and the cafeteria; all of them looked the same. It would take him weeks to learn his way around.

He sighed. Room 638 was out there—somewhere. But right now it could be on Mars for all the good it did him.

Not wanting to ask anyone on the bus for directions, he had hoped to blunder into either the right room or some sort of map. So far his search had gone unrewarded, and the bell announcing the start of Home Room had sounded three minutes ago. The covered walks were mostly empty, except for a few other students hurrying to class, a teacher's aide pushing a film projecter to its logged-in destination . . .

And the sudden voice of God Incarnate.

"You'd better have a good reason for being out here." The teacher seemed to have simply materialized, so abruptly did he come around the corner. Probably lying in wait for me, Chris thought. Probably does this a lot, just for fun. He was a square, stocky man who wore a thin tie over a white shirt, the sleeves rolled up to a point just above his elbows. His face was framed by a thick jaw and an impossibly flat crew-cut.

Ex-Marine, Chris decided.

Chris held out his schedule, the pink sheet limp in his hand, feeling like some ancient, none-too-bright swordsman confronting a troll with a paper knife. "I'm—"

He didn't have time to finish the sentence. The teacher snatched the paper from his hands, glanced at it briefly, and handed it back. "There," he said, pointing over Chris's shoulder.

"Thanks," Chris said, and started to turn away.

"I suggest you pick up a map of the campus at the administration office before first period."

Chris nodded, smiled. It was what he did best under such circumstances, and he saw no reason to change his strategy. "Right."

"Just so you don't have any excuses next time I catch you wandering around when you should be in class. And I'd better not catch you. Is that clear?"

Chris nodded, smiled.

"I'm *Mister* Huntington," he said, stressing the "Mister." Chris didn't know anyone could actually speak in italics. "Just so you'll know . . . One more thing—I keep a baseball bat in my classroom."

Mr. Huntington disappeared around the corner, vanishing like some terrible specter sent to welcome him properly and, having done its job, returning to whatever darkness had first spawned it. But why make a point of mentioning the baseball bat?

Unless . . .

"Oh, shit," Chris muttered, and glanced at his schedule: AMERICAN HISTORY, ROOM 314, 13:00. C. HUNTINGTON.

Chris stuffed the schedule into his shirt pocket, wondered how many more things could go wrong in one day, and set off across the yard for room 638.

Five full minutes late.

"Christopher Martino?"

The teacher was seated at the front of Room 638, Chris's home room. G. EDWARDS, the schedule had said. He was mildly relieved to see that G. EDWARDS seemed to know how to smile, a trait unacquired by C. HUNTINGTON. From the door, Chris couldn't see a baseball bat, either.

But that proved nothing. Teachers were a sneaky bunch.

One wall of the classroom was mostly window, looking out on the athletic field. The room was bright and airy, but still smelled the same as every classroom he'd ever been in. Something about the interrelationships of chalk and plastic chairs, he concluded, wishing he could sit down.

But G. EDWARDS wasn't finished with him yet.

"You're late."

When in doubt . . . Chris throught, and nodded. Smiled.

Someone in the back of the room snickered.

"I'll let it go this time because you're new, but let's not make this a habit, all right?" Edwards said, and glanced down at his seating chart. "Do you prefer Christopher or Chris?"

"Chris, I guess."

"All right, Chris it is." He made a note in his chart. "We don't go alphabetically here, so pick whatever available seat you'd like."

Chris glanced over at the rows of seats, at the faces that turned toward him, and felt himself go vague. The faces blurred. He wished he were anywhere else rather than standing here, in front of everyone, feeling stupid.

He started toward an empty seat at the back of the room, feeling them watching him. Thankfully, he did not trip. He reached the desk, slid his books into the rack below the seat, and sat—to the sound of sudden, loud laughter.

"He did it!" someone said.

"I don't believe it! Right next to Horseface!"

Chris looked across the aisle at the boy beside him. It was true. The kid *did* look a little horsey. But what did that—

"You know what they say—birds of a feather!" And this time, Chris got a good look at the speaker. It was the same kid who had been smoking the joint on the bus. He looked across two rows at Chris. "What're you staring at, shithead?"

There was more laughter, diminishing only with movement at the front of the room. "All right, that's enough," Edwards said. "Chris is new to California—and this isn't exactly what I'd call a warm welcome."

Why is he going on like this? Chris wondered, wishing they would just move on to something else. Wishing that the earth would open up and swallow him whole.

No such luck.

4

Lunch came mercifully soon. Picking up a hamburger, a pint of milk, and a slice of apple pie at the concession end of the cafeteria, Chris carried his tray in search of a likely place to eat in relative peace. He spotted a pleasant greensward just the other side of an archway, and started toward it.

"I wouldn't do that if I were you."

He turned to the source of the unwanted advice, recognizing the kid as the one the others had referred to as Horseface. He was sitting on a slight rise, beneath a eucalyptus tree, chewing on a sandwich. "Why not? It's a free country."

"Not around here, it's not." He pointed past Chris to the green-sward. "Senior Park. The Green. Only seniors allowed. Set one foot in there and in thirty seconds they'll have you in that trash can over there." He took another bite. "Thirty seconds exactly. I timed it."

Chris gave Senior Park a brief look. Another eleven months before he could sit in that place of status that could not be taken from him because it was his simply by virtue of being the right age.

For now, he was the wrong age.

And he had a decision to make: Horseface—or whatever his real name was—had just saved him considerable trauma. It was only polite to stop here and have lunch. He certainly could use someone who knew the ins and outs of Lennox High.

But someone called *Horseface?*

What the hell, he thought, and headed up the rise, sitting not far from Horseface. "Thanks," he said, unwrapping the hamburger.

"Forget it. I'd just rather not give those assholes any more op-

14

portunities to show off." He took another bite of his sandwich. "You're Chris, right?"

"Right. Chris Martino."

"Italian?"

"One half, yeah."

"Well, I guess I won't hold that against you." He took a sip from a can of Pepsi. Close up, Chris could see how he got the nickname Horseface. His jaw stuck out, and his head was squared toward the back, giving the impression that his whole face was sloping to a point around the mouth—a muzzle effect. His hair was dark, and looked as if it hadn't been washed in a while. He wore thick, tortoise-shell glasses and a gray shirt over what looked like heavy green work pants. "The name's Roger. Roger Obst. Rog is okay. Obst is acceptable. Horseface is not. It means you're no smarter than the rest of those jerks, and I'd rather not waste my time. Got it?"

"Got it. So how come you don't talk like anybody else I've met?"

"You mean the absence of 'fer shurr's and 'uh's? Damned right. You just watch. All those jocks who can't read, can't write, can't think much beyond what's on TV—in ten years they'll be pumping gas at the stations I drive into in my Volvo. I'll hit the full-serve line, not the self-serve, and the whole time they're washing my windshield, I'll be laughing my ass off."

Chris looked up. "You drive a Volvo?"

"Well, not yet," Roger admitted. "But as soon as I'm out of here I'm going to start working on it. I said *ten* years, not next year. Just wait." He crunched the lunch sack into a ball and balanced it atop his Pepsi can. "You from around here?"

"New Jersey. A place called Matawan—you've probably never heard of it."

"You're right. How was it?"

"Okay. I liked the mascot better—a husky. Our colors were maroon and silver. Looked great." He glanced at the drawing on the book cover he'd picked up when his mother had brought him to be enrolled. A helmet and lance. The Lennox Lancers. Dark yellow and blue. A crummy combination.

Rog made a disgusted noise in the back of his throat. "Who gives a shit about mascots? It's just a part of the game, that's all. Get everyone all fired up over nothing. 'We're the Lancers, so we're better than the Huskies!' Bullshit. Who cares? What's it got to do with anything?"

Chris cut a response off at the knees. No point in defending Matawan, that was gone now. And what had Matawan done for *him* lately? The last thing he wanted was to come across like some gee-whiz rah-rah kid. That had always been his problem before. So he said nothing. Just looked down again to the book cover wrapping his assigned *Adventures in Reading*.

Dirty-yellow and blue.

"Shit," he muttered, and returned to his hamburger.

"Exactly," Rog said. "Egg-zactly."

2

Susan Warrick brushed a few bread crumbs from her uniform, then sat forward in despair at the sight in front of her. "That's going to kill you, you know."

"Then I'll die happy," Jordan said. He stuffed the last of the chili dog into his mouth, then gestured to the waiter for another salvo. "Sure you don't want one? It'll put hair on your chest."

"Pass."

"Last chance. It'll make you a better cop."

She drummed her fingernails on the table. "I'd remind you that we're both armed. Pursue this any further and it could turn messy."

"Point taken," Jordan said.

The Legends Deli on Hollywood near Highland was one of their favorite stops when they went 10-10 for lunch, even if it was a bit of a drive from their usual beat. Short of Pink's hot dog stand, it was one of the best places to get a proper hot dog. A *proper* hot dog, as Jordan explained, meant kosher beef, chili just short of eye-watering, mustard, relish, onions, and anything else that wasn't nailed down or on fire. Susan wondered how his stomach could stand the abuse, three times a week. She'd read something about spontaneous combustion once— people who went up in flames for no discernible reason—and since meeting Jordan Cayle she'd wondered if they had been habitual chili dog eaters.

She groaned as the next dog arrived, and the waiter took away her plate, bearing the remains of her tuna on rye.

"So how'd last night go?" Jordan asked.

"Okay, I guess. My friend Karen set me up with him. An entertainment attorney, works over at ICM. A nice guy."

"Think you'll see him again?"

"I—it's hard to say. Maybe. I haven't thought about it a lot." In truth, it had been an unexceptional night all around. He'd spent nearly as much time talking about his ex-wife as he did his work, and hadn't asked her more than two questions the whole night. So she had sat, and listened, and counted the seconds until the end of the evening.

The only thing that made it worthwhile was the look on his face when he found out he wouldn't be spending the night. He'd been genuinely surprised. After all, as he'd let drop several times during the evening, he earned in the upper six figures. Of course she would want to go to bed with him.

The midnight movie on channel 5 had never looked so good.

She picked her nightstick up off the seat. "Think I'll take a walk."

"Don't go far."

"I won't. You're welcome to come, you know."

"Pass. I think I'll just sit here and recover from lunch."

"Okay. See you in twenty."

Outside the deli, it was painfully bright. Eighty-five in the shade. Unusually high for September in LA, thanks to the Santa Ana winds. A couple of skateboarders shot past her, slowing considerably at the sight of a badge. One of them nudged the other, called back a wolf whistle before zipping around the corner.

There's just something about a woman in uniform, she guessed.

From the deli she walked west, toward Highland and the Chinese Theater, stopping in to say hello at the restaurants and gift shops. Prior to their reassignment to the Inglewood Precinct, this had been their beat, and she quickly stepped into the familiar role as beat cop. It was one she liked.

In a city as big as Los Angeles, patrol cars were a necessity. But she always felt cut off when she was inside a unit. She'd grown up remembering the cop who used to stop and buy lemonade at her stand when she was a girl. He knew her name, and her family, and her friends, and what time school let out, and when she was supposed to be inside, and when somebody who didn't belong in the neighborhood was hanging around. He made her feel *safe*, that if she ever got into trouble, all she'd have to do was yell, and he'd be there, looming big against the sky, her personal bodyguard.

Since becoming a cop herself, she'd always tried to return the favor.

She was just looking in on the cashier working the Snow White cafeteria when the walkie-talkie on her hip beeped. She snatched it up, cued the receiver. The dispatcher's voice crackled over the speaker. "Two-David-seven, four-fifteen-F at 16115 Century, see the manager, code two."

She punched the SEND button. "Ten-four."

She backtracked at a run, hitting the parking lot in front of Legends just as Jordan was pulling out. She jumped into the passenger seat and slammed the door. Jordan hit lights and sirens and sped south toward the freeway.

"Domestic," Jordan said. "Man, I hate domestics."

Susan nodded. It was the kind of call she worried about the most. You never knew what you were going to walk into on a domestic. A kid caught trying to run away from home. A husband/wife squabble that escalated into violence. Somebody who thought somebody else's TV was up too loud, and figured to let the cops do the dirty work for them. Drunks, wife beaters, husband beaters, abusers, druggies, loud-mouths, yoyos, bozos, yipyops, and kadodies. Domestic had 'em all.

It was an apartment building, one of the two-story brownstones that lined some of LA's older streets. Brick courtyard, no air conditioning, renters who came and went with regularity. Jordan took the stairs to the second floor, Susan following. If there weren't a lot of steps to climb, better to avoid elevators where possible. Too enclosed. They reached the second floor, and found a crowd congregated in the middle of the hall. Shouts came from down the corridor, behind the closed doors of an apartment, the words too muffled to make out.

Susan buttonholed the man nearest her: heavy-set, in T-shirt and work pants. "Where's the manager?"

He turned toward her. "You found him." He nodded at the far door. "Apartment 207. Alla time he's been here, he's been quiet. Now, boom! He starts yellin' about a gun, about killin' everybody."

A gun. Why was there always a gun?

"What's his name? Who does he have in there?"

"Frank something-or-other. Just by himself, I think. He's got the door locked from inside, don't know what he's gonna do."

Jordan came up beside her. "I heard. Radioed for backup. Better give me a hand here, the lookey-loos don't want to go away."

"You got it." They started toward the crowd. "All right everybody, get back, please give us some room. There might be some danger. Please, everyone—"

She didn't have time to repeat the order. A gunshot from Apartment 207 scattered everyone. The bullet slammed into a fire door behind her. She dropped, hugging the wall. Jordan tucked-and-rolled to the other side of the hall. There were cries of panic from the crowd; they raced back into their apartments.

Told you, Susan thought, service revolver in hand. The door to 207 was open a crack—just enough to fire out a shot and check the results. She didn't dare fire back; no way of telling who was behind the door, in the line of fire.

"Leave me *alone!*" It was Frank's voice. "It's no use, don't you understand? No goddamned use!"

"How's that?" Susan called back, wishing their backup would get here with the negotiating team. This was their jurisdiction, not hers. Except that she was here, and they weren't. "What's no use? Frank? That is your name, isn't it? Frank?"

Silence.

Jordan held up his gun, let Frank see it wasn't aimed at him. "Listen—why don't you tell us about it? Maybe it's not as hopeless as you think. Maybe we can find some solutions."

From inside the apartment: sobbing. "Liars! Can't you see what's going on? It's over! For all of us! It's all closing in on us, getting dark. I won't let it happen to me! I won't!"

Susan edged forward, trying to see through the crack. "I can understand your concern, Frank, but you're going about this all wrong. You're scaring people, Frank. Your friends. Your neighbors. If you don't want anybody to suffer, then why don't you open the door so we can discuss this." She slid forward another half-inch.

"Stay back!"

Susan froze. "Okay, okay. I'm not moving. Just trying to get a little more comfortable—kind of in an awkward position."

No response.

"If you could just tell me what's wrong, maybe I could help," she said. "In a little while this place will be swarming with people—reporters, TV people, everyone. They'll want to understand, too. If I can tell them something, that'll help. You want them to know what you're doing, don't you? And why? I can talk to them for you, so they won't think the wrong sort of things about you."

Another long pause. When Frank's voice came again, it sounded not angry, but tired. Scared. "Just—just tell 'em I saw it. Started last week. The blood. God, blood everywhere, so thick you could drown in it. And there were—*things* that talked to me, told me what was going to happen. *Showed* me. Oh god, so—horrible. Fire, everywhere. Smoke, and fire, and everybody dying. At first, I was scared—I didn't know what to . . ." His voice faded out for a moment, then came back.

"I love my family. Just tell them that, all right?"

"I won't have to. You'll—"

"I just couldn't let them see it happen to me. Not with what's coming. I can't."

Then, from inside the apartment: laughter.

Abruptly, the door slammed. With the sudden movement, Susan got a whiff of it for the first time.

Gasoline.

"Shit!"

Jordan was moving up the hall, toward the door.

"No! Get *down*!" She leapt at him, tackling him mid-body.

They hit the ground and rolled as the fireball erupted, exploding out of the gas-soaked room like a living thing. The impact blew out the door, hurling papers and debris down the hall like shrapnel.

Smoke billowed out, choking her lungs. She scrambled to her feet. There were screams all around them.

"Got to get everybody out of here!" Jordan yelled over the roar of the flames.

Susan nodded, trying to get her bearings. They quickly began backtracking, checking apartments, and retreating from the oven that had moments before been Apartment 207. Christ, she thought distantly, he must've had at least a dozen gas cans in there, big ones. The smoke thickened quickly; she couldn't see. It surrounded her,

21

choking off her breath. She dropped, seeking fresh air, and crawled forward on her hands and knees.

It became almost impossible to keep going. The floor tilted under her, her eyes were tearing, and her lungs felt ready to explode. She hit a wall, couldn't figure out which way was out, and she was getting so tired, so hard to think—

She heard someone calling her name. Then her hand found someone's leg. Next thing she knew, she was being hauled to her feet and rushed forward. Jordan, his face barely visible under an oxygen mask, threw her arm over his shoulder and dragged her down the corridor and downstairs, to the street outside. Fire trucks were lined up in front of the building, pouring water through the shattered windows upstairs.

"You okay?" he asked her.

She nodded, fighting for breath. Her throat was raw, hot. Someone gave her an oxygen mask. She sucked air as if it were water. It felt good.

"Anybody alive inside?"

"Not now," she said. Down the street, squad cars were arriving in force. People stood beyond the barricades, looking up at the flames curling from the second floor. Windows on both sides of the apartment had exploded from the heat, spraying glass everywhere.

Bits of paper floated down from the exploded apartment. Some of it landed at their feet. She glanced down at what was left of a scorched sheet of paper, a flier by the look of it, covered in tight, precise handwriting.

hat there will be nothing left, and in the end there is just the darkness and Jesus said He loved everyone but there are some even Jesus does not love and John 3:1 lied where are you do you feel it its not in your thoughts its real and its here and we're real and you know they hate but to hate is to fall but is that not better than being crucified listen listen there is no love there is no hate there is only me and there is only you listen listen

Gibberish.

Smoke and fire, he had yelled through the doorway. And he had been right. Only it had been a self-fulfilling prophecy. Another End-of-the-World nut determined to destroy his own personal universe in order to see the prediction through.

He must have been in terrible torment, she thought. In that moment just before the door slammed shut, and he'd laughed, he had sounded so relieved, so calm. Almost happy.

Why? she wondered, knowing there would never be an answer.

There never was.

3

Three-twenty.

God, how Roger hated three-twenty.

It was the worst kind of irony. Three-twenty P.M. was when school let out; it was supposed to be a happy time, when he was at last freed from the company of cretins, freed to go home and read or work on his models or stop by the newsstand and sneak a copy of *Hustler* out inside the latest issue of *Discover*.

They had deprived him even of that.

Three-twenty P.M. was the signal for the running of the gauntlet.

"Bastards," he said, and slammed the hall locker shut. He gave the combination lock a vicious turn, imagining it to be someone's nose, then shouldered his backpack. The hall was almost empty. Anyone who didn't believe in faster-than-light travel had never been in a high school after last period. By now, everyone he knew was probably halfway home.

And here he was, wanting to go home but reluctant to leave the safety of the building.

Because he knew they would be out there, waiting for him.

They were *always* waiting for him.

He'd tried to outwait them a few times, and when there was

something good on television, or when someone decided to get a game going or sneak in a few joints, he'd actually managed to go home unmolested. But invariably they would get him twice as bad the next day.

He glanced at his watch. Three-thirty. He'd stalled long enough. He'd take the back route this time, cutting through the playing field. That would be the last place they'd expect to find him. He cared about sports nearly as much as he cared about school.

He stuffed his hands in his pockets and started down the long hall toward the double doors.

"Hey! Roger!"

Oh crap, they decided not to wait, he thought, an instant before recognizing the voice behind him. Chris ran up the hall after him.

"Boy, am I glad to see you," Chris said, breathless. "Just missed my bus. Chased it halfway down the driveway, but it didn't even slow down."

"Typical. What happened?"

"Got lost again."

Roger rolled his eyes. "Jesus, what a dweeb. Okay, where do you live?"

Chris gave him the address. Roger thought about it for a minute.

"Take the two-twelve. You catch it over on Sixteenth, and it'll get you within a block of your place. Right around Maple. You know how to find your way home from there?"

"I think so, yeah."

"Good."

Chris nodded. "So which way to Sixteenth Street?"

Roger started to tell him, then caught himself. "Just follow me. I go right by there."

"Hey, that'd be great. Thanks."

"No problem." Roger pushed open the glass and steel door and headed out on the lawn that ran behind the school. What he was doing wasn't exactly fair, but as his Dad-the-Drunk liked to say, *Two heads are harder than one.* Maybe having somebody along with him might make Them think twice about hassling him.

And maybe there really *is* a tooth fairy, he thought.

Chris jogged a little to catch up. "You know all the bus routes?"

"Sure. Sometimes I need to get around."

"Doesn't your dad give you lifts?"

25

"When he's sober."

"Oh."

They walked on a little farther, until the sudden silence began to annoy Roger. He hated it when people didn't know what to say. "What about your dad?"

"He's an engineer. Still back in New Jersey."

"Folks divorced?"

"My mom says they kind of grew apart."

"Think they'll get together again?"

A pause. "I really don't want to talk about it."

"Okay." They had reached the playing field, marked by a chalky diamond. Chris picked up a rock, heaved it. It bounced off the pitcher's mound.

A little farther, and they'd be past the playing field and on the last stretch. If they could make it as far as 16th Street, they'd be clear.

Chris took up another rock, threw it. It bounced off the backstop. "You think your folks are gonna get divorced?"

"Not a chance. My dad's having too good a time. You should see my place on the weekend. Saturday Night Fights, man. Just beats on her."

"Why doesn't she leave?"

"No guts, no brains. My Mother, the Vacuum Tube. Ask me, she ought to just take a gun and blow his brains out, but it's not gonna happen, so why think about it? I'm just hanging out until I'm eighteen, and then I'm getting the hell out of there so fast I'll leave a Doppler effect."

"A what?"

"Skip it."

They walked on silently for a while. Then Chris said, "You'd *really* want somebody to kill your dad?"

"Why? You got a name?"

Chris laughed. "No. It's just—I've never heard anybody say that before. Say it and *mean* it."

"Sure, I mean it. I wouldn't want to do it personally—they catch you, and you're royally screwed—but sometimes, when he's out all night, I think about somebody getting him outside a bar and blowing his brains out." He made a gun out of his hand, squinting along his forefinger at an imagined target. "Just squeeze the trigger, and BLAM! Dad Pudding. But he always makes it back."

He glanced at Chris, whose face was all squinched up, like he'd eaten something sour but didn't want to spit it out in front of other people.

"Hey!" someone yelled.

Shit, Roger thought. *They* were here. At the other end of the open lot that emptied out on 16th Street. Three of them, and not the usual ones. He recognized them from home room. They were friends of the other kids, the ones who usually nailed him.

They're turning this into a goddamned social event. Why don't they just lease me out and cut me in for a piece of the profits?

"Hey, Horseface!" one of them yelled. Steve, that was his name. The two guys with him were Jack and Paul. All three were seniors.

Chris looked at him, must've seen the worry on his face. "Roger?"

"Just keep walking."

He quickened his pace, angling toward the far side of the lot. They moved to cut him off. Not running, because that wasn't cool. But he knew that if they wanted to, they could run him down easily.

Bastards, he thought.

"I'm *talking* to you, Horseface," Steve said. "Where the hell do you think you're going?"

"Home."

" 'Home,' " Steve mimicked. The others laughed. Roger imagined stuffing a shrapnel grenade into their mouths and pulling the pin. "Give me a dollar, Horseface."

"My name's not Horseface."

"Okay, *Shithead,* give me a dollar or I'll beat the crap out of you." The other guys laughed again. Steve was coming closer, his fists at his side. He was wearing a ripped T-shirt that showed his muscles.

Chris stepped up beside Roger. "Look, guys, we don't want any trouble, okay?"

"I don't give a fuck what you want, asshole. Now you either give me a buck, both of you, or we'll send you home in a Hefty bag."

Chris reddened. Roger could see him balancing on one foot, ready to run.

"No way!" Chris said, and started running.

"Son of a bitch!" Steve said, and raced after him, catching him before he got more than ten feet away. He yanked Chris back by the shirt. Chris stumbled, then fell in the dirt lot, on one knee. Steve rabbit-punched him behind the left shoulder. Chris gave a yowl.

27

"I told you, man, don't screw with me," Steve said. He was enjoying it. Roger could see it in his face.

Steve hauled back, fist hovering over Chris, his other hand holding on to Chris's shirt. "You got two seconds."

Chris reached into his back pocket and came out with a dollar. He handed it back over his shoulder to Steve, who took it—and rabbit-punched him anyway. "Jerk," Steve said, and turned his attention to Roger.

"A dollar, Horseface," Steve said. "Now."

Roger looked up at the rock-hard face, the sloping brow, the piggy eyes. "Go fuck yourself."

Pain exploded. He flew back, landed hard in the dirt. Lights danced behind his eyes and his chest felt like a hole had been drilled into the muscles. He tried to catch his breath but Steve was there, grabbing his shirt and yanking him up to look right in his eyes. "What did you say, Horseface?" he asked, real quiet.

"Nothing," Roger said.

"Sure sounded like something to me."

"Then get your ears fixed."

He didn't even see Steve's hand as it whipped him across the side of the head. The slap sent his glasses flying. His ear was ringing now, and his eyes were beginning to water.

Leave me alone, damn you, why won't you just leave me alone? What did I ever do to you?

Steve was breathing hard now, fist raised again, this time aimed right between Roger's eyes. "Don't get smart with me, asshole, or I swear to God I'll beat the living shit out of you. Just give me the goddamned dollar."

Roger looked up at that cocked fist. Swallowed. "No way."

The fist swung back—

"Leave him alone!"

The punch didn't come. Steve looked behind him to the source of the challenge. It was Chris. He stood a little ways off, a dollar bill clutched in his hand. "Here! You want it? Here."

For a moment, Steve considered it. Seemed to weigh the advantages of an easy dollar against the joy of beating it out of Roger's hide. Then he dropped Roger, stood up and went over to Chris, snatching the dollar bill. He made a point of inspecting it—and suddenly backhanded Chris across the neck.

"Don't ever, ever talk to me like that again, asshole," Steve said. "Got that?"

Chris nodded.

Steve waved to the others, who followed him out of the lot. Roger could hear them laughing. More than anything else in the world, he wished for an Uzi. *Let's see how tough you are with a few hundred holes in those muscles, fat-ass.*

He struggled to his feet to find Chris standing next to him, holding his glasses. "Found these," he said.

Roger put the glasses on. "Thanks."

Chris looked after the three seniors, who were now crossing the street into the video arcade. "Jerks," he said.

"Yeah."

"You okay?"

Roger nodded. His ear was still ringing, but that would pass. It always did.

"So how come you just didn't give 'em a dollar?"

"Because I didn't have it, okay? Satisfied now? I only get enough for lunch and those assholes take it away from me every time anyway!" He kicked a Pepsi can, sent it hurling into a wall on the near side of the lot. His face was burning. Damn them all!

"Sorry," Chris said.

Roger shook his head. "No, it's not you."

"Why didn't you tell them you didn't have it?"

"Because they would've just beat me anyway, just on principle. They don't care about a crummy dollar, it's just an excuse to kick ass. I figured, hell, they're going to beat me up anyway, might as well tell 'em where to stick it."

He stuffed his hands in his pockets, and they continued out of the lot to the street. He looked away. "By the way," Roger said, "thanks. I mean, for what you did back there."

"Forget it."

"No, really. I won't forget that. I never forget my friends."

Chris smiled. "Okay."

Roger pointed to a bus stop in front of a post office. "You get the bus over there. I think it runs about every twenty minutes this time of day."

"Great. Just one problem."

"What?"

29

"Gave that asshole my bus money."

Roger grinned, even though it made his cheek hurt. "Jerk."

"Tell me about it."

"C'mon." Roger started across the street. "We'll go to my place. If my dad's home, he's probably asleep. If I'm real quiet, I can slip a dollar out of his wallet. If not, maybe I can get something out of my mom's purse."

"What if they catch you?"

"Hey, couldn't get any worse, could it?"

2

Roger's house was three blocks north of the bus stop, a two-bedroom split-level with dirty whitewashed sideboarding and an overgrown backyard. They cut across it, through the high grass and past an old swing set that had rusted through years ago.

Roger held a finger to his lips. "We get in, we get the money, we get out. No noise, okay?"

Chris nodded.

Roger opened the rear door slowly, then stepped inside, holding it open for Chris.

"Roger?" a woman's voice called down the hall. "Roger, honey, is that you?"

"Shit," Roger said. "The woman's got fucking sonar, I swear to God."

"Maybe you could sell her to the Russians?"

Roger thought about it. "I like that. Remind me to bring it up to the President at the next staff meeting."

"Roger?"

"Yeah, Mom, just a sec." He trudged down the hall in the direction of the voice, motioning for Chris to follow.

They came into the living room, which was dark and musky. Venetian blinds shut behind yellowing curtains pulled tight behind heavy drapes. Like a goddamn tomb, Roger thought. What're you afraid of, Mom? Afraid somebody'll see inside, maybe see something they don't like? Sometimes he thought she wasn't afraid of anyone seeing in; that she was, in fact, afraid to see out. Sometimes he saw her in his mind as some grotesquely huge canary, its wings mottled and greying, with a curtain drawn around its cage in the hope that the outside world would go away and it wouldn't have to be reminded that it was living in a cage, and eating in a cage, and would eventually die in a cage.

Not me, though, he thought. No way.

She put down the book she'd been reading and smiled across the room at Chris. It was the kind of smile Roger hated—thin and bloodless. "Hello, I'm Roger's mother."

"Hi," Chris said, and introduced himself. "I'm in the same home room as Roger."

"That's nice," she said. "It's nice that Roger is finally making some friends."

"Mom—"

"Well, it's true," she said, her face drawn almost exaggeratedly into worry. "He's a good boy," she said, "but the other boys in school keep picking on him. I think they're jealous. He's a very smart boy."

"Yeah, well, we'd better get going," Roger said. "Want to show Chris my room."

"I can make some sandwiches, would you like that, Roger? And some Kool-Aid. We've got black cherry, your favorite."

"Maybe later," Roger said. already backing up toward the door. "Chris can't stay long."

"Are you sure? He could stay for dinner. We could call his mother—"

"Mom . . ."

She looked down, pouting, then picked up her book. "All right, dear," she said, and there was that whipped quality in her voice that he hated, the same tone she had with his father. "You have a good time."

"It was nice to meet you, Mrs. Obst," Chris said.

From the doorway, Roger mouthed, *Come on!*

Chris followed him back into the hall. They stopped in front of a door marked with a yellow-and-black radiation symbol and the words FALLOUT SHELTER. "Swiped it from the library," Roger said, and opened the door.

Chris stepped inside and let out a long, low whistle. "Wow," he said. "Where'd you *get* all this stuff?"

Roger closed the door and followed Chris's gaze as it swept the room that was covered by posters and signs and models and movie stills. There were huge black-and-white photos of Lon Chaney, Jr. as the Werewolf and Bela Lugosi as Dracula and Boris Karloff as the Monster; stacks and stacks of old magazines, *Creepy* and *Eerie* and *Famous Monsters of Filmland* and *Fangoria*, and models from the old movies that he'd put together and painted himself. One whole wall was inaccessible due to the boxes of comics piled up in front of it, each comic catalogued and priced and preserved in a polystyrene pouch.

And there were the books. Lovecraft, Poe, King, Dunsany, Koontz, Bloch, Matheson, on and on and on, spilling across four shelves made from two-by-fours and cinderblocks. He'd read them all, over and over and over.

"Pretty neat, huh?" Roger asked.

Chris nodded. "My mom would kill me if she saw half this stuff in my room."

"Look around," Roger said. "I'll be right back."

He stepped back into the hallway, closed the door behind him, and took a deep breath.

This was always the part he hated.

He continued down the hall toward the other bedroom. Even if he hadn't known where it was, he could have found it by following the sound. His father's snoring could be heard clearly even through the closed door.

He pushed the door open slowly. His father was in his undershorts, sheets tossed all over the place. The smell of booze was thick in the room. Across the room, on top of the dresser, was the prize Roger sought: the wallet.

Roger tiptoed toward it, knowing from experience which floorboards to avoid. He slid a set of keys off the wallet, and carefully opened it. A handful of bills had been carelessly shoved into one corner. Perfect. His father had probably stuffed his change there before heading home last night, and probably wouldn't remember what or how much was there.

He thumbed through the bills before deciding on a five. He shoved the bill in his pocket and quietly replaced the wallet, putting the keys back on it in just the same way they'd been left. He then retraced his steps to the door and out, closing it behind him.

The perfect crime, he thought.

He couldn't have been more wrong.

"You want the rest of those fries?"

Chris was eyeing the remains of his Big Mac Attack. The money Roger had taken had been enough to buy both of them some munchies as well as get Chris home. Now, with a cheeseburger burbling in his stomach, the idea of food seemed repugnant. "It's all yours," Roger said.

Chris scooped up the grease-stained bag and emptied them into his mouth, then sat back with a nearly beatific expression on his face. "Thanks."

"Skip it." Roger looked past Chris, through the plate-glass window to the outside world. A creepy-looking man was making his way down the street, plastering stuff onto walls and lampposts. He looked like the derelicts Roger sometimes saw down around the bus depot. It was hard to tell from here, but it looked like he was putting up posters . . .

"Hey, Horseface, how's it hanging? When you can find it, I mean!"

Roger turned around in his seat. Coming up behind him was Jim Bertierie, also from his home room. He was a big kid, not as big as Steve, but big enough, and maybe a little smarter in the candlepower department, which made him even more of a pain. He was holding an empty fry bag on his face like a feedbag, and making whinnying noises into it. Then he broke up, laughing at his own routine.

What an asshole, Roger thought.

"Screw yourself, Bertierie."

Bertierie's eyes widened with mock shock. "Ooooooh! Tough guy! Looka me, I'm shakin' in my shoes!" He turned his attention to Chris. "You're the new kid, right?"

Chris nodded.

"Better learn fast about who you pick for friends. There're laws about hanging out with mutants, y'know."

Chris looked over at Roger and shrugged. "He's okay."

Good for you, Roger thought.

"Aw," Bertierie said, "well, I'll let you two lovebirds finish your supper." He glanced back at Chris. " 'Sides, I've gotta go say hi to your mom on my way home. Me and about half the senior class."

Chris reddened, and was halfway out of his chair when Roger grabbed him by the sleeve. "Don't."

"Let go!"

"Yeah," Bertierie said, "let him go. C'mon, punk, you want to make something out of it?"

A clerk came forward from the counter, probably a senior from another school. "Okay, no fighting in here. You got a problem, you take it outside, you hear me?"

Bertierie nodded and, after a moment, headed out. Grinning.

Roger pulled Chris back into his seat. "Dumb, man, real dumb."

"What?"

"You gave him a lever. You know what a lever is, right? 'Give me a big enough lever and I can move the world' and all that shit? Well, your mom just became the lever, and you became the world, dummy."

"But you heard what he said—"

"Yeah, I heard, and you have to let it go. Assholes like him just look for the way to bug you, get you to start a fight so you get the blame, not them. So you have to make believe like it doesn't bother you, and if you're lucky they'll try something else that doesn't really bother you as much. But now he knows all he has to do is talk about fucking your mom, and you'll go off the deep end. Got it?"

Chris bit his lip. "Yeah," he said finally, "I got it. And it stinks."

"Next time, just shine it on, okay?"

"Okay, okay." He was still angry, though.

"From your reaction, I bet your mom's a real fox, isn't she?"

That look again. "Don't start with me, Roger."

"All right," Roger said, and laughed. "Just asking. Loosen up a little. Jesus." He looked at Bertierie standing at the bus stop. It was the same one Chris would have to wait at; he was probably waiting for the same bus, Roger decided.

Sometimes life had a really rotten sense of humor.

If Chris was lucky, Bertierie would have to get off first, removing any chance of an ambush. If not . . .

He noticed the Shabby Man cross the street and start putting up one of his posters on the telephone pole beside the bus stop. It looked like a plain sheet of legal-sized paper covered with handwriting. He'd seen that kind of thing a lot, especially the last week or so. The stuff was popping up all over the place.

A nutcase, Roger thought.

The Shabby Man finished slathering glue on the pole and tacked the sign up. He'd just started away when Bertierie said something to him. The Shabby Man stopped but didn't look around. They were too far away for Roger to hear what Bertierie had said, but it wasn't polite. It seemed Bertierie was determined to start trouble.

Roger hoped that the Shabby Man would skrag the little fucker. After a moment, Bertierie said something else, and the Shabby Man turned slowly toward him. Looked at him.

"Uh-oh," Roger said.

"What?"

Roger pointed toward the window. "I think Bertierie just got himself in big trouble." But the Shabby Man merely locked eyes with Bertierie, as though only now becoming aware of his presence.

Bertierie stuck out his chin and returned the stare. Started to say something else—

And then stopped.

For what seemed like the longest time, the two of them just looked at each other. It was as if—and this was really crazy, Roger thought— but it was as if something were being said without words. Just a flash of sudden connection.

Okay, Roger thought, so who's gonna punch who? Let's get on with it, already.

But no one punched anyone. Another moment, and the staring ended. The Shabby Man gathered up his posters and his bucket of glue and walked off down the street. Bertierie watched him go, then turned around, dazed, to look toward where the bus was rapidly approaching.

The bus!

"Shit," Roger said, the exchange forgotten, "that's your bus!"

They burst out of the McDonald's and raced to the corner, where the bus was beginning to pull away. Roger slapped the side of the bus, yelling until it stopped. The doors popped open; Chris trotted up the steps and inside.

Roger watched until the bus rounded a corner, then he turned and started away—

And remembered.

Oh, hell, he thought. Bertierie! I forgot to tell Chris about Bertierie being on the bus!

Too late now, though. Chris would certainly figure it out soon enough. After that . . .

35

Oh, well, he thought, stuffing his hands into his pockets, it isn't my problem.

He paused and glanced up at the telephone pole beside him. There was the poster the Shabby Man had put up.

I am we and we are you and we have been looking for you
for you for so long so long goodbye farewell it doesn't matter
nothing matters unless you can see us but we are among you
but not of you and the Word is made flesh but the flesh is
weak nothing matters nothing matters in the end He said it
He said that there will be nothing left, and in the end there
is just the darkness and Jesus said He loved everyone but
there are some even Jesus does not love and John 3:1 lied
where are you do you feel it its not in your thoughts its real
and its here and we're real

It was like all the others he'd seen at one time or another. Didn't make any sense. They never did.

He glanced at his watch, and was startled to realize that he'd been standing here, staring at this stupid poster, for nearly fifteen minutes, though it had felt like only a minute.

His gaze returned almost against his will to the poster. No, it didn't make any sense. But there was something about it that seemed, somewhere inside his head, to *almost* make sense. Better get out of here, he thought. This stuff might be contagious.

4

The baby upstairs was crying again. Tony Soznick buried his head in his pillow, and tried to wish it away.

Go to sleep, for Christ's sake, please, just leave me alone.

The crying continued.

He was tired. God, but he was tired. And still he couldn't sleep. Seven days of work, of walking up and down miles of sidewalk, plastering and setting and moving on . . .

His hands were callused, encrusted with glue that even washing with lye couldn't get off. It covered his nails and fingertips like chiton. Sometimes he was afraid to go to sleep, afraid he'd cut himself with the sharp edges of his no longer recognizable hands.

They had been soft hands, once, used to delicate work.

Seven days.

Even God rested on the seventh day.

But there was no rest for the wicked, was there?

I'M NOT WICKED, he thought. *I've been going through some bad times lately, but I'm not a bad man I'm not a wicked man.* He thought of a movie he'd seen once (how long ago? he could barely remember), *The Elephant Man. I am not an animal, I am a human being!*

Yeah? he thought. Really?

Prove it.

So long ago . . .

He'd been a telephone repairman. That was it. He closed his eyes against the darkness and tried to pull the memories out from the greater dark behind his eyelids. He had been born in Connecticut, he had one sister and one brother and his brother died when he was sixteen

(and ah, but the thirst was there, and it knew, didn't it?)

and he had gone on to finish high school in a household that was more dead than alive, then two years of junior college before dropping out and working at little odd jobs but they were okay, he never wanted much

(certainly not this, no, no, never this)

and when the job opening came at Ma Bell, he'd taken it. It was honest work. He drove around in a clean white van, and worked out in the open, installing phones or fixing damaged lines, and he could go home

(wherever that was)

and not have to think about anything but what was on TV that night.

Then he'd gotten the call.

The weather had been bad. A storm was raging up and down the coast, dropping sheets of rain and auroras of lightning, and screwing up the phone service for miles. Lines went down, unwilling to compete with the several zillion volts flashing through the night sky all around them. Crews worked all night, on double shifts, to restore even the most rudimentary service. Emergency services got first priority; hospitals and fire departments and crisis hotlines—

And that was the one that had done him in.

The twelve lines leading in and out of the Sacred Heart Crisis Center had blinked once and gone out, and they had to be restored, fast. It was the only local resource for suicides and overdoses and runaways, the desperate and the frightened.

So there he'd been, at three in the morning, strapped to the top of a telephone pole, frantically repairing wires. Cut, splice, tape, check. Checking meant feeding his handset phone into the line and direct-dialing each of the twelve numbers to make sure the connection was solid. It was numbing work, and he had to keep wiping the lines to keep them dry so the splice would hold. Line one, secure. Line two, secure. Line three, four, five—secure, secure, and again secure.

He connected his handset phone to check line six—and it rang, startling him. It was a rare thing to get a ring on a cold-connection.

Only one of two things could cause it: a sudden power spike in the line . . . or someone was calling in on the crisis center line he was fixing.

He looked at the phone as the ringing vibrated his hand. If it was just a spike, all he had to do was toggle the ON switch, and he'd just get static.

But if someone *was* calling in . . .

Six rings. Seven.

Can't just hang up, he'd thought. What if it were somebody in trouble? But he didn't want to deal with it. *Couldn't* deal with it. Most likely it was just static. The odds of someone calling in during the ten seconds his handset would be connected . . .

Nine rings.

He toggled the ON switch. "Unit four-seven-nine," he said.

There was a woman's voice at the other end. Sobbing, frightened, desperate. It sounded far away, rising and falling like waves hitting the shoreline.

" . . . help me. Please God, help me, someone."

Damn, he thought. "Listen, ma'am, I'm sorry, but there's no one here who can talk to you. If you could call one of the other numbers—"

"All those people," the voice continued, "ohgod, it wasn't my fault, I didn't mean . . . *I didn't know it was going to happen!* It's not my fault, please, you've got to believe me!"

"Ma'am, I'm sorry, really, but there's nothing I can do. I'm just fixing the lines."

But he doubted she was even listening. She was sobbing at the other end of the line. The sound was oddly muffled, as though she were leaning forward, the mouthpiece cradled against her chin. He had a sudden image of a woman in her late thirties, in pain, shivering, alone in a kitchen. It struck him like a retinal afterflash, most visible when he shut his eyes. She was sitting at the table, her face partly covered by her left hand, and the reason he couldn't hear her properly, the reason the sound was muffled, was because the phone was cradled against her chin, her right hand not holding the phone, but something else—

(*Gun, she's got a gun!*)

Crazy! he thought. You're so wrought up, you're not thinking straight. "Please," he said, "if you could just call back in five minutes."

When she next spoke, her voice was colder. As though a decision had been made, and was now to be enforced. "No," she said. "If I wait, I might change my mind. Or *it* might change its mind. I can't—I just can't deal with it anymore. I'm sorry. Please, tell them that for me. I'm so sorry."

"Ma'am?" Nothing. *"Ma'am?"*

He heard the receiver drop, striking the table and tumbling to the floor—

And then one gunshot.

He jumped so that he almost dropped the handset. "Ma'am? Hello? Is anybody there?"

He clicked the receiver. Listened hard. This couldn't be happening to him. He started to pull the receiver away, to dial 911, when he thought he heard something on the line. He pressed the receiver to his ear, straining for the slightest sound. Let her be alive, please, whoever it was.

At first he couldn't make it out. It was a rushing noise, building slowly, and after a moment he knew what it reminded him of: a sound like distant thunder, growing nearer.

Crazy, he thought—and then it slammed into his ear. Like a thin, white-hot pick, it drilled through his eardrum and rocketed into his skull, a tornado in his head, whipping and thrashing and—

Laughing.

Tony screamed. Dropped the receiver and cradled his head as the whole world tripped over itself and went sliding away, going from grey to black to—

Laughing, god, laughing in his head, and he couldn't make it stop.

He twisted in the leather harness, trying to get away, lost his footing, and was only vaguely aware of falling, falling farther than the twenty-five feet to the ground, falling for miles and light years and galaxies and oh god, it was inside his head, inside . . .

When he finally hit ground, Tony Soznick, repair unit 479, went somewhere far away.

Three days later, he woke up in a hospital bed.

Four days after that, the blackouts started, first only a few minutes long, then increasing in duration.

Two days after that, he began to suspect that he was not alone in his own head. Just before bed, he decided he would talk to someone about it.

When he woke up it was a month later, and he was in Minneapolis, Minnesota, with five hundred of the handwritten posters stacked neatly on a dresser, a set of clothes he didn't recognize, and two hundred dollars in cash.

And the glue, always on his fingers, like a second skin.

Under the sheets, he picked at the roughness on his hands. He tried to remember what he had used to get off the glue when he was twelve, making model airplanes. It was turpentine, yes, he was sure that was it. Turpentine.

He'd pick some up first thing tomorrow.

It would be a busy day tomorrow. Plenty to do, lots of ground to cover.

Go to sleep, he thought.

Upstairs, the baby stopped crying.

Thank you God, he thought.

And a voice whispered in his ear, *"You're welcome."*

2

"Your rack," Susan said.

"Got it." Jordan moved down the table, pulling the balls out of the pockets and rolling them down toward the foot cushion. The other two pool tables were empty. Three green-shaded lamps overhead broke the darkness, which bled off into the rest of the bar. Susan could catch glimpses of a few other customers here and there in the shadows. The place was quiet, even for a Monday. Fine, she thought. No need to embarrass him in public.

"Five bucks this time?"

He grinned. "Glutton for punishment, eh?"

"Maybe," she said, trying for an innocent quality in her voice. It was tough. It'd been a while since she'd been innocent. But this was too good an opportunity to lose. She started away from the table and toward the back door. "Forgot something in the car," she said. "Back in a sec."

Once outside, in the parking lot, the smile she'd worked all night to suppress finally slipped out. Three days she'd been waiting for this!

Every Monday and Wednesday nights after shift, when the guns and the badges had been put away, they would stop in at the Riverside Tavern in Burbank. And every Monday and Wednesday, Jordan would haul out a leather bag containing his favorite pool cue. He'd unzip the bag with something like reverence, chalk the cue with precise attention . . . and then proceed to whomp her five games out of seven.

She said it was because of the tavern's crummy house cues.

He said it was superior ability, and if she didn't like it, then she should buy her own stick.

So this past weekend, that was exactly what she'd done.

She found the sleek black leather case and headed back into the bar.

In retrospect, two hundred and fifty dollars was a lot to drop on a pool cue. But she figured she could just afford it if she cut back a little on eating out. The expression she caught on Jordan's face as she came in carrying the case was worth it.

One by one she snapped open the combination locks. "The Campione Deluxe graphite cue," she said, reciting the owner's manual by memory, "is designed in Italy by Caudillo Paulini—famous for his high-tech sports equipment design."

Now the plush, grey suede interior was revealed. And there, nestled like lovers, were the two emerald-green halves of the cue. "Craftsmen mold each cue of graphite over a core of ceramic glass fibers—thirty-seven times stronger than steel."

She fitted the butt and shaft together. The joint and ferrule were brass, and she'd had her initials engraved on them. SAW. "As you shoot, the graphite construction provides a dampening effect, which adds touch and control to your form. This precision-balanced cue withstands the hardest break shot without vibrating. Temperature and humidity resistant, and *one hundred percent straight*."

She propped the cue against her leg, waiting for a reaction.

"Five bucks, huh?" Jordan said.

Susan nodded.

"Make it ten. I don't care if that thing's got radar control, computer chips, diodes, and a Ouija board—it don't mean shit if you shoot like Helen Keller."

"You're on." She leaned over and shot. The break came with a solid, satisfying *crack*.

The seven ball went in immediately.

One hundred percent straight, she thought, and lined up her next shot.

"Why didn't you just buy a goddamned Laws rocket and get it over with?"

Susan folded up the forty dollars, reached under her chair, and slipped it into her purse. Which means I'm only two hundred and ten dollars in the hole, she thought. "You're not really upset, are you?" He didn't answer. "C'mon, Jordan, talk to me. What's up?"

Jordan took a long swallow from the bottle of Coors. "Lieutenant called me into the office just as the shift was getting out."

"The sergeant's test—"

He shook his head. "No, not that. Results still aren't in. And I don't expect much out of 'em anyway. If I don't make it this time, I'm gonna give it a rest for a while. Who knows, maybe I'm just not sergeant material. But like I said—that wasn't it. We're being reassigned."

"*Again?* Jordy, we just *got* here!"

"Don't worry, it's not to another precinct. They're taking us off patrol and putting us on Juvie. He said it's just temporary; they're shorthanded downtown."

"So what? We're shorthanded *every*where."

"Could be worse," Jordan said. "They could be shipping us over to the street gang detail."

Susan dragged a finger through the water on the table top, sketching concentric circles. He was right. She'd seen cops coming off six months on gang detail. It wasn't pretty.

She turned over the empty glass in front of her, then sat back. "We'd better go."

Outside, it was wonderfully cool, a relief from the Santa Ana heat of the day. She returned the leather case to the trunk and climbed into the Pontiac. As she waited for the car to warm up, she watched Jordan's car pull out and head off down the street, its taillights vanishing into the night. She did the same thing at airports. After dropping someone off, she always waited until the plane took off, never taking her eyes off it until it disappeared into the clouds. She liked to be one hundred percent sure that she had done her job properly.

One hundred percent straight, she thought, remembering her spiel about the pool cue. She smiled at the idea.

Two years, and he's never asked me out once. But romance and police work didn't go together, not when you were out in the street together. It got in the way of good judgment. Sometimes he talked about the women he dated, and sometimes she regaled him with her own stories, but that was the extent of it. That was what led to the pool nights in the first place.

She'd just broken up with Michael, and it had been painful. It still was. He'd told her that he was being faithful, that he was willing to make a commitment—and she'd come by his apartment early one morning, as a surprise, to find him boffing someone else. For a while after that, she stopped taking care of herself the way she always had, and found herself mistrusting all men. It was affecting her work.

So Jordy had started dragging her out once a week, figuring that his company alone would force her to begin seeking out other dates. It had worked.

He's a good cop, she thought. And he'd be a damn good sergeant, too, if he'd just get off his ass and work at it.

Maybe tomorrow would bring some good news about the sergeant's test, she thought, and pointed her car toward the freeway.

3

Lying in bed, Chris Martino finished the last page of the latest issue of *The Adventures of Superman*, and set it down on the pile of comics beside his bed. As usual, he was annoyed. So why keep buying it? Because he was hoping it would get better. Because it couldn't get any worse.

Truth was, Superman just hadn't been the same since they'd decided to "renovate" him. With every succeeding issue he was turning into more of a wimp. Everybody was beating up on him, everybody was stronger than he was, more interesting, more dynamic. And then they had killed Supergirl, and Robin, and the Flash . . .

It was almost enough to make him start buying Marvel.

"Honey? You still up?"

The door opened, his mom stuck her head in. From downstairs he could just hear the theme music from the David Letterman show. "You really ought to get some sleep. We've got to get you back on a regular schedule, and school comes awfully early."

"I know." During the move from Matawan, he'd been allowed to stay up later than usual, and had quickly become used to it.

"Can I turn off the lights?"

He nodded. The lights went out.

" 'Night," she said, and closed the coor.

"G'night."

Feeling the seconds crawl past, his mind kept turning in upon itself. He was still coming down from his first day back at school, and discovering that he dreaded day two even more. He'd tried to make it sound better than it was when his mom had asked how his day had been, but the truth of it was that this school was going to be the pits. He'd pissed off at least half a dozen kids, he was sure one of his teachers had it in for him (C. HUNTINGTON strikes again), he'd already been in one fight, and his only friend was known as Horseface.

And on top of all *that*, they were screwing up Superman.

He tried breathing regularly, which helped, but only a little. His mind kept returning to the events of the day, and like a scratched record, kept sliding into one particular groove over and over.

It was on the bus ride home, after he'd left Roger outside the McDonald's. He'd dropped his eighty-five cents into the box and had just taken his seat when he realized that Jim Bertierie was sitting two seats ahead of him. He'd resigned himself to the abuse that now seemed inevitable—but nothing had happened. Bertierie seemed oblivious to his presence.

As the minutes passed, Chris kept waiting for the hammer to fall, but it never did. If anything, Bertierie seemed to get more distant the longer he sat there.

When the bus reached his stop, Chris started for the back door, still reluctant to take any chances, then changed his mind and went to the front. As the doors opened, he glanced back at Bertierie, who was still unaware of him.

Chris's thoughts kept going back to the curious look on Bertierie's face. At the time, it looked as though he had forgotten something very important, and was trying desperately to remember what it was.

But now, lying in his bed, Chris finally realized what it was that Bertierie's expression reminded him of. He'd seen the same look on his mother, when she was listening intently to someone on the telephone. Head down, eyes fixed on nothing in particular, distant but attentive to what was being said.

Yes, he thought, surrendering at last to sleep, that was it. The very look.

Except that it was silly, of course.

Buses didn't have telephones.

4

Roger shifted the headphones on his ears, trying to get them to sit more comfortably. He had hot-wired them up to the old black-and-white television set in his bedroom six months ago, to put an end to his mother's ceaseless complaining about being able to hear it at even the lowest volume.

The sound was tinny and harsh, and after a while the headphones made his ears burn, especially when he wore them in bed, but it was better than being complained at all the time.

On the screen, Godzilla was coming out of Tokyo Bay, smashing his way through electrical towers and tank fire, past rockets and bullets and gas bombs, set on a course for downtown Tokyo, the wrath of God Incarnate come to pay its respects.

He'd seen the movie at least five times, but he never got tired of watching the fire lizard stomping Japan. There were times he could imagine himself trading places with it, that it was him up there on the screen, and instead of Tokyo, it was Lennox High School that was being torched and crushed beneath the unleashed force of his righteous anger and his limitless power. He would turn his face upon his enemies, and at a single gesture they would burst into flames and smoke and vanish from the earth.

And he would move on, unconcerned. Invulnerable.

Of course, there was always that scientist with the air-destroying pill lurking in the second act, wasn't there?

Well, stomp him, too. That was the answer to any given problem, including this one. *If a train is moving at fifty miles per hour going west, and you are in a car going at thirty-five miles per hour in an easterly direction, and the train leaves at twelve o'clock, and you leave at one-fifteen, at what time will you intersect the train if both vehicles are one hundred miles apart when they start? Please remember that your answer is one half of your grade.*

What was the answer?

Stomp the car, stomp the train, and incinerate the teacher while you were at it, just for good measure, being sure to scatter the ashes on the off-chance she might regenerate. You could never tell when a math teacher might try something sneaky, like becoming a scientist and inventing an air-destroying pill.

After a while, he noticed that there was a pounding in his ears that didn't match the pounding on the screen. Admittedly, the voices of the actors never quite matched the movements of their mouths either, but . . .

He pulled off the headphones.

The pounding was coming from down the hall, in the kitchen. The sound of a fist pounding on the dining room table.

Dad's up, he thought. He could hear his father clearly now, as could most of the neighborhood, he suspected.

"WHERE IS IT?"

His mother was answering. The words were indistinguishable, but the beaten tone in her voice was evident even through the walls.

"DON'T LIE TO ME, YOU GODDAMN COW, YOU FUCK-ING BITCH, WHERE THE HELL IS IT? WHAT DID YOU DO WITH IT?"

Then: the sound of flesh hitting flesh. He was hitting her. Again.

The Saturday Night Fights had arrived five days early.

She was crying now, pleading. The hitting continued.

He started to replace the headphones, pretend that it had nothing to do with him, screw them, screw them both—when he heard something that made his heart feel as though it were being squeezed in a vise.

"IT WAS MY POKER BILL, YOU UNDERSTAND?" Slap. "FIRST FUCKING BILL I EVER GOT HAD PRACTICALLY ALL NINES! I WON FIFTEEN DOLLARS LAST NIGHT"—slap—"AND NOW YOU"—slap—"YOU GO AND STEAL THE GODDAMN THING! WHAT THE HELL DID YOU THINK YOU WERE DOING?"

No, he thought.

It couldn't be.

His father played bill-poker with some of his other drunkbuddies. They'd each pull out a bill at random, check the serial number, and whoever had the highest numbers won.

And now he remembered noticing that there had been at least six nines on the bill he'd handed to the clerk at the McDonald's.

Suddenly, the slapping and yelling stopped. He listened to the wall, but the only sound he could hear was his mother's voice. She was talking fast, explaining something—

No. Terror clawed at his chest from the inside out. NO!

Please, God, no.

Footsteps in the hall. Coming toward his bedroom.

His father stood there in the doorway, his belt swinging free in his hand, buckle out, his T-shirt covered with sweat.

"YOU!" he yelled, face red. "SON OF A BITCH!"

Roger scooted back along his bed, but there was nowhere to run, nowhere to go. "Please, Dad, no, wait, *please!*"

He should have known better.

There was no negotiating with Godzilla.

5

Jim Bertierie peered through the dark at the clock beside his bed: 2:37 A.M. He listened for any sound from elsewhere in the house.

Nothing.

He grinned. He had been patient, and he had waited, and he had gone to bed early, and he had waited some more, and now it was time. He could begin his trip.

He pulled away the covers. Beneath the sheets he was completely dressed: Reeboks, black socks, his cleanest Levi's, and the black T-shirt he'd bought as a joke last year, with an upside-down raven over the white-on-black letters that spelled out DEATH RECORDS . . .

Perfect.

He took a step forward, letting his foot come down slowly on the floorboards to prevent creaking. Each step took ten seconds. In forty seconds he had crossed to the other side of his room, where he pulled out the knapsack he'd filled and set beside his dresser. He pulled the Velcro flap open. The process took another thirty seconds; you could barely hear the whisper of parting fabric in the room.

Everything was there, of course. But he had to check, had to be sure, because everything had to be . . .

perfect

in every detail. He shone a penlight into the knapsack, revealing the prized items: a screwdriver, seven paperclips that he had meticulously unfolded until they were straight silver lines with only the slightest of bumps to indicate their original shape, a pair of socks, a bar of soap, a map of Los Angeles, a can of Raid, three Band-Aids, a condom, and a kazoo.

A *kazoo*, he thought, and stifled a giggle. How radical, how bizarre, how utterly

perfect.

Satisfied that he had everything he would need, he closed the knapsack, slung it over one shoulder and walked

ten seconds per step

toward the bedroom door. He twisted the knob.

Sixty seconds.

Opened the door.

Sixty seconds.

Stepped outside into the hall.

Thirty seconds, and ten seconds per step down the hall toward the staircase, down the steps, his mind filling in the prolonged silences by estimating that at his current rate he would average a mile every fourteen and a half hours. Fortunately, he didn't need to go that far. Not yet.

But soon, he would be going fast.

He reached the garage door, stepped through, closed and locked it after him. He could afford to move a little faster now. The garage walls were pretty thick. Just right for his needs.

He made his way to the car and opened the door on the driver's side. He climbed in and shut the door after him. He was inside. Finally. He ran his hands along the steering wheel, and a happiness welled up inside him that was so profound he thought he might start crying. His heart swelled with love for everyone, including his dad, even though he had wanted to drive this car for so long, and his dad had said no, not until you're out of school, for wasn't his dad looking out for him, for his own best interests?

Of course he was. And for a moment, he wished he could invite his dad to come with him.

But it was not to be.

He removed the spare set of car keys from the pocket of his Levi's, where he'd hidden them earlier, and found the ignition. He held the key without moving it for a moment. This was the critical moment. If they heard him—

He turned the key. The engine caught on the first attempt, as he'd known it would. He waited. But there was no knock at the garage door, no lights switched on, no voices.

Almost there, he thought. Almost there.

He stepped out of the car and made his way to the garage door. All he had to do was open it.

Except . . . then it wouldn't be

perfect

anymore, would it? Just as he wasn't

perfect

either.

After all, with the door open, he couldn't go anyplace that was worth going to, could he? He had to go someplace special, a secret place. And he couldn't let anyone see him, or they'd interfere. They wouldn't understand.

He found the box of rags and laid them out at the base of the garage door, pushing them into the cracks so that no one could see in. This done, he returned to the car, climbed back into the driver's seat, and closed the door. The engine thrummed smoothly, its sound muffled again behind the glass.

He leaned back in the seat and gripped the steering wheel hard, imagining his hands made of concrete cast around it. He ignored the stick shift. There was no gear marked that would transport him where he wanted to go. No, the car would *know* how to take him.

Sure enough, the car was accelerating around him.

The speed pushed him back into his seat, but he refused to let go of the steering wheel. That would be dangerous. And it was too nice a day to drive recklessly. He opened the window to let in the sweet summer air.

All so perfect.

He wasn't perfect. He knew that now. He had always wondered why he hadn't felt right, hadn't felt as though he belonged anywhere, and now he knew. It was because he wasn't perfect. But now he was going someplace where he *would* be perfect, where he would be recast and reborn and *made* perfect.

Gently, he pushed down on the gas pedal. The engine revved beneath his foot.

Faster and faster now, the landscape blurring all around him.

And the people . . . yes, there were *people* walking alongside the road, but he was passing them so fast now that they were all just blurs. And he was going still faster now, so fast that he doubted he would soon be able to see them at all.

5

G. EDWARDS was late. Roger was late. And Home Room was rapidly deteriorating.

Chris wondered what was going on. Some of the kids who'd come in late said they'd seen most of the home room teachers standing outside the vice-principal's office, and that there were a couple of cops there, too. When Vincent Elmayo tried to find out what was happening, C. HUNTINGTON had practically thrown him down the stairs.

The class quieted down when the door opened—only to go back to full volume when they saw it was Roger. He walked straight to his seat, head down, not noticing the balls of wadded-up paper tossed in his direction.

"Roger?" Chris asked. He didn't answer. He was sitting with his face turned to one side, so that Chris could only see the back of his head. "What's wrong?"

Roger shook his head, then resignedly turned to face Chris. "Satisfied?"

There was a bruise on his right cheek, and his eye was swollen. Both eyes were red, as though he'd been crying.

"Jesus," Chris said. "What happened?"

"Nothing."

"What do you mean, nothing?"

"I fell down, okay? That's what the note from my mom says, right here, you want to see it?" He whipped a sheet of notepaper out of his pocket.

Chris shook his head. "C'mon, I don't want to see the—"

"No, you gotta look at it, see, she signed it and everything, and it's—it's like a story, see—all about how I wasn't looking where I was going, and I fell, and—and—" He stopped, choking on anger. "Damn it," he said, and shoved the paper back into his pocket. "Just damn them all to fucking hell."

Roger stared out the window for a moment, clearly fighting back tears. "So where the hell's Mr. Edwards? He fall down, too?"

Before Chris could answer, the door opened again. Chris thought Edwards looked pretty upset about something. He hardly noticed them, just walked straight to his desk, but didn't sit down, only stood looking distractedly at the roll sheets. Then he paced for what felt like a full minute before finally turning toward them.

Something's happened, Chris thought.

"Can I have your attention, please," he said, although he already had it. The rest of the class had begun to pick up on the same nervousness Chris had noticed.

Mr. Edwards cleared his throat. "Ah, sometimes, things happen, and we have no control over them. Sometimes they happen to people we don't know, so it seems far away, and sometimes they happen to people we do know. Last night," he stopped, and gestured toward the empty second seat in the third row, "last night, Jim Bertierie passed away."

Holy shit! Chris thought.

It took a moment for it to sink in. Then someone asked, "How—"

"They're not sure yet. It seems to have been an accident. We're trying to find out everything we can, to try and—put all the pieces together. So we'll need some help from some of you who were friends of Jim's. We're going to have a short day today, the principal has decided to close school at noon. If you knew Jim, or if you saw Jim yesterday after school, we'd appreciate it if you could come by the front office. There are some people who'd like to talk to you, just to get some information. Any help you can give, anything you might know, would be appreciated by a lot of people, particularly Jim's family."

Above them, the bell rang, signaling first period. For a moment, no one moved. Then, slowly, they began gathering up books and papers and heading out, still silent. A couple of girls who sat near Jim were crying.

The faces Chris passed in the hall were as numb as his. Apparently everyone had been told at the same time. Roger came alongside him. "Big Jim Bertierie bites the big one," he said. "Un-be-fucking-lievable."

"Yeah."

"Best part is, we get half a day off."

"Not funny, Roger."

"So who's trying to be funny? He was an asshole."

"Roger—"

"If he *wasn't* an asshole, they would've given us the whole day off. Assholes only merit half a day."

Chris stopped. "Look, cut it out, okay?"

"No. You didn't know him. You just met him for ten minutes. And he was frigging nice compared to the some of the others! Do you know how many times he beat me up? No! You know how many times he tripped me, or ripped me off? I say it's about time some of these jerks got what's coming to them!" His face was red, and Chris saw that his hands were shaking. He'd never seen anyone this enraged before. The swelling around his eye made his expression even blacker, and he rubbed at it where it was watering.

"They just—they just get me mad," he said finally. "I just want to hurt them sometimes, the way they hurt me."

Then he started walking again, and Chris hurried to keep up with him.

Chris wondered if maybe Roger was right, to some extent. He had hardly met Bertierie. And hadn't he been worried all the way home last night that Bertierie was going to hassle him? All true. So why get upset?

Because you were *supposed* to get upset when someone died, he thought. That, at least, was the theory.

"You going to talk to them about last night?" he asked.

"What about it?"

"He said anybody who saw Bertierie last night should go by the principal's office and—"

"Oh, man, you've got to be putting me on."

"Roger, we *saw* him."

"Yeah, and he was fine. So what good is that? It was an accident, you heard him."

"I know, I know." Chris headed out of the door and started across the greensward to his first class. Roger angled off, heading for the building at the far side. "See you later."

"Right," Roger said.

Chris walked on a few more paces, then stopped. Screw it, he thought. "Roger," he called back.

"What?"

"I'm going to talk to them. You can come if you want."

"What an asshole," Roger said. But finally he grinned. "Okay, I'll go with you."

"Thanks."

The grin broadened a little, though it seemed to hurt his face where it was bruised. "Guess it *is* pretty sick, isn't it? Being glad somebody's dead if it gives you half a day off from school?"

"Extremely." The bell rang behind them. Another two minutes and they'd be late. "Later," Chris said.

"Yeah, later."

Chris jogged the rest of the way to first class.

Jim Bertierie was dead.

Un-be-fucking-lievable.

2

As the next three hours crawled by, teachers set aside their lesson plans to encourage their students to talk about their feelings. To depressurize, like fish brought up from a mile underwater, slowly and carefully, so they wouldn't explode like water balloons when they were pulled out into the real world.

What do you feel about what happened? Over and over, the same question. Some of the students seemed genuinely upset by the whole thing, but that included a few who got upset by just about anything, and relished the opportunity to cry and go on about how they were just so shocked and stunned and confused.

Derek Veltner was the only one who finally put up his hand, waited to be called on, and then said it the way he saw it. "Bertierie was a jerk-off," he said.

For this, Derek got to leave earlier than anyone else. Chris caught a glimpse of Derek as he raced from the building, turning around just long enough to wave at those trapped inside before running off into the P.E. field to shoot baskets.

Somehow, this struck Chris as just a little unfair.

He wondered if right now Roger was telling them all what *he* really thought of Bertierie.

If so, Roger would probably get the rest of the *year* off.

The one teacher seemingly untouched by the crisis atmosphere that held all the other classes was C. HUNTINGTON. Mr. Huntington picked up precisely where he had left off the day before: the burning of Atlanta in the final days of the Civil War.

"November fifteenth, 1864," he said, writing the date on the blackboard. "The city was in flames. General William Tecumseh Sherman rode into the city after wreaking havoc over half the South, taking Vicksburg and Chattanooga. The greycoats were on the run. And he didn't stop there, either. No, this was where he brought his men together, and, with a force of sixty *thousand* men strong, left Atlanta and began his famous march to the sea, which led to capturing Savannah in December and—"

A raised hand in the first row finally got his attention. "Yes, Carol?"

Carol Farrell was one of the weepers. She had cried all through Home Room, first period, second period, and now seemed determined to cry her way through Sherman's march. When Mr. Huntington called on her, she had her handkerchief in hand. "What—what about Jim?"

"Bertierie?"

She nodded. "Yes."

Chris looked back at Mr. Huntington; he thought he had never seen a face as hard or as unforgiving as the one that stared blankly back at Carol Farrell. "What about him?"

Carol's mouth worked for a moment as she tried to process this. He wasn't playing his assigned role. "He's *dead*."

"I know. What of it?"

"But shouldn't we—"

56

"Do you know how many thousands of people were killed or maimed or left homeless after Sherman torched Atlanta? Do you have any idea how many men and boys were killed over the course of the Civil War? Over three-hundred-and-sixty-four thousand." He stood before the blackboard, only the thinning of his lips betraying his anger. "Three-hundred-and-sixty-four *thousand*. Run that figure around in your head for a moment. And no one asked 'Please, can we stop to discuss our feelings?' "

"But Jim—" Carol looked confused. Not only was he denying her the discussion of her feelings, it seemed he was actually *angry* at her, for no good reason that she could see. "He was just sixteen."

"THREE-HUNDRED-AND-SIXTY-FOUR-THOUSAND-FIVE-HUNDRED-AND-ELEVEN MEN AND BOYS, Miss Farrell!" Carol sat back as if slapped. "Yes, it's a terrible thing when someone dies, when they get sick or they get hit by a car or they're in the wrong color uniform on the wrong day on the wrong side of the line, and it's terrible when we can't do anything about it, but at least you have some consolation in saying, well, maybe it was an act of God that little Billy got sick, or maybe he died fighting for a cause or a country or a flag or *something*—then you *have* to mourn and you *have* to show respect, because they went down fighting, they didn't just throw their lives away in an act of cowardice or fear or—"

He stopped. For a moment, his mouth just hung there, fighting with something he wanted to say. Then it snapped shut, as though his mouth had finally received its much-delayed orders from his brain.

Shut up, the orders must have read, because that's exactly what Mr. Huntington did. Two seats in front of him, Carol was crying, the tears real this time.

"You didn't have to yell at me," she said.

He nodded, then began erasing the blackboard, where he had painstakingly traced out Sherman's route. "Class dismissed," he said.

3

Chris waited until twelve-thirty before Roger finally joined him outside the principal's office. He looked pissed, as always. Chris wondered if Roger ever felt anything other than mad.

"What took you?" he asked.

Roger shrugged. "Got into some trouble with that jerk, Steve. He was going around telling everyone how he gave me this black eye. So I called him a liar. Next thing I knew they were all over me."

"Just don't know when to shut up, do you?"

"He was *laughing* about it, Chris! Saying, 'Oh, yeah, I beat this little shithead up *real* good. Just look at that face.' I get beat up enough as it is—you let 'em think this happens all the time, they'll never get off your back. What was I supposed to do?"

"Did you tell them it was an accident?"

Roger snorted. "Give me a break."

"But—"

"Look, just—let it go, will you? Jesus . . ." He shifted his books under his arm. "You talked to the principal yet?"

"No, I was waiting for you."

"Okay, okay, so I'm here, all right? C'mon."

They checked in with the administration secretary, were told to wait until Mr. Gerber was finished with some other students. After fifteen minutes Chris had almost decided to leave when the door to Mr. Gerber's office opened, and a pair of students were ushered out into the foyer. Mr. Gerber stood in the doorway. He was a gaunt man, with dark curly hair, who kept moving all the time, like someone late for several appointments. He checked a note clutched in one hand. "Chris Martino and—Roger Obst?"

"Here," Chris said, as he and Roger were ushered into the office.

Inside was Mr. Evanier, the vice-principal, and two cops.

What the hell? Chris thought.

One of the cops—a woman—came over to shake their hands. Mr. Evanier cleared his throat. He was a large man, and his shirt didn't seem quite capable of closing, creating a little triangle of skin just above his belt. "Roger, Chris, this is Officer Susan Warrick, and Officer Jordan Cayle."

"Hi," she said. "We're very sorry to hear what happened to your friend."

Chris shrugged. Roger didn't say a word.

"We're not here to get him in trouble, or you. As far as we know, no one's done anything wrong. We're just here because we need to understand a few things. Any information you can give us about Jim would be appreciated."

She gestured at a couple of chairs in front of Mr. Gerber's desk. They sat. The room was uncomfortably warm, Chris thought.

"Were you friends for very long?" Warrick asked.

"We weren't *friends*," Roger said. "He was a—"

Chris shot him a look.

"—we knew him from class, that's all," Roger finished.

"But we saw him yesterday, after school," Chris said.

"Do you remember what time it was?"

Chris thought about it, gave her the time as near as he could remember it. The other cop wrote the information down on his notepad.

"Do you know where he was going?"

"Home, I guess."

"When you saw him yesterday afternoon, how did he look to you?"

"You mean, did he look sick or something?"

"I'll let you find your own words."

"He seemed okay."

"He didn't appear upset, or angry, or depressed?"

"No more than usual," Roger said.

"How so?" she asked.

Roger looked uncomfortable. In the back of the room, Mr. Gerber cleared his throat. "It's all right, just say whatever you want."

"He was a jerk, okay?" Roger said. "He picked on a lot of kids, me included."

"So did you and he have a fight?"

"No," Chris said. "He kind of hassled us at McDonald's, but that was it. Then he left."

"And was that the last you saw of him?"

"No, not really. I mean, I didn't talk to him anymore, but I saw him on the bus. We were on the same one, and—" He hesitated, remembering the strange look on Bertierie's face.

"Go on."

"Well, I don't know . . . it's just when I saw him on the bus, it's like he didn't know I was there. He just looked . . . weird, I guess."

"How so?"

"It's hard to say."

"All right, would you say he looked happy, or sad?"

59

Chris thought about it. "Sad, I guess. Real distant."

"Resigned?"

"Yeah, I guess. And serious. Like he'd just gotten a bad grade, and was trying to figure out how to tell his folks."

She glanced to the other cop, who checked his notebook and shook his head. "So let me see if I have this sequence correct," she said. "When you were in the restaurant together, he was hassling you. Was he enjoying himself? Laughing?"

"Yeah," Roger said, "he seemed to be having a real good time."

"And then when you saw him on the bus just a few moments later, you say he seemed kind of sad, resigned, like he was worried about something."

Chris considered it. It was curious that Bertierie's mood had changed so quickly, like a switch had been thrown inside him. "Yes."

"Did he see or talk to anyone else before he got on the bus?"

"Yeah," Roger said. "But it was nobody from the school. Just some guy."

"Can you be a little more exact?"

"I don't—no, he was just some guy. Looked kind of like a bum. He was standing by the bus stop, and I think Jim said something to him."

"Did the man say anything back?"

Roger shrugged. "I don't know. Maybe. Then they just stood there for a minute, and the bus came."

"And that was it?"

Both of them nodded.

"And you didn't see Jim after that?"

"No, ma'am," Chris said.

She stepped across the room and stood before them, hands crossed behind her back. "One last thing. As far as you know, did Jim seem unusually upset about anything lately? Family? Friends? Grades?"

"Nope," Roger said. "He was just like everybody else." Chris knew what Roger meant by that, and knew that Roger was probably grinning inside at it. *He was an asshole, just like everybody else, Miss Cop, and my, aren't you looking especially puckered this fine afternoon?*

"All right," she said, and turned to Mr. Gerber and the rest. "Anyone want to ask anything else? Jordan?"

They declined. The other cop closed his notebook and put it back into his pocket.

"You're free to go," she said. "Thank you for your cooperation. You've been very helpful."

The door opened, and they were led back into the hall.

Once they were alone, Chris let out a long, low whistle. "Man, what was *that* all about?" He looked over to see that Roger was grinning. "What? Come on, give."

"You know what *I* think? I think old Bertierie didn't just have an accident. I think something else happened to him."

"Like what?"

"I say it was drugs or he killed himself."

"Get out of here!"

"I bet you five dollars."

He could see that Roger was quite serious. Back in Matawan, drugs were still pretty new. He hadn't known anyone who had ever died from them, though he knew it happened a lot, especially in a town like L.A. But Bertierie hadn't looked stoned at the time.

"What makes you think so?"

"You heard what they were asking in there. How was he when you saw him last? What kind of mood was he in? Did he have any problems? What does that have to do with an accident?"

"Nothing, I guess."

"Egg-zactly."

"But they said—"

"Oh, come on. You believe everything you're told? Look, last semester there was a senior girl who left school in the middle of her last semester. All the teachers said it was because she got sick and went away to get better, when everybody *knew* she left because she got an abortion, and her folks split up because of it. But the teachers never *tell* you that kind of stuff. So if Bertierie did O.D., or jump off a roof somewhere, you think they'd tell *us*?"

Roger stopped. He looked at Chris, and his eyes widened. "Hey, what if Bertierie got killed by somebody? What about that, huh?"

"Then it'd be on the news," Chris said. "That kind of stuff you can't cover up."

"Yeah," Roger said. He sounded actually disappointed. "Hey, maybe Bertierie finally realized he was an asshole and figured he'd clean up the gene pool a little. Maybe he hung himself. Or—no, wait— what if he got a gun and blew his brains all over the living room? Wouldn't that be boss?"

4

By the time they reached Roger's house, the topic had finally changed to other matters. Roger explained how Mr. Winston had gotten his Creative Writing class to form a circle, to better discuss their feelings about Bertierie. Roger had ended up sitting directly across from Patricia McKinley, who he'd been wet-dreaming about since junior high, and she was wearing a short skirt and *no panties.*

Sitting on his bed in his room, Roger said it almost reverently. "No panties." Chris doubted Roger would have been any more moved if he had seen a flying saucer.

"You think she saw you?" Chris asked. He picked up one of the books stuffed into the shelves beside the chair. *Make-Up Secrets Revealed,* by Lawrence Radmussen. There was a picture of a man in a *Creature from the Black Lagoon* costume on the cover.

"If she had, I wouldn't be *alive* right now. She's going with one of the hormone cases from the basketball team. What's between those legs is strictly private property, and if she'd seen me, she'd've had him dribble me all over the basketball court and leave me there to rot." He tapped his glasses. "It's one of the benefits of wearing glasses. You can point your face in one direction, while all the time you're looking somewhere else."

Chris turned his attention back to the book in his hands. It was filled with diagrams and pictures from old horror movies. Beside it was a book on stage magic.

"Pretty boss, huh?" Roger asked.

"You ever actually *try* any of this stuff?"

"Some of them, yeah. Here," he said, "let me show you something." He ripped a sheet of paper out of his spiral-bound notebook and went to the door. "Be right back," he said, and stepped outside.

While Roger was gone, Chris continued his inspection of the room. Everywhere his gaze fell there was something interesting. There were stills from science fiction movies. Piles of comics sandwiched in between textbooks and library books. Paper everywhere. *One well-placed match . . .,* he thought.

Roger reentered the bedroom, the sheet of paper folded twice. He handed it to Chris. "Read it," he said.

Chris unfolded the paper. It was blank on both sides. "Funny," he said.

"Look at it again. See anything?"

Chris examined the page more carefully. There was a slight dampness to it, but that was all. He squinted at the blue lines in case anything had been written in letters so tiny he hadn't seen them the first time. Still nothing.

"Okay," Roger said. "Give it back."

He handed it back, and watched as Roger pulled a cigarette lighter out of his pocket. "Now watch," he said, and held it under the paper. He moved it back and forth, and up and down, keeping it just far enough away to avoid singeing the paper. A bitter, slightly acrid smell filled the air.

"All right," Roger said, handing back the sheet of paper, "*now* look."

This time there was writing on the page. Brown, jagged letters had appeared, some thick, some thin, but still readable. It said:

WHAT ARE YOU LOOKING AT, ASSHOLE?

Roger burst into laughter. "Is that great, or what?"

"Yeah. How'd you do it?"

"Magic."

"C'mon, Roger, don't shit me. How'd you do it?"

"Lemon juice," he said, and sat back down on the bed. He pulled an eyedropper from his pocket. "It's easy. You just squeeze a little lemon inside, then use it like a pen. You can see it for a minute while it's wet, so you can keep track of what you write, but after that it dries up and turns invisible. Until you heat it up. Then the lemon juice turns brown, and you can read it again. I found out about it in *Secret Codes and Brain-Tangles*. Used to use it to pass notes in class. That way if a teacher got hold of it, all they'd see was a blank page. Used to drive 'em crazy. 'Course, you couldn't read it until after class, they have this thing about starting fires—"

The smile on Roger's face vanished with the sound of the front door opening down the hall. Chris could make out the sound of a man's voice. A moment later, there was the sound of footsteps coming down the hall. Roger seemed to hold his breath as they approached, then continued on past the door to his bedroom. Another door slammed elsewhere down the hall.

"My dad's home," Roger said. He looked down at the lemon-filled eyedropper in his hand, and impulsively capped it and handed it to Chris. "Here. Take it."

"No, I—"

"It's okay. I've got a bunch more. Go on."

Chris took it. "Thanks."

Roger smiled a little, but it was just a flicker of politeness. "You'd better go now," he said.

At the screen door that opened on the front porch, Chris tucked the eyedropper into his pocket. "You can come to my place. My mom won't be home for a while yet."

"No," Roger said, and his voice was flat. "I can't. Sometimes—I think sometimes I'm never getting out of here."

"See you tomorrow," Chris said, but by then the inner door had clicked shut. He lingered for a moment, then started down the short steps to the sidewalk.

A few paces away, he stopped and looked back.

There was shouting coming from inside the house. The very sound of it made Chris feel queasy.

The rest of the way home, he thought about Roger's books, especially of *Make-Up Secrets Revealed*. Roger must have studied that one carefully, because he had learned how to make a lot of masks. There was the superior one he wore around the other kids, there was the angry one he wore when he was picked on, there was the friendly one that peeked out when he and Chris were joking around—and that was the one that had fallen off when they'd both heard the door slam.

Dad's home. And wasn't that a curious mask he had put on at that moment? Blank. Empty, except for the one thing it had in common with all the rest of Roger's masks.

They were all swollen around the right eye.

6

So far, everything matched—and nothing matched.

While Gene Edwards poured another cup of coffee, Susan checked her notes to see if there were anything she had forgotten to ask. Edwards, the dead kid's home room teacher, had been helpful and detailed. He was the kind of teacher she'd liked best when she was in school—accessible, and interested in his students. He was taking this hard. One of his students had slipped through his fingers, and he couldn't understand why, or how.

The lounge was deserted, except for the two of them. The rest of the teachers had gone home, and Jordan was still in with the principal. It was standard department policy to investigate any suicide, especially juveniles, because often they were symptoms of other, more far-reaching problems: abuse at home, drugs, gang activities. But the stakes had been raised even further because of what she'd learned this morning, when they'd been briefed on the reasons for their transfer to Juvie. There had been three teenage suicides in seven days. One at Inglewood High, another at Hoover Junior High, and this one.

None of them fit the pattern.

Bertierie, like the rest, was an average student. No sudden dropoff in grades, no unusual absenteeism problems, no apparent drug abuse, though they were still waiting for the coroner's report. He seemed to have, gotten along well with his parents, who did not have any overwhelming financial burdens.

So what was the button? she wondered. What made a perfectly ordinary sixteen-year-old kid decide to take a drive in his garage with the door closed tight?

Gene came back with his coffee. "Sure I can't get you anything?"

Susan shook her head. Gene took his seat at the far end of the couch. "Can I ask *you* a question now?"

"Sure."

"Why couldn't we tell the kids the real reason Jim died? Why the cover story about an accident? You know it'll leak out in time."

"It was a departmental decision," she said. "There's a lot of concern about patterning. Statistics indicate that for whatever reason, juvenile suicides sometimes come in clumps. It happens a lot more often than you hear about. One kid kills himself, and then other kids—maybe feeling trapped in their own situations, or in need of affection or attention—suddenly find themselves with a new possibility. They see parents crying, and think, 'Yeah, that'll teach them. Then they'll miss me.' Next thing you know, one becomes two becomes three. Eventually it'll get out—but by that time it'll have lost some of its emotional context, and maybe there'll be less chance that others will get the same idea."

Though we've lost that battle a couple of times already, she thought, which was all the more reason to keep this one quiet. Though there didn't seem much chance of Bertierie having heard about the other two suicides.

"All right," Gene said, "I'll keep to the cover story. What else can I do to help?"

"Keep an eye on the students for us, as we asked the other teachers to do. He may have talked to someone, indicated what he was planning to do. If so, then eventually they'll say something. Meanwhile, if you think of anything else that might help, give me a call." She handed him her card, with her home phone number written in pencil.

He tucked the card into his jacket pocket. "Will do," he said, extending his hand. "And I want to thank you for taking the time to look into this as thoroughly as you have. It's good to know the department will do all this for one kid."

She accepted the hand. "We try," she said, thinking, But we try a lot more when there's three bodies lying on slabs in the mortuary instead of one.

2

Jordan looked up from his hamburger as Susan climbed into the squad car. "You get anything?"

She closed the door. "Nothing useful. Just a kid, that's all." She noticed the hamburger. "Jesus, is there anytime you *don't* eat?"

He licked mustard and ketchup off his right thumb. "School cafeteria was just going to throw away some of this stuff, since most everyone's leaving at lunch. So I figured, why not? Where else can you get a hamburger like this for a buck and a quarter?"

"So did you find out anything?"

"Nothing special. No connection I can see to the other two deaths. My guess is it's a coincidence. When I was a rookie, I saw three silver Mercedes in head-on collisions on the same day in the same neighborhood. No connection, they just happened at the same time. Synchronicity."

"Maybe," Susan said. "Let's hope so, anyway."

3

Tony Soznick woke up with a start. The sound was gone now, but there was the sense of a door having been slammed shut.

Crazy, he thought. Just fell asleep, that's all. Must've been dreaming.

Then he realized he was lying on the floor.

But he'd sat down on the bed, just for a minute, just to close his eyes after finishing up for the day.

And hadn't the sky outside his window been much lighter than it was now?

He closed his eyes, mentally backtracking. He remembered collapsing on the bed at around three-thirty; it was now almost five-forty-five.

Just fell asleep, he thought. And he'd fallen out of bed. That had to be it. The fall was the bang he thought he'd heard. Yes, that seemed to make sense.

He sat up, and saw two bundles of papers stacked beside the door, each containing maybe two thousand sheets of the usual fliers. Beside them was a fresh bucket of glue, and a Thomas Brothers book of maps.

They had not been there when he had gone to sleep.

He licked his lips, an image coming unbidden to him: he lies down on his bed, closes his eyes, then suddenly his eyes open, *even though he's still asleep*, and he goes—somewhere—eventually coming back carrying all this stuff, and slamming the door behind him as he slumps to the floor.

It was determined to squeeze every drop out of him, awake or asleep, wasn't it?

He went to the Thomas Brothers book beside the bundles of fliers. Three maps had been ripped out and stuck inside the other pages. The first was page 34. A red ink circle had been drawn around the intersection of Sunset Boulevard and Highland.

Next was page 56. The red circle this time appeared at 111th Street and Buford.

Page 57 was last. The circle was at Grevillea Avenue and Manchester Boulevard.

The longer he looked, the more he began to realize that the red circles had something in common. The mark on 34 was beside Hollywood High School, the one on 56 was on top of Lennox High School, and the final circle marked Inglewood High School.

He felt his skin go cold.

Sometimes they were hospitals. Sometimes they were schools, or asylums or retirement homes . . . sometimes there wasn't a pattern to it at all, or at least none that he could see.

He ran his fingers over the circles. They had been made by pressing the pen so hard into the page that the circles were almost holes. If he pushed, they would pop out. For a giddy moment, he considered doing just that, pushing out the holes in two of the pages and holding them up in front of him like a mask; running out into the hall yelling "Trick or treat! Give us some candy, because we're not alone, even though we look like it. Give us some candy or we'll look at you through the map, we'll make you wake up in Miami. Give us some candy or we'll—"

What?

Stop it, part of his brain was screaming. *You'd think you'd be used to it by now.*

And that was the terrible part of it, he thought. He was used to it. The only thing that kept the terror of it from squeezing his heart until it burst was his ignorance of what the circles *meant*, or what the fliers meant, or what *any*thing meant.

He picked up page 34. Might as well go alphabetically, by school, he thought, and held the page up to the fading light of day, letting it filter in through the cuts in the red circle. He held it up to his eye, squinting through the strands of fiber. It made the world look the same as it did through the X-ray specs he'd once ordered as a kid from some place in White Plains, New York.

He pressed the page against his face, and in spite of himself, started to giggle again.

Trick or treat.

BOOK TWO
CONTACT

The land of darkness, and the shadow of death.
The Book of Job, 10:21

7

There were fifteen minutes left before lunch was over, and Chris was still scavenging around the racquetball courts, trying not to panic. *Damn them,* he thought. His stomach was knotted up inside; he had missed lunch to come here and search—uselessly, it now seemed— for his pen.

It had been a birthday present from his father, a silver-and-gold Cross ballpoint, top of the line. Less than a month later his father had walked out. Chris wondered sometimes if the gift had been a way to salve his father's conscience.

Whatever the reason, it had been a gift from his father, whose only request was that he not lose it. And he hadn't. Not through two moves. And he hadn't lost it now, either, he thought, and the anger returned.

Damn that Steve Mackey, he thought, his cheeks burning, *damn them all to hell.*

They had been in the locker room after P.E. As Chris picked up his books the pen fell out of his folder. Steve saw it, and snatched it up off the concrete floor.

"Whoa," Steve said, showing it to one of his fellow Neanderthals. "Nice stuff."

Chris asked for it back. They laughed and started throwing it back and forth, just beyond his reach. At one point they tossed it over a row of lockers, and Chris raced around it as fast as he could—but Steve was faster.

"You want it?" he asked again. "Fetch!" he yelled, and threw it out through the upper window that faced the racquetball field. Chris ran after it, barely beginning his search when the bell rang for next period. His only hope was to come back at lunch and hope that someone else didn't claim it in the interim.

He was just about ready to give up when he saw a silver glint at the base of one of the side walls. The pen had rolled into a crack in the concrete base. He couldn't quite get at it with his fingers, so he unfolded a paperclip and used it to get behind the pen and knock it far enough out for him to get a grip on it. The silver coating was scuffed in places, and the opening at the bottom was dented, but it was otherwise intact. He turned the pen. The cartridge came out with some difficulty. He'd have to see if there was some way to reshape the opening without further damaging the pen.

But he *had* it, he thought. For once here was something Steve hadn't managed to take away from him.

He decided to cut back across the playing field toward the cafeteria. If he were lucky, there might still be time to grab a hamburger before the bell rang. Halfway across the field, though, he stopped at the sound of voices coming from behind a line of bushes, mixed with the scent of grass. He peeked through the bushes.

Steve and two of his buddies were leaning against the wall of the English building, passing a joint back and forth. Soda cans and hamburger wrappers littered the ground.

Chris froze, his heart beating triphammer hard as an idea settled in behind his eyes. There were ten minutes before lunch was over; ten minutes before they'd leave; ten minutes during which Chris might be able to find a teacher, and get him back here. Ten minutes between Now and the possibility of Steve being suspended or expelled. Ten minutes to freedom.

Do it! he thought. *Serve him right!*

Then from behind him: "Hey!"

Paul Geyer was running toward him.

Chris cursed. He should have noticed that Paul was missing from the usual bunch Steve hung out with.

Steve stood up, saw Chris on the other side of the bushes. "Son of a BITCH!" He started toward Chris.

Chris ran.

He paralleled the English building, glancing back only once to see Steve and the rest of his bunch closing the gap behind him. Getting out from behind the bushes must've cost them an extra second—but they were bigger than he was, and gaining fast.

". . . kill you, you fucker!" Steve was yelling. "Goddamn son of a bitch *spying* on us!"

Chris hit the door to the English building and cut inside, ducking into the first open room. Mr. Edwards was at his desk, eating a sandwich. He looked up as Steve and the rest charged in through the door after him.

"Something I can do for you?" Mr. Edwards asked them.

Steve shot Chris a look. If he had something to say, he swallowed it, and headed back out again. As the door closed, Chris saw him hold up a threatening finger. *One word*, he mouthed. It was enough. The meaning was clear.

Chris was aware that his knees were shaking, and that Mr. Edwards was looking at him.

"You want to talk about it?" he asked.

"No thanks."

"They're trouble," Edwards said. "My bet is they'll get expelled or screwed up before they graduate. Until then, you'd do well to steer clear of them and avoid pissing them off."

It was, Chris thought distantly, the first time he had ever heard a teacher use the term "pissed off."

"Have you had lunch already?" Edwards asked. Chris shook his head. Edwards picked up the other half of his tuna fish sandwich and handed it to him. "I hope you like it without mayonnaise."

Chris took a bite. "Thanks."

"Any time," Mr. Edwards said. Chris thought it sounded as if he actually meant it.

When he had caught his breath and finished most of the sandwich, Chris started to tell him about the Cross pen, and what had kept him from lunch.

But he didn't mention the grass.

"Mr. Edwards?"

Gene stopped, midway into his car, as a police woman approached. "Yes?"

"Susan Warrick. We met last week."

Behind them, another cop headed into the school. "Yes, of course. What can I do for you?"

A group of students were lounging within earshot. "Can we walk for a second?"

"Sure," he said. She kept pace with him, eyes down. She hasn't slept much, he thought.

"We had another one last night."

"God . . ." The thought of another dead kid made him sick. *Such madness.* "You're sure it's a suicide?"

"Coroner confirmed the cause of death this morning, though no one had any real doubt. It was pretty ugly. Girl's name was Pamela Manriquez. Inglewood High. Ring any bells?"

"None."

"The kids in your class didn't know her?"

"I can't be *absolutely* sure—I mean, most kids don't talk about each other to their teachers—but I don't recall hearing the name."

"Okay, just thought I'd try." She looked out toward the playing field. "At first we thought it was gang related, but that connection didn't pan out."

"Drugs?"

"Thought about that, too. Coroner says there were traces of coke in her bloodstream, but so minute it was hardly worth mentioning. Must've just tried it a couple of times and stopped." She smiled without humor. "Probably decided it wasn't good for her health."

She looked around the campus. "This is a nice place. A lot better than some of the schools around here."

Gene smiled. "The gangs tend to leave us alone—so far, at any rate." He started walking again, leading them back to the parking lot. "Any chance the girl could've heard about what happened here?"

"That's what my partner's trying to find out now. He's checking to see if there were any other family members here, any friends. If not . . ." She frowned. "It's just weird, that's all. If there's *no* connection, if they didn't even know about one another, then how the hell do you explain four kids in a ten-mile radius all deciding to kill themselves within a two-week period? We've been good about containing this so far, but I have a hunch that this last one's going to slip out. Too many witnesses this time."

"You two handling this pretty much by yourselves?"

"Not a chance. We've got five detectives coordinating the investigation. They do all the direct contact with the kids' families, but they can't be everywhere at once. Most of the emphasis is on gang detail these days, and since none of the deaths have been homicides, everybody has to make do with what's available. That means us and about four others doing the preliminary interviews. If we turn anything up, the detectives move in and do the followups."

They arrived at the squad car just as her partner came back out of the administration building. "Nothing," he said. "Principal says the incident here is still under wraps, and there's no connection he can think of, but he'll check around some more just in case."

"Okay," she said. Her partner got behind the wheel. "Thanks for your help, Mr. Edwards. If we need anything else, we'll be in touch."

"Just sorry I couldn't do more," he said.

He headed back to his car and in spite of himself his thoughts wandered to the dead girl. He wondered how it had happened this time.

Coroner confirmed the cause of death this morning, she'd said, *though no one had any real doubt. It was pretty ugly.*

All things considered, he'd rather not know.

3

In the last two weeks, walking most of the way home after school had become a habit for Chris and Roger. The routine they had fallen into rarely varied, nor was there much need to change it. So far, the routine had kept them safe.

It was Chris who had discovered the workroom door that led into the back of the gym. The lock was rusted; with a little effort, it would come free of its slot and open up on the gym. With the last bell, most kids were either on their way home, or were out on the playing field outside. So they had the whole place to themselves.

Chris generally put in the twenty or so minutes shooting baskets.

It was the only time he could practice without (as Roger put it) getting big laughs. He wasn't good at it, but there was something relaxing about shooting the ball with no one around trying to take it away.

Roger read. Roger, Chris discovered, was *always* reading. Lovecraft, Poe, King, Dunsany, Derleth, on and on. He'd once made the mistake of asking Roger if he wanted to join in, shoot a few baskets—and Roger had pulled a face so twisted that it seemed almost to fall in upon itself.

Roger hated sports. Even on short notice he could invariably provide a note from his parents prohibiting him from whatever the gym teacher wanted him to do—basketball, football, baseball, track, wrestling, whatever. Chris sometimes suspected he had gone through the encyclopedia, pulled out references to every known sport, and made up a standard form for his mother to sign, adding a few extra sports just in case someone invented them when he wasn't looking.

Please excuse my son from playing Motorized Jai-Lai. Thank you very much. Roger's mom. P.S., please keep him away from girls, as they make him breathe too hard.

So for twenty minutes, the only sounds in the gym were a whoosh, a thump, and (if Chris was lucky) a swish from one end, while from the other came the rhythmic turning of pages.

Afterward, when they could be reasonably certain that the Dumbass Deathsquad had grown tired of waiting for them, they would start the walk home. They would talk about anything and everything during these walks, though mostly they talked about girls, movie monsters, and did Roger *really* think Luke Skywalker slept with Princess Leia before finding out she was actually his sister?

"Of course he did," Roger was saying. They were cutting across an open lot, heading for the main street. "Look, they had all that time on Hoth, and you could see they were close. Real close. In *Return of the Jedi* they were practically all over each other—and with Han Solo out of the way, wouldn't you take advantage of the situation? I say he slept with her, and that's the reason we haven't seen a new movie since—I think she's pregnant, and they don't know how to handle it."

Chris grinned. "Jesus, the way you talk, you'd think this stuff was real."

"It is. Well, not *really* real, everyone knows that. But it's almost as good. It's like—"

Abruptly, he stopped beside a telephone pole. "Hey," Roger said, "look at this."

Chris came over to where he was looking at a poster glued to the telephone pole. "What about it?"

"Read it."

It didn't make a lot of sense—just a jumble of words and images tumbling one over another in a way that didn't add up to anything Chris could understand.

And yet there was something about it—

. . . in the end there is just the darkness . . .

He squinted at the words, but they seemed to run together.

"I've seen this before," Roger said. "Can't remember where, but somewhere."

. . . there is no love there is no hate there is only me and there is only you listen listen . . .

It must have been the cramped, uneven printing, but the text momentarily seemed to swim in front of him. For a moment it seemed he was actually seeing past the words, as though there were something written underneath them, inside the paper—

And suddenly there was a shadow on the paper.

Someone behind them.

Chris turned, startled. A man, dressed haphazardly, loomed behind them, black against the sun. He was so close that he could touch them by just reaching out a few inches. He wore a hat that hid his face, and a pile of papers were tucked under his right arm. His other hand carried a bucket of glue.

Oh, shit, Chris thought, and gradually realized the specter before them was talking.

"Do you like it?" he said.

"Well, I, uh, I guess."

His eyes, Chris thought. Beneath the brim of his hat they seemed to burn out, brighter than they had any right to be. It was as though the man were straining to look *into* him, straining so hard Chris thought those eyes would burn a hole through his body.

This is crazy, he thought. *Stop looking at him.*

But he couldn't. And now, suddenly, he felt cold, the kind of chill his father used to say was like someone walking over your grave.

"It's okay," Roger said, his voice seeming to come from a place far underground. The man shifted his gaze to Roger, and now those eyes burrowed into him. Chris could feel the gaze clamping onto Roger like an octopus.

"I'm glad you like it," the man said, never taking his eyes off Roger. "It's important that you like it."

Crazy, Chris thought again. The conversation was benign; no one could tell from looking at them that they were drowning in the strangeness of the moment.

Roger opened his mouth to say something, but nothing came out. His jaw hung open for a second, and his brow furrowed, as if something he hadn't thought about for a long time had suddenly come up from somewhere deep inside, and he was surprised to see it.

Then, with a last look at both—

Those eyes, get away from those eyes, not right, they're not right

—the man said "Thank you," and walked away. The shadow lifted off them like a long-accustomed weight.

Chris took a long, slow breath, feeling himself coming back from . . . where? The entire encounter couldn't have lasted more than thirty seconds. "What the hell was *that*?" he asked Roger.

"Just . . . some guy," Roger said. "Weird, huh?"

"Yeah," Chris said. He started walking again. Suddenly he wanted nothing more than to get home and surround himself with the sight of familiar things.

Roger didn't move. "You coming?" Chris called.

"Huh?" Roger roused himself. "Oh, yeah. Hang on."

He jogged up to Chris. They walked along the sidewalk without speaking. After a while, Roger gamely continued his argument in favor of cosmic incest, but it seemed his heart just wasn't in it.

Real weird, Chris thought, then forced himself to put it out of his mind.

He would never see the man again.

8

Susan caught the phone on the third ring, and immediately recognized Gene Edwards's voice.

"What's up?" she asked, grateful for the diversion. She'd been going over her notes from the day's interviews until she was dizzy.

"Nothing important," Gene said, "I was just wondering if you'd like to get together for dinner sometime." There was a small laugh at the other end. "Never asked a cop to go out to dinner before. Feels kind of funny."

"It'll pass," she said, and hesitated before going on. There were departmental policies about socializing with subjects under investigation, but Gene was only tangential to the inquiry. He seemed like a nice enough man. And there was hardly ever anything good on television these days. And weren't there always plenty of rationalizations lying around when you really needed them? *Strictly business, Captain, exchanging views on stress factors and their impact on the student population. Sir.*

"Sure," she said, "why not?"

"Great! I'll give you a call tomorrow—"

"Better if I call you," she said. "I'm on the move a lot, so it's hard to pin down where I'll be. Barring unforeseen incidents, I'll give you a call tomorrow afternoon, and we'll take it from there."

"Talk to you then," he said, and hung up.

She was getting too used to being a cop, she thought.

Barring unforeseen incidents.

A nice, clean metaphor for, *Unless another adolescent corpse crops up.*

Screw it, she thought, and switched on the TV to catch the evening news.

2

It hurts, Chris thought. He lay in bed, staring up at the ceiling, and thinking IT HURTS until the letters burned in his brain. His head was throbbing, the pain squeezing him right between the eyes. No matter what position he lay in, the pain continued.

IT HURTS was at two miles and climbing.

He pressed the palm of his hand against his forehead. It seemed to help a little. He pressed harder. Harder still—

With a sudden *crack* he felt something give.

OH SHIT! he thought, and sat bolt upright. *Oh shit, oh shit, oh shit, I broke something.* Panic tore at his chest. He pushed at the center of his forehead—gently, gently—and it gave slightly under his fingers. He was shaking now.

Oh shit, I broke something and I'm gonna die.

Moving slowly, he stood up and walked toward the door, both hands holding his head as though it might split. His knees were trembling so badly that it was nearly impossible to stand.

He made it to the bathroom (*can't tell Mom, oh jeez, what am I gonna do*) and switched on the light. Closed the door. He leaned against the sink, looking at the mirror. He turned his head slowly from side to side. Yes, there was a definite depression there in the middle of his forehead. Horrified, he touched it again, pushed gingerly against it with one finger—

And it gave under his touch.

Oh god, he thought.

Then it split open with a sickening, soft tearing sound.

His finger sank an inch into the hole before he could stop himself.

He tried to cry out but the sound died in his throat. The world spun around him, and he thought he would faint. They would find him like that in the morning with his finger in his forehead—

Stop it.

Slowly, he pulled his finger out. It came out with a sucking noise, leaving a hole in the middle of his forehead. With horrified fascination, unable to stop himself, he tugged gently at the edges of the hole—and they folded down, widening the hole, which seemed to penetrate in a straight line, a round tunnel made of bone and tissue and

(no, no way, please God)

—and in spite of himself he slid his finger back into the hole, slowly, the tissue soft and yielding and moist, and when he pulled it out again it glistened greyly in the light over the sink. He looked again at the hole, angling his head so that the light could reach into it.

And there was another light inside. Dull, and red, but definitely there.

For the last time, he slid his finger into the hole, farther and farther, past the first knuckle, the second—

"*No!*" he cried out, and sat upright.

He was in bed. His mom was sitting beside him.

"You okay, honey?" She ran a hand across his forehead. He flinched, then allowed the touch. His skull was solid beneath her touch, even if covered with perspiration. "Bad dream?"

He nodded, blinking. It had seemed so *real*, so mind-numbingly, frighteningly real.

"Do you want some water?" she asked.

"No, I—I don't think so." Her hand was cool and reassuring on his forehead. "Did I yell?"

"Only after I started to wake you." The reassuring smile flickered for a moment, then returned. "I was watching the news. I guess it upset me a little, and I just came upstairs to see if you were all right. Looks like I did the right thing."

"Yeah," he said, and slid back under the covers.

"You sure you're okay now?"

"Uh-huh."

"Positive?"

He nodded.

"All right," she said, and started for the door.

"Mom?"

She paused in the doorway. "Yes?"

"What did you see on the news?"

"Nothing you need to worry about," she said, softly. "Good night,

Chris." Then she stepped back into the hallway, leaving the door open a few inches behind her.

He waited until her footsteps had receded down the stairs, then closed his eyes. Stupid dream, he thought . . . then gently pressed the palm of his hand against his forehead.

It didn't give.

But he didn't press too hard, either.

You could never be too sure about these things.

3

perfect

4

Roger's legs were falling asleep, he was uncomfortable, his neck was sore, it was well past midnight, and part of him ached to go back to bed.

But that other part had other ideas.

He'd been nearly asleep when he'd heard the car door slam, heard two voices laughing and heading toward the house next door. He'd waited for a long time before concluding that the car wasn't going anywhere, that this was going to be one of his Special Nights.

Lisa Williams had moved in two months ago, renting the house from the couple who had lived there before. Not long afterward, he discovered that she had changed the curtains in her bedroom window to something translucent, and that they were often left opened.

Roger's bedroom was about ten feet to the left of the window, which meant that though he couldn't see the whole room, by virtually shoving himself against the glass, and standing on tiptoe, he could see most of it. And the first night she'd brought someone home with her, that had been quite a lot.

The first time he'd watched her, he thought he would die of excitement. She switched on a red light, and slowly undressed in front of the mirror. He could see everything. He could see hands roaming over her body, finally pulling her toward the bed. He could see most but not all of the bed, just the bottom half—which left him a view of legs entwining around one another, then one pair slipping between the other, then her legs wrapping around his waist, pulling him into her. Somehow, not being able to see all of it made it even more exciting. If he opened his window, he could hear the sound of her moaning in a throaty way that made his hands tremble.

That had been the first of his Special Nights.

There had been three more since then.

He was hoping that tonight would be number five.

He shifted uncomfortably at the window, his legs racing fire up through his hips. He had to lean forward to get a decent view, and after twenty minutes his legs were starting to quiver from the strain. The windowsill had left long creases in his palms where he rested against it. What the hell was *taking* her so long?

Then he thought, They couldn't be doing it in the living room, could they? Where he couldn't see them?

No. They couldn't do that to him. They wouldn't.

Would they?

Five minutes, that's all. Five minutes more and then I'm going to bed.

The bedroom light switched on. A moment later, she appeared in his line of sight. She was wearing a long dress that looked satiny in the dim light, her shoulder-length blond hair tousled from the touch of another's hands. She stepped out of her heels as the man—whoever he was this time—went to her and pulled her to him. Through the window, he could hear the windchime sound of her laughter. The man reached behind her, and her dress fell off her shoulders, stopping just short of her breasts.

Roger licked his lips, his groin tightening, the shaking in his knees all but forgotten.

The man whispered something to her. She shook her head. He whispered again, and then she nodded.

Roger wondered what he was talking her into. It had to be something good.

She almost never had to be talked into *anything*.

They moved toward the bed, and the man lay down. She went around to the other side and—

No! No way!

The light went out.

YOU CAN'T DO THIS TO ME!

She did. The bedroom was dark, but the sound of laughter continued.

Mocking him. He was sure of it.

And now the moaning.

He stepped back and kicked the dresser. "Damn them," he said, oblivious to the pain in his foot, "damn them all to hell!"

Half an hour he had been standing there, his legs on fire, waiting for her, and this is what he gets! His fists balled up in impotent rage. They did it deliberately. They all did it deliberately.

He looked at the plastic models on his shelves, and a flash of hatred seared his thoughts. It wasn't fair. All he got were these stupid models, while some asshole was in there screwing her brains out. In that moment he hated the grotesquely painted figures silhouetted against the shadows. They were stupid. And weren't they leering at him? Mocking him?

Laughing at him?

"I hate you!" He grabbed one of them and threw it to the floor. It cracked upon impact. A head—was it the Wolfman?—skittered under the bed. He stomped on the torso, grinding his slipper-clad foot into it until its arms and legs snapped off.

He grabbed another, and smashed it against the wall over his bed. It bounced, landing on the sheets. It was his prize, the battery-powered Frankenstein model that would drop its pants and blush red when activated.

And now it did just that. Lying there on his bed, its black trousers dropped, revealing the heart-covered boxer shorts beneath. Its face leered red at him, the same shade of red that he'd seen in her bedroom. Its hands were gripping its own shorts grotesquely. *Bet she'd love what I got in here, eh, short stuff? Let her see a real man. Hell,* several *real men.*

Then: a final moan from the house next door. It cut through Roger like a knife.

Damn her.

He stood in the middle of the room and felt the rage bleed out of him, as though her release had triggered one of his own. In a moment, there was nothing but the familiar feeling of helplessness.

But someday that would change. Someday he would have Power, and on that day his wrath would fall like fire from the sky. Someday, she and all the other girls he saw snickering at him would come to him, and then he would teach them. They would beg for the honor of giving him whatever he wanted.

He would have them all.

In a room with a red light.

But for now, he was trapped. And with that knowledge, the fire diminished a little.

What time is it? he wondered, and glanced at the bedside clock. Nearly one-thirty. Christ, and on a school night no less.

He picked up the Frankenstein model, switching it off and putting it back on the shelf with its back to him, its trousers still down around its ankles. Let it sit that way until morning, he thought. Then, with a pang, he knelt down and felt along the carpet for the pieces of the werewolf model. He had spent hours putting it together, and could recognize each piece by feel.

After a few minutes, he had all but one of the pieces.

All but the head.

He peered into the darkness under the bed. It had to be in there somewhere. He put out a hand. Nothing. He reached farther in, sliding his hand back and forth across the carpet. C'mon, where the hell are you?

His fingers fumbled over something hard and round.

Got it! he thought, closing his hand around it—and cried out as a sudden pain lanced up his arm. He yanked his hand back, but the pain didn't stop.

My hand, oh shit, it hurts!

It was hanging on to his hand, biting into the fleshy part between his thumb and forefinger. He grabbed at it with his other hand; it came off with a tearing of skin like a series of tiny paper cuts.

"Damn!" he muttered, and looked at his hand in the moonlight. A neat ring of tiny holes had been poked into it, the circle about an inch in diameter. Small droplets of blood were starting to form on each of them. He'd have to wash it out to prevent an infection.

Then he turned his attention to the object he had pulled off.

It was the plastic werewolf head that he had painted so meticulously, now turned traitor. Its jagged mouth was tinged a slight red, and there was something caught in one of its teeth. Presumably part of his hand.

Must've caught it wrong when I closed my hand, he thought. The teeth were plastic, but still sharp. They glistened wetly. *Nice appetizer, bub, but where's the main course?*

Moving slowly, he put the head in a box along with the other parts. He would try and reassemble them later.

What a night, he thought bitterly.

Across the way, in the house next door, Lisa Williams was laughing.

5

perfect

6

At a quarter to two in the morning, Tony Soznick was still trying to go to bed. It was simple. All he had to do was get up out of the chair he was sitting in, cross the ten feet to his bed, and lie down.

Simple.

Except he couldn't get up.

So silly. Such a simple thing. Just get up. That's all. Just. Get. Up.

He continued to sit as he had since coming in the door two hours earlier.

He hadn't even been that tired. It had been a light day, all things considered. He'd only put up about half the day's quota of fliers when he'd suddenly felt that it was okay to stop. It was . . . when?

That's right. After they had talked to him.

There had been two of them, he remembered. That was right, wasn't it? Somehow it seemed important that he remember. Yes. Two of them. They had seen one of his fliers, and he had spoken to them. One of them had even said he'd liked what he'd read. That was important too, wasn't it? Then they went away.

And he knew, somehow *knew*, that it was all right to stop.

Afterward, he had come back up to the room, put down the fliers and the glue, and gone back out again. He'd actually felt—well, *good* for a change. He'd even gone out for dinner, not a hamburger, or a hot dog, but a *real dinner*, which—

(it almost never let him do)

—he almost never did. He'd marched down the street to The Sizzler, and ordered the biggest steak they had, and a baked potato, and some shrimp on the side, and a salad with Italian dressing. They had looked at him a little funny, since he wasn't exactly dressed for the dinner crowd, but his money was as good as anyone else's. He had taken his time eating. After his third cup of coffee, he had paid his bill and walked back to the hotel, feeling at peace.

The compulsion was gone. He knew it would surely return, probably first thing in the morning, but for the moment, he would take his vacation at face value.

He had considered lying down as soon as he got inside, but he didn't think that would be wise after such a heavy meal, so he'd settled down in the worn chair beside the window and, for the first time in six months, allowed himself to relax.

That had been two hours ago.

It was harder to tell at what point motionlessness had gone from lethargy to inability. He remembered that after sitting for about ten minutes, he had decided to cross his legs. But then, as though from far away, a voice said that he was just fine the way he was, perfectly comfortable.

Then he had wanted a cigarette, but the dresser had seemed so far away, and he was comfortable. Better to wait until later.

It was only gradually, as his arms and legs started to get stiff, that he realized he hadn't moved an inch in the better part of an hour.

I will cross my legs, he decided.

His legs did not move.

And that was when the fear began to gnaw at him.

Now it was a quarter to two, and he was growing more acutely aware of his discomfort. His back hurt where it joined with his buttocks. If he could push back just a little that would help. But even that was denied him. He felt as though his body had been cut off below his chin, and that he was floating just a fraction of an inch above it. Even his head refused to move, providing a view of only his hands, his legs, the top of his calves, and the television running silently against the far wall. He looked at his limbs with distant interest, as though they belonged to someone else.

Just a few feet to the bed. So silly. Just get up.

He was taking this remarkably calmly, he thought, and with good reason. He had been through so much lately, he doubted that much could still bother him. It was probably playing with him, as it had in the past. Sooner or later it would tire of the game, and he could go and lie down, and continue his work in the morning. He was necessary.

And he could wait.

Not that he had much choice in the matter.

Ten feet. So silly.

He hoped that it would stop playing soon. A growing sense of discomfort was making itself known in his groin, something more compelling at the moment than the need to lie down.

He knew he shouldn't have had quite so much coffee with dinner.

He had to go to the bathroom.

7

At two A.M., the video recorder in Susan Warrick's apartment switched on. She'd turned the volume down so that it wouldn't wake her. Besides, she had heard it once. She only needed it now for reference.

The videocassette whirred softly in the VCR.

The following is a rebroadcast of the Channel 4 evening news, with Marjorie Whitehead and Alan Chu.

Good evening. More news tonight on that cocaine bust in Santa Monica. Police are holding a yacht and a load of coke valued at approximately a quarter of a million dollars confiscated just off the coast as part of the Coast Guard's newly announced sweep of the area. Four as-yet unidentified men have been arrested in connection with the discovery, and are being held pending arraignment. Police say that nearly forty thousand dollars in cash and five AK-47 automatic rifles were also seized in the arrest. Alan?

Thanks, Marjorie. Tragic news tonight in the shooting death of thirteen-year-old Pamela Manriquez of Inglewood last night. The County Coroner's office has ruled the incident a suicide, eliminating speculation that the incident was related to a recent upswing in gang activity in that area. According to a report just issued by the coroner's office, death resulted from a single head wound made by a handgun registered to the girl's father. The father is not currently considered a suspect.

Police had no comment when asked about rumors that this was one more in a number of incidents of juvenile suicide in recent days.

Back to you, Marjorie.

9

Chris sat in the back of the classroom, only distantly aware of what was being taught up front. After last night, he was too tired for much concentrated thought. He had slept fitfully, fearing to sleep too deeply in case the dream returned.

He pulled out one of the thin slips of paper he kept in his shirt pocket, and the eyedropper filled with lemon juice. He almost always passed Roger on his way to Huntington's class, and would slip the note to him there. He composed the sentence in his head first. When you wrote in lemon, there wasn't much room for mistakes.

Where were you for Home Room? Will be late for lunch. Wait for me. Did you hear about the girl?

"The girl" had been a favorite topic of discussion on the bus this morning. There had been considerable speculation as to how she'd killed herself. One of the guys doing the talking said that he'd heard she'd put a gun to the middle of her forehead and had blown her brains out through the back of her head.

"C'mon, man, stop shittin' us," Steve said. Chris tried to stay as far away from Steve as possible. So far, Steve had seemed utterly unaware of him, pretending he didn't even exist. "The news don't give out that kind of stuff."

"Heard it from my sister," the other guy said, offended.

"Oh, yeah, your sister," Steve said with a snicker. "Well, then it's gotta be true. Everybody talks to your sister. But the way I hear, they just talk so's they can get her to bring down her price." He laughed, then put a finger up against his head in a mock-gun, and pulled the trigger. "Boom! Hey, three holes for the price of two!"

Chris tuned out the rest of the conversation. The gesture, and the whole discussion, reminded him too much of his dream.

He uncapped the eyedropper, and carefully squeezed the bulb as he wrote out in lemon, WHERE WERE—

"Christopher?"

Chris started upright in his seat. "Yes?"

Mrs. Stacey pointed to the blackboard. "In this sentence, is the word 'fence' the object or the subject?"

He looked at the sentence, worked it over in his head. "Subject?"

"Is that an answer or a question?"

"Subject," he said.

"Correct." She turned her attention to one of the other students.

Chris sat back, relieved. For once the hammer hadn't fallen on him. But the slip of paper he'd been writing on was wet where he had squeezed the eyedropper bulb in surprise at being called upon. Lemon juice dripped across it. He folded it up and put it back in his pocket, deciding to toss it away later. Then he took out another slip of paper, and tried again.

WHERE WERE YOU FOR HOME ROOM?
WILL BE LATE FOR LUNCH. WAIT FOR ME.
DID YOU HEAR ABOUT THE GIRL?

2

Chris had intended to be no more than fifteen minutes late, but that was now stretching into half an hour.

He'd found Mr. Edwards eating his lunch in his room, as always. "I like to stay accessible to the students," he explained. His desk was covered with a map of England, and Chris noticed that he had circled a number of cities on it

"Planning my agenda," Edwards explained. "About every three years, I try to get away to England."

"You've actually *been* there?" Somehow it seemed farther than Mars.
"Four times so far."

Chris had been in love with England for as long as he had been able to read. He had read all of the Sherlock Holmes stories, and for a year had been fascinated by the riddle of Jack the Ripper. It was frivolous, he supposed, all the more so since he'd never been there. But now, to find someone who had actually *been* to England . . .

Chris wanted to hear about London first: St. James's Park, Buckingham Palace, bobbies, even the taxicabs.

"The amazing thing," Edwards said, "is that they always know *exactly* where you have to go. They never check a map, never ask you for directions. So one day, when I was getting a ride back from Porter's, this wonderful little restaurant over by Covent Garden, which makes the best chocolate pudding I've ever had—they serve it warm, the way it's supposed to be served—I asked the driver how this could be. He pointed up the street to this man on a bicycle with a sheet of paper tacked to the handlebars.

" 'See him?' he asked. I said yes, I did.

" 'Before a man can drive a cab in London, he 'as to spend two years on a bicycle, just like that one, pedaling his heart out all over London. He 'as to cover every street, every alley, until he knows 'em all by heart. And let me tell you, mate, once you've bounced your bum all over these cobblestoned streets and back alleys where nobody's been since Henry the bleedin' Eighth, mark my word, you remember every single bump and chuckhole.' "

Chris laughed. Roger can wait a few more minutes, he decided, and asked Mr. Edwards if he'd ever been to Baker Street.

3

He found Roger at their usual spot, a grassy rise not far from Senior Park. "Sorry," Chris said, flopping down on the grass beside him. He began unwrapping his hamburger. "Got tied up."

"Mmm." Roger pulled an apple out of his lunch bag and chewed at it.

Great, Chris thought, he's pissed at me. "Look, I said I'm sorry. I told you I was going to be late, but—"

"No, you didn't."

"What do you mean, no I didn't? Didn't you read my note?"

"Sure. It only takes about a minute." He threw the rest of the apple into the sack and crumpled it up.

"So you read it."

"Right. And if it's supposed to be a joke, I don't get it."

"Look, I don't know if it's you, or me, but either way I don't know *what* the hell you're talking about."

Roger fished in his pocket and pulled out a slip of paper. "You gave me this, right?"

"Right."

He tossed it into Chris's lap. "So you explain it to me."

Chris picked up the paper and unfolded it. Roger had held the match too closely to the paper. It was so singed in places that it was brittle, almost burned through. But the words were still legible.

WHERE ArE YOU?

WE CAn HEaR YOU BUT wE CANNOT SeE YOU

WHO ArE YOU?

Chris felt his stomach drop. This had to be a joke. But Roger wasn't smiling.

"Roger, I didn't write this."

"You handed it to me, you wrote it."

"No, I—" He looked at the note again. The "WHERE" *was* recognizably his printing. But the rest . . .

"Wait a minute." He fumbled in his pocket and came out with another slip of paper. "Got a match?"

Roger handed across a book of matches. Chris struck one and held it under the paper. It was the second note, the one he had intended to give to Roger.

"I put them both in my pocket, and when I saw you in the hall, I must've given you the wrong one," Chris said.

"Oh. So who else are you passing notes to?"

"Nobody! That's the whole point! Look, after I wrote one word—see, it's the same on both papers, the same writing—I accidentally spilled some of the lemon juice. It dripped all over the paper. So I folded it up and stuck it in my pocket. I figured I'd ruined it."

"And you're saying that's the one I got."

"Right."

"The one you'd spilled the lemon on."

"Right."

"So where did the words come from?"

Chris threw up his hands. "I don't know."

"They don't come out of nowhere," Roger said. "You don't get words by accident."

"I know. But I swear, Roger, I didn't write that stuff. Honest to God."

Roger studied him a moment. "You're not shitting me?"

"I swear."

Roger frowned, and took back the slip of paper. Chris looked at it over his shoulder.

WHERE ArE YOU?

WE CAn HEaR YOU BUT wE CANNOT SeE YOU

WHO ArE YOU?

"Okay," Roger said, "so if it wasn't you, then who *did* write it?"

"I don't know."

Overhead, the bell rang, announcing the start of the next period.

4

For the next three hours, Chris found it almost impossible to concentrate. He wished now that he had taken the note back instead of letting Roger hold on to it. He wanted to examine it again. It had given him the strangest feeling, seeing his own handwriting side by side with . . . the rest of it.

More than once, he wondered if Roger was running a number on him. But he had seen the look on Roger's face, and knew it wasn't a joke.

There would be no easy answers to this one.

When the last bell rang, Chris raced to meet Roger at the usual place, behind the gym.

"I want to try it again," Roger said. "How much lemon do you have left?"

Chris produced the eyedropper. There was barely a quarter of an inch left, not enough to write anything.

"Crap," Roger said.

"What about yours?"

"Forgot it," Roger said. "Didn't get to sleep until real early this morning, then I overslept. By the time I remembered it I was halfway here. We'll go to my place."

Chris nodded, though part of him was reluctant to try it again. There was something creepy about it, something just *not right*. But he needed to know what had happened.

And if it could happen again.

They cut across the athletic field and came out the other side, hardly talking to one another. Anything they might have to say would depend on what happened when they tried the experiment.

You're overreacting, Chris thought. Just a trick. Nothing weird like this really happens. They would figure it out sooner or later.

They crossed the street and headed up an alley. It was a shortcut they always used after—

"Oh hell," Chris said, "we forgot!"

"What?" Roger asked—and the answer came to him the same time that the sound did.

It came from behind them, at the other end of the alley. "Hey, you little faggots, where d'you think *you're* going?"

Shit, Chris thought. In their excitement, they'd just started walking and forgotten about the twenty-minute Safety Zone.

Jack came around the corner of the building to their left. To the right was a fence that ran alongside a junkyard. The only way out was straight ahead.

And *that*, he saw now, was where Steve waited, Paul beside him. Even from here, Chris could see his face was flushed, his eyes big.

Christ, he's stoned on something major.

"Told you I'd see you later," Steve said. He was walking slowly toward them. "You were gonna snitch on us, weren't you?"

"No," Chris said. "Honest! I just got lost."

"Yeah, right," Steve said, and kept repeating it, caught up in the rhythm of the words. "Yeah right, yeah right, yeahright, y'right." He was sweating.

"We're in serious trouble," Roger whispered. Chris nodded. He saw Roger glance left, toward a small break between two buildings, then right. Chris got the meaning behind the look. *Split up, hope one of us gets out.*

"Go!" Roger yelled.

97

Chris split off toward the junkyard, and the fence. Roger ran as fast as he could toward the breezeway.

Chris hit the gully where the high grass came up to his thighs. "Get him!" Steve yelled at someone behind him. He dared a look back to see Steve chasing after him, the rest going after Roger.

"You're all mine, you fuckin' snitch!"

Chris ran harder. He came to the fence, ran alongside it. It was a wire fence, held in place by posts that went halfway up. *Gotta try it.*

His lungs on fire, he cut across the last of the high grass and grabbed on to the fence. The metal strips cut into his palms as he pulled himself up. It twisted in his hands. Above the poles there was nothing to support it, or him. He got to the top just as Steve hit the fence behind him, and for a second Chris thought he would fall. Then with a final pull he launched himself over the top and down the other side. He landed hard, twisting his ankle. He could still run, if he had to, but not fast. If Steve followed him over—

Steve tried to climb after him, but the upper part of the fence wouldn't support his greater weight. It just bent and dropped him back down again. He tried twice, and both times Chris watched with horrified fascination. He was high on something, all right. He was snarling at the fence, at him, cursing nonstop. It was like watching a mad dog unable to accept the idea that it wasn't going to be able to get over to where the prey was.

Steve rushed the fence one last time, trying to grab at Chris through the openings. Chris stayed just out of range. Then, as if the realization that Chris was beyond his reach had at last gotten through, he stopped struggling with a startling suddenness. He stuck his face up against the fence and grinned at Chris in a way he didn't like. "You got to go to school someday, asshooooole," he said, low and slow, "you got to be alooooone someday, asshooooole."

And again that grin.

He's fucking crazy, Chris thought.

He shivered, but tried not to let Steve see it.

"We got him!" one of the others yelled.

Steve looked back at Chris. "See you around." Then he ran to catch up with the others.

Roger. They had Roger.

What were they going to do with him? They had been mainly

after Chris. If they'd gotten him, they might even have let Roger go. But now—

Okay, so what're you going to do about it? As much as he hated the idea, and himself, the only answer he could come up with was, nothing. What *could* he do? Go help Roger fight them off? Get help? By the time he got to a phone booth, they'd probably be done with him anyway—and who would he call? The police? Roger's mom? His dad?

He spotted a fire alarm at the rear of the building just on the other side of the fence. If he pulled it, the noise would probably scare them off. And even if it didn't, the firemen would come, and that would stop them.

But wouldn't they arrest him if he pulled the alarm and there wasn't a fire?

He and Roger might be able to get away before then.

But maybe not.

And what if he got caught before he reached the alarm?

That thought stopped him. He looked past the fence, measuring the distance to the alarm. Maybe. If he wasn't seen. If nobody was hiding in wait for him.

He reached for the fence . . . and stopped.

He couldn't do it. It was just too dangerous.

In the distance, he could hear someone crying out.

Roger.

Feeling sick, Chris turned and began to pick his way through the junkyard. Gradually Roger's cries receded into silence behind him, and Chris realized that he, too, was crying.

There was nothing he could do. Nothing.

He hoped Roger would understand.

5

Chris waited for Roger at his house. Roger's parents weren't there, so Chris sat on the front porch, letting his trembling knees calm down, and waited.

Nearly an hour passed before he saw Roger walking toward the house, walking deliberately, in pain.

"You okay?" Chris asked.

"Yeah. Fine." It was barely a whisper. Roger didn't look at him, only continued across the front porch. At the door, he found a key, and let them both in.

"Meet you in my room," Roger said, and continued down the hall.

"Roger?" He had never seen Roger like this.

"In a minute," Roger said, without looking back. He stepped into the bathroom and closed the door. A moment later, Chris heard water running.

Christ, he thought, what did they *do* to him?

He went inside Roger's room to wait.

After what felt like a long time, the sound of water stopped. A little later, the door opened. Roger came in, wearing only a towel. There were bruises and scrapes all over his back and thighs. He grabbed a pair of shorts and a shirt out of his dresser and stepped outside to put them on.

It was as though someone had closed a door in him, and the sign out front said ROGER'S NOT HERE AT THE MOMENT.

Roger came back into the room and sat on the bed. Chris didn't speak, didn't push it. Roger would talk when he was ready.

Finally, without looking at Chris, he said, "They made me piss my pants."

"Oh, jeez."

"They held me down, and they started hitting me, and they kept hitting me, and hitting me, and they said they were going to keep hitting me until I pissed my pants, and I wouldn't, I wouldn't do it, they couldn't make me, then Steve came over and unzipped and he said if I didn't piss my pants he would, and he was crazy, you could see it, and I was scared, god I was so scared and I pissed my pants and they started laughing, and calling me a baby, and I kept on pissing, and the more I pissed the more they laughed."

Tears were running down his face, but his expression was as without emotion as it had been earlier.

"I'm sorry," Chris said.

Roger shrugged. "It happens. Maybe after a while I'll get used to it. That would be nice. And it wouldn't hurt me anymore."

Silence hung uncomfortably between them. "Are—are you mad at me? For leaving?"

Another shrug. "I'd have done the same thing. Besides, you couldn't do anything anyway, right?"

Chris nodded, hating himself for the coward he was.

6

Chris called his mom, and explained he would be having dinner with Roger's folks, even though so far he had not seen either of them.

After another hour, Roger seemed to rouse himself, though much of him was still somewhere else. He asked Chris if he could see the paper with the lemon writing again. It was in his shirt pocket, in the bathroom. Chris could understand why he wouldn't want to retrieve it himself.

Chris found it, and Roger read it over again, running his fingers over the brown, burnt-lemon letters. "Get me some lemon juice. It's in the fridge."

Chris obliged, filling the eyedropper. He took a notepad from the front room and a book of matches from a drawer in the kitchen, and brought them back with him.

Roger tore out a sheet of notepad paper. "Okay," he said, handing it to Chris. "Do it again. Just the way you did before."

"All right."

"And Chris," Roger said, "if I find out now that this really was all a joke, I want you to know that I'm going to have to kill you. Kill you dead right here, right now. But it's nothing personal."

"Fair deal."

"Do it."

Chris repeated his actions of that morning. He aimed the eyedropper at the upper rim of the paper, and squeezed the bulb. Lemon juice spat out and ran down the paper in thin rivulets. After a second, he folded the paper in two, then again, and stuck it back in his pocket.

"That's it?" Roger asked.

"That's it. Now we just wait a few minutes until it dries."

They sat on the bed, staring at the pile of comics stacked on top of the foot locker. At last Chris reached into his pocket, pulled the paper out, checked to make sure it was fully dry, and then handed it to Roger.

Roger unfolded it, then held a lighted match under the paper, warming it.

"Not too close," Chris said. "Don't burn it!"

"Quiet."

Gradually, brown lines staining the paper began to appear. They spread across the paper, seemed almost to crawl across the surface, intersecting and connecting with one another.

Forming words.

WHERE ArE YOU?

WE CAn HEaR YOU BUT wE CANNOT SeE YOU

WHO ArE YOU?

"Holy shit!" Roger dropped the paper and shook out the match. "Did you see it?"

"Yeah, I saw it, I saw it."

"It's real."

"I know."

"Scared the piss out of me."

"Well, then you're oh-for-two, aren't you?"

Roger grunted an affirmation. "I guess you could say that, yeah."

"So what're we gonna do about it?"

Roger thought about it, then picked up the sheet of paper. Held it up in front of him. "My name is Roger—"

"What the hell are you doing?"

"Shush! It asked a question, remember? *Who are you?* So let's see what happens." He looked back to the paper. "My name is Roger Obst. I'm—hell, what am I supposed to say to 'where are you'?—I'm at home. In my room. In Lennox. California. Planet Earth."

Chris rolled his eyes. " 'Planet Earth.' Give me a break."

"You think you can do better?" He thrust the paper into Chris's hands. "You try."

"I don't want to."

"Why? You afraid?"

Chris frowned. *What the hell,* he thought. "My name's Christopher Martino. I live near here. I'd give you my phone number but my mom wants it unlisted."

He grinned at Roger, who was peering out at him over the top of his glasses. "Dog meat," Roger said. "I swear to God, one more crack and you're dog meat."

"Sorry."

Roger thrust the lemon juice and another sheet of paper at him. "Do it again."

Chris repeated the process. They waited for it to dry.

"Time," Roger said, and took back the paper. He heated it carefully. Again the tracery of lines spread out over the paper.

rOGEr
CHrISTOpH
WHErE
CANnOT SEE

Chris felt his stomach fall straight into his shoes.

It knows our names.

"I think we better stop," Chris said. "This is getting too weird."

"Not yet."

"I mean it, Roger. I don't think we should do this anymore." He stood up.

"Just one more, okay? Come here. I got an idea."

Roger walked around the bed and stood in front of the mirror. "Come on."

Reluctantly, Chris obliged. They stood so that they were both framed in the mirror. Roger looked at the paper again. "Can you see us now?"

No way, Chris thought. *No way.*

Lemon.

Paper.

Match:

YeS
BETtER

"That's it," Chris said. "I'm out of here."

"Wait a minute, you can't leave now! What if it only works if we both do it?"

"Then I'm not doing it. This is too creepy. Are you going to try it again?"

"Hell, yes."

"Then like I said—I'm out of here."

"What the hell kind of friend are you, anyway?"

"I'm scared! Okay?" Chris felt his face flush red. He wasn't aware of just how scared he was until he said it. "I just don't want to do this anymore. Not now, at least. Could we just, like, wait until tomorrow? Let's think about this for a while."

Roger frowned, looked away, and finally nodded. "Okay," he said, though obviously not happy about it. "Fine. Go home. It's getting late anyway, your mom'll probably wonder what's taking so long."

"All right," Chris said, heading for the bedroom door. "Are you mad at me?"

Roger took a moment, then shook his head. "No, I guess not. I guess I'm a little scared, too. So we'll wait. I'll talk to you tomorrow, Chris."

"Okay. See you in Home Room."

He closed the bedroom door and let himself out of the house. It was getting dark outside. If he hurried, he could get home before night fell.

He wasn't in the mood to be alone in the night.

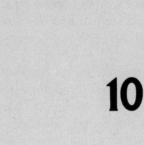

10

Susan glanced at her watch as the waiter took away the remains of their Chinese dinner. Forty-three minutes since they'd started dinner. Seven more minutes and Gene would have broken the record for the longest time anyone had waited before asking The Question.

"So," he'd said as he poured the tea, "have you ever had to actually use that gun?"

"Twice," she answered finally. "Once was a warning shot. The guy we were chasing got the message. The second time, my partner—Jordan, you met him in the car—and I walked right into the middle of a robbery at a 7-Eleven. We hadn't even gotten a call, Jordan just wanted to stop for some doughnuts. You could tell right off the perp was crazy stoned on something—PCP, we found out later. He started yelling and shooting wild. Jordan jumped left, I jumped right, and the guy behind the counter kissed the ground. Trouble was, we were both behind these counters and the only way to get a clear shot at him was to stand up right in clear view."

"Not a good thing."

"No. Meanwhile, this guy's shooting everything in sight. Pretty soon, somebody's going to get hit, or we're going to have to take him down hard. Then I saw this coffeemaker right on the edge of the counter, you know, the kind where you can buy a cup of coffee from the guy at the register. I couldn't get a clear shot at the perp, but this was right in my line of sight, not more than two feet away from him. So I took a chance and fired at the coffeepot. It was practically full, and when the bullet hit it, the thing just exploded and shot hot coffee all over him. Startled the hell out of him. Before he knew what hit him, Jordan was all over him, and we had him down on the floor in cuffs."

"That's it?"

"Don't sound so disappointed. As far as I'm concerned, that's enough. Used to be most cops could go through their whole careers and never have to fire a shot. Now most of the cops I know have had to fire their gun at least once, usually hurting someone. It's not something we like to think about a lot."

Gene shook his head. "I don't think I could do it."

"Shoot someone?"

"Uh-huh. You?"

She shrugged. "When you're at the academy, they spend a lot of time teaching you how *not* to shoot someone. They teach you how to deal with a hostage situation, how to avoid inflaming a perp, how to disable someone with a baton, all the rest of it. *Then* they take you aside and teach you how to shoot to wound, and shoot to kill. They teach you about guns. You learn that if someone's right-handed and pointing a gun at you, you move fast to his left, because when the gun goes off, his hand will jerk to his right and away from you. And in that one second . . ."

She sipped at her tea. "It's always dead quiet in class when they teach you that stuff. You realize pretty fast that you *may* have to kill someone someday, to protect yourself or someone else, and you shouldn't be wearing a badge unless you're prepared to do that."

She looked up to find him studying her. "I didn't mean to upset you," he said. "I'm sorry."

"It's okay." She straightened a little in her seat. "Not off to the best of starts, are we? I've seen you three times so far, and every time we end up talking about somebody dying. I suspect we're falling into a rut."

"Agreed."

"So let's start with you passing me a fortune cookie."

He was divorced. No kids. L. A. born, but with a passion for traveling. Dedicated to his work. And she liked the way he smelled. Lord knew why. She thought she'd outgrown the smell of chalk and old notebooks years ago.

When he'd mentioned he was divorced, she had instinctively braced herself for the expected flood of recollections, recriminations and still-unresolved arguments. But he proved to be one of the happy exceptions. The reference was only in passing, and he moved on, asking what kinds of movies she liked. As usual, whenever asked for titles, her brain froze up like a glacier. "Good ones" was all she was able to come up with, and let him change the subject with another question.

That was something else she liked about Gene. He asked questions, and seemed genuinely interested in her answers. At one point, she'd thought, Of course he's being polite, you twit—he knows you travel armed. She sent the offending thought to its room without dinner.

When they reached her apartment, she unlocked the door, then hesitated, knowing he would want to come inside, "just for a while," like the others, and it would take dynamite to get him to leave and she just didn't think she was ready for him to spend the night and—

"Well," he said, before she could get a word out, "I know you have to get up early. Same here. So I'll thank you for a terrific evening. I hope we can do it again, soon." Then a quick kiss on the lips and a smile, and he walked back to his car.

She stood there for a moment, flummoxed, wanting to call out, *Hey! Wait a minute! You can't leave yet! You haven't tried anything! I haven't even thrown you out yet!*

But by the time the comment jumped the six inches from her brain to her mouth, he was in the car and pulling out into the street.

"Son of a gun," she said to the night, and smiled.

Still smiling, she opened the door and stepped inside. Her foot kicked up something on the floor. An envelope. She picked it up, recognizing the handwriting as Jordan's.

Now what? she thought, and opened it.

Inside she found a magazine clipping and a Polaroid photograph of Jordan standing beside their usual pool table. In his hands was a burgundy cue. The clipping was from a sporting catalog. *The Sterling Pool Cue is considered one of the finest instruments of its kind, used in professional matches throughout the world. Designed by English billiards champion Frederick Sterling . . .* She couldn't see a price—it had been torn off—but she could make a good guess that it cost at least as much as hers.

She looked back at the photograph of Jordan. He was wearing a smile so big that she couldn't help but smile herself. She turned the photo over. *YOU REALIZE, OF COURSE, THIS MEANS WAR* was written on the back.

"You're on," she said to the photograph, and laughed.

Two sons of guns in one night.

My cup runneth over, she thought, and, still laughing, began to undress for bed.

11

Everything hurt.

In twenty-four hours, Tony had gone beyond pain to something worse. He still sat in his chair by the window. Time and again he had tried to move some limb, even a finger or a toe, something to indicate that he was more than a mind dwelling in a house of flesh that was no longer aware of his presence. But only the most basic involuntary responses were left to him. Breathing. Blinking. Heartbeat.

And one other.

Unable to move his head, he had come to memorize every detail of what was in front of him, to explore the limited world that was visible from where he sat, without moving. Out of the corner of his right eye, he could see a little of the street outside his apartment. With peripheral vision he had traced the arc of sun from dawn to night, tracked the shadows as they raced across the room. It had been hot, which meant that at least his skin was still transmitting information to him, though he wished now that it had remained mute. The back of his neck was burned where the sunlight had come in through the window. Without looking at it he knew that it was bright red now, and blistered, the flesh beginning to weep. It was an agony that itched and seethed through his skin right into his thoughts. Hot, and down below, the wetness—

Don't think about it, don't think about it.

He would just think about the room.

The television was still on, as he'd left it, with the sound down. He'd watched the station end its broadcasting day with a religious benediction and "The Star Spangled Banner." Then it had come on again a few hours later, beginning a parade of soundless faces. By noon—he must have been nearly mad at the time, with the sun burning into his brain—he had gotten the strangest idea that the people on the TV were talking about him. Discussing the curious dilemma he found himself in.

Gee, Skipper, he's stuck to his chair! What're we gonna do?

Stuck to the . . .! Gilligan, where's that glue the Professor made for the raft?

It was an accident, Skipper, honest!

GILLIGAN!

He'd liked that one. But there had been others, not as funny, They, too, had been talking about him.

All readings would seem to indicate that he is dying, Captain.

Are—are you sure, Spock? The tricorder—

Is functioning quite efficiently, Captain. It is most regrettable, but he is dying. And there appears to be little or nothing we can do about it.

I can't accept that. There has to be a solution. Bones?

Damn it, Jim, it's that alien physiology. Readings are all over the place. Can't tell what works and what doesn't. If he could just give me a sign, if he could just communicate—

Spock! The Vulcan mind-meld!

Negative, Captain. It would appear that the alien is rapidly going mad, and to attempt the mind-meld would result in damage to us both. I'm afraid there really is nothing to be done.

Damn. All right. I'll be on the bridge. Bones, if there's any change, any change at all, let me know immediately.

That one bothered Tony a lot.

Fortunately the woman with the paper towels didn't seem to think he was beyond hope. *It's the quicker-picker-upper!*

But then, she hadn't seen the mess he'd made, had she?

As the afternoon news rolled by, he got the impression that the people on the news seemed to think he had something to do with the Middle East, but he couldn't quite figure out what.

He couldn't remember anything between about four and seven; he assumed he had passed out. When he woke up, the people on TV weren't talking about him anymore.

But then he had done it again.

Don't think about it.

He couldn't help but think about it.

Why had he drunk so much coffee the night before?

It must've been about two in the morning when the pain in his groin had first become so intense that he would have screamed if he'd been able to. Then, finally, when the pressure became too great to stand anymore, the system had put itself on automatic and he had wet himself. For a moment, he wasn't sure which was the worse—the pain of a moment before, or the humiliation.

He decided on the pain. If it had gone on a second longer, he was sure he would have exploded.

And that was when he had The Thought.

Urination was one thing. He could do that without thinking, and his position in no way interfered with that. It was the other—

Oh god, he thought.

Why the *hell* did you have to cross your legs when you sat down?

It was a silly thought, the sort you have when you're a kid, and you're afraid to go to the bathroom because whatever lived in the toilet bowl might grab you and pull you down into the water where it lived.

He didn't *think* it was possible, but he didn't know for sure, and that made it all the worse, as The Thought began to run in faster and faster circles in his head.

Mom, I gotta go to the bathroom!

You'll just have to wait.

But MOM, if I don't, I'm gonna EXPLODE.

Oh god, he thought. *Oh god, oh god, oh god.*

Perhaps, he thought, perhaps someone will see me in the window, and think, Why, he's been there for the whole day, never moving once. Maybe he's dead or something. Maybe we ought to call the police.

It was possible.

Gilligan! Where's the pitchblende we were going to burn so the plane would see it when it passed over the island?

Gee, I'm sorry, Skipper, but you said the Professor's hut was leaking, and since it was his birthday and everything—

Oh no . . .

So now we're stuck here on this rotten island and it's all my fault and what's that smell? Did somebody pee in his pants?

GILLIGAN!

12

Chris awoke to the sound of tapping at his window.

Don't be a jerk, he thought, clinging to sleep. You're on the second floor. There's no one at the window.

Tap. Tap. Tap-tap.

Chris sat up. Feeling his way through the darkness, he made it to the window, and pushed aside the curtains just as another pebble bounced off the glass, *tap*. He looked down. Roger stood a few feet away from the house, one hand filled with pebbles.

Chris opened the window. "What're you *doing* here?" he whispered. If his mom found him up—

"Come outside for a second," Roger said.

"No way!"

"C'mon! I've got to talk to you!"

"Okay, okay. Just give me a minute!"

He stepped away from the window and started pulling on his clothes. Moving as quietly as he could, he grabbed a flashlight from the closet and crept down the stairs. He opened the front door to find Roger standing just outside. In the glow of the porch light, Roger's face was flushed, excited.

"This way," Roger said, and led Chris to a dark breezeway between the houses, where they couldn't be seen. Chris wished he'd brought a jacket. California days were warm enough, but at nearly one in the morning, it was chilly.

"Okay," Chris said, "What the hell's going on? This better be good."

Roger's face split into a wide grin, made almost maniacal by the reflection of the flashlight in his glasses. "It works without you, Chris. I waited until after you were gone, and then I tried it again. And it worked."

It took Chris a second to figure out what he was talking about. "The lemon writing?"

Roger nodded. "At first, I thought maybe we both had to be there for it to work. And in a way, I might still be right. But I went ahead and tried anyway. And look what happened."

He dug in his pocket and pulled out a fistful of singed papers. Chris didn't want to see what was on them, wanted only to forget any and all of what had happened . . . but his curiosity was too great, and he shone the flashlight on the pile. On the backs of the papers he recognized Roger's handwriting. And on the front, the *other* writing.

"I found out that sometimes it could hear me better if I wrote the questions down."

"It?"

"Yeah," Roger said, and his voice was hushed. "It. I don't know its name yet, but . . . something. And it's trying to talk to us. To me. Here, see for yourself."

He started handing Chris the papers, one at a time. Chris read both sides, questions, then answers.

Is this better?
a LiTtLE
Where are you?
WhERe YOU ArE
Is that a question or an answer?
YES
You said you didn't know where we were.
yeS
But now you do.
YES
Who are you?
WhO ARE yOU?

I already answered that.
sO DID wE
I don't understand.
wE CAn HELP yOU
How?
WhO I aM IS wHErE i Am iS wHo i am
Explain.
wHErE iS ThE oTHEr
Chris?
YES
If I get him, will you answer the question?
YES

Chris stared numbly at the last four papers, feeling a cold knot growing in his stomach. It knew his name, and it had sent Roger to get him before it would tell Roger its name.

"I don't want to do this stuff anymore," Chris said. "It's scary."

"You can't back out now," Roger said. "You started it! You've got to see it through now!"

"Forget it." He started back toward the apartment. "You want to play with this stuff, fine, but leave me out of it."

"You don't want to do that," Roger said. "There were other messages. I didn't show them to you. But I think it would be a good idea for you to help me."

"Let me see."

"Maybe later. It's better you don't, for now."

He's bluffing, Chris thought. *Trying to scare me.* And doing a damn good job of it, too. He shone the flashlight on Roger's face. Roger didn't even blink. It hadn't sounded exactly like a threat—but maybe there was something there, something he should know about. And in spite of himself, he wanted to find out what it had to say.

What the hell, he decided. I'll help out and it'll put up some stupid answer, and I can go to sleep and tomorrow maybe I can talk him into stopping it.

"Okay," Chris said, "but just one question, and then I'm going back inside." He stood alongside Roger. "Go ahead."

Roger seemed so genuinely pleased that Chris couldn't help but feel a momentary flash of warmth. He was Roger's only friend. Who else was he going to turn to?

Roger pulled a sheet of paper out of his pocket. The question—

What is your name?—was already written on one side. He splashed lemon juice onto the paper and folded it up. They waited a minute or two for it to dry. Then he unfolded it again. As Chris held the flashlight steady, Roger warmed up the paper with a match. Gradually, the reply came back:

OtHERsYDE

"What kind of a name is that?"

Roger didn't look up. "Maybe that's what it meant. It's in a place called the other side. Or 'othersyde.' I don't know why the Y is there; it's an archaic spelling. Unless it's real old. But because that's where it *is*, that's what it calls itself."

"The other side of *what?*"

"I don't know. Maybe if we ask—"

"Uh-uh. I said *one* question. And I meant it. I've got to get back upstairs. I mean, c'mon, I've got to get up early. We both do! And if my mom finds out I'm gone—"

"What a wuss!" Roger shook his head. "Chris, I came all the way out here!"

"Tomorrow. Tomorrow we'll do it some more, but not now, okay? That's all I ask."

Roger glared at him. "All right, you win. First thing after class. Meanwhile, I'm going to start putting all this stuff down in a notebook."

"Fine," Chris said. He was starting to shiver now, and he realized it wasn't entirely due to the cold. The implications of what he had seen were starting to get to him. "See you tomorrow," he said, and started away.

"Chris?"

Chris turned, called back in a whisper, "What?"

He could barely make out Roger standing in the glow of the flashlight—and for the first time, Chris could see fear in his face, too . . . fear, and excitement. "I think this could be important," Roger said. "I mean, I think this could be *really* important."

"Yeah," Chris said at last, softly. "Yeah, I think maybe it could, too."

Roger grinned again, and shoved his glasses back up the bridge of his nose. "See you tomorrow," he said, and walked off into the night.

13

From the journal of Roger Obst:
I am going to write down everything that I say or ask the OtherSyde, and then what it says when it answers. This will be only the new things, after we found out what its name was. This will be just my personal book (Roger L. Obst), though maybe I will put in what Chris says to it, too, and what it says to Chris. Maybe.

Any one reading this who's not supposed to will have happen to him what happened to the guy in *The Color Out of Space.*

Stop now. You wouldn't like it.

Okay. Here goes.

         #   #   #

What do you want?
WHO ARE YOU
My name is Roger.
WHAT DO YOU WANT
That's not what I asked.
YES IT IS
Can you describe where you are?
LOOK AROUND YOU
Are you here?

117

YES NO
Are you someplace else?
NO YES
This is frustrating.
THERE ARE WORSE THINGS
Such as?
THE OTHERS
More like you?
LIKE YOU
Explain.
YOU WANT TO HURT THEM
No.
(no response)
Maybe.
YES NO   NO YES
Where do you come from?
WE ARE HERE
We? You said you were one.
YES NO
Explain.
NO
Why?
SLOW
Is there another way to communicate with you?
YES
Will you tell me what to do?
YES QUESTION
What?
NEED NAMES
Whose names?
THE OTHERS
Why?
TO HELP
Help me? Or you?
YES NO YES
I don't understand.
WAIT

118

14

Gene finished filling his tray from the lunch buffet in the teachers' lounge, then looked across the rows of tables for a clear space to sit down. He found an opening across from Chet Huntington.

"This taken?"

Huntington looked up at him with tired eyes. "Help yourself."

Gene did. He pulled the plastic cover off the plate to reveal a slab of meat loaf, whipped potatoes, and mixed vegetables. "Same old stuff," he said. "But at least it looks like food this time."

Huntington nodded and kept eating, not looking up. Gene noticed that his eyes were red-rimmed, and his shirt looked as though it had been slept in.

They can't still be riding him over what happened, can they? he wondered.

"How're you doing?" Gene asked.

"Okay. Fine."

"I stopped by your house the other night to say hello. I saw the light on, but when I rang the doorbell, there wasn't an answer. Guess I must've just missed you."

"No. I was home. I heard you downstairs. Just . . . didn't want to see anybody, that's all."

Gene put down his fork. "You want to talk about it?"

"No. Look, I'm fine, okay?"

"No, you're not fine. I know you better than that. Is it Evanier? Is he still hassling you over what happened?"

"I just don't want to talk about it, all right?" He was speaking more loudly now. A few heads turned farther down the table.

"Suit yourself," Gene said.

They sat in silence, fragments of other conversations from around the room drifting across to them. After about a minute, Huntington stopped eating, his lunch barely touched. "Damn noisy in here," he said.

"Yeah, it is."

Huntington pushed away the tray and rubbed his face. "Marie's thinking of leaving me."

"Oh Jesus, Chet, I'm sorry."

"Don't be. She's right. She's one hundred percent right."

"Is it over what happened last week?"

"Sort of. It just brought everything back, you know?"

Gene did. Though he wasn't privy to all of the details, he knew that there had been what Vice Principal Evanier politely referred to as an "outburst" in Huntington's class the day Jim Bertierie died. He didn't know exactly what Chet had said, but apparently it had been enough to unnerve some of the students, who complained to their parents, who in turn started calling Evanier. Evanier had reprimanded Huntington for "disruptive behavior unbecoming a teacher."

Huntington had responded hotly, resulting in a two-day suspension. In the week since then, Gene had thought the problem taken care of. But now that he thought about it, he realized that it couldn't have just gone away. Not for Chet.

Hadn't there been two more suicides?

It's a wonder he's still in one piece, Gene thought.

"Marie suggested we start seeing a counselor again," Huntington said, "try to close the old wounds. She said it's the only way she'll stay. Won't work, of course. Hell, we went to a counselor for six months after Jenny died—didn't do any good then, why should it now?" He shook his head. "Christ, Gene, every time I hear about one of those kids, all I can think about is finding Jenny in her room and—" He wiped at his face with the back of his hand. "Sorry."

"Don't be. It's okay."

"No. No, it's not okay." He let out a long, low breath. "Damn kids. They don't understand. There's nothing they can do, nothing that can happen, that's so bad they have to kill themselves over it. So you flunk algebra—is that a reason to end it all? If they were users, maybe they weren't in their right minds, then I could see it. But I talked to the police. None of them were like that. They were just . . . *kids*. Just like Jenny. And it makes you wonder, Gene, it really does make you wonder what the hell we're doing here, how the hell we're supposed to make it better. What am I supposed to do, when I couldn't even help . . ." His voice trailed off.

"It was a long time ago, Chet. I know it hurts, but you've got to let it go."

"Marie's been telling me that for three years, and especially now, once we started hearing about the others. But it just keeps getting worse. I can't sleep. Can barely eat. I think I've started yelling at her a lot more than usual, but I don't really remember a lot of the last few days. All I remember is the look on her face a couple of days ago when she told me it was see a counselor or else. So now I'm thinking, maybe I should just let her go. Maybe she's right. I can't keep doing this to her forever, can I? It's not right."

"I don't think that's for you to decide. I think that's something you both have to work out, give her a choice in the matter—but give her a chance, too."

If Huntington had any response, there was no sign of it. He looked up only when the bell behind them rang, signaling the end of lunch.

"We'd better get going," Huntington said, picking up his tray.

"If you need anything . . ."

Huntington nodded, and turned away. Outside, Gene noticed Chris, sitting alone on a slight rise. Probably waiting for Roger, he thought. Roger had been absent from Home Room.

Probably out sick, Gene concluded. As he stepped out into the hall, he thought of Jenny, whom he'd met only once at a faculty party four years ago. She was thirteen.

She had been only fourteen when she'd taken her own life by swallowing her mother's sleeping pills. They never did find out why.

Poor Chet, he thought.

It never ends.

Chris waited as long as he could before heading on to his next class. He was late already, the second bell having rung two minutes ago. Roger had said he'd come to class today. He'd said they would talk about all this OtherSyde stuff. So far, though, not a sign of him.

He walked toward the 300-building, running the events of last night through his head until they blurred together. In the daylight, the whole thing seemed like one of the make-believe games he played when he was a kid. *What if Superman were real?* or, *What if I could fly?*

Except that this was real, and he didn't know what to do about it.

The way he saw it, he had only a few options. One, tell Roger he didn't want to mess with the notes anymore, and pretend none of it had happened. (But that didn't answer the question of what was really going on, did it? And he *was* curious to find out.) Two, he could give it a while longer, see what happened, and then cut out if it got too weird. Or three, as his father used to say, just get on the horse and see where it takes you.

Some choices.

The curious thing about all of the options was that each indicated that he accepted as real what was going on. But then, he had seen it with his own eyes. Roger was not a magician.

So who, or what, were they in contact with?

And did he really want to find out?

He stepped into the building and stopped. Blocking his way were Steve and the Dumbass Deathsquad. They had been waiting for him. But they didn't try to jump him.

"You," Steve said, never taking his eyes off Chris, "your ass is grass as of this moment. And what you'll get will be twice as bad as we gave to your little queer friend. You got something coming, you take it like a man, you don't run like a goddamned chicken. You gotta remember, unless you wanna ditch school and run away like the little faggot coward you are, you're stuck here for the duration. I can get you any time I want, any day I want." He pointed a finger at Chris, his face as rigid as stone. "Your ass is mine, shithead."

With that he headed down the hall, shouldering Chris aside as he passed. The others followed, each in turn going out of his way to elbow Chris.

The fear that had been kept down by surprise and a rush of adrenaline surfaced and turned quickly into anger. Anger with them, with the move, with California and palm trees and Roger and his goddamned lemon writing—

He started after them.

"What the hell is *wrong* with you guys?" he shouted. "I never did anything to you! Why're you picking on me? I didn't do anything, damn it, I didn't do anything! It's not fair!" Steve didn't turn around, only kept walking down the hall. Slowly. Infuriatingly.

"It's not fair!" Chris said. "It's not fucking *fair!* LISTEN TO ME!"

And without thinking, as though watching himself from somewhere outside, he rushed Steve and shoved him from behind. Steve staggered a step, surprised, then whirled around, fist cocked back. "Okay, that's it, asshole!"

One of the doors opened and Mr. Huntington came out into the hall. Gripped in one meaty hand was a baseball bat. "What's going on out here?" he said.

Steve glanced from Chris to Huntington and back again. "Nothing."

"Then get going. Go on. You bunch go that way. Martino, you go back that way. And if I hear another sound from out here, I'm getting you both suspended for a month. Move!"

"But I didn't—"

"Move."

Chris backtracked along the hall toward where his class was already in session, still angry at Steve and, now, at Huntington, even though the teacher had probably saved him from being splattered across the lockers.

It *wasn't* his fault, damn it! None of this was. He didn't want trouble. He hadn't done anything to anyone. How did these things happen? How do you get an enemy without even trying? Where was it written that at every school there always has to be one guy who gets you in his crosshairs and sets out to make your life miserable?

And where did Huntington keep that bat, anyway?

3

The clerk behind the counter at Mach Five Electronics looked up from his issue of the Sharper Image catalog and sniffed at the air. There was just a whiff of an acrid smell in the store, not quite like someone lighting up a cigarette, sourer somehow, and yet familiar.

He got up and went around the counter into the stacks of electronic parts and kits. The smell was stronger here. He followed it down Aisle 9, HOBBIES. He looked down the aisle, expecting to see someone smoking a joint—and instead found a teenager pulling out boxes and arranging them on the floor as though searching through them. There was a match at his feet.

"Hey, you!" he said. "What are you doing?"

The kid looked around. "Me?"

"You smoking something?"

"No, I—"

"Then what's that match doing over there? You trying to burn me down or something? I could smell the smoke halfway down the store."

"Wasn't me," the kid said, "must've been that other guy. He left just before you got here."

He's a crummy liar, the clerk thought. "Look, I don't give a rat's ass what you're smoking, but you do it outside my store, got that? Now if you're gonna buy something, buy it, otherwise I think you better get out."

The kid nodded and picked up one of the boxes at his feet. He replaced the rest, then followed the clerk back to the counter. "Twelve ninety-five," the clerk said.

The kid produced the money and headed out with his purchase. It was only after he'd left that the clerk realized he'd been so distracted by the smoke and the smell and the kid that he hadn't bothered to notice what was *in* the kit. He'd seen only the price.

Didn't matter, he thought, and went back to his catalog. It'd show up on inventory eventually.

It was a little later that he realized what the smell had reminded him of.

Lemon. Burnt lemon.

Chris fired off another basketball. It hit the backboard, rolled around the rim, and bounced out. He chased the ball down the empty gym and headed back to the foul line for another try. He would get it right yet.

It was already four o'clock, twenty minutes after he would normally have left with Roger. But Roger wasn't here, had all but abandoned him, and he knew that Steve and his bunch would be out there somewhere, waiting for him.

He tried another shot, and missed that one, too.

He wondered how long he would have to stay inside to wait out Steve. In his mind he could see the newspapers already:

MISSING STUDENT FOUND IN HIGH SCHOOL GYM
Christopher Martino, missing since last September, was found late Friday night by a janitor at Lennox High School. When questioned by authorities, the confused student could only look around nervously and ask, repeatedly, "Is he gone yet?"

Terrific, he thought, and chased down the ball.

He was lining up his next shot when he heard the squeak of sneakers on the floor behind him.

Damn! he thought, and whirled around.

Roger walked toward him, grinning. "Did I scare you?"

"No, I always look this color," Chris said. "So what're you doing here?"

"Came to get you."

"How'd you know I'd still be here?"

Roger squinted evilly. "Ve haff vays, my friend." Then he laughed. "C'mon, I got something to show you."

"Can't. Steve and the D.D.S. are waiting for me out there."

Roger snorted. "Forget those guys. Look, I got in, right? I can get us both out again. C'mon. What do you have to lose, except your life?"

Chris reluctantly agreed. He really *couldn't* stay here forever, and if Roger knew some safe way out, that was fine with him.

They stepped out of the gym and walked across the greensward toward the administration building. When they came to a break between two buildings, Roger pulled out a slip of paper. He glanced at it, then folded it up and stuck it into another pocket. "Left," he said, and angled off in that direction.

At the library, he pulled out another sheet of paper. "Right, then wait ten seconds, then right again."

They made it off the school grounds and onto the street, moving at odd angles like soldiers picking their way through a mine field. Chris didn't have to examine the papers to know what they were. The obvious scorch marks confirmed his suspicions.

"Made 'em up ahead of time," Roger said. "One set for getting in, another for getting out. I just pull them out as needed. It keeps track of where Steve is, so all we have to do is go around him."

It, Chris thought. Great.

I'm going to die, I know it.

But he *didn't* die, and wasn't seen, and before he knew it they were two-thirds of the way to Roger's house. In another few minutes, they had reached his front porch.

"Home free!" Roger announced. "What d'you think?"

"Not bad," Chris said. Whatever *it* was, however it worked, it had saved him considerable pain.

"Come on," Roger said, and opened the front door. He led Chris back to his room. "You got to see this."

The bed was covered with sheets of paper and an empty box. Beside the mess, something was hidden by a pillowcase. It was about a foot long, if the lump beneath the fabric was any indication.

With great deliberateness, Roger pulled off the pillowcase, revealing the object beneath. "Well? What do you think?"

Chris stepped closer. As far as he could tell, it looked like a telegraph key, the kind you would buy from a Radio Shack and put together from a kit. It looked clumsy and had clearly been assembled in haste; glue and tape still held parts of it together.

He looked for the wires that would lead from this key to another, but failed to see them. "Where's the other end?"

"There isn't one. That's all there is." Roger grinned again, in a way Chris was starting to find annoying.

"So what good is it? The only way this'll work is with two keys at either end of a line. This isn't connected to anything."

"Isn't it?" Roger said.

No, Chris started to say, when he heard it.

126

Tick.

He looked down at the key on the bed, the key that wasn't connected to anything. It jumped again. *Tick. Tick-tick-tick. Tick. Tick. Tick-tick-tick.*

Roger listened, and then spelled, slowly, deciphering the Morse code, "H-E-L-L-O C-H-R-I-S-T-O-P-H."

The key fell silent.

"Oh shit," Chris said.

"Exactly," Roger said, grinning again, "egg-zactly."

15

It was hot.

And he hurt. Oh god, how he hurt.

Tony's stomach floated in nausea and cramps and *pain* beyond reason, *pain* that shuttled down deep into his colon and knotted itself up into something with spikes that burned where they penetrated.

Around morning he had felt something pop inside him, something that came with the release of pressure but also with a searing agony that sent him spiraling into unconsciousness. He'd been fading in and out ever since.

Something happened to me, he thought distantly, something bad, real bad.

I think I'm dying.

Then he went away again, to a place where nothing hurt, where he was able to get up and walk out of that chair and that room and it was all just a nightmare, gone and done with.

When he awoke, the pain returned four-fold.

Pain, and thirst. His tongue had swollen so thickly in his mouth that he was afraid he might choke on it. His lips were sore and cracked. And the nape of his neck where the sun had shone on it for two days straight was a weeping blister that inched up under his hair, which scratched incessantly at it.

He squinted out at the world through barely open eyes, at the television which continued to mock him. Every time he woke up, there were images of water, of 7-Up and water skiing and Gatorade and swimming and ice cream and he was burning up inside and out.

Just get it over with, please.

Then the room blurred, and when his sight cleared again the shadow had moved another inch across the far wall. A fly slipped in through the window and buzzed him, alighting on his chest and arms. It scuttled up his face, across the bridge of his nose, and for one terrible moment he was sure it was going to walk right across his open eye, but then it changed course—and went instead into his ear.

Its buzzing was as loud as a jet, vibrating his ear so that he thought he would surely go mad.

He could feel it moving around on the inside of his ear, poking and buzzing like an explorer calling into a cave. *Hello in there! Anyone home?*

Not for long, Tony thought.

After a while, the buzzing died down. Dizzy, sick, he focused back on the television, where Dan Rather was doing the news. As before, he could seem to hear the voice in his head.

Dan was speaking to him again.

So nice of him to stop by.

This is a special edition of the CBS Evening News, Dan was saying, never taking his eyes off Tony.

Good evening, I guess you're wondering why I called you here.

You bet, Tony thought.

Well, we'll have more on that in a moment. First, though, a sad report. Roving Correspondent Anthony L. Soznick, who had been sending us field reports from around the country for the last year or so, passed away this afternoon at— Dan listened to his earplug for a moment, then straightened. *Just getting in this word from our producer—make that is about to pass away from exposure and dehydration and a rupture of the colon leading to septic infection.*

Jumped the gun, didn't you? Tony thought, a sick giddiness sliding through his brain. Serves you right for manufacturing the news.

For those of you who may not recognize the name, Tony was our field correspondent, one of many who go out into the country to keep us in touch with what's really happening.

One of many? Excuse me?

It's a difficult, time-consuming job that requires a very special kind of person. And Tony was that person, willing to go wherever the story was. A fine reporter. With a final tribute, we turn to Special Correspondent Pierce Landry in Chicago.

The picture changed to a series of shots of streets, of ghettos and well-tended middle-class blocks and expensive neighborhoods. Tony recognized some of them. Others were unfamiliar, but part of him, that part that had been kept in darkness during the months on the move, the months he could never remember, stepped into the light and seemed to respond. Yes, we were there.

Chicago, Detroit, Los Angeles, Minneapolis, New Orleans—no place was too far or too small for Tony Soznick, the unseen narrator said. *As roving correspondent, he introduced us to so many of you out there. Here are just a few pictures in the scrapbook Tony was able to put together for us.*

Then, one after another, snapshots appeared on the screen, with names under each of them.

GINA MOSES	Age 18	Deceased
TONY RUIZ	Age 13	Deceased
MARGIE PAPISH	Age 15	Deceased
DAVID PARSON	Age 20	Deceased
LUANN TYCE	Age 18	Deceased
JEFF WYKES	Age 14	Deceased
JAMES BERTIERIE	Age 15	Deceased
PAMELA MANRIQUEZ	Age 13	Deceased

The names continued to scroll past. He tried to look away, but there was nowhere else to look.

Please god, no, it can't be. I didn't.

Each of them met our correspondent, and each one shared a special moment with him. They touched us and, through Tony, we were able to touch them as well. They were not perfect, they were not the ones we were looking for, but that was no fault of their own. Our standards are high, and such things take time. Still, each in his or her own way was able, even encouraged, to find peace in spite of their imperfections. That is the strength of our country, and our system, that even the deprived—especially the deprived—are never excluded from the selection process. And in so doing, they provided a moment of . . . shared joy and entertainment. They gave of themselves, and we accepted their gifts.

In the past, the search for the perfect vessel has worn out other, lesser corre-

spondents. *There are many of them among our viewers, but because we can only go out among you through our special representatives, it takes time and effort to individually meet all of you. And by the time you've finished one pass-through, a whole new generation has been born, and the process begins all over again.*

But Tony was up to the challenge, and found not one but—we believe, the final results are still coming in—two such specimens. It was quite an achievement, and all of us here are very proud of Tony, who was recently recognized for his work at a dinner in his honor. Back to you, Dan.

Dan Rather appeared again, his face somber. *A touching testimonial for one of our own, Pierce, thank you. Regrettably, we must now turn to other developing stories which require our full attention. As every good reporter knows, when you're hunting down a story, there's no room for distractions. The past dies, and the future is continually reborn.*

Distantly, Tony became aware of an acrid smell in the tiny apartment. Smoke? He managed to focus past the screen, to where a thin trail of blue-white smoke rose from the wall socket where the TV was plugged in.

He imagined this might be important, but his thoughts were scattered, and it was getting difficult to pull them together. The room was sliding in and out of a blackness that lived just behind his eyes. Better to turn his attention to Dan. He would be going soon, wouldn't he? Couldn't be rude to Dan.

Dan pressed his earplug to his ear again, listening. *This just in, apparently a fire has broken out in an apartment building in southeast Los Angeles at this hour. We'll try to update this story as circumstances permit. Meanwhile, thank you for joining us.*

For CBS News, this is Dan Rather. Good night.

Good night, Tony thought, as the television burst into flames.

BOOK THREE
ROGER SENDS A MESSAGE

He shall return no more to his house, neither shall his place know him anymore.

The Book of Job, 7:10

16

Carlyn Martino risked a glance at the clock as she stirred the rapidly heating pot of chocolate pudding. Chris had said he'd be home early. She was making his favorite: burnt meat loaf, a dish she had prepared on special occasions ever since his tenth birthday. On that day, like most days, she'd spent much of the afternoon arguing with his father. When she finally realized she'd forgotten to make anything special, she had hurriedly whipped up some meat loaf. And then had gotten into another argument with Bill.

By the time she remembered the meat loaf and pulled it out of the oven it was almost black. Naturally, Bill put on his disgusted look and went out, leaving her with burnt meat loaf and a ten-year-old son confident that Mom was whipping up something extravagant.

She'd cried for nearly half an hour before calling Chris in to dinner. I'll make it up to him, she'd thought at the time. Somehow.

But when he took his first bite, his face lit up. "This is *great*," he said, crunching happily, "why don't you make it like this all the time?"

It was all she could do to keep from hugging him right into another incarnation. She couldn't recall loving him more than she did at that instant, except for the moment he was born.

So whenever it seemed he was having a bad day, or she wanted to be especially nice to him, she would stick a meat loaf in the oven, and force herself to read a book and ignore the smell of smoke and evaporating ketchup that escaped from the kitchen.

On the whole, she decided, there was nothing wonkier than being a mother.

She hoped the dinner would help, at least a little, though she would have been more comfortable if she knew *what it was* that she was supposed to be helping. Over the last few days, Chris seemed to be steadily withdrawing into himself. True, he was in a new school, trying to deal with a major change in his life, trying to make new friends—and it was understandable, at his age, to try and cut the apron strings as much as possible. But still she was concerned. Thus far, she had tried to give him as much room as possible to find his own way, which apparently meant spending a lot of time with Roger, who seemed a decent sort, if a little reserved, bookish in a nervous kind of way. She supposed Chris had a little of that in him, too.

For a while she'd worried that Roger was having a bad effect on him. She'd awakened a couple of times in the middle of the night and, upon checking, had found Chris's bed empty. A quick glance out his window had revealed Chris and Roger talking. It had happened again just the other night, and though the window was too far up to hear what they were saying, it was clear they were arguing. Both times she'd seen Roger lately he'd been carrying an oblong box. She wondered what he was carrying around in it, and why he needed it whenever he was with Chris.

Initially, she'd considered asking about it. But so far there was no indication that it was anything other than standard adolescent adventuring. She didn't want to put Chris in the position of feeling he had to lie to her in order to protect his friend. So she would allow it. For the moment.

He'll be fine, she thought, and poured the pudding out into a bowl to cool.

She heard the front door open and close. "Chris? That you?"

"Yeah, Mom," he called back. Even from here she could make out that curious distance in his voice.

"Better get washed, dinner'll be on in a sec."

There was no answer from the front room, but she could hear him climbing up the stairs. Probably didn't hear me, she decided.

When the table was set, she came out into the living room to get him, and found him still upstairs. She called him to dinner. He called back something she didn't quite catch, but it sounded as though he was on his way.

As she stepped back toward the kitchen, she noticed a package behind one of the chairs, the bag from a downtown electronics store. She couldn't tell if Chris had casually dropped it there, or if he had been making a deliberate, if clumsy, effort to conceal it from her.

No, she decided. If he'd been trying to hide it he would have just taken it upstairs. It was therefore okay to peek in and see what it was.

She tugged at a corner of the bag and saw a smiling face on a red-and-blue box. 1,001 EXPERIMENTS! the box proclaimed. MAKE OVER A THOUSAND SCIENTIFIC DEVICES—TRANSISTORS AND PEGBOARD IN-CLUDED!

THESE ARE JUST SOME OF THE THINGS YOU CAN MAKE WITH 1,001 EXPERIMENTS:
- RADIO!
- SPEAKER BOX!
- TELEPHONE!
- SOUND-ACTIVATED LIGHT!
- TELEGRAPH KEY!
- AND MANY, MANY MORE!

She pushed the bag back into its original position and headed for the kitchen, feeling better than she had a few moments earlier.

It was good to see Chris getting into some hobbies.

2

Steve Mackey took another swallow off the can of Budweiser and settled back against the cold stone wall that ran alongside the beach. It was getting dark, the afternoon's warmth fading to a brisk wind that whipped up over the water. Everyone else had started to clear out, packing up umbrellas and ice chests for the drive back into the city. In a little while, only a few fishermen and die-hard surfers would be left.

About then, he would walk back to the car and head off to Paul's place. Paul's folks were out of town for the weekend, and he had the house to himself. That meant a party. And maybe getting laid. The way things had been going lately, Steve figured he could use a little of the old in-and-out.

What would happen afterward, of course, was another question.

Sooner or later he would have to go home.

Screw it, he thought, and poked at the sand with a stick. In a few more months he'd be eighteen, and he could do what he wanted. Not that he had any clear idea what that was—except to be as far away from here as a full tank of gas could carry him.

It had not been a good week.

First the mid-semester progress report came in; the explosion followed. He'd seen it in the mailbox, and had hoped to sneak it away before his old man got a look at it, but he was too slow. It said he'd either be held back a year and not allowed to graduate, or do a semester of summer school. He didn't like the idea any more than his old man did, but what the hell was he supposed to do? The shit they taught in school was about as relevant to his life as a fart. As soon as he got out of school, he could probably kill a couple of years at a local junior college, maybe L. A. C. C. That would give him a chance to get out of the house, get his own place for a while. After that . . .

That was always where the plan ran out. Right now nothing much appealed to him as a career. He snorted at the word. Career. For him that would probably mean the military, working at the brake shop with his old man the rest of his life, or working in a department store or a restaurant or a gas station.

It was an ugly thought, and he tried to keep it out of his head.

He dug deeper into the sand, his stomach knotting. His grades weren't even the worst of it.

Yesterday his old man had found his stash.

It wasn't much—a half-dozen joints, a couple of 'ludes, some other stuff—but it was the coke that made his old man lose it. It was just a quarter-gram, but you'd've thought he'd been caught smuggling a half-ton of primo heroin. All of a sudden his father had something to blame everything on—Steve's grades, his attitude, it was all due to that ol' debbil drugs!

He got loud. So Steve got loud. He shoved. So Steve shoved back. Only he must've shoved back harder than he thought because the next thing he knew he was on his ass with the wind knocked out of him, and his old man was standing over him, yelling and screaming for him to get out of the house, just get the hell out and never come back.

So Steve got the hell out. Always willing to oblige. But *never come back?* He figured that once his folks cooled down, they'd let him return, though they'd be murder for the next few months. They'd watchdog him endlessly, check his eyes, search his room. It wasn't something he looked forward to—but he couldn't see any way around it. Later, when he turned eighteen and could leave on his own terms, well, that'd be different.

Damn straight, he thought, and stopped digging when his stick hit something hard. Probably a soda can, he decided, and started to outline its shape with the stick, only to find it was square.

He dug around the object, which was about six inches across, until it loosened and he was able to drag it out of the sand. It was a metal box, beaded with moisture on the outside. He brushed away the sand. There were no markings; it was an ordinary sort of box, the kind you might make in metal shop. It was dented in places, and when he shook it, something inside rattled. Couldn't be much, though; the box was light.

He tried to open it, but the hinges were rusted. He pulled harder, wondering why someone had decided to bury it. Abruptly, the box snapped open so suddenly that he drove the palm of his hand into one of the sharp corners. "Shit!" he yelled, dropping the box. It wasn't a deep cut, but blood was already seeping out of it, dropping onto the sand. Some was smeared over the top of the box.

Great, he thought, just my luck, now I'll get tetanus. Pulling a tissue out of his pocket, he pressed it against the cut and closed his fist. With his free hand, he picked up the box.

Whatever was inside, it better be worth all this, he thought.

It was a photograph. Nothing more. A Polaroid. It took him a moment to realize what he was looking at.

It was a picture of a car; more specifically, a picture of *his* car. Or what was left of it. It was wrapped around a center divider, the hood buckled and the rear punched in pretty badly. But he could see the KIIS-FM bumper sticker he'd customized by replacing the FM with the words "MY ASS." The hubcaps were the same, the interior was the same, the paint job was the same . . .

There were just a few problems.

139

One, his car had never been in a wreck.

Two, where was *he* in this?

And, more important, who had taken the picture, and how had it gotten in the box?

"What the fuck?" he said aloud, and started at the sound of his own voice. It had to be a gag. But who could know he'd come to this spot, on this day, and start poking around in the dirt with a stick?

He turned the photo over, but the back of it was blank; there was no indication where it came from or who took it. Each time he turned it over again, he expected to find he had misread the photo, and it wasn't really his car. But it remained, stubbornly and stead-fastly, his.

Then he realized that if, somehow, someone *had* put it there for him to find, wouldn't they be watching to make sure he did, indeed, find it?

Damn straight, he thought. He looked up and down the beach, and behind him to the parking lot. Everybody seemed too busy with their own affairs to even notice him. But wasn't that what he should expect, to be observed inconspicuously?

You're getting paranoid, he thought out of one half of his brain, as the other half responded, With good reason.

Oh, and by the way, you are being watched.

He glanced up toward the pier, squinting against the sun which was now nearly level with the horizon. Wasn't there someone standing there, beside the pilings? A silhouette against the glittering surf?

"Hey!" Steve yelled. "Hey, you!"

Nothing moved. He held up his hand to shield his eyes and jogged a few steps closer to the pier.

No, there was nothing there. He was sure of it now. Though he would have sworn otherwise a moment ago, would have been willing to bet that there had been someone short, and round, wearing glasses that had briefly seemed to reflect the fading sunlight.

But there was no one here now, he was certain, and no way for anyone to get away without being seen.

Weird, he thought.

Clutching the photograph and the metal box (his hand was starting to hurt now, though the bleeding had stopped), he walked toward the parking lot.

It took him a moment to steel himself enough to get inside the car, start the engine, and drive off.

Just a gag, he thought. But weird. Real eff-ing weird.

Behind him, the sun slid beneath the horizon.

3

Chet Huntington watched the tiny brass drum turn in his daughter's music box. It was curious, he thought, that a sound so small and delicate could fill the bedroom. In that way, it was a lot like Jenny. Even now, the room held her imprint: the crack in the wall from where she'd smashed a spider with her first high-heel shoe, the pictures, the stuffed toys on the bed, just as she left them.

I'm going to have to clean this room out some day, he thought, as painful as that would be. It was getting close to that time when keeping her room as it was would pass from mourning into the macabre. They had tried twice before to pack everything away. Each time their hearts just weren't up to the task.

"Chet?" Marie called from downstairs. " 'Sixty Minutes' is on. You told me to remind you when it started."

"Be right down."

Marie had been able to sustain Jenny's death with the fewest visible wounds. She was a strong woman. He'd tried to comfort her, but in the end he suspected he ended up drawing more strength from her than she from him. Frank, who was a couple of years older than Jenny, took it the worst. And now, between that and being away at college, he had all but disappeared from their lives. There were still the occasional phone calls, but they were awkward, strained, punctuated with silences.

He closed the lid to the music box, and silence rushed into the room, as though it had been waiting greedily outside for the chance to reclaim its dominion.

Why did you go away, Jenny? Why did you leave us alone?

In the three years since her death, he had not been able to come up with an answer to that.

There was only the silence, and the pain that he knew would come again tonight, in the midnight hour when he would miss her

141

most. He remembered the weeks after her birth, when he would wake up in the middle of the night and go into her room to make sure that she was still breathing. He would stand there in the darkness, watching her sleep, returning again and again over the years to that place, just to look at her as she grew, to be sure she was safe, there in the midnight silence.

Then one night he woke up and made his nightly round only to find the bed empty. And then he remembered. Marie had found him sitting on Jenny's bed, crying in huge, wracking sobs until she had finally been able to get him back to their own bedroom, where she held him until dawn, when he was finally able to sleep.

They had never spoken about that night.

"I miss you, baby," he said, quietly. Then, feeling old, he stepped out into the hall, closing the door behind him. He could almost imagine the relief that the silence inside felt at his departure, the freedom to run its fingers across her clothes, her dolls, her bed.

Jenny belonged to the silence now. It, too, was a jealous god.

4

Susan decided that she really should be heading home—and, of course, did nothing about it.

You're a fool, she thought—and did nothing about it.

The wine felt good, and she'd had too much of it already. They had returned from the movies early, and this time they had come to Gene's apartment afterward. She let her head fall back against the sofa, allowing her gaze to take in the details of his living room as he worked to uncork a bottle of chablis in the kitchen.

It was a nice place. The furniture was all new (post-divorce, she assumed), paintings and movie posters shared space on the walls, and potted ferns lurked behind chairs and hid in the corners. She couldn't keep plants on a bet. They always turned brown and died within a couple of weeks.

She giggled at the idea of having an official burial for her plants. HERE LIES FERN, the headstone would say, PLANTED AT LAST.

You're drunk, pronounced the part of her mind that always sounded like her mother. She nodded. Darn right. So what else is new?

"Be just a sec," Gene called from the kitchen. Apparently the cork had decided to be difficult. If his hands were as nervous in there as they had been in here a few minutes earlier, it would be an even fight. Oh yes, she had felt the tension in his hands as he had begun to touch her. She had almost said it. *You haven't done this much since your divorce, have you?* But she held it in. She wasn't that drunk.

The night before, they had gone out again, this time to a bar he knew where they played wonderful jazz. Afterward, they had gone to her place, and they stood inside and talked, and talked, and finally she thought that if he did not kiss her she would go mad from the suspense. At that point it wasn't even lust; it was just a desire to get past that stage of things. And to find out the kinds of things you could only learn by kissing.

Finally, when it had gotten quiet for a long time, he had done just that. It had been nice. Very nice.

And now here she was, in his apartment, late, half-drunk, and facing the inevitable question: What now, Sherlock? Never mind the chatter now, Watson. The game's afoot! We must move swiftly.

"Mission accomplished," Gene said, and stepped back into the room with the open bottle. "Took a while, but it finally surrendered."

He filled her glass, then his, and sat down, leaving the bottle on the table. "Now, where were we?"

"You were making fun of Stallone."

"No I wasn't," he said, taking a sip. "For what he does, he's good enough. I wouldn't make fun of him. It would be inappropriate."

"And he would come and rip your arms off."

"That, too," he said, and smiled.

It was quiet again in the room. *That* kind of quiet. They both looked down at their glasses, both—she suspected—reluctant to meet one another's gaze.

Finally, she looked up, only to find him staring at her. "No fair," she said.

"I know," he said, and stroked the side of her face. She closed her eyes, instinctively raising her head to allow access to her neck and throat, the way a cat might. She could feel his fingers tracing an ever-lengthening line down her throat and around, to the nape of her neck. Then his lips were on hers, and she parted her mouth slightly, feeling his breath.

She reached behind his head and held his hair, pulling him closer as his hands crossed her breasts before sweeping smoothly across her stomach. Then his fingers rode her hips to her legs, to the back of her knees; she shivered at his touch. Her pulse quickened, and she could feel herself starting to move in response, reaching out to stroke his leg—

No, she thought, and pulled away. His hand stopped instantly. "I'm—sorry," she said. Despite herself, she remembered Michael. Remembered seeing him with that other woman. Remembered betrayal and tears and swearing she'd never fall for it again . . .

He looked in her eyes, barely inches away. "Are you all right?"

"No. Yes. I'm . . . just a little drunk, I think."

"Yes, you are."

"And I think I'd rather wait, until—well, I just don't want to wake up in the morning and think we did it because I was drunk. I'd just—rather not. Am I making any sense?"

He considered it. "I think so."

"Thank you. I'm so sorry, I—"

"No reason to apologize."

She straightened her skirt. Somehow it had gotten hiked up around her thighs. Her hands felt numb, as though they didn't really belong to her. "I should probably go," she said.

"I don't think you can be trusted to drive at the moment."

He was, unfortunately, right. Until she got some coffee, or some sleep, she would be a menace. "Okay, I give up. If you can get me a cab—"

"Or you can sleep here."

She focused on him. "Gene . . ."

He held up his hands. "Not like that." He patted the sofa. "This turns into a sleeper. I bought it since I have friends from out of town who sometimes stay over, and I don't have a guest room. You're welcome to it. I have a couple of spare robes in here somewhere. You'll just sleep over, with me in there." He pointed toward what was probably the bedroom. "Deal?"

She knew that the safe thing would be to leave now, rather than endanger the rough truce that had been arrived at. On the other hand, she trusted him, or at least, *wanted* to trust him. And this was one sure way of testing it.

"Deal," she said.

5

Steve sat on the floor, back to the wall, letting the vibrations from the stereo speaker beside him fill his head. Screw it, so what if he wasn't going to get laid tonight? No big deal, just a crummy ache inside him to ignore, that's all. Just a pang the approximate size of King Kong, that's all.

Screw it, he thought again, and let his eyes slit open to check on the party's progress. It was getting late, and most everyone was splitting for home. His hopes for getting laid had vanished when he found out that Karen wasn't going to show. Homework, or somesuch dipshit excuse. Karen was the only girl he'd ever met who was hornier than he was. He knew he could rely on her to do anything he wanted.

Typical, he thought. The one night he needed her, really needed her, she wasn't there. The photograph he found on the beach was still burning in his pocket. He wanted to talk to someone about it, but Paul and Jack were too zonked out to be of much use, and nobody else would give a shit. They'd probably think he was jerking them around, trying to run a number on them.

He took another hit off the joint. The more he thought about the photograph, the more he came to the realization that somebody was trying to play with his head. Maybe somebody he knew. He began to see a way somebody could've set him up. He usually hung out at the same part of the beach, so that factored in. The details of how they could time it and put it in exactly the right place were still fuzzy, but it was possible. Hell, he'd once seen a guy on TV make the Statue of Liberty disappear; by comparison, this was nothing. And you could do just about anything you wanted with a picture. Everybody knew that.

The question now was who did it, and why?

He'd figure it out. He was good at figuring out stuff like this.

He let his gaze wander toward the patio door. To his surprise, Karen was standing there, smiling through the crowd at him. He got unsteadily to his feet, and made his way toward her. So far, no one else seemed to have noticed her, so probably no one would notice her missing for a little while.

"Hi," he said, his head buzzing from the grass.

"Hi," she said back. She looked good. The way she smiled always seemed to have *Fuck Me* written in neon just behind her eyes.

"Want to go outside?"

"Sure."

He led her out back, to where it was darkest. If he kept close to the hedge he could avoid being seen by the neighbors, and he would also be at just the right angle not to be seen from the house, either. "How you been?"

"Just fine." She was standing close to him, infuriatingly close, her perfume causing his groin to ache. "How're *you?*"

He grinned at her. "You want to find out?"

She nodded, and he was all over her in a second. He pulled her into the shadows, kissing her as his hands went to her breasts. She struggled, but he knew that was how she liked it, and he pressed on, pulling her down with him to the grass, everything red behind his eyes, the only sound his own heartbeat as he slid his hands between her legs and moved them apart. Then he was working at his own zipper, looking for a way in, fumbling with her—

"What the hell are you doing down there?! Hey! You!"

He looked up. One of the neighbors yelled out his back window at them, then vanished back inside as another scream, this time from below him, caught Steve's attention.

She was sobbing, her dress torn, hair looped around his fingers. "Daddy!" she was screaming, "DADDY!"

She wasn't Karen.

She was one of the kids who'd come around earlier that evening.

She was twelve, if he was lucky.

"Oh shit," he said, stumbling backward, his pants catching him behind the knees. Already some of the kids were coming out of Paul's house. Lights came on in the surrounding houses and now there were other voices crying out, yelling at him to leave her alone.

The man from next door ran toward him. He had a gun.

It's her father, Steve thought, as from far away.

Get away! Get out of here! MOVE!

He raced back through the crowd inside the house, knocking over the coffee table, buckling his pants as he caromed off the front door and across the lawn. He dived into his car and started the engine just as the father came bursting out of the house after him.

"Stop! Stop or I swear to God I'll shoot, you son of a bitch!"

He floored the gas pedal, not looking back. If the old man did shoot at him, Steve didn't hear it over the roar of the engine. He made for the main road, doing sixty on surface streets.

Oh shit, he thought, *oh shit, oh shit, oh shit, what am I gonna do, I thought it was Karen, oh shit, what am I gonna do they'll put me in jail.*

Police lights and sirens appeared in his rear window. He could hear them on the megaphone, ordering him to pull over. But he couldn't. He had to get away, that was the only thing he knew, the two words that filled his head to the exclusion of all else, GET AWAY, GET AWAY!

They moved up, closing in on him.

He pushed the accelerator. Seventy. He hit the freeway on-ramp and pushed it farther. Eighty. They were still behind him, two of them now. He looked back to judge their distance, then forward to—

Car!

It swerved out of its lane into his and he was heading straight for it. He hit the brakes, and the car centerpunched his right side, and now he was swerving, spinning clockwise as he fought the wheel, braking, braking, turning into the spin, trying to slow down, slow the hell down—and suddenly there was a sound of metal tearing and a sound like the end of the world.

Then it was quiet. He was lying on the pavement, and he was looking up at a cop's face. The cop was saying something to him, but he couldn't make out what it was. Slowly, so slowly it seemed almost a dream, he moved his head and looked across the road, past the cars now backed up behind the accident, to where his car was wrapped around the center divider, the door popped open where he had been thrown out.

It was the same view as the photograph.

Isn't that interesting? he thought, and felt himself go far away.

17

Chris never liked to revel in anyone's bad news—that sort of thing had a way of backfiring on you. But it was hard not to find some pleasure in the news he overheard in Home Room.

"Did you hear what happened to Steve Mackey?" one of the guys in front of him had said.

"No, what?"

"Got caught trying to pork some junior high girl last night. Ended up getting busted up real bad after a really radical car chase. Guy I know was there, says it was like something out of *Dirty Harry*."

"He gonna live?"

"Nobody knows."

"No shit?"

"No shit."

No shit, indeed, Chris thought, and decided it couldn't have happened to a nicer guy. It would have been even more enjoyable if Roger had been there to share it with. But he was absent, as he'd been the last few days of the preceding week. Roger said he didn't have to come to school anymore, and therefore he chose not to. The OtherSyde would take care of it, he said. But Mr. Edwards was taking roll, same as any other day, and marking down Roger's absent days. Sooner or later, somebody would have to notice.

And would Roger much care if they did? All he ever seemed to talk about now was the OtherSyde. The OtherSyde said this, the OtherSyde said that. Chris still thought it was pretty creepy, but the longer he saw the tapping telegraph key in action, the more ordinary it became. It reminded him of the first time he had seen Palisades Amusement Park, how big and awesome it had seemed at the time. Then, after the fourth or fifth trip there, it was no longer anything special, just the same old tricks and rides.

Was that how life was, he wondered? You find something weird, or strange, and soon enough you stop noticing how weird and strange it is? His mom was always saying how his dad took her for granted, to the point where he hardly even saw her anymore, even when she was in the same room. Was that the same thing?

Do we just get used to everything? It was a question he would have liked to ask Roger. But Roger wasn't there.

Roger, it seemed, had gotten used to it a lot faster than he had, which was to be expected. Roger had put together his key days ago. Chris had barely cracked the plastic wrapping on his kit, let alone tried to put it together.

He wanted to wait. If Roger was ready to believe everything the OtherSyde seemed to promise, that was fine. But Chris wanted some evidence first.

That was what they had argued about Friday night.

"What do you want?" Roger said. "For Christ to come off his frigging cross and give you a pat on the head, say 'It's okay, Chris, do what you want'?"

"I just want to be sure this works the way you say."

"How? How sure? What do you need?"

Chris thought about it. "I took a geography test, we're supposed to get back the results Monday. I don't think I did real well. If it can fix that, then fine, I'll put mine together."

Roger said he'd get back to him.

Sunday night, Roger called. "What kind of test was it?" he asked. The connection sounded strange, as though he were calling from far away.

"Multiple choice."

"Computer form? The kind you fill out with a pencil and the computer scans it?"

"Right."

"Just a sec." Roger put down the phone, and Chris could hear him repeating the information. Then there was a pause, followed by a series of rapid-fire *ticks*. A moment later, Roger came back on the line. "No sweat. You're just lucky it wasn't an essay test, or you'd be screwed. Talk to you after."

"Wait a minute, I—"

"Sorry, Chris, gotta go, got to go to a party. Bye."

Click and disconnect from the other end.

It had sounded good at the time. But now Chris sat anxiously at his desk, waiting as Mr. St. Clair passed out the graded forms.

If he was lucky, he probably got a 65 or a 68. He would need at least a 70 to keep his total grade from slipping too far.

Mr. St. Clair handed him his form. "An improvement, Chris," he said, and kept on moving, "very good."

Chris glanced at the grade computer-printed on the top of the narrow sheet of paper: 100%.

No way, Chris thought. *No way*. He looked to another student across the aisle, whose test was marked 98%. "Can I borrow that for a sec?" Chris asked.

"Sure," he said, and handed Chris his form.

Chris held them up to the light, one atop the other. Since there were fifty questions, two points each, then there should only be one discrepancy between his and the other kid's.

There were sixteen discrepancies, which meant his grade should actually have been around 68, as he'd expected. Yet the form said 100%. There had to be some sort of computer error. It hadn't scanned his form properly.

You're just lucky it wasn't an essay test, or you'd be screwed.

"Son of a bitch," Chris muttered.

With Roger gone, Chris stopped by Mr. Edwards's class again for the last part of lunch. In recent days, the visits had become more regular. He was still having a hard time getting to know anyone else, and Edwards went out of his way to make himself available to anyone who wanted to visit. Sometimes there were kids from his other classes, and sometimes it was just him.

This time, though, Edwards was gone, a note on his door explaining that there was a pressing faculty meeting.

With twenty minutes to kill, Chris wandered the halls, reading the graffiti on the lockers and glancing in at the other classrooms, most of them empty, a few occupied by other kids in meetings. Sheets of paper taped to the doors announced KEY CLUB MEETING HERE! or PEP CLUB or CAMPUS LIFE. One whole row was taken up by the foreign language clubs: German, Spanish, French, and Italian. He'd wondered if he should try to join one of the campus clubs. It seemed a good way to meet people—and much as he liked Roger, he sometimes wondered if the word "people" really applied to him. It was an assessment Roger would agree with enthusiastically.

"You want to look at stuff, I got something better than that, Chris."

Chris turned, startled to find Roger standing behind him. "What're you doing here?"

"Slumming. What does it look like?"

"What if you get caught?"

Roger snorted. "I won't. C'mon."

"C'mon where?"

"Just follow and shut up, we don't have much time!" He headed out the door. Chris hesitated only a moment before following. If Roger had actually come to class, then there had to be one heck of a reason for it, and he didn't want to miss it.

He caught up with him as they cut across the lawn toward the gym. The athletic field and volleyball courts were empty now; in another few minutes, they would be filled with students. For a moment, Chris thought Roger was leading him to the boys' locker room, but then he went past it without slowing, heading around to the other side of the gym.

The girls' locker room.

Chris hurried to keep up with him. "Where the hell are we going?"

"Where does it look like?"

"Are you crazy? We can't go in there! If they catch us, they'll throw us out of school!"

"They won't catch us."

"Yeah? How do you know?"

"OtherSyde said so."

"You can't be serious. They'll see us, man!"

151

"Only if they *decide* to see us."

"What the hell does *that* mean?" Chris asked. Already they were at the entrance.

Roger looked around. No one in sight. "You'll find out. Now, you coming, or what?" He held the door open.

Chris hesitated.

"Okay, fine, then I'll go in by myself—and I'm not going to tell you what I see, either." He stepped quickly inside.

Chris looked around, balancing from foot to foot, then grabbed the door handle and followed. *If he gets me expelled I swear to God I'll kill him.*

The inside looked like the boys' locker room, with rows of lockers facing long wooden benches. The first thing that struck Chris was the smell—a mix of sweat, old clothes, perfume, and powdered soap. The showers stood empty at the far end of the room. At one side were the offices for the gym teacher and her assistant, and a storage room for basketballs and other equipment. The door to the storage room was made of louvered wooden slats.

Roger pointed at it. "In there."

"What if someone needs something? What if someone looks inside?"

"They won't."

"How can you be so sure?"

Roger tried the door. It stuck for a moment, then pulled open. Above them, the bell rang announcing the start of the next period. "Better make up your mind fast—this place is gonna be crawling with tits in about ten seconds."

Already Chris could hear footsteps coming down the corridor.

"All right, all right," Chris said. They closed the door after them, the slats in the door providing a clear view of the locker room and the showers. Chris figured if they hunched down low enough, and let the shadows inside work against anyone on the brightly lit other side, they might not be seen . . . unless someone opened the door and looked inside, because in here there was absolutely nowhere to hide.

I'll say he forced me to come with him. No, I tried to stop him, and I nearly had him out when the bell rang, so we hid. Maybe they'll believe me.

Fat chance, he decided, as the door to the locker room swung open, and the girls started to come in. He recognized some of them from his own classes. There were quite a few senior girls among them. Most of them were at least as tall as Chris.

"They'll tear us to shreds," Chris whispered.

"Shh!" Roger said. "Just watch and learn."

The girls started taking their clothes off. Chris had always thought that girls must move slowly and sensually when they disrobed, but they were dropping skirts and pants and pulling off tops just like guys did. Watching them made Chris's mouth go dry. Bras were removed or replaced by sturdier ones, revealing breasts that took his breath away. And when they sat down to pull off skirts and hose and panties. . . .

Chris felt his knees go weak. He leaned against the door for support. It creaked slightly, and it sounded to him like a cannon going off. But no one outside seemed to notice.

Chris licked his lips, finding them dry, only vaguely aware of Roger in the same room. There was such an abundance of movement and skin and laughter and clothes that it was hard to focus on any of it—he would pick one girl, then flit to another before getting a good look, then back only to find she'd turned away.

Suddenly someone blew a whistle right outside the door; Chris thought his heart would explode.

It was the gym teacher. She came in the locker room trailing a cart filled with basketballs. "Okay, here's the lineup. Team one plays team eight, team two plays team seven, three plays six, four plays five. I want everyone done by ten till, then everyone do one lap around the field before coming in."

One girl—Chris recognized her from history class—put her hand up. Unlike the rest, she was still dressed in her street clothes. "Can I be excused from playing?" she said.

"Cramps?"

The girl nodded.

"Okay, everybody else out on the field. Let's go!" The teacher handed out basketballs to the girls as they headed out toward the courts. One girl who took it stopped and examined hers. "Mrs. Archer?"

"Yes?"

"This ball's got gunk all over it."

"It won't kill you, Janice."

She pouted. "But Mrs. *Archerrrr.*"

Mrs. Archer sighed. "All right, go get another one. But hurry up."

Janice started to jog toward the storage room.

"Shit!" Chris whispered. "Oh, shit-shit-shit!"

Ten feet away, she slowed. Her face seemed momentarily to cloud over, as though she were trying to remember something. "Screw it," she said, "it's not worth the hassle."

Then she ran out of the locker room, dribbling the basketball in front of her.

Chris exhaled, realizing that he'd been holding his breath. His legs were trembling so badly he wished he could sit down, but there was no place available except the floor.

It was good enough.

Chris sat heavily, back hunched against the door. "Jesus, Roger, that was close."

"No sweat," Roger said. "Like I said, they'll only see us if they *decide* to see us. Meanwhile, they'll keep looking wherever we're not."

Right, Chris thought. *Makes sense to me.*

Roger was still looking out through the slats, his mouth open, eyes glittering in the semi-dark.

"What is it?" Chris said.

"See for yourself."

Chris hauled himself off the floor and peered out through the slats. The locker room was all but deserted. Only one girl was left. She'd arrived later than the rest, and was just finishing changing.

She was sitting on one of the wooden benches, in the far corner of the locker room, where she couldn't be seen from the main door. She had another girl's locker open, and with one hand she was touching the girl's clothes to her face and neck. Her other hand was buried beneath the elastic waistband of her shorts. Even from here Chris could see her hand working quickly beneath the fabric, her head leaning to one side against the cold locker.

Oh my god.

It seemed like only a moment later when her back arched, and she bit down on her lower lip. The movement beneath her shorts grew even more rapid. Then her lower lip dropped open and her eyes closed, the tension going out of her face. She kept her hand in her shorts a little longer, moving slowly now, before finally withdrawing it. She replaced the clothing she'd borrowed, then sat back against the locker for a moment more before standing, her face still flushed, and straightening her shorts. With a final check in the mirror, she headed out toward the playing fields.

"I'd say that was worth the price of admission, wouldn't you?" Roger said.

"Yeah," Chris said, his voice sounding husky to his own ears. His groin felt as if it had been knotted up a dozen times and tied with barbed wire. "We better go now."

"Okay," Roger said. "I think it's probably safe."

He opened the door, looked around, and trotted quickly to the main door. He peered outside. "Okay, it's clear. Go!"

They jogged outside. Chris risked a glance behind them, to the playing field. The girls were shooting baskets, their backs toward them, and wasn't that a singular coincidence, wondered the part of him that wasn't still reeling from what he'd just seen, that at the moment when he and Roger left the locker room, they would all be looking in the other direction?

"Pretty good, huh, Chris?" Roger asked. His face was flushed, and he was sweating.

"Okay, I guess," Chris said, and allowed a smile. The possibility was dawning on him—as it obviously already had on Roger—that maybe it *was* true, maybe now they *could* do all kinds of incredible stuff. The opportunities were enormous.

"And this is only the start. If you knew what else we could do—"

"Like what?"

"You'll see," Roger said. "You coming by the house after school?"

"I'll try, but my mom wants me to pick up some stuff at the store for her."

"Your loss," Roger said. "See you later." He headed away down the hall.

"Wait a second, aren't you staying for the rest of the day?"

"Are you kidding? No way." He waved back at Chris before turning the corner and disappearing from view.

Chris continued on his way to class, remembering that he'd forgotten to mention what happened to Steve Mackey over the weekend.

He shrugged. Knowing Roger, he'd hear about it soon on his own.

Roger walked with his hands stuffed in his pockets, passing classrooms filled with students going through the motions of learning something they did not care about, and would never use again. The big shots, the soshes, the rah-rah types, and the ten-watts-on-the-I.Q.-scale athletes, they were all stuck in those hot, stuffy little rooms. And here he was, on the outside looking in, able to go where he wanted, and do what he wanted.

In the latter was the greatest pleasure of all.

He had barely even *started*.

He stopped first at his locker to pick up the box, and anything else he might want to bring home with him; he doubted he'd be in the neighborhood again anytime soon. But aside from the box he'd stashed there when he got on campus, there was nothing he considered of value or interest. Just stacks of books that after just four days looked alien and unfamiliar, as though he were looking at someone else's locker. *Fundamentals of History, English II, Our United States, Calculus I.* What did they have to do with him anymore?

He removed the shoebox. The only visible marks on it were the two small air holes he had punched in one end, before realizing to his chagrin that what was inside didn't need air.

As if in response to his thoughts, the box vibrated against his hands, and he heard a soft *tick tick-tick* from inside.

Hello to you, too. He slammed the locker door shut, then retraced his steps toward the school library. Phase One had been a success, even if he hadn't known what he was doing when he had done it, and hadn't known what form the results would take. A sheet of unexposed Polaroid film, an old metal box, the long bus ride to the beach—it had taken him hours to get the last of the sand out of his shoes. But it was all he could have hoped for. Steve wouldn't be bothering him again.

Now it was time for Phase Two.

In the library he found what he needed: last year's school yearbook. He tucked it under the box, and walked calmly through the detectors at the door. They failed to register the unauthorized checkout, as he had known they would. It was all taken care of.

From now on, everything, and everyone, would be taken care of just fine.

Outside, the sun was bright and warm on his back. No one challenged him as he left the campus and headed home. It was nice to be able to walk out of school and not have to worry about being punched out.

Halfway home, he stopped at a small park and sat down on a grassy rise. From his pocket he pulled a Zagnut bar and a red pen. And then slowly, page by page, with the methodical attention to detail that would normally have been reserved for homework, he went through the rows of photographs that filled the yearbook. Most of the faces that peered out at him were little more than strangers, other students that he'd seen around school, and had done him neither wrong nor right.

Label them Civilians.

Then one by one, like a movie detective working a lineup of suspects, he noted the names and faces of the others.

Label them the Enemy.

Gary Stavros. This one had deliberately tripped him in the hall. He'd torn his pants at the knee, and later others had made fun of him, asking why his father couldn't afford to buy him new clothes.

Red circle.

This one had pantsed him in the athletic field.

This one had gone out of his way to ram into Roger at first base during baseball practice. Roger's ears had rung for nearly an hour afterward.

Two more red circles.

Paul Geyer, second in command of the Dumbass Deathsquad. A bright red circle.

And this one—oh yes, this one was the first girl he had ever asked out. Patricia Alberts. He'd started by leaving her anonymous notes. Then, finally, he had his chance when he found her at her locker, away from her usual entourage of friends. She'd stared blankly at him as he'd stuttered his way through an explanation, that it was he who had left the notes, and he who wanted desperately to take her to a movie or a dance or—

"You *creep!*" she'd said. "You fucking *creep*, how *dare* you!" And then she had hit him. He fell trying to back out of the way, and then everyone had gathered around and she kept yelling at him, yelling and *enjoying* the yelling, and they had all laughed at him.

Not long after that she dropped out of school. He learned later she'd gotten pregnant, and married the guy who'd done it, a senior. Now they were living in hopes of his someday becoming assistant manager at the McDonald's or someplace similar.

At the time, that news had seemed sufficient retribution. But now he had the chance to balance out the scales just a little more.

A nice, big red circle for Patricia Alberts.

He went back to turning pages.

Red circle. Red circle. Two more red circles. Insults, slights, offenses, assaults, rebuffs, he had catalogued them all.

The only regret he felt was the need to keep all this from Chris. Chris was okay, but he was kind of slow to pick up on what they had stumbled into. Roger understood, because he'd talked to it a lot more. Their conversations now filled ten pages of his journal. But Roger had an advantage. He'd read all those stories by Lovecraft, Dunsany, Smith, and the rest. They knew what forces were out there, waiting to be turned to one person's will—the *right person's* will. And he was that right person. He'd demonstrated that several times over. Even the OtherSyde had said so.

Perfect, it had called him. Perfect.

Chris was close to perfect, but not there yet. He'd figure it out, though, given enough time; the incident in the girls' locker room had probably started him thinking about all the possibilities it presented. Roger would help him figure it out. Chris was his friend, and he owed him that much.

You have to look after your friends, he thought.

Then drew another red circle.

18

Jordan hated computers.

So of course when he arrived at the Lennox High admissions office, they'd put him behind a computer, told him how to access the files, handed him a bunch of folders with the latest roll sheets from all the home rooms, and bade him happy hunting.

Thanks ever. After a few classes back in college, he could handle himself around computers, but he still hated the things. He was always worried about hitting the wrong button and wiping out the entire database.

Now that the newspapers had broken the story about the increase in juvenile suicides, the city council was applying even more heat to the investigation. More officers had been assigned to Juvie and broken into teams, each assigned to a different school. Since he and Susan had covered it before, they'd been assigned to Lennox.

Handy enough, Jordan thought, and smiled. Susan seemed a little uncomfortable with the arrangement, though, and he wondered why. Maybe she thinks it'll compromise the work.

Maybe she's not ready for this much exposure to what's-his-name.

And maybe you ought to get back to work and mind your own business.

He closed the file he'd just been working on and picked up another. So far, nothing unusual. He checked the teacher's name on the next folder. G. EDWARDS. There's timing for you, he thought, and started flipping through the pages.

There was something curious in the roll sheets.

He followed a horizontal line backwards along a row of dates, and found one absence after another for two weeks straight. He traced the line back to the one name that intersected all the checkmarks under *Absent*. OBST, ROGER. Something about the name was familiar, but he couldn't place it.

Okay, let's start there, he decided, and called up OBST, ROGER on the computer. His file appeared on the screen. Better than average grades, a few black marks for fighting, but nothing unusual.

Then he checked the *Absent* column on the file.

DAYS ABSENT: 0

That wasn't right. The teacher's log book showed ten absences for the last two weeks.

He flagged down the woman who had helped set him up at the computer. "Mrs. Kim? Can I see you for a second?"

She stood behind him at the terminal. "Is there a problem?"

He showed her the log book, and pointed to the corresponding line on the computer screen. "Didn't you say these files are updated every day?"

"Absolutely. We'd just finished putting in today's records when you got here. Half an hour later and the roll books would've been given back to the teachers." She studied the screen. "Can I get in there?"

He moved to make room for her. She called for a backup file, hit RETURN. The same screen was displayed. "How curious," she said. "I'm glad you brought this to our attention. I'll have to talk to the girls, somebody hasn't been doing her job properly."

With that she began to type in the correct figures: DAYS ABSENT: *10 unexcused*.

She hit RETURN.

The new entry clicked into the proper part of the screen.

Then, for just a moment, Jordan thought the computer screen blurred. He rubbed at his eyes. *Must be more tired than I thought.*

"Well, would you look at that?" Mrs. Kim said.

He glanced up at the screen.

The entry read DAYS ABSENT: 0.

"Let me try it again," she said. She repeated the same routine.

The figures held for only a moment, then the screen blurred again, and the Days Absent line clicked back to zero. It was as though the numbers just slid off the screen.

"Must be a computer error of some kind," Mrs. Kim said. "I really don't know that much about how the system works, and the man who programmed it isn't here right now. Best I can do is have someone take a look at it later. Let me know if it happens on any of the other files."

Jordan moved back into his chair and she returned to her post behind the main counter. He saw her talk to someone at the counter, then glance back at him with a look of annoyance. Probably thinks I did it, he thought.

He hated computers.

He moved on to the next file, adding OBST, ROGER to the list of students he'd have to talk to.

2

"Roger, where are we going?" Chris asked.

Roger shook his head, refused to answer. "You'll see."

Chris sighed and continued following Roger through the maze of alleys, streets, and breezeways. He was so turned around he was sure he'd never be able to find his way back. It felt as if they'd walked at least a mile and a half. Wherever Roger was taking him, it had damn well better be worth the walk, Chris thought.

The walk was taking them out of Lennox and into Inglewood. The buildings were grimier, the streets covered with litter, and the looks they got from some of the older guys hanging out on the corners made Chris nervous. His mom had warned him to stay out of that part of town because of the gangs.

"Through here," Roger said, and darted ahead to a narrow space between two buildings.

They came out on an empty lot flanked by a wooden fence on three sides, where a building had been torn down. Chris followed him to a round concrete rise located between the debris and the alley. Roger kicked away some cardboard boxes piled on top of it to reveal a hole and metal steps going down into the dark. It looked like some kind of service tunnel.

"C'mon!" Roger said, and before Chris could do anything to stop him, he descended into the hole.

"No way!" Chris said. "Are you crazy? There could be rats down there!"

No reply from below.

"Roger."

Then, from somewhere beneath his feet, "Ooooga, boooga, nobody here but us monsters. *Will you get down here, you dweeb?"*

Chris's lips tightened. If Roger was down there, he reasoned, it couldn't be *too* bad. Roger was an even bigger wuss than he was.

"I hate this," Chris said, and swung his legs over the hole until they caught on the steps, then levered himself down. The steps seemed to go on forever until his foot finally hit bottom. He looked around, without letting go of the railing, his one anchor in the blackness. The light filtering in from above was all but useless. There was no trace of Roger.

"Roger?" Silence. "Roger?" He squinted into the darkness. "Rog—"

"Boo!"

"NOT FUNNY!"

"Sorry." A moment, then a light appeared in the darkness. He could see Roger now, holding a kerosene lamp and turning up the fire. "Couldn't help myself," Roger said.

He moved around the room, lighting other lanterns. "I can probably get some electric current once I figure out which outlet is safe to use."

The concrete bunker had to be at least twenty feet long in one direction, and at its end intersected with a maintenance tunnel that stretched on beyond Chris's ability to see. A few folding chairs were set up in the room, and he noticed fast food containers and magazines scattered throughout. *Hustler, Playboy, Penthouse, High Society.* There was a transistor radio in one corner, and a case of Pepsi on the floor.

Roger picked up two of the cans and opened one, offering Chris the other. "No thanks," Chris said. "Christ, you don't know what's been walking over that stuff."

"Nothing," Roger said. "The place is clean. No bugs, no rats, no spiders—nothing. Nothing here for them to eat."

162

"Not until now, maybe, but pretty soon, with all this food around—"

Roger shook his head, determined. "No. It's clean and it'll stay clean. Nothing gets in here that I don't know about. Nothing, and nobody. It makes sure of that."

"Oh." *It* again.

Chris went over to the nearest pile of magazines and picked one at random. *The Girls of Penthouse.* "How'd you get these?"

"I got 'em."

"How? You found somebody who'll sell them to you?" There was hope in his voice.

"No. I just go in and take 'em. I stick them under my notebook, as many as I want, and I just walk out the door."

"Are you nuts? That's shoplifting! What if they catch you?"

Roger sat on one of the folding chairs in the middle of the room. "They don't see me because I don't want them to see me. It takes care of that, too."

Chris remembered how *it* made all the girls look the other way during gym class. One guy in a 7-Eleven was hardly even a challenge.

He put down the magazine. "So what's up?"

Roger took a sip of the Pepsi. "You haven't put together the telegraph key yet, have you?"

"How did—"

He stopped. Stupid question. Of course he knew. It would have told him.

"I've just been busy, that's all," Chris said.

"Bullshit."

"It's true! Look, I've had homework up the wazoo, I've been up three nights in the last week talking to you, my mom's starting to think I've gone off the deep end—when was I supposed to find time to put together a stupid telegraph key?"

"It's not stupid," Roger said. "And you know it."

Chris raised his hands. "Okay. Drop that part."

Roger nodded, satisfied. Then he crushed the Pepsi can under his foot. "Look," he said, "I don't want to hassle you. But either you're in, or you're out. I need to know, one way or another. We *both* need to know."

Chris wished Roger wouldn't keep referring to it that way, as if it were a real person. It made Chris feel as though it were looking at him over Roger's shoulder. "All right, I'll put it together."

"When?"

"Tonight."

"You promise?"

"I promise already! Jeez, give it a break, will you?"

Roger chewed his lip. "Okay. I believe you. Now, you want a Pepsi or not?"

"No thanks," Chris said. "I gotta get home."

"Want to take one of the magazines home with you? You can take your pick."

Chris considered it, then sighed. "No, my mom would find it sooner or later, and she'd probably have a cow right on the spot."

"Suit yourself." He kicked through a pile of *Hustlers*. "You can come by anytime you want, look at any of them. I'll be bringing in some more stuff over the next couple of weeks. You won't believe this place when I get done with it."

Of that Chris had no doubt. To listen to Roger, you'd think he'd just moved out of his house and was talking about an apartment he'd rented. Except he hadn't moved out, and this wasn't an apartment. It was a tunnel; maybe once it had even been a sewer. When he was younger, Chris had had clubhouses, and treehouses, but he'd outgrown both—and this place didn't feel right.

"I gotta go," Chris repeated, and headed for the ladder that would lead him back to the lot.

"I just want you to know that I'm not giving you a hard time because I want to," Roger said. "I'm your only friend, Chris, remember that. Your only friend, and I'm looking out for you, trying to get you up to speed, that's all. Okay?"

"Okay," Chris said, and started up the ladder.

He was glad to be above ground again. It wasn't that the air below had been stale—it had, in fact, been surprisingly fresh—but to Chris it had felt heavy. Coming out was like a swimmer coming up for air.

He'd gone only a few steps when he remembered what part of town he was in. *Nuts*, he thought. He was pretty sure that he would probably be able to find his way back, but he didn't want to go by himself. This wasn't the right neighborhood for that.

Reluctantly, he turned and headed back toward the entrance to the bunker. He'd find some excuse to get Roger to go with him.

He stopped short of the hole and was about to swing himself over when he heard sounds from beneath his feet.

Roger's voice.

He couldn't make out the words, but it was definitely Roger. *Has he got a phone in there, too?*

Then Roger's voice fell silent, replaced by another sound.

Tick. Tick. Tick-tick. Tick.

Goddamn! He had it with him down there the whole time! He must've been hiding it somewhere!

The thought unnerved him, though he knew it shouldn't. It always seemed to know what he was up to, and anything else Roger would probably tell it.

Still, knowing it had been there the whole time made Chris feel as though he had been spied on.

And soon you'll have your OWN key, and it'll be with you all the time! Won't THAT be swell?

He started out of the empty lot.

For the moment, he would take his chances with the junkies and the gangs rather than go back down.

3

"Chris?" his mother called up from downstairs. "Your show is on. You want to watch it?"

Chris looked at the maze of transistors, springs, and bits of metal spread out over his bed. "Babylon 5" was one of his favorite programs, the only decent science-fiction series on TV. But he still had to work his way through the instructions on the electronics kit, and he was only halfway finished.

Like it or not, he *had* promised Roger.

"No thanks," he called, and turned his attention back to the instruction booklet which, he'd discovered, was mainly in Japanese, with a few perfunctory translations into English along the way.

Insert Transistor A into circuit board C, so that legs 5, 6, and 7 are aligned with slots D and E, without touching leads F or G.

He worked that one over for nearly half an hour before figuring out that there wasn't a lead for F or G because they were the ones that were supposed to go to another key, and he didn't have to *worry* about leads F or G because he hadn't bought another key in the first place.

He moved on to the next set of instructions.

By now, he had all but managed to push aside the *reason* he was making it, and concentrate only on the task itself. It had become a challenge, one he intended to overcome.

He would put that key together if it took him all night.

4

Roger couldn't sleep.

It wasn't his father's snoring that kept him awake—he had learned long ago to tune it out.

It was the waiting.

He was scared, but eager. Anxious to get it over with.

For a moment, this afternoon, he had almost told Chris what he was going to do. But Chris wasn't ready for it. He'd have to get him used to it gradually, in stages.

To his mother's surprise, he had gone to bed early, though he took off only his shirt and shoes when he climbed into bed. He wanted to be ready when the moment came. He'd even intended to get a little sleep beforehand. Lately it seemed he was feeling tired a lot more often than ever before.

It's just the excitement of the last few weeks, he decided, and closed his eyes.

But sleep eluded him, and when he finally looked at the clock, it was 1:30 A.M.

Time.

He slipped out of bed, pulled on his shirt and shoes, and took his jacket out of the closet. It would be cold outside.

It was.

He walked across the street, and waited under the streetlamp for the bus that would come in exactly two minutes.

It did.

He dropped his fare into the cash box, ignoring the curious look from the driver, and settled into a seat at the front of the bus. He got off when they reached the hospital.

*   *   *

He had been told the back door would be open, and it was.

He had been told that no one would see him slip inside, and no one did.

He had been told that the room he wanted was at the end of the hall on the third floor, and it was.

He had been told what to do when he got there, and now he could not do it.

He stood beside the bed, staring down at Steve Mackey's shattered face. It looked like someone had taken five pounds of ground round, stuck it into a plastic bag to give it shape, and formed a nose and eyes in it.

It sickened him, and he could not do it.

He traced the flow of oxygen from the mask clamped over Steve's face back to the tank beside the bed. There was a little nozzle in the clear plastic tube. All he had to do was turn the nozzle. That's all.

The air would stop.

And so would Steve.

He felt cold, inside and out, and he couldn't make his knees stop trembling.

Don't be such a baby! he thought. *Just do it! Remember all the shit he did to you and DO IT!*

He tried to summon up the rage that had always swelled up inside him at the sight of Steve. He forced himself to remember the beatings, the taunts, the constant humiliation in front of everyone he knew.

It wasn't enough. In spite of himself, he felt pity for the broken form on the bed.

Do it! he thought. *He's going to die anyway! It told you he would! What difference does it make if it's today or tomorrow?*

The difference was that he was here.

It had been easier when it had all been done for him. Once the box had been buried where it said Steve would find it, the rest just— *happened.*

This was different.

This time he was *right here.*

He could not do it.

He fought back tears as the rage finally appeared, directed not at Steve, but at himself. Rage at his own impotence, his own powerlessness. He talked big, but when it came right down to the moment, he couldn't do it. Just couldn't do it.

Wuss.

His eyes burned, and he wiped at them with the heel of his hand. But his eyes didn't seem to want to clear. He blinked hard, and for a moment, just a moment, the world kicked slantwise beneath him. He felt dizzy, nauseous, as though he were about to throw up.

Then it was gone.

His eyes cleared at last.

And Steve Mackey wasn't breathing.

He looked frantically at the nozzle. It had been turned. He listened, but the telltale hiss of oxygen flowing through the tube was absent.

Oh Christ, Roger thought. *I did it—I must've done it when I wasn't thinking about it, just reached out and did it.*

The heart monitor beside Steve's bed began to flutter where it had once been regular.

Abruptly, it flat-lined.

A buzzer suddenly went off.

Get out! Get out before they see you, get out, get out, get out!

He nearly fell as he ran down the hall, away from the room. He risked a glance behind to see three nurses and a doctor come on the run from the other end of the hall. They burst into Steve's room and disappeared from view.

They hadn't seen him.

As he'd been told they wouldn't.

Numb, trembling violently, Roger staggered down the access stairs and out on the grassy lawn behind the hospital. He got only a few feet before falling to his knees and throwing up.

He thought he would go on vomiting forever.

Finally, when he thought he had nothing more left inside him, it stopped. He crouched, dry-heaving, still unnoticed by anyone. He sat forward, pushing his face down into the cool grass.

Oh god, oh god, oh god, ohgod.

He had done it. He had truly and honestly done it.

He had done it . . . and he had gotten away with it.

Unless you stick around here for too long, upchucking your guts into the lawn. It was three A.M. The OtherSyde was good, but he doubted that even it could prevent him from being noticed if someone came by.

Chris awoke, and thought his heart would stop.

The telegraph key was buzzing, over and over and over, buzzing maniacally, frenziedly, so loud he thought it would wake the whole neighborhood.

He couldn't figure out how to make it stop, then finally yanked the battery out.

It went silent.

Chris's heart was pounding.

"Chris?" his mother called from down the hall, her voice sleepy. "Chris? You okay?"

"Yeah, Mom. The alarm clock went off by accident."

She mumbled something from the other bedroom, and then was quiet again.

Chris sat down on the bed, jumpy, scared, adrenaline pumping. What the hell had it done *that* for?

Assuming, he corrected itself, that *it* had done anything at all, and the sound wasn't simply a malfunction. Since he had put the telegraph key together, it had been completely dead. Not a sound from the OtherSyde, until now.

He put the telegraph key back on his side table and crawled back into bed. Sure that he would never be able to get back to sleep, he thought about the sound the buzzer had made.

It had gone crazy, as though someone were beating on it in excitement, or anger, or exhilaration, or . . .

Laughter?

Chris squinted out past the sheets to the bedside clock. He *had* to be mistaken.

There was nothing—absolutely nothing—funny about three o'clock in the morning.

19

Chris ate his lunch alone, on the small rise where he and Roger usually hung out. Only now Roger was never there, and today even Mr. Edwards was unavailable, called off for another staff meeting.

He looked around at the other students sitting in twos and threes on the lawn. The lunch crowd was definitely quieter than usual.

It was the news, he supposed.

Word of Steve Mackey's death had affected everyone, even those who didn't know him, or hadn't much liked him. First Jim Bertierie, then the kids at those other schools he'd heard about on the news, and now Steve—after a while it was like being hit with a hammer, over and over, until finally everything went numb and the only thing you wanted was to be left alone.

Jim Bertierie.

Steve Mackey.

It was strange. Since he'd arrived, Chris had met maybe ten people that he knew by face, not always for pleasant reasons. And now two of them were gone.

What were the odds on that? he wondered.

At the sound of the bell, he picked up his bags and headed across the lawn toward class.

"Chris?" Roger called to him just before he went into the Humanities building.

"What the hell happened to you?" Chris asked. Roger was pale, his face drawn. He looked as though he'd lost twenty pounds and, from the dark sags under his eyes, he hadn't slept the night before.

"Long night," Roger said. "Kept waking up every five minutes. Having these dreams . . ." His eyes kept moving, shifting from Chris to the other kids filing into the building. He squinted at the light as though it were painful. "Just wanted to let you know not to stop by this afternoon. I'm going to be busy, then I'm going to try and get some sleep."

"You look like you could use it."

"Yeah," Roger said, then forced a smile. "You put the key together last night, just like you promised. I knew you would. You're a good friend."

Chris smiled, shrugged. There was something in Roger's manner that seemed especially sad. Having a friend seemed painfully important to him. "I gotta get to class," Chris said.

"Hmm?" Roger looked up, as though rousing from a distant thought. "Oh. Right, yeah. Well, I guess I'll see you this weekend, and—"

Oh Christ, Chris thought. "I can't."

"Why not?"

"It's Thanksgiving, and my mom's taking me to Yosemite."

"What?"

"She said it was something I ought to see, but I think she's mainly going because she wants to see it herself."

"Shit," Roger said, and his eyes got that distant look again. He slid down, back against the wall, until he was sitting on the grass. "This screws up everything. I had to tell you . . ." He glanced up. "You're sure you can't get out of it?"

"Not a chance."

"Umm." He sighed, an old man's sigh, long and resigned. "All right. I'll talk to you when you get back."

"Why don't you talk to all of us?" asked a voice behind him.

Mr. Huntington.

It was five minutes past the start of the next period.

How the hell does he walk so quietly? Chris wondered.

"Do you want to share your thoughts with the rest of us?" Huntington asked.

Roger didn't stand. "Nope."

"What about you?" He turned to Chris. "Don't you have a class you should be getting to?"

Chris nodded. "Just on my way."

"Then get going," Huntington said. "You, too."

Roger glared at him. "Screw you."

For a moment, Huntington didn't move. His mouth worked, but nothing came out. "That's it," he said at last. "I'll see you in the vice-principal's office after class."

Roger's face reddened. Chris felt his stomach tighten; he had never seen Roger like this, not with an adult, and certainly not with a teacher.

"Is that what I get for saying 'Screw you'?"

"That's right."

"So what do I get for saying 'Fuck you'?"

"Don't start with me!"

"FUCK YOU!"

"That's it!" Huntington said. "You're going to the office with me right now. You hear me? Right now!"

Roger didn't move.

Huntington was so enraged that he was trembling. Suddenly, he grabbed hold of Roger by the arm and hauled him to his feet. "DON'T YOU TALK TO ME LIKE THAT, YOU GODDAMNED PUNK! DON'T YOU EVER TALK TO ME LIKE THAT!"

Roger met his gaze without flinching. "Let. Me. Go," he said.

"No way. You're—"

"I said, let me GO!"

Roger yanked free, surprising even Chris. He didn't think Roger was that strong. He could see finger bruises on Roger's arm, and Roger saw them as well.

"You touched me," Roger said.

"Look, don't give me any—"

"YOU TOUCHED ME! *Nobody* touches me! You understand that? Nobody!"

He stalked away. Perhaps fearing his own temper, Huntington did not follow.

Roger looked back at them, and pointed a finger trembling with rage. "You're on the list, Huntington! I want you to know that when the time comes! You're on the list! You get a big, *fat* red circle!"

He afforded one quick glance at Chris. "See you around, Chris," he said, then walked away.

Chris felt cold, all the way through, as though an icy fist had grabbed his stomach and twisted.

Huntington looked no better. He said nothing to Chris, seemed hardly aware of his presence. He went back the way he came and disappeared inside the Humanities building.

This is getting out of control, Chris thought.

Then another voice, deeper inside, whispered back, *What do you mean 'getting'?*

20

At five-thirty A.M., Carlyn Martino locked up the house and started toward the car. They'd packed everything up the night before, so they could leave before first light. They had a long drive ahead of them.

She poked her head in the door of the car. "You ready, Chris? We—"

She smiled. He was asleep in the passenger seat.

They were halfway to the highway before he stirred. Then, all at once, he sat bolt upright.

"Mom?"

"Yes, dear?"

"My shoebox—the one by the sofa. Did you get it before we left?"

She vaguely remembered having seen it, but hadn't attached any particular importance to it. "No, I didn't know you wanted to bring it along."

"Sh—" Chris started, then caught himself. "Shoot."

"Was it important? If it was, we can go back and get it."

"No, I guess it'll be okay."

"What was it?"

He glanced across the seat at her, and for a second she caught the strangest look in his eyes. "Just a science project, that's all. Thought I'd work on it while we were up at Yosemite."

"No schoolwork," she said. "That was our deal, remember? You've been working hard, and I'm very proud of you, and you deserve a break."

"Hmm," he said, hardly acknowledging the compliment. He turned his attention to the passing scenery. In another few minutes, the steady rhythm of the car had lulled him back to sleep.

Carlyn watched as the grey half-light of morning finally gave form to the highway surrounding them, hoping that the clouds scudding across the western sky didn't mean rain. Something in Chris's expression troubled her, though she couldn't pin down what it was. She didn't think Chris was lying to her—he had no reason to. If there had been anything illegal in the box, he certainly wouldn't have wanted to bring it along.

He's just a born worrier, she decided, *and you're a born paranoid.*

2

"Roger?" His mother stood in the doorway to his room, wringing her hands. She always wrung her hands, whether there was a problem or not, and always with this *look,* as if she'd just heard on the news that missiles had been spotted coming from Russia. "Roger, why don't you come out in the front room with everyone else? Your aunt and uncle are wondering where you are."

"Because I don't feel like it." He sat on his bed, reading *The Incredible Hulk.*

"They only get to see you twice a year. It wouldn't hurt you to come out and talk to them for a while."

Roger flipped pages.

"Please, Roger . . . it's Thanksgiving." Then, lower, "We don't want your father upset on Thanksgiving."

That was always her court of last resort. That whiny, stricken voice that said, without ever saying it, *If you make him angry he'll hit me, and it'll be your fault. I won't ever mention it, oh no, but when you see the bruises you'll know it was your fault.*

He sighed. "All right, I'll be out in a sec."

She brightened, and at that moment he could feel only loathing toward her. "I'll go tell them," she said, and stepped out, closing the door behind her.

Roger glanced at the last page of the comic before setting it down. The Thinker was offering to team up with the Hulk, and the Hulk seemed about to agree, on the condition that he cure the Hulk of having to change back to Bruce Banner ever again. Of course in the end, the Thinker would betray him, and he would be left with Bruce Banner still inside.

You'd think the Hulk would've learned by now. Nobody gives you anything without a price. Then again, he thought, looking at the skinny, scrawny, bespectacled Banner on page twelve, he could see why the Hulk kept falling for it.

Who'd want to be like *that?*

He climbed off the bed and slid into his loafers. As he went to the door, he passed the closet—and heard the familiar rapping sound from inside.

Soon, it was saying. *Soon.*

Roger grinned.

3

Susan signed out, and stepped back into the squad room before leaving the station. Nearly everyone from her shift was already gone. Only Jordan seemed in no particular hurry, buried behind a pile of manila folders.

She crossed to his desk. "Shift's up, Jordy," she said. "I thought you were going home early."

"Wanted to finish this stuff first. So far, I've got about six kids to check up on first thing Monday morning. Might be nothing more than your basic truancy, in which case we'll turn it back over to Juvie." He closed the folder and looked up at her. "So how about you? Any family reunions planned for the weekend?"

She shook her head. Just about everyone she was still close to lived on the East Coast or in the Pacific Northwest, and there wasn't enough money for airfare. Not since the pool cue, anyway. "Just a couple of open invitations from some friends to have Thanksgiving with their families," she said. It would be the usual thing: two people she knew in a house of thirty or more strangers, and always one three-year-old kid, overexcited and sick from nibbling at cakes.

"You can't just spend Thanksgiving by yourself," Jordan said.

"I know," she said, and let it trail off there. "There was one thing I was thinking about, but . . . I don't know."

Jordan studied her for a moment, then his eyes widened as he got it. That was the beautiful thing about partners. After a while they could tell what you were thinking without you having to say anything.

"Have you called him?"

"No. Hell, I don't know, he could be having ten thousand relatives over there, and I felt awkward about inviting myself. He probably has plans."

"Then again, maybe not."

"Maybe. But beyond that I'm—well, frankly, I'm not sure I'm ready for *that* right now."

"So who said you had to go to bed with him?"

"That's not what I was talking about."

"Says you," he said, and grinned at her.

That was the problem with partners, she decided. After a while they could tell what you were thinking without having to say anything.

"Go," he said. "Worst that'll happen is that he'll have a pair of cheerleaders in there and you'll embarrass yourself. In which case be sure you get their phone numbers for me later."

"You're a big help," she said, and headed for the door.

"And Happy Thanksgiving to you, too," he called after her.

4

"Dear? Are you all right?"

Chet Huntington stood looking out the window in Jenny's bedroom. It was raining outside. "Just thinking," he said. "Remember how Jenny always loved the rain? At an age when most kids would hide from the lightning, she'd be standing by the window with the biggest smile on her face."

Marie took his arm. "I remember. But right now there are people downstairs waiting for you to carve the turkey."

He nodded. "I've decided," he started, then paused, as though gathering strength, "I've decided that this Tuesday, after I get back from work, we'll start packing her stuff away."

She met his gaze as though trying to peer down into his soul. "Are you sure?"

"Yes," he said. "I think it's time, don't you?"

"I think so."

He ran his fingers over the dresser, the stuffed dolls. "We'll give whatever we can to this fund I heard about at the school. They give clothes to homeless kids. I think Jenny would want that."

"I agree," Marie said, and kissed him. "Now, I think you should come downstairs."

"All right," he said, and allowed himself to be led out of the room. It was time to start living again. He owed Marie that much.

He owed them *both* that much.

5

For nearly half an hour Susan sat in her car, in the dark, parked across the street from Gene's apartment. The lights were on, so he was home. And so far she hadn't seen anyone enter, or leave.

This is stupid, she thought. You're not on stakeout.

But at least now she knew what she needed to know.

He was alone. On Thanksgiving evening.

It's simple. All you have to do is open the door, cross the street, go up the stairs, and knock on his door. Simple. Except—

Except the last time she'd gotten too close to someone, it had turned her so far inside out that she thought she'd never get out. Part of her needed to trust again, but it was so much safer not to.

She sat up straighter behind the wheel. Okay, Officer, we've got a Situation here, and there's one of two ways we can go. You can start the car and drive off and go have dinner at somebody's house and kick yourself for being a coward the rest of the year or go up there and see what happens. But either way, you can't keep pushing everyone away for the rest of your life.

She smiled, and wondered why the voice in her head sounded so much like Jordy.

Okay, she thought. You win.

She climbed out. The wind was cold against her skin, and she pulled the coat tighter around her. Heels clicking on the wet street, she walked to Gene's building and up the stairs to the front door. Not wanting to give herself the chance to reconsider, she quickly rapped on the door.

Please don't let him be there with somebody else, God, it'll be so embarrassing.

He opened the door. He was surprised to see her, but thankfully it wasn't the kind of surprise that comes with an unwelcome face.

"Hope I'm not disturbing you," she said.

"No, not at all, come on in."

It was warm inside, and dry, and he looked so pleased to see her that she wanted to hold him until they were both breathless.

But there would be time for that later.

6

Chris looked out the cabin window, to where the first of a row of high trees rose up against the night sky. The newscaster had said that it looked as if there would be another big storm.

For the last part of the drive up to Yosemite, when it was too late to turn back, the rain had been nearly impossible to see through, the road visible only in occasional lightning flashes that smeared the sky a bone-bright white. When they finally reached the safety of the campground, he thought they'd need a crowbar to pry his mom's fingers off the steering wheel. Since then it had cleared up, but now the clouds were returning.

A door closed behind him, and he saw her come toward him in the reflection in the night-black glass of the window. "Time you were getting to bed," she said. "Weather permitting, we've got an early morning tomorrow. A hike up the mountain, maybe some barbecued hot dogs for lunch, followed by a proper dinner later. How's that sound?"

"Fine," Chris said, wishing he could summon up more enthusiasm. Beyond the frosted glass of the window, a lightning flash ripped a jagged tear in the night. Thunder rumbled off the window a moment later, then faded away, echoing off the mountains. He doubted the elements would permit much of anything beyond huddling around the fire and waiting for the storm to pass.

Perhaps it was only the weather, but he continued to be plagued by the terrible feeling that something was wrong, that there was something he should be doing, or should have done, and now was too late.

But he couldn't find anything specific to hang the feeling on. His mom would say it was adrenaline left over from the long drive.

She might even be right.

But he doubted it.

7

From the journal of Roger Obst:

It tells me I'm ready.

It tells me it's only as strong as I am.

It tells me that it has been watching me for a long time, ever since I was born. It says that I'm special. That I can learn what others couldn't.

I know it's right. Tonight I saw them.

After dinner, after everybody else had left (how I hated every minute of it, listening to them, playing stupid, like I didn't know something *they* didn't know, didn't know what they really thought of me), I came back to my room and did what it told me to do. I turned off the lights, all but one. It was dark. Almost midnight.

It asked me if I was strong.

I said yes.

It asked me if I was ready.

I said yes.

Listen, it said. *Listen*.

Then it got quiet. Quieter than it should have been. Quieter than it could have been. The cars outside, the rain, I couldn't hear any of it.

Then I heard them.

They're strange—if you try to look right at them, you can't see them, the way you can't see a star if you look right at it. You have to look just a little to one side, like you're not really looking at them at all. And then all you see are shapes, a sense of movement. Small. But fast.

And the sound. Like whispering. Real low. When I heard them moving behind me, I got scared for a minute, then I remembered what it said, that I was ready, that I was strong, that they were there to do only what I wanted. And I stopped being scared anymore.

Name them, it said.

180

I thought about it real hard. And then I thought about the sound they made, like they were chewing on something. All the time, chewing, biting, their teeth grinding so loud and so soft all at the same time. I wondered what somebody like Lovecraft would have named them, and I thought of it.

Eaters in the dark.

A good name, it said. I think it was pleased.

That's when the funny thing happened.

I wanted them to go away, now that I had seen them. But it said that was impossible.

They can't leave without serving, it said.

Summoned, they come. Summoned, they serve. Summoned, they must be fed.

I said I didn't know what it meant. It got real quiet for a minute. Then it said, *Red circle, red circle, red circle, redcircle redcircle.*

They were moving all around me.

A name, it said. *They require a name.*

I thought about it. And then I gave them one.

I said the name, and as soon as I did, they were gone. I could feel them leave, though I couldn't see them do it. Then the room got cold for a minute, real cold, and then that was gone, too.

What now? I asked it.

It didn't answer.

What will they do?

It didn't answer.

But I guess I'll find out.

8

The bottle of chablis stood half-full on the coffee table. Susan had permitted herself just one glass. No more.

Gene had bought a baked turkey at the deli a few blocks away, more than enough for two. And carrot salad, macaroni salad, a half-dozen kaiser rolls, niblets corn, and a pumpkin pie with whipped cream for dessert.

Then came the wine.

Then came midnight.

She picked up the glasses and carried them into the kitchen, where Gene was making coffee.

"Thanks," he said, as she put the glasses into a sink filled with soapy water and dinner dishes.

"No problem."

He nodded absently for a moment, trying to look interested in measuring out exactly the right amounts of coffee. "So," he said at last, "when do you have to be getting back?"

"I guess that depends on you."

She brushed her fingers across his hair, past his ear.

He put down the scoop. "Does this mean you don't want coffee?"

"Maybe later."

He reached out and took her face in his hands and kissed her, his fingers twining in the hair behind her neck. She could feel his lips part hers, feel the warmth of his breath mingling with her own.

After a moment, he pulled back. He looked into her eyes, barely inches from his own. "I think you ought to know, I haven't done this since, well, since the divorce."

"I know."

"How?"

"I could just tell. And now we'll say no more about it."

"Deal," he said, and his face brushed hers. Then she could feel him pulling her close, bodies molding to one another. His hands flowed down her, strange and yet instantly familiar, knowing just where to linger before moving on. She could feel the warmth of his skin radiating through his shirt, his hands, his face. Then his hands slipped beneath her skirt, and raised it slowly, until his fingers traced delicate lines along the backs of her thighs, so firm and yet so gentle that it made her shiver.

Not letting go, she let herself be led to the bedroom, kicking off her shoes as she went.

In the light spilling in from the hallway, he undressed her, and she responded in kind, and they raced for the sheets in the cool night of the bedroom. For a moment they huddled against each other, warming quickly. Then their mouths met again, and she wrapped her legs around his thigh. As she pressed against him she could feel that she was ready.

He entered her surely, but gently, as though she might break, and she smiled at the thought even as she felt his warmth inside her. Then they began to move, seeking one another's rhythms, and finding them. And then, as they quickened, he touched her there, where the need grew incessantly, never once slowing, a counterpoint to their movements, knowing just when to quicken the pace—

—as suddenly her back arched and she gasped and shivered forward, biting his shoulder, instinctively tightening, knowing what it would do to him, and he stiffened above her and moaned. She thought it would go on and on forever, until finally he slowed and lay still.

Her eyes closed, she felt both their hearts beating. The thought came to Susan in spite of herself: *If he asks "How was it," or falls asleep, I'm leaving.*

He did neither.

9

When Chet Huntington awoke, it was to the sound of thunder rumbling over the house. It came with a flash of blue-white lightning that strobed through the bedroom curtains. He opened his eyes enough to make out the clock on the bedside table. 2:30 A.M. Marie was still asleep. She could probably sleep through the Normandy invasion, he decided.

He was just drifting back to sleep when he heard delicate laughter from down the hall.

I told her, he thought on the edge of sleep, *told Jenny not to stay up watching the storms.*

It came again, alternating with the thunder. Jenny's laugh, gay but distant, muffled. Then a long, low rumble.

I should check on her, he thought, and sat up in bed, moving slowly so as not to wake Marie. After fumbling around, he found his slippers with his feet. His head felt numb, his thoughts hard to pull together.

"Daddy," the voice called softly down the hall, "come look at the storm! Come see, Daddy!"

"Coming," Chet muttered. The room seemed to tilt beneath him. He felt his way across it, closing his eyes against the occasional lightning flash from outside.

He couldn't shake the numbness that kept his thoughts from connecting clearly with one another. *Must've drunk too much.*

But he hadn't been drinking, had he?

He remembered something about Thanksgiving, and Jenny's room—they were going to do something to it—

"Daddy!" The voice called, full of promise and excitement. "Come see! It's so pretty!"

He shook his head to clear it, the thoughts fragmenting. None of them made any sense. He moved toward Jenny's bedroom, found it, and nudged the door open.

He couldn't see Jenny.

"Pumpkin?" he whispered. "Where are you? It's too late to play games."

She giggled, and for a moment it seemed the darkness surged and pulsed around him.

"Jenny?"

"Over here, Daddy! Where you can see best!"

In the momentary brilliance of a lightning flash he saw a shadow cast on the floor in front of him.

From the window.

Outside the window.

"Jenny, honey?" He staggered over to the window and peered through the glass. He couldn't see her. But that was right, wasn't it? Wasn't Jenny

(gone)

there in the glow of the lightning, her features thrown in high contrast as lightning arced across the sky. She looked in at him, smiling broadly.

"Isn't it pretty, Daddy? Look at it."

He pressed his hand to the glass. Was she standing on the ledge? He couldn't tell, couldn't see her

(no, she's gone)

and then suddenly her face was right next to his, pressed on the other side of the glass, her eyes inches from his own. "Come see, Daddy. You can't see from in there. You have to come out."

"No, Jenny," he said, "you have to come in now, it's not safe out there on the ledge. Come on."

"Make me."

"This isn't the time for games." It was a thirty-foot drop to the driveway.

"Chet?" Marie called from their bedroom. "What are you doing up?"

"There," he whispered, "you see? You've woken Mommy. Now come inside."

184

"Okay," she said, and held out her hand. "Take my hand, Daddy."

"I have to open the window first, pumpkin," he said.

She smiled, and in the smile was something terrible.

"No, you don't, Daddy. Let me show you."

She reached out, reached through the glass without breaking it, grabbed his arm. The grip was strong, impossibly strong, and he was pulled off his feet, pulled forward. He cried out and threw his arms in front of his face, but it was too late and he plunged into the window and it shattered and he was through, feeling the glass cutting into his arms, feeling the cold wind striking his face, feeling her grip on his arm tighten as he hung suspended for the barest flicker of a moment before falling. She held him all the way down, and when she smiled at him in the instant before they struck the ground her teeth were small, and sharp, and her whispered voice was the last thing he heard.

"Tell me you love me, Daddy," she said.

21

It wasn't good enough.

It had said Roger would know soon enough what had been done, that Huntington had been dealt with, and that he had played his part well.

Red x in the red circle, was all it said.

It wasn't good enough.

He hadn't *been* there, hadn't seen it happen. Not seeing it made it less real, less satisfying. That was why he'd wanted to wait before acting on the red circles, so he could make sure he'd be in a position to enjoy it. Timing, he knew, was everything. But the Eaters had demanded something for appetizers.

To make up for it, he wanted something more.

And he knew just what it was.

He stood in the darkness of his room, leaning forward over the storage locker on the floor and peering out the window. The woman next door had come home ten minutes ago, with yet another man. He had gone immediately to his usual position by the window; soon the show would begin in earnest.

Then he remembered what it had told him.

Anything is yours provided you are strong enough to take it.

His decision was made even before he saw the bedroom light go on.

"I want her," he said.

No further explanation was needed. It would know what he was talking about.

From the box behind his bed, a ticking.

Yes.

"Now."

A long pause, then: *Wait.*

He kept watch through the window. She stepped out of view, and the light went off. Another moment passed.

The room grew suddenly cold, as it had earlier. He rubbed his arms through the fabric of his shirt.

Then, so suddenly that it startled him, the command came. *Go.*

Roger moved as quietly as he could. He stepped down the hall, and out the back door, letting the screen door close without banging. It was chilly outside. A brisk wind flapped his shirt against his chest as he navigated his way in the darkness down the slight drop between the two houses, coming up by the side door. He tried the knob, found it unlocked, and slowly opened it.

He poked his head inside, half-expecting someone to throw him out. But it was quiet inside. Even the ticking of the wall clock sounded muffled, as though wrapped in cotton. He took a cautious step, gently closing the door behind him. The house was sparsely furnished, just an old sofa and two director's chairs in the living room, arranged in front of the TV.

He moved forward another few paces, cringing at every creak in the floorboards, even though he suspected, given the silence around him, that those inside the house probably wouldn't hear him if he had been twice as noisy.

Roger passed the bathroom and jumped when he saw a man sitting on the floor beside the sink, his head lolling on his chest, his shirt half off. His eyes were closed, as though in sleep. Roger determined the man was still breathing before moving on.

Toward the bedroom.

She was lying on the bed, dressed only in a bra and half-slip, her dress caught around one foot where she had been removing it. Her underclothes were red, and shimmered where the moonlight touched them. Satin. He stepped closer. Her mouth was formed in a curious half-smile, and Roger wondered if she had been smiling like that when *it* had touched her, had been smiling in anticipation of what was to come.

But now, eyes closed, she was smiling only for him.

He went to her, and dared himself to touch her leg. It was warm to his hand, and softer than he had imagined. He let his hand slide up, roaming where he wished, lingering over the crests and valleys of her body. His groin ached, and his movements became faster. He tugged at the satin waistband until her panties were pulled to her feet. Her bra was still fastened behind her, where he couldn't get to it, so he contented himself with sliding it up over her breasts so that it rested below her chin like a bib.

He kneaded, stroked. At last he had access to everything he had ever wanted, everything he had dreamed of and squinted at through the wire mesh screen of his window.

And yet it was wrong. No matter what he did, she continued to lie without moving, her expression dreamy and uninterested. It wasn't right. She should react when he touched her. They were *supposed* to react.

He shucked his pants and shorts and climbed on top of her. He felt between her legs but couldn't find where everything was supposed to go. He ground against her, growing more frustrated. Her smile now seemed almost to mock him, as though she knew he had never done this before, knew that he was lost.

She wouldn't laugh if it was HIM, Roger thought, remembering the man he had seen in the bathroom.

Then, as if in response, she moved beneath him. For a moment, he was terrified. Had it stopped working? Had it abandoned him suddenly? She peered out through heavy-lidded eyes at a place where his head would have been if he were ten inches taller. "Richard," she murmured, "yessssss."

Must be the name of the guy in the bathroom.

Then she reached down to guide him, but as soon as her hand touched him, he felt himself tense, then suddenly explode.

"Shit!" Roger said, "shit!" He hadn't even gotten close.

"Ooooh, poor baby," she said, slurring her words sleepily, seeing not him but another. "It's okay . . . happens to everyone some time or other . . . come on."

She reached for him, but he pulled back, repelled. She lay cradling nothing in her arms. He crawled off the bed, cursing himself and sobbing, and tripped backwards over his pants. He landed hard on the floor.

Above him, she giggled, murmuring something to the night.

"Bitch," he cried. His face was wet. He'd dreamed about being with a woman for so long, reading the magazines, waiting, wondering—*it wasn't supposed to be like this!*

She began to move on the bed, as though her lover—her *real* lover—were on top, moving with her. Her sounds were infuriating; they drilled into his heart like a blade.

With a cry, Roger lunged from the room, past the bathroom, and out the side door, not slowing until he had found his own front door, and ran inside. He rushed to his room and slammed the door, throwing himself on his bed.

He cried until nearly morning.

Stupid, he thought, *stupid, stupid, stupid.*

As the sun rose, he heard a sound from the closet, a reassuring sound that was his only other friend, the only one who had not mocked him.

Next time, it said. *Next time.*

BOOK FOUR
CHRIS GETS AN ANSWER

The king of terrors.

The Book of Job, 18:14

22

It had rained nonstop for the last two days, and now Chris sat by the window, waiting for his mother to come back from the main cabin, where a police scanner monitored road conditions leading out of Yosemite. Originally, her plan was to drive back into Los Angeles last night, in time for classes today, but the rain had washed out the part of the road that led down to the highway. The road crews hoped to open it soon, but whether *soon* meant two hours or ten hours was something neither of them had been able to determine.

Although he was happy to miss a day of school, he couldn't fight a sense of urgency that clawed at his thoughts. He kept returning to the expression on Roger's face during his confrontation with Huntington, the look of hatred, a rage more intense than he had ever seen in Roger. What bothered him most was that the whole incident was really Roger's fault. Huntington hadn't started out to harass Roger; he had just been doing his job. It was Roger who had exacerbated the situation.

If Roger had been the innocent victim, that would be one thing. But it was almost as if Roger had been looking for a fight, and Chris found it difficult to sympathize with him.

Still, he worried. But what he had now, that he didn't have before, was a sense of perspective that let him look back on recent events more clearly. Getting away from school for a few days had given him room to breathe, and to think. Sure there were assholes at school. But there were assholes *everywhere*, and if you let them get to you, then you'd destroy yourself a hell of a lot faster than they ever could.

It was, he decided, a mature attitude to take, and he was sure that once he got back to school it'd last about five minutes before he was ready to break someone's legs, but at least he would return with the right attitude. Like a fresh pencil box on his first day of school, he would at least be prepared.

The door opened behind him, and his mother entered the cabin, a flurry of windblown leaves dogging her footsteps. "Buck up," she said, noting his expression. "You just got an extra day on your vacation. The crew says they won't have the road cleared until four o'clock."

Chris tried to smile.

2

Gene was putting on a pot of fresh coffee when the phone rang. Susan was still in the shower. She had come back again last night to make sure that what they had experienced the night before hadn't been a fluke. It wasn't.

What are you getting yourself into now? he wondered, and picked up the phone. "Hello?"

"It's me, Gene." The principal's voice sounded tired. "We're calling everyone to let them know not to show up for class today. We're canceling class for the next few days, hell, maybe the whole week."

Gene put down the can of ground coffee. "What's happened?"

"Chet's dead."

Oh Christ.

"Happened over the weekend," Gerber said. "We're still getting the details, but from what we've been able to piece together it looks like a suicide."

Gene felt his skin go cold. "How's Marie taking it?"

"She's pretty shaken up. There's been some . . . tension there for a while now, but she thought he was finally coming out of it. Then, all of a sudden, she wakes up and hears him crashing out through the window. Now she's wondering if maybe it was her fault, that maybe she didn't recognize the signs. They say when somebody decides to kill himself, they get real calm all of a sudden, like the problem's over. Then wham, they're gone."

"I'll call her right now," Gene said.

"I wouldn't. Not yet, anyway. She's been up the last twenty-four hours straight, talking to police, crying—give her a little room, and some time to sleep. This afternoon will probably be better."

Gerber paused. "This is going to be a bitch to explain to the kids. That's why we decided to cancel classes for a while, drastic as it is. I'll probably catch heat for it, but there's just been too much—too much of this *kind* of thing lately. One of the cops I spoke with joked that maybe it's contagious. Now I'm wondering if it's really a joke anymore.

"Anyway, I spoke to a couple of people on the Board. They agreed that until they can meet officially the best thing to do is keep everyone apart until the situation cools off."

Susan came out of the shower, wearing one of his oversized towels. Reading his expression, she mouthed, *What's up?* He held up a finger, *wait*.

"I agree completely," Gene said into the phone. "Meanwhile, if there's anything I can do, let me know."

"I will, Gene. Thanks. Right now I just wish I knew what the hell was going on around here. Everything's gone out of control, somehow, and I don't know what to do to get it back again. I'll be in touch."

Gene hung up, feeling numb.

"What happened?"

He told her. Susan's face didn't change, but he could see the steel slide down behind her eyes. She's gone into police mode, he thought.

"Can I use your phone?" she asked.

He nodded. She dialed her apartment, and checked the answering machine. "The call came in about an hour ago," she said, listening. "Same information you got. I'm supposed to show up at the station in an hour. Good thing I checked. I'd better let Jordan know."

She dialed again, waited, then hung up. "Not home," she said. "Damn. He likes to get an early start, so there's no way of knowing if he got the other call or not."

"Anything I can do?"

"No," she said, "except a cup of coffee would be nice. Just let me get dressed and out of here." She paused, and stroked his cheek. "I'm sorry our weekend had to end like this."

195

When she was out of sight, he ran his last few conversations with Chet through his head, looking for clues, wondering if he had missed anything. But he found nothing.

Chet was dead, and though he knew the hell Chet had gone through since Jenny's death, he still couldn't understand why he would kill himself. It wasn't like Chet to give up like this.

One more death.

Who's next?

3

The address on the house across from the squad car matched the printout from the school computer: OBST, WALTER AND DORIS. It was the third name on the list of parents of chronic absentees.

Jordan finished his doughnut and coffee, then headed for the house. It was one of those off-pink stucco bungalows that had begun losing their popularity in the fifties, the lawn only marginally tended.

He knocked and, after a moment, a woman's face appeared at the door. Jordan was surprised; she looked much older than he would have expected of the mother of a high school sophomore. She peered out at him through a crack in the door, the chain latch still in place. "Yes?"

"Mrs. Doris Obst?" She nodded. "I'm here to talk to you about your son, Roger. Can I come inside?"

"Just a moment," she said, and closed the door. When it opened again, her husband stood there, unshaven, his hair rumpled, a robe covering pajamas.

"Mr. Obst?"

The man nodded. "Yeah?"

"I'm here to talk to you about your son, Roger. Can I come in?"

"Is he in some kind of trouble? What'd he do?"

"We're not saying he did anything, Mr. Obst. We were just in the process of running checks on students who've missed an unusual number of school days without explanation, and your son's name came up in the search."

The man rubbed at his face. "Just a second," he said, and closed the door. Jordan could hear voices on the other side, but he couldn't make out the words. A moment later, the door opened all the way. "Come on in," Walter said. Behind him stood Doris Obst.

Jordan stepped inside. The living room was dim and heavily curtained. "Where's Roger right now?" Jordan said.

"At school. Least, that's what the little bastard's been telling us all this time."

Jordan allowed himself a smile. He could understand hooky, and though he doubted Roger would be happy to have his afternoon excursions revealed, Jordan was relieved that it was nothing more ominous than that.

Walter Obst, however, was not smiling at all.

4

It was dark when Roger headed down the sidewalk toward home, kicking a spray of leaves ahead of him. Sometimes, since finding the OtherSyde, he'd felt down and depressed. Other times, like now, when he thought about what he had lucked into, what he could *do* with it, he felt big, as if he could snatch the stars and throw them in his path like marbles.

Maybe he could.

Just before he'd left the Keep, as he called his secret place, the OtherSyde had chattered a last message at him. It had said that something wonderful was about to happen. Something that would change his life forever.

He lifted his face to the nightwind. He felt *big*.

He took the porch steps two at a time and banged through the screen door.

Instantly he knew that something was wrong.

His mother and father were sitting silently at the dining room table. Her face was bruised, and she had been crying. His father was still in his pajamas, his face dark. They looked at Roger but said nothing. His mother turned away when he met her gaze.

"Hi," Roger said, running on residual cockiness. "What's up? Somebody die?"

His father backhanded him across the face so fast Roger didn't see it coming. He crashed to the floor, notebooks scattering.

"You lying son of a bitch." His father stood up. "What've you been doing?"

"What?" Roger scuttled backwards along the floor, his ears ringing from the slap. In an instant all his confidence had fled, leaving nothing behind but the familiar fear. "What'd I *do?*"

"Don't lie to me," his father said, and threw his beer glass. It shattered against the wall.

"Don't!" his mother cried. Tears ran down her face.

"You stay out of this, you stupid bitch! 'Cause of you he's been running around like some kind of animal, lying, doing Christ knows what." He looked back to Roger. "Police came by here today, looking for you."

Police? Roger thought. *What—*

His father's lips skinned back over his teeth. "A cop! Coming to *my* door, waking *me* up, when I got to work nights. I don't have enough to worry about, I have to wake up to find a goddamned COP asking me all kinds of questions because you've been out running around the streets like some kind of animal when you're supposed to be in school?"

Oh jeez. "Dad—"

"Do I have to put up with that kind of shit? Do I?"

He was ripping his belt out of the waistband of his pants.

"No, wait, please," Roger said, trying to get to his feet. "I can explain!"

"I don't want to hear any more of your goddamned lies! Animals like you only understand one thing." He swung the belt. Roger jumped, but the buckle caught him across the leg. He cried out; his leg burned as though it had been branded.

"What've you been doing? Huh?"

Swing and *slap*.

"Talk, you son of a bitch!"

"Dad—"

Swing and *slap!*

"You doing drugs? Huh? That it?"

"No!"

Swing and *slap!* Swing and *slap!*

Roger huddled in the corner of the dining room, nowhere to go, covering his head with his hands.

"Teach you to lie to me!"

A blow caught him across the face, sent the room spinning.

"Walter! Please!"

"Shut up!"

"Stop it! Dad, stop!"

"Lying bastard!"

Swing and *slap*!

"Stop it! Stop it! GODDAMN YOU! STOP IT!"

Roger leapt forward, and shoved his father, hard. For a moment, his father seemed stunned, but Roger knew he was only surprised. He had never raised a hand to his father before.

"Bastard," his father said, so low Roger barely heard it. Then his face twisted in rage. "You think you can pull that shit on me? Huh? Touch *me*? Who the hell do you think you are?"

In the corner, the box Roger had been carrying with his books had fallen open. He could hear the key clicking madly, too fast to follow.

"Teach you once and for all!"

It was there. If he was strong enough.

His father threw aside the belt, and ran toward him, fists balled.

Roger stood, watching as the end of the world came rushing toward him.

He was strong enough.

"Don't you fucking touch me!"

Suddenly the world seemed to explode behind his eyes.

Everything strobed for a second, then moved in slow motion, or maybe he was suddenly moving very fast, but either way it was the same. His father moved as though underwater, his movements slow and cumbersome. Roger moved out of his way and lashed out. He kicked at his father's leg, sent him sprawling.

Roger watched him fall, and he felt big again.

Then they came to him, the Eaters surrounded him, summoned by rage. He felt at the center of a great black cloud, and the cloud was part of him, and it would do what he wanted, what he never could.

"Damn you!" he screamed—and the darkness around him uncoiled, separated from the shadows, and struck with fury, slashing like a thousand tiny claws, each one with its own mind, but they were all of his mind, his claws.

In a second they covered the floor, the walls, dropped out of the ceiling and onto the table, the stove, and though his eyes were closed with the effort of summoning them, he could *see* them crawling over his father like great black ants, mandibles working at flesh and hair and bone, and he was screaming, and it was glorious, and they fed, and his father ran unseeing into the wall, tearing at them, but they were too strong, and they were multiplying, filling the room, and his mother was screaming, immobile, and had he wanted to he could have struck her, too, but it was not time, and his father was shrieking as the tiny claws that were Roger's/not-Roger's dug and snapped, and they were under the table and in the cabinets and under his feet and crawling down the walls, hundreds and hundreds of them, under the carpet, behind the stove, chewing, as his father bled and bled and they chewed on the pipes, through the pipes—

Get out, get out now, quickly.

Roger moved back, smelling gas, unable to take his gaze off the twisting mass of flesh on the floor.

Summoned, they must be fed.

Now Roger saw wires sparking in the walls where they had been ripped through, and it was too late to run when the others came to him and covered him, covered every inch of his skin like a new layer of flesh, black and mobile and glittering, carapaces fusing into a protective husk, and all their eyes were turned in upon him, his eyes staring at his eyes, staring at his eyes and moving him forward, almost without his being aware of it, out the door and into the darkness outside, and the darkness parted just for a moment, just long enough for him to look out at the house as it burst into flames. Then the only sounds were the crackle of the fire as it ate at the structure, and the fading echoes of his father's screaming, which soon disappeared altogether.

Then the living darkness was gone, and he stood shivering in the cold. Across the street, people came out of houses and backyards to look at the fire. Some of them were comforting his mother, who was screaming unintelligible things, eyes wide with horror and incomprehension. He could hear sirens approaching.

Have to get out of here, he thought, as from a great distance. *Have to get out of here. Now.*

He ran, thinking of nothing but escape, but he only got as far as a block away when the impact of what he had seen and done burst through from where he had been suppressing it. Sobbing, he stumbled and fell by the side of the road.

"Oh god," he gasped, fighting for air. The smell of smoke burned his nostrils. He hadn't meant for it to go that far, but he was tired of being hit, and he had been so angry, and they seemed to feed on his anger, sending it back to him stronger.

What'm I gonna do now? Oh Christ, I didn't mean to do it! I didn't mean to do it!

He had to get away, had to get someplace where it was safe, where he could think for a minute.

There was only one possible place.

5

The telegraph key was waiting for Roger, there in the cool subterranean darkness of his Keep. He had last seen it on the floor of the house, surrounded by fire. But now, here it was. Intact. Unscorched. Waiting for him.

Welcome home, it said.

23

Chris hesitated at the entrance to Roger's Keep.

Everything was happening so fast.

He had barely gotten home last night with his mom when Roger called. He had explained everything; or, more likely, as much as Roger wanted to explain, which wasn't much.

He'd told Chris about the beating his father had given him, and that much Chris had believed. It wasn't an uncommon event at Roger's place. And then a fire had started. Somehow. Roger had been vague about that point. However it happened, the house had burned to the ground before they could stop it. Roger was sure that he'd be blamed for it. He had to hide out for a while.

He'd asked Chris to bring him a few things—a couple of six-packs of Coke, munchies, and some comics.

This morning, after finding out that school had been canceled for the week, Chris made the rounds as Roger had asked, catching the bus to Roger's Keep. And now, just above the first step, he hesitated.

Maybe it had something to do with finding out *why* school had been canceled the rest of the week.

Maybe it had a lot to do with that.

"You coming down or not?" Roger called from below.

Nuts, Chris thought, and wondered how long Roger had known he had been standing there. "Just a sec." He scooted around over the lip of the opening, found the first step with his toe, and climbed down.

A single kerosene lamp, turned down low, was the only light in the room. "Roger?"

"Over here." Another kerosene lamp glowed slowly to life. Roger sat on a chair set atop a pile of wooden boxes like a throne, so it was higher than anything else in the room.

Even allowing for the poor light, Roger looked terrible. The flickering lamp cast erratic shadows that chased each other across Roger's face; his eyes seemed deep-set within his head, as though he were peering out at Chris from somewhere far inside his skull. "You got the stuff?"

"Yeah." Chris put the package down on a pile of boxes along one wall. "How long you think you'll have to stay here?"

"I don't know. I haven't figured that part out yet. Not long, I guess." He shifted uncomfortably in his chair. "I spent the night here. I've never done that before, not here. It was—"

"What? It was what?"

Roger raised his head and his eyes caught the glow of the kerosene lamps. "You remember when you were a kid, and you were afraid of the dark, and your mom would tell you that you were just being silly, that there was nothing there in the dark that wasn't there in the light?"

"Yeah."

"She lied."

Chris waited to see if he would continue, but when the silence stretched into minutes, he finally spoke. "I was waiting for the school bus this morning, and nobody else was there, and the bus never came. Then Jim Tilly, this kid who lives down the block from me, I've seen him on the bus, rode by on his bike and said that school'd been canceled the rest of the week."

Roger nodded absently.

"Jim said he'd heard his folks talking, and they said that Mr. Huntington died over the weekend."

"That so?"

"Well, that's what he *said*, anyway. If it's true, though, isn't it kinda weird? I mean—"

"He had it coming," Roger said.

"For what? Look, Roger—"

"I don't want to talk about it anymore."

Chris threw up his hands. "All right, all right, I'll drop it." He pulled out the six-pack and yanked off one of the Cokes. "So what about your folks?"

Roger stiffened. "What about them?"

"They've probably got everybody from the FBI to the CIA looking for you. You can't just run away and figure they won't notice. You have to go back sooner or later."

"Who says?"

"Because that's the way things *are*. Look, if you're afraid of your dad, maybe you can get somebody to talk to him."

"I did," Roger said, and smiled for the first time.

"Do you think it'll do any good?"

"I think so."

"Then what's the—"

"I don't want to talk about him anymore."

"Okay. Great. What else don't you want to talk about?"

Roger said nothing.

"I'm sorry I yelled," Chris said at last. "I know you've been through a lot. It's just that this is all getting too weird. Everything's been out of control ever since—"

"Ever since what?"

Chris glanced at the telegraph key sitting on a crate near Roger. "Nothing," he said. "Listen, I was thinking of going by your place on my way home. Should I look around, see if I can find anything that isn't toast?"

"No," Roger said, a little too quickly, Chris thought. "There's nothing I need there." He sat up in his chair. "Thanks for bringing the stuff, Chris. You're a good friend. I really appreciate it."

"S'okay," Chris said, and started up the steps that led out of the bunker. He stopped after climbing only a few rungs. "Rog?"

"Yeah?"

"This is maybe a stupid question, but . . . did you . . . *do* anything to Mr. Huntington?"

Roger's eyes lifted. "I never touched him, Chris. I swear."

"Okay," Chris said. "See you tomorrow." He continued up the steps until he came to the surface and swung himself over the top. He sat for a moment, legs dangling into the dark below, frowning.

Everything was *definitely* happening too fast.

2

Chris dreamed that he was trying to make a phone call, but no matter how he tried, he couldn't seem to punch in the right numbers. Whenever he held the phone to his ear, all he could hear was a clicking and, under it all, a vague tremor of distant voices, among them a woman's voice, calling for help; then a man asking over and over to please let him go to the bathroom; then a harsh voice, accusing, *You lying son of a bitch.*

Then: fire!

He started awake. The clicking he'd heard was not just in his dream.

It was coming from his closet.

The telegraph key.

He must have heard it in his sleep, and integrated it into his dreams. He wondered how long it had been tapping, there in a dark corner of his closet? He shuddered. The idea that it was chattering at him in his sleep, whispering code into his ears, bothered him.

When he sat up, the rhythm of dots and dashes slowed, as though it sensed that he had awakened. Then it picked up speed again. Chris had to listen hard to pick out the sequences. *What do you want?* it was asking. *What do you want?*

"I want to go back to sleep," Chris said.

What do you want?

"What's it to you?"

We are you and you are us.

"And we are the eggmen, big deal."

The ticking stopped. In the ominous silence that followed, Chris thought he saw the darkness in front of him deepen, as though the night had turned sullen.

TICK!TICK!TICK!TICK!TICK!TICK!TICK!TICK!

The key was pounding out a rhythm on the other side of the door, too fast to make any sense of it, loud enough to be heard down the hall, as though the key were being slammed down by invisible fists.

He leapt out of bed and threw open the closet door. It was piercingly loud now. He put his hands over his ears, peered into the corner, searching for the key. When he saw it he grabbed the key and ripped it off its base, stripping the wires. Silence filled the small bedroom.

He stood still for a moment, waiting for the sound of his mother's footsteps, but they didn't come. *Still recovering from the long drive, I guess,* Chris thought. He peered at the two halves of the key. They were warm to the touch, almost as though alive.

Friction. It was the friction. Had to be.

He tossed the base back into the closet, and set the broken key down separately on top of his desk before collapsing back into bed.

Tick. Tick-tick.

He rolled over and looked toward his desk. The key was moving by itself, tapping against the wooden top of the desk. Its movements were awkward, cumbersome, like a legless insect trying to stand erect. But it wasn't trying for anything complex. Just three letters, over and over.

B. A. D.

B. A. D.

B. A. D.

After another moment, it stopped, and this time remained silent.

3

From the journal of Roger Obst:

Now I understand.

It told me that something wonderful was going to happen, and when everything went weird at home, I thought that it had lied to me. But it wasn't lying. All of this is part of the process.

I had to get away, I see that now. I had to get out of there. This is the first step. Now I can start being what I'm supposed to be.

It talks to me at night.

It talks to me all the time. Sometimes I'm not even aware that it's doing it, and then I see it is. I think it's teaching me what I need to know. It's talking even now. It used to make sounds that meant letters that meant words when you put them all together. But now it's like the sound has become words, and I hear them in my head as well as in my ear, always whispering to me.

I think I'm smarter than I was.

This is what I was born for. I see that now. All these years, I knew I was special, that I was different. *They* knew it, too, and they hated me for it. Because I was special. Well, I hated them, too. I hate them now.

Difference is, then I couldn't do anything about it.

Difference is, now I can.

I can't remember the last time I slept. Doesn't matter. I can't remember what day it is, if it's day or night. This morning I went outside and it was so bright, I had to go back down again.

I guess that means we're in for another month of winter.

It's talking to me again, as I write this, telling me incredible things.

It tells me I have a destiny.

I get little mental pictures of it, sometimes, when I listen carefully enough—fire and glory and death and honor and power and oh, won't they be surprised to see me, won't they be surprised to see what I've become?

I have to go now.

I wish I could sleep. Just for a little while. But there's so much work ahead. So much to do.

Later. I will sleep later.

(P.S. Chris didn't come today. He hadn't said he would, but I expected him anyway. I asked it why, but it just played its answer/non-answer game until I stopped asking. Maybe he'll come tomorrow.)

24

Chris was in his room, reading, when he heard the doorbell downstairs. A moment later, he could distinguish voices, then the familiar sound of his mother's footsteps approaching the stairs.

"Chris? Could you come down here for a minute?" Her voice was tentative.

He discovered the reason when he reached the bottom of the stairs. Mr. Edwards was there, sitting on the couch, flanked by two uniformed police, one a man, the other a woman. She looked familiar.

"Hi, Chris," Mr. Edwards said. "You got a minute?"

"Sure."

"We'd prefer if we could talk to Chris alone, Mrs. Martino," Gene said. "He might feel more comfortable."

She glanced at Chris. "Well, if Chris wants me to leave—"

"No, it's okay," Chris said. "What's up?"

"My name's Susan," the police woman said. "We met once before, didn't we? In the principal's office? You were a friend of that other boy—"

"Jim Bertierie," Chris said. "And he wasn't a friend. He was just somebody I met."

"All right," Susan said. "But you do know Roger Obst, don't you?"

Chris felt his heart quicken. "Yeah."

"You're friends, aren't you?"

"I guess."

"Do you know where he is right now?"

Chris chewed on his lip. "No."

"You're sure?"

"Haven't got a clue."

The two officers shared a glance, then the man stood up. "Chris, my name's Jordan. It's very important that we find your friend Roger. Do you have any idea at all where he might be?"

"Chris was out of town until just the other day," Chris's mother said. "We went up to Yosemite together."

Jordan didn't seem to hear. "Chris, do you know what happened at Roger's place?"

"I know there was a fire, but that's all. I went by the other day on my bike, and saw the mess."

"I was there before the fire," Jordan said. "I talked to Roger's parents. They said he's been troubled lately. Do you know anything about that?"

Chris shook his head.

"Did you know that Roger's father was killed in the fire?"

Chris paled. "No. No, I didn't."

Why didn't Roger tell me?

Maybe Roger didn't know, Chris thought. Then he remembered the way Roger hadn't wanted to talk about his father, the weird look on his face when he'd told Chris that the problem had been dealt with. *He knew. Of course he knew. And he didn't tell me!*

Apparently his surprise was sufficiently sincere to convince the officers he was telling the truth. "We're sorry to break the news to you like this, but you understand now why we have to find Roger. There are some questions we have to ask him. We're still trying to figure out what happened."

"What about his mom?" Chris asked.

"She's in a state of shock," Susan said. "She's talking, but she's not making a lot of sense. So it's very important that we talk to Roger. Now, if you really don't know where he is, then all I ask is that if you should hear something, please let us know. But if you *do* know where he is, then you should tell us, for Roger's sake. I know you two are friends, but believe me, helping him hide is the worst thing you can do. It's not going to help him. We're not trying to accuse him of anything. We're worried that Roger's wandering around scared, without anyone to look out for him, or hiding because he thinks he's in trouble. We only want to find him and help him."

She met his gaze, and held it. "So I'm going to ask you again, Chris. Do you have any idea at all where Roger is?"

Chris hesitated. "No."

Susan studied him a moment longer. "All right. I believe you. But if anything should come up, I want you to call me at this number immediately, okay?" She pulled a card out of her pocket and handed it to him. He accepted it numbly and stuffed it in his back pocket.

The officers turned to go. "Thanks for your help, Mrs. Martino," Jordan said, then followed Susan out the door.

Mr. Edwards patted Chris on the shoulder. "This is tough for you," he said, "but it'll all work out. If you need to talk about anything, you know where to find me, all right?"

"Okay," Chris said.

When they had gone, his mother turned to Chris. "I want you to listen to me," she said, talking slowly and deliberately, the way she sometimes did when she was mad at him, but this time he could tell that she was worried, not mad. "If you say you don't know where Roger is, then I believe you, too. But if the two of you are in some kind of trouble, I don't want you to be afraid to tell them, or me. There's nothing so terrible that we can't work things out somehow. All right?"

"All right," Chris said.

And for a moment, he almost *did* tell her all of it; he wanted to. But he said nothing, and after a moment he walked back upstairs to his room.

He had to talk to Roger. But not immediately. They might follow him.

And he had to think very hard about what he was going to say.

2

It was Susan's turn to drive. "How long have you known Chris?" she asked Gene.

"Only a couple of months. Seems like a good kid. A little with-drawn, your typical new kid on the block, but otherwise normal. Why?"

"I don't know," she said. "It's just that his name keeps coming up, his and Roger's, and I don't know what it means. Maybe it doesn't mean anything at all. But he knew the Bertierie kid, he knew Roger, and you said yourself that the other boy, the one who got himself wrapped around a streetlamp, had been harassing him."

"It's a small community," Gene said. "Especially in high school. You're in six classes a day, with thirty, sometimes forty kids to a class—so you're meeting over two hundred kids a day right there. Then you add on their friends, the friends of their friends, the lunch crowd—after a while, there's nobody you don't know."

"Maybe," Susan said. She glanced at Jordan, sitting in the back seat. "So what did you make of Chris's reactions?"

"Hard to say, but I'd give it a better than even chance that he either knows where the Obst kid is, or knows something else that he's holding back from us."

"Ditto," Susan said.

"So what's your next move?" Gene asked.

"We wait. The way I figure it, sooner or later Roger's going to have to show up, or try to leave town, or Chris'll say something he shouldn't, and lead us to him."

"You make it sound like he's a criminal," Gene said. "He's just a kid. And not much of a threat to anyone, from what I've seen."

"No one said he was. But there are only so many options you can pursue, and you have to be efficient about it," Susan said, pulling up in front of Gene's apartment. "Jordy and I are going to shoot a few rounds of pool tonight. You want to join us?"

Gene shook his head. "I don't think I'm up to it. Can you stop by and say hello on your way?"

"I'll try," Susan said. "By the way, you never said what *you* thought of Chris's reaction."

"Much as I hate to say it, I think he's lying. About what, though, I don't know. And I wish I did." He left the car and headed toward the apartment.

"I'd say we have a consensus," Susan said, and backed the car out on the street. She had no doubt that Roger would turn up sooner or later. Or that Chris would lead them to him. From what Gene said, and her own brief meeting, neither of them were the sort to tough it out for very long. Bookworms both.

She made a private bet that they'd hear from one of them by the end of the day.

3

From the journal of Roger Obst:

Chris didn't come by today, either. I wonder if something's wrong. It tells me that Chris did something bad, but it won't tell me what. Whatever it is, I'm sure Chris will explain it when he shows up.

Ran out of food this afternoon, and had to go outside during the day. Just went into a store and took what I needed. No one saw. Reminded me that it's been days since I went outside before it got dark. Took me a long time to get used to it. Everywhere I walked, it was like I was visiting someplace I'd never been to before. It all looked different. I thought maybe it had changed while I've been here. But it hasn't changed.

I have.

I'm growing. I feel taller. And smarter. It's like this place is my cocoon. I'm growing in here. Hello, world! Wait until you see what's coming out of here.

I don't think I *think* like I used to. I looked over these pages earlier today, and lately it all reads more mature. More adult.

I was noticing earlier that my skin feels different. I was pinching the skin on my arm, the way it seems to move too much when I touch it, and suddenly I was afraid that if I pushed too hard the skin would peel off like a lizard shedding its skin. It still feels funny when I touch it.

Does that make sense?

I don't think it would *really* come off.

But why take chances?

Maybe he'll come tomorrow.

Of course he'll come tomorrow. He's my friend.

Still haven't slept. Maybe I don't need it anymore.

Still changing.

Not important. Have to get ready. Have to go soon. Big night ahead of me.

<hr>

4

Eight o'clock. Chris had to get to Roger. But he might as well be in maximum security prison for all the chance he had of leaving. His mother was in watchdog mode. If he so much as stuck his nose out, she'd be there to see what he was up to.

But he had to find Roger and get him out of that hole. He needed to get some help, maybe talk to a doctor. If Roger's father really was dead, and Chris saw no reason for the police to lie to him, then maybe it had pushed Roger over the edge.

The first chance he got, Chris was going to rip Roger's telegraph key to pieces. Shut off Roger's supply of whispers.

It was over. One way or another, he would make sure of that.

If he could just get out of the house without his mother seeing him.

5

From the journal of Roger Obst:
    I'm ready.

6

Susan extricated one leg from the sheets and wrapped it around Gene's, resting her chin on his shoulder. At the motion, he opened one eye and kissed her. She sighed. She'd promised herself that she would only stop by for a few minutes on her way to shoot a few racks with Jordan. Then they had gotten talking. Then they had stopped talking, and started taking each other's clothes off.

Now it was nearly nine o'clock, half an hour after she'd told Jordan she'd try to stop in at the bar. He'd teased her that she wouldn't make it past Gene's. He'd been very smug about it, she recalled. By now Jordan had probably figured out that she had indeed gotten sidetracked, and was taking somebody else for five bucks a rack.

She'd hear about it tomorrow. Endlessly.

She opened her eyes and looked at Gene, his face relaxed for the first time that day. Let Jordan say what he wanted. It was worth it.

It was a little before two A.M. when Jordan left the bar, thirty dollars richer than when he'd arrived. He'd have to thank Susan for provoking him into buying a better stick. Knowing that her attempt to unnerve him had actually helped him would annoy her no end.

He hadn't meant to stay this late, but he'd had to buy a few more rounds than usual in order to convince some of the guys to shoot with him, and Jordan had a rule about not driving drunk, or even a little tipsy.

He pulled out of the driveway and turned south, onto the almost-empty highway. He was nearly to his exit when his vision blurred momentarily. It cleared just in time for him to see his off-ramp go by to his right.

Damn. Must be more tired than I thought.

He aimed for the next exit, intending to double back and catch the exit from the other direction.

He came down the off-ramp and turned onto a darkened street, pausing at the intersection. He couldn't see a sign for the on-ramp, but he knew it had to be close. He turned left, and kept going for a few blocks until admitting that he'd gone the wrong way.

He tried to double back, turning onto a smaller, one-way street, lined with boarded-up industrial warehouses and factories. It wasn't the sort of neighborhood he wanted to be cruising through at two in the morning. Finally he saw another street. He turned, trying to keep in mind his position relative to the highway. *Another left, then back to the main road, make a right.*

It was a narrow street, little more than an alley. On the left were two abandoned factories, the opposite side bordered by the concrete wash that contained the L.A. River during the rainy season, now little more than a trickle of water running between clumps of moss and discarded shopping carts. In the distance, he could see the stoplight that marked the main road. He breathed a little easier at the sight.

Then something went *clunk* beneath the hood.

The car shuddered, then died in the middle of the long block.

Shit!

Jordan slammed the gear back into park, turned the ignition key. The engine groaned, but didn't catch. He tried again. This time there was no sound at all.

Well, that's just great, Jordan thought, and popped the hood. He climbed out of the car. Battery? Fan belt? Maybe the whole thing just up and went all at once.

He reached underneath the hood, feeling for the latch—then cried out as his finger hit something sharp.

He jerked his hand out. The tip of his index finger was bleeding. He squeezed a few drops of blood as a hedge against infection, then wiped the rest off on a handkerchief. *What the hell did I catch it on?* His fingers wrapped in the handkerchief, he reached under the hood, fumbling until he found the latch. He pushed. For a moment it seemed reluctant to give, then finally popped free. Jordan lifted the hood.

The darkness was moving inside. It was as though a black sheet had been thrown over the engine, and was somehow pulsating.

Then they boiled out of the frame like hundreds of sleek black spiders, each the size of his hand. They spilled out over the headlights and clattered on the asphalt. They surged up, as though pushed from below, legs grasping for purchase in grillwork and hoses, flowing out and over the engine.

Jordan jumped back as they poured out of the car, flinching when some of them hit the ground barely inches from his feet. "Christ!" he muttered, momentarily frozen at the sight before him. They hopped and wriggled out on both sides of the narrow alley, moving in his direction.

He walked backwards, never taking his eyes off them.

They matched his pace.

And now he could hear them, as though they were murmuring, whispering to one another.

He was running even before he realized he was doing it.

He ran toward the stoplight at the end of the alley, toward the main street.

They surged up behind him like a wave.

He ran.

Something snagged his ankle from behind. He stumbled, kept his balance, ran.

Toward the light. Green-yellow-red-green-yellow—

The alley floor moved in front of him.

No. *Not* the alley. A sheet of black, chitinous shapes, so numerous that they seemed solid. Until they began moving.

And whispering.

Murmuring.

In front of him.

He staggered to a stop. Glanced behind. They were moving up faster now.

"Hey!" Jordan yelled, "Somebody! Anybody! Help!"

They kept coming.

To his left was the rear wall of the factory. No doors, no windows.

To his right was the wash.

He jumped up onto the retaining wall, pulling himself up over the wire mesh. He tried not to look down. It was a seventy-five-foot drop to the bottom.

They reached the wall in front and behind him, and boiled up its sides, climbing over one another in their rush to get to the top, where *he* was. The mesh slowed them for a moment.

C'mon, Jordan thought. *Just a little farther.*

A little farther, to the drainage pipe that spanned the wash across to the other side, to lights and cars and safety.

They surged up over the mesh and fell onto the retaining wall, righting themselves and moving toward him again from both sides.

Don't look at them, Jordan thought. *And don't look down. Just keep moving.*

Five steps. Ten.

He reached the drainage pipe. It was concrete, five feet around. Holding on to the mesh for one last moment, he braced one foot on top of the pipe, then the other, and stepped out.

He held out his arms. The pipe was narrow, but not too narrow to keep his balance.

One foot in front of the other, no problem, just keep moving.

He didn't dare risk a look back, but from the vibration that came up through his shoes, he knew they had reached the pipe behind him.

C'mon, C'MON!

Again, something snapped at his ankle—and came away with flesh.

Jordan screamed. Then stifled it.

Another bite. He wobbled on the pipe, found his balance. Tried not to think about the fall.

Then something sank deep into the flesh above his ankle. He stumbled, arms pinwheeling for balance—and fell. He plunged forward, grabbing on to the pipe with both hands.

They were on him in a second.

They ran over his legs and his back, biting everywhere, even through his jacket. He felt one of them skitter under his pants cuff, and pain lanced up his calf.

They were on his hands, on the back of his neck.

He fought to stand, but there were too many of them. They surged over him, his balance wavering, hands bleeding from the bites—

One of them moved around to his face, and he could see twin rows of small, white teeth snapping at him. Teeth, set in a white head that reminded him distantly of fungus, but there was something about it, something familiar—

He jerked back in pain as it got hold of his ear, coming away with a piece of it. He tried to bat it away, but he could barely move on the pipe without losing his balance.

Then it scuttled farther up, moving sideways.

It was looking at his eye.

It lunged.

"NO!"

His grip failed. He rolled down the side of the pipe, fighting desperately for a handhold.

Please God, he prayed, insanely, as he fell, *don't let me break my back, please God . . .*

It was the only prayer God would answer.

25

The call came a little before four A.M. Susan had only gotten to bed a couple of hours earlier, but she came wide awake. No one called at that hour of the morning to wish you happy birthday.

The voice at the other end told her what had happened. She didn't know him; she didn't know most of the cops on night shift. He told her everything he knew, his voice calm and concerned but professional.

"Where?" she said. She had to say it twice before she could get her voice loud enough for him to hear.

He gave her the address. She had a hard time seeing the paper to write it down.

She hung up, and all the strength went out of her legs. She slid down the side of the bed to the floor, her arms pulled tight around her shoulders. "Oh Christ, Jordy," she said, the first sob breaking out of her throat. "Oh god, Jordy."

Tears kept running down her cheeks, no matter how often she brushed them away. Great, gasping sobs wracked her body as she sat on the floor, shivering as much from shock as from the cold. She looked at the pool cue, propped up over in a corner. *It's my fault. If I'd been there, I could've stopped it. I could've done something.*

"God, Jordy, I'm sorry, I'm so sorry."

After a while, when the dry-heaving stopped long enough for her to stand up, she went into the bathroom and washed her face, then came back into the bedroom and began changing into her uniform.

I'll find them, Jordy. I swear to God, I'll find them.

2

In another hour, the sun would be coming up. The wind whipped up the concrete wash and blew cold up over the retaining wall. The air smelled of concrete, and moisture, and moss gone old and rotten. *Like a cemetery*, Susan thought.

Below, a clump of yellow ribbon marked POLICE BARRICADE—DO NOT CROSS had been bunched together and strung between clumps of wet moss to mark where Jordan had fallen. There would be no chalk outline of a body on this one; the small but steady stream of water that still flowed through the wash made that impossible. Identical ribbons had been strung across the wire mesh fence, and the drainage pipe that, judging from his position in the middle of the wash, he must have been walking on when he fell.

What the hell were you up to, Jordy? she wondered. *What were you doing, all the way out here? And what were you running from? Or to?*

The lieutenant dispatched from the local precinct came toward her, making a note in his book. "How long were you and the other officer partnered?"

"Two years, maybe a little more."

Another note. "Did he ever show up for work drunk? Any reason to think he did drugs?"

She glared at him. "Jordan was as straight arrow as you could get. He liked his beer, but only off duty, and I never saw him get drunk. Drugs scared the hell out of him. He was a good cop, Lieutenant."

"I'm sure he was. But we have to look into everything." He closed the notebook, fastening it with a leather snap that went over the top. "You'll be hearing from I.A.D. this afternoon. Just an informational meeting."

"What about the guys who did this?" she asked. "Any leads on them? Anything at all?"

He shook his head. "Homicide's going over every inch of the

place. But so far they haven't turned up a thing. One set of footprints on the retaining wall and the pipe, no sign of anyone forcing the car to a stop. It's almost like he just stopped his car, got out, walked out into the middle of the pipe, and did a half-gainer into the basin." He looked away from her. "Which is why we're not ruling out suicide at this time."

"Not a chance," she said. "Jordy wasn't the type."

"They never are. But if there were any family problems, bad debts, they'll show up pretty soon." He glanced at his watch. "I'd better get going, file my report. The coroner'll want all the details."

"What about—" She hesitated, then forced herself to finish. "What about the body? Was it the fall that killed him?"

"Hard to say right now. We're waiting for the autopsy before we can be sure. Might've been. Except—well, we found some cuts on his legs we can't account for, unless he got them coming over the fence. Beyond that, there's reason to believe there may have been, well, you have to understand, there are all kinds of little animals that live in these washes—rats, owls, you name it. They may be responsible for some of the rest."

"What rest?"

"You don't want to know."

"Yes, I do."

He avoided her gaze. "It looks like something . . . may have chewed his eyes out. They weren't there when we found him."

She felt her knees buckle, and fought not to throw up.

"You want to sit down?" he asked.

She shook her head. "Anything else . . . out of the ordinary?"

"Just one thing. His shield was missing. The case was there, but the shield was gone. We don't know if he left it home, or someone stole it, or maybe it fell somewhere down in the wash and we haven't found it yet."

"Check the wash again," Susan said. "He never went anywhere without his shield. If the case was there, it was there, too."

"All right. Will do. You need a ride anywhere?"

"No, I brought my own car."

"Okay. If you want, I can get you a copy of the full report as soon as it's finished."

"I'd appreciate that. Thanks."

There was an awkward silence. "I'm sorry," he said at last.

"Yeah," she said. "Me, too."

He put a hand on her shoulder, then headed away. She stood alone beside the wall. The sky was starting to lighten. Down below, part of the clump of yellow ribbon started to untangle, the ends whipped by the wind that came up the wash.

You'd think he was waving goodbye.

3

Chris waited until the bus doors were about to close before jumping out the back door and down an alley. He levered himself through a gap in the fence and cut through a Woolworth's before he let himself slow down and catch his breath.

He hadn't seen anyone watching outside his house, but that didn't mean they weren't there. By now, though, he was sure that if there had been anyone following, he had lost them.

At first, he'd thought he wouldn't be able to get away. But when his mother had tried to take off work one more day, her boss had complained about being shorthanded. The flu was making the rounds again. So she agreed to come in for half a day.

Stay close to home, she'd told Chris. *And stay out of trouble.*

He'd already broken the first promise, but he was determined to avoid breaking the second.

He trotted over to the access tunnel to Roger's Keep, and knelt down by the entrance. "Roger?" he called down.

Silence.

He swung his legs over the opening, found the steps, and lowered himself into the darkness.

The smell inside was even worse than before. More piles of fast food containers littered the floor. From one of the tunnels that led into the main chamber, Chris caught a whiff of excrement. He blanched at the smell; it had never before occurred to him to ask where Roger went to the bathroom.

Roger was nowhere to be seen. Chris stepped forward. Beaver magazines were scattered around the room. He picked up one. The pages were sticky with peanut butter. He tossed it back into the corner and moved farther into the room. "Roger?"

The chair—Roger's "throne"—was empty. Half-expecting Roger

to leap out of the shadows at any moment, just to scare him, Chris stepped up on the raised platform on which the chair sat. More of the beaver magazines were spread out there. And something that caught Chris's eye: the current school yearbook.

It was lying open and upside-down, and when he turned it over, he saw that it was open to the faculty section.

A red circle had been drawn around Mr. Huntington's photo. Inside the circle, an X had been drawn over his face with such force that the tip of the pen had torn through the page. He flipped back through the book. There were more circles every few pages. Most surrounded pictures of the senior class. Then a bunch in the junior class. He figured roughly twenty, twenty-five red circles in all.

And two more bright red X's inside red circles: one over Jim Bertierie's picture, another over Steve Mackey's.

Three X's.

Three deaths.

He's keeping track, Chris thought, and the idea made him feel cold, almost as cold as the thought that followed: *But which came first? The deaths? Or the X's?*

He started at a sound from the main tunnel. He quickly turned the book over, leaving it just as he'd found it.

Chris moved toward the tunnel at the far end of the room. "Roger?" The sound came again, a rustle of movement on the fringe of what he could hear. He moved forward cautiously. The walls on either side were narrow, and spiderwebs had grown in among the pipes and conduits carrying telephone and electrical wires. Just beyond a bend in the tunnel, he could see a faint glow of light.

He pressed on, his footsteps echoing in the narrow tunnel, until he turned the corner.

The passage was wider up ahead, and a cot had been set up in the middle. Barely visible in the darkness, lit only by a small kerosene lamp, Roger sat on the cot, his hands outstretched to . . .

To what?

Smoke. But it didn't dissipate. It hovered beside the cot, its form wavering and shifting but not moving from that place, where Roger's hands seemed almost to be caressing it.

Chris took a step forward—

It looked at him.

Chris thought his heart would explode. There were no eyes that he could see, just two dark pools amid the swirling vapor, but he had the undeniable feeling that it was staring at him. The gaze was cold.

Then, an instant later, it was gone, dissolving into the shadows. But the cold remained.

"Hello, Chris."

"Rog."

"It's been a while. I was starting to think you'd forgotten all about me."

"I've been kinda busy. A lot of it has to do with you."

A pause. "Oh?"

"Roger," Chris started, then hesitated. He decided finally to just come out with it. "Rog, your dad's dead. Your mom's in the hospital. The cops are looking for you. They want to ask you some questions. And I think you ought to get out of this place. Now."

Roger laughed, low and brittle and breathy, the sound like dry leaves rustling down a sidewalk. "You always were a kidder."

"I'm not kidding. I want you to come with me, out of here. This is crazy."

"I'm not going. This is *my* place now, and nobody's going to take it away from me. For the first time in my life, I get to do what I want, not what somebody else wants me to do. Nobody pushes me around anymore. I'm free!"

"You call this free? You're living in a hole in the ground!"

Roger sighed, sat back on the cot. "You don't understand." He peered out into the shadows. "Come here, where I can see you a little better."

Chris stepped forward. Closer now, he could now see Roger in more detail as well, caught in the flickering glow of the kerosene lamp.

Roger looked bad.

His skin was pale, so white it was almost luminous. Roger had never been in good physical condition, but now it seemed all muscle tone had gone out of his body. His skin looked too soft, almost pulpy, but smooth, right down to the thick, rounded fingertips. His face was flaccid, his lips thick. His glasses were gritty and smeared. His appearance reminded Chris of a grubworm he'd once seen. And set in the middle of that too-white face was the one thing that still reminded Chris of the old Roger: the grin, only now it seemed to reflect some inner amusement that was less than wholesome.

"I saw you looking at her when you came in," Roger whispered, as if sharing a confidence.

"Looking at who?"

But Roger didn't seem to hear. "Beautiful, isn't she? And I can have her any time I want."

"But—" Chris stopped, and remembered the smoke that had seemed to look at him. Oh jeez, Chris thought, he can't be talking about *that*, can he?

Can he?

"Roger, your dad's *dead*."

"I know."

"Doesn't that bother you?"

A shrug. "It wasn't my fault. But I know whose fault it was. And that's been taken care of now. He was very bad. He told on me, and got me in trouble with my dad. That's not good. But now everything's settled. Everything's fine now."

"Damn it, everything's *not* fine! Nothing's fine! And nothing's going to *be* fine as long as you stay down here."

Roger shook his head. "This is my *home* now. At least for a little while. I have everything I want. This is what it's all about. And then, later . . . I have such plans."

He stared out into the shadows, and for a moment his thoughts were far away. Then, slowly, he lowered his eyes until he focused on Chris. Chris felt a shiver at the thought that the coldness in those eyes was the same cold he had seen earlier, in the dark form beside the cot.

"Why did you break the key?" Roger asked.

"Because it was making me crazy, just like it's making *you* crazy."

"I was really upset when it told me what happened. And I can't afford to get upset anymore. Bad things . . . bad things happen when I get upset." His brow furrowed, and he looked more closely at Chris in the light of the lamp. "You're still my friend, aren't you?"

"Yeah, of course. I'm still your friend. I just—"

"Then I forgive you." Roger sat back on the cot. "It's hard, at first. I know. It can be pretty confusing. There's so much to learn. But I forgive you. I—"

Abruptly, Roger turned on the cot, and looked to where the telegraph key sat on a nearby box. It was silent. Nonetheless, Roger watched it attentively for a moment, and then smiled. Looked back at Chris. "It says it forgives you, too."

Chris felt his jaw go slack. "Roger, *it didn't move.*"

"Yes, it did. I heard it."

"Look, I know what I saw."

Roger opened his mouth to reply, then closed it as he looked at the telegraph key. There was a moment of prolonged silence.

This is crazy, Chris thought. *This is nuts! It's not DOING anything! It's just sitting there!*

Roger frowned. "It says I should ask you about the fire alarm, and why you didn't pull it?"

"What fire alarm?" Chris asked.

And then he remembered.

That's right, Steve and the rest, they were beating Roger up, and I got away, and I could've snuck back in and pulled the fire alarm and scared them off, but I was afraid they'd catch me, afraid I'd get in trouble, and I didn't, and I let them beat up Roger but I never told him I never told Mom I never told anybody and it knows, it knows!

"Chris?"

Chris started. "I, uh, I don't remember. I mean, it's hard enough to keep track of what I *do*—trying to remember something I *didn't* do, and why—I don't know. Did it . . . say anything else?"

"No," Roger said, and glanced back at the telegraph key. Chris felt his stomach tighten, not knowing if the silence was just silence, or if even now it was telling Roger about how he had run, leaving Roger to get beaten up. *He'd understand if I explained it to him, I'm sure he would.*

"Nope. Nothing. I guess it wasn't important."

Chris smiled thinly. "Guess not."

"But we'll get you a new key as soon as possible."

"I don't want one."

"But you *have* to have one. It's important."

"I said no, and I meant it. Look, Roger, I'm serious. I want out of this mess. And I think you should get out, too, while you still can."

"I thought you were my friend."

"I *am* your friend! You think I'd put up with all this if I *wasn't?*"

Roger considered it for a moment. "No. You wouldn't. But for the first time, I'm doing what I want. Nobody's telling me what to do, or where to go. I have a place here, a special place, and I won't give that up."

Another argument came to Chris's lips, but he fought it back. "Okay, fine, stay in a hole in the ground, see if I care." He started back along the tunnel the way he came.

"Will you stop by tomorrow?" Roger asked. "There's some stuff I've been waiting to show you. Stuff that'll knock your socks off. There's things you need to know." Chris kept on walking. "You'll change your mind when you understand." A pause. *"Will you come by tomorrow?"*

Chris stopped at a bend in the tunnel. "Yeah, I'll come by tomorrow. If I can get out of the house."

"Good enough," Roger said, and for a moment he looked so pleased that he reminded Chris of a puppy. "See you tomorrow."

Chris waved, and continued down the tunnel to the main room, where he paused by the chair, the school yearbook lying just where he'd left it. The pictures, and the red marks, still bothered him. But he didn't know exactly what they meant, or how to bring them up.

Maybe they meant nothing at all.

And maybe they did.

I know whose fault it was, Roger had said. *And that's been taken care of now. He was very bad. He told on me, and got me in trouble with my dad. That's not good. But now everything's settled. Everything's fine now.*

Chris wondered who *he* was, and whether or not *his* picture was also in the yearbook.

4

Susan hung up, then sat forward at her desk, palming her eyes. They burned. She'd almost fallen apart again when she told Gene, which was why it was better to tell him over the phone; in person, she wouldn't have been able to hold back the tears. But she was determined not to let that happen, not until she'd gotten some answers. The phone made everything feel more removed.

Gene had sounded almost as stunned by the news as she had been. There were the usual words of comfort, the repeated long silences, and the offer of his place for the night. She declined. In part she still blamed herself for not being with Jordan the night before. Being with

Gene again so soon afterward would only color their time together. But he would meet her after work, and then—

"Susan?"

She glanced up. Captain Phillips stood in the doorway. "Can I see you a minute?"

She entered his office, closing the translucent glass door behind her. The sound from the squad room outside fell to a low murmur through the glass.

"Have a seat," he said. She took the single chair that faced his desk. He had a manila folder in his hands, and she thought his face looked paler than it should.

"How're you holding up?" he asked.

"All right."

"You look like you could use some sleep."

"So do you."

"Yeah, I wouldn't be surprised," he said. It was a moment before he continued. "I want you to take the rest of the day off. You're going on two hours sleep, you've been through hell, and you're not doing either of us any good by being here."

"Captain—"

"And take tomorrow, too, if you need it. Right now, I'm making that part voluntary. If you give me any trouble about taking today off, it'll become mandatory."

"Understood."

"Good. Now, when you come back, you'll be off the streets for a few days, just long enough for I.A.D. to finish looking into the matter, and to give you some time to adjust. End of the week, we'll find someone else to partner you with. If you have any preferences, let me know."

"I will. Anything else, Captain?"

His gaze fell on the manila folder. "One more thing. We got the coroner's report a few minutes ago. I just finished going over it." He fidgeted in the chair. "Christ, Susan, I don't know where to begin."

"Was it the fall that killed him?"

"No. Coroner says it was a contributing cause, broken ribs, one broken leg, and some internal bleeding, but nothing terminal by itself. It"—he drew in a deep breath, and let it out slowly—"Susan, the coroner's report indicates suffocation as cause of death."

"I don't understand."

"Yeah, well, neither does the coroner." He slid the folder across the desk. "I guess you might as well see it for yourself. You've got at least that much right."

She opened the folder. As always, she was struck by the detached quality of the report. Name, date, age, weight, color of hair, color of eyes . . . nowhere in it did it say that he was a gentle, funny man who loved to shoot pool and eat chili dogs.

Her gaze scanned down the entries until she reached the line marked CAUSE OF DEATH.

Asphyxiation, the result of blockage of the trachea. Blockage caused by compacting of material within the trachea, extending as far down as the cardiac plexus, and as high as the epiglottis. Due to the organic appearance of the blocking material, said substance was forwarded for further analysis. [See attachment B.]

She flipped through the sheets of paper.

"It's the last page," Phillips said.

She found it.

Based on preliminary analysis, material definitely organic in origin, belonging to either the arachnea family or orthopteria blattaria.

"I had to call the coroner's office and ask them what they were talking about," Phillips said. "Can't speak English, any of them. *Arachnea* is the family name for spiders. *Orthopteria blattaria* is the family name for cockroaches. It was as though someone had taken all of that and . . . and ground it up and shoved it down his throat."

He went on, but Susan barely heard him. She was aware only of the rushing sound in her ears, the cold that moved down her arms, the slow movement of the folder as it slipped from her hand and fell to the floor, and the way the world suddenly began to spin around her, threatening to pull her down, down . . .

When she looked up again, the captain was standing over her with a paper cup filled with water. "You better drink this," he said.

She took a sip, and found it wasn't water. Straight scotch. It seared her throat as it went down. She closed her eyes and let it burn, hoping it would take away the cold that seemed to reach all the way into her bones.

Goddamn it, Jordy, what what WHAT in god's good name happened to you?

From the journal of Roger Obst:
This afternoon it told me about the fire alarm.

Chris paced anxiously up and down the sidewalk in front of Mr. Edwards's apartment. He'd gotten the address from directory information, but Mr. Edwards hadn't been home when he arrived over an hour ago, and there was still no sign of him. Chris had managed to snag a neighbor heading out for groceries, and learned that Mr. Edwards had left not ten minutes before he arrived, "looking pretty upset about something," the neighbor had said.

Where *was* he? Another twenty minutes and Chris would have to leave in order to get home before his mom did. She was worried enough as it was, he didn't want to add to it.

Which was why he'd decided on the way over that he was going to tell Mr. Edwards everything. Well, almost everything. Chris knew a lot of what had been happening, but there was far more, and far worse, that he only suspected. If even a fraction of it were true, then . . .

Then what?

Are you gonna tell them that Roger killed Huntington, or had him killed? And Bertierie? And his old man? Are you gonna tell them about the key, and the lemon writing, and the OtherSyde?

They'd think he was nuts. But he had to do something to help Roger, whether Roger appreciated it or not. So he would tell them only what was absolutely necessary: where Roger was, and that he looked weirded-out, so they should be careful when they went and got him.

Question was, by *not* telling them the rest, was he putting them at risk?

His thoughts kept chasing themselves around in ever-smaller circles. He couldn't tell them. He couldn't afford *not* to tell them. He couldn't afford to tell them everything. He couldn't afford *not* to tell them everything.

"I hate this," Chris muttered. The twenty minutes were up. Already, the sky was starting to darken. He couldn't wait any longer.

He started up the street toward the bus stop, and home. He would try again tomorrow. Maybe things would look better in the morning.

Fat chance, he thought, and stuffed his hands in his pockets. He walked on another few paces and then stopped. It had gotten quiet. A moment earlier, there had been the sounds of birds, of distant traffic; the noise of the wind as it brushed through the trees lining the street.

Now everything was silent. It was as though someone had put a bell jar over him, and he was isolated from the rest of the world. He was aware only of the sound of his own heartbeat, his own breathing, and the sense that it had suddenly gotten very hot.

He quickened his pace, heading for the end of the street. But no matter how fast he walked, the corner seemed just as distant. Chris was perspiring now. Then: a sound. To his right, in the underbrush. A quick-flash sound of movement. He jumped, but could see nothing. He walked on. The sound came again, paralleling his steps. He got the impression of something sliding through the brush, tracking him. He felt eyes fixed on his neck, though he could not see them. He walked faster. Now the sound was louder, and Chris couldn't tell if it were closer, or there were suddenly more of them. He caught a blur of movement in the brush, a sway of branch and leaf, and now he was running, his heartbeat loud in his ears, the only other sound the rustling at his feet, nearer, faster, just behind—

Chris reached the corner and was practically knocked back again by the sudden explosion of sound all around him. Cars, horns, whistles, ghetto blasters, footsteps, an airplane overhead—they crashed over him like a wave, stunning but welcome. Chris risked a glance over his shoulder. No movement. No trace of pursuit.

He leaned against a storefront, and put a hand to his chest. It came away wet with sweat. He forced his breathing to slow down. *It was nothing, nothing, just your imagination, don't get paranoid.*

A bus rumbled up to the corner. He jogged the few paces to the stop and climbed in, moving to the back. The seats were covered with graffiti. He slumped into an empty seat and closed his eyes, letting his heart slow.

Then he opened his eyes, and saw what was scrawled on the back of the seat in front of him, there amid the profanities:

HELLO, CHRIS

Fear returned to squeeze his heart until he thought it would burst. Roger knew.

7

Chris didn't remember the rest of the ride home. He didn't remember walking the two blocks to his house. Didn't remember dinner, or what his mom talked about. Nothing held his attention but those two words.

Hello, Chris.

He lay in bed, wide awake, the bedside clock reading 2:17 A.M. A moment ago it had been 1:35. A second before that it had been 12:43.

What am I gonna do? Oh Christ, what am I gonna DO?

Chris started at the sound of a pebble striking the window. Three more struck in rapid succession before he could get to the window and look down.

Roger stood in the backyard, which was covered with a thick mist that hovered around Roger's feet. Even from here, Chris could see movement within the mist. Roger was looking up at the window. When he saw Chris, he waved to him to come down.

Chris hesitated.

Another pebble, larger this time, struck the window. A hairline crack appeared in the glass.

But that wasn't what frightened Chris.

Roger hadn't thrown the pebble. It had come from somewhere within the mist that roiled at his feet.

Chris looked back at Roger, who waved to him exactly as he had before. And his lips formed the words, *"Come down."*

Chris pulled on a shirt and pants, his fingers unsteady on the buttons. He stepped into his shoes and moved quietly out of the bedroom, trying not to make any noise. *Please, God, don't let her wake up, don't let her get into this.* He hesitated at the back door, then forced himself to open it and step out on the porch.

Roger stood twenty feet away, unmoving, like a stone idol rising out of the fog. "Come here," he said.

Chris stepped gingerly off the porch, his feet sinking into the moist grass, and walked a few paces until he reached the border of the

231

mist. It boiled and surged a few inches from his feet. Chris stepped forward. The mist was cold, and damp, and clung to his feet like oil. As he walked forward, something inside the mist brushed against his feet, something hard and thin and spiny, but invisible within the greyness.

He stopped a few paces away from Roger. "Hi."

"I thought you were my friend!"

"Roger—"

"It told me, Chris! It *told* me about the fire alarm, and Steve! You could've helped me! And you didn't! You just left me there! And you were going to tell Edwards everything, weren't you? *Weren't you?*"

"I don't know!" Chris shouted back. "I don't know *what* I was going to tell him. I just . . . wanted to talk. I was trying to help you."

"Like you helped me before?"

Chris felt something brush his foot again, the feel of it sharp against his exposed ankle. He bit down and tried to ignore it. "Roger, I'm sorry. Okay? I'm sorry. I was afraid. I figured if I tried to get to the alarm they'd get me too, and maybe it was the wrong thing to do—okay, it *was* the wrong thing to do—but I was afraid and I wasn't thinking straight. If I could go back in time and fix it, I would. But I can't. All I can do is say I'm sorry."

Roger glared at him. "You should've at least told me."

"I was afraid you'd get mad. Fact is, ever since all this started, I've been afraid a *lot.* Some times I have to work hard to think about a time when I *wasn't* afraid."

Chris thought he saw genuine surprise in Roger's face—and hurt. "Are you afraid of me?"

"Of you? No," Chris said. "Of what you're turning into—yes."

"You just want to hold me back," Roger said. "Like everyone else. You don't understand. I thought you would. I figured you, of all people, would understand. But you don't."

He walked a few paces away, the mist at his feet parting ahead of him. Finally, he stopped, and looked back at Chris. "Don't come around the Keep anymore," he said. "I don't want to hurt you. You were my friend, and I still respect that. But I can't be responsible for what happens if you don't stay clear."

He disappeared into the line of trees that framed the backyard. "Stay away from the Keep," he called back, "and don't tell on me to anyone, or you won't have anyone to blame but yourself for what happens. I'm sorry it had to go this way. Really sorry."

He was gone.

Chris looked down at the grass. The mist was withdrawing like a curtain, falling back to the line of trees. Just before it vanished, he thought he glimpsed something within the mist that turned and glared at him. Just an impression of eyes and a hard, shiny carapace, and then it faded into the night.

Then Chris saw an object lying a few feet away. Previously covered by the mist, it was now exposed by the dim glow from the back porch light: one of his mother's favorite blouses. It had been shredded until it was hardly recognizable. Only the pattern—roses set against an off-white background—identified it for what it was.

She had worn it to work that day. He had seen it in the hamper when he brushed his teeth for bed.

The only way it could be out here would be if Roger had gone inside the house and taken it. *Impossible*, Chris thought, then remembered the incident at the girls' gym.

It was a reminder, that Roger could go wherever he wanted, and no one would notice.

He looked again at the violated blouse.

The meaning was unambiguous.

Though the night was not cold, he shivered violently.

26

Susan stood in the middle of Jordy's living room trying unsuccessfully to reconcile it with the man she knew. In the years they'd been partners, he'd never brought her to his place. She was his partner, and because she was also a woman that meant keeping a certain distance to avoid complicating their working relationship. She'd always imagined it as rumpled as he was—but now she found that was far from the truth.

The apartment was organized, and ordered, and (to her chagrin) neater than her own. Magazines were stacked neatly on the coffee table, the dishes were washed and in the rack (long since dried), the corner of the table he apparently used for his work contained folders and papers meticulously stacked, everything alphabetical, edges flush . . .

Should've known, Susan thought. He was always so organized, always knew where everything was. That kind of discipline doesn't come by nature. You have to work at it. And Jordy did. He was a good cop. This just underlines it. And some cop I was, not to have figured it out.

It was easy to imagine him having stepped out for a minute,

---

heading across the street for a sandwich and a cup of coffee, due to return at any moment.

Except he's not coming back, is he? Her throat tightened painfully.

The two investigating officers came out of the bedroom behind her. The tall one in the suit, the one who didn't talk much and never referred to her by name, was from the Internal Affairs Division. The other one, shorter and wearing a blazer over slacks and an open shirt, was Lieutenant-Detective Guerra, from the homicide division of the precinct where Jordan's body had been found.

She looked past them to the bedroom. Where it had previously been as neat as the front room, now drawers were pulled open, closets partly emptied, boxes spilled onto the floor. They were looking for anything that might be suspicious—notes, stashes of money, drugs. From their expressions, Susan could tell that they had turned up nothing. The investigator from I.A.D. seemed surprised, even disappointed.

That's because you didn't know Jordy, she decided, and the thought warmed her.

"We've got a few more questions for you," the man from I.A.D. said. "Do you know if Jordan was having problems at work with anyone else? Did he ever seem unusually worried, especially about money?"

"No to both," Susan said.

"No mention of debts?"

"None."

"You said he gambled."

"I said that once in a while he shot pool for a few bucks a rack. Usually he broke even, and I never saw him lose more than twenty dollars in a night."

"Drugs?"

"Not that I ever saw."

The investigator frowned. It gave his face a pinched look, as though he'd just swallowed something bitter. "I want you to understand that your testimony goes directly into the record. If there's anything you're hiding, you're not doing your partner's memory any good, and you're doing yourself a lot of harm."

Susan stiffened. "I told you the truth. Jordan was a clean cop."

"He sure didn't die a clean death."

She flushed. "I didn't know the two went together."

"You two ever sleep together?"

"What the hell kind of question is that?"

"A standard one. You know the routine." He paused. "Look, to hear you talk about him, he sounds like a goddamned saint. I've been on the force fifteen years, and I've never once met a saint. You say he was, fine, but I'd like to be sure there was more than hormones involved. Give me a reason to believe you."

"The answer is no," she said. "We never slept together. Our time off-duty was confined to lunches, a few beers here and there, and a little pool. That's it. He wasn't a saint. He was just a good cop."

The investigator nodded, closed his notebook and glanced at the homicide detective. "I'll have my report in by the end of the day," he said, and headed out of the apartment.

Guerra waited until the door was closed, then turned to Susan. "Mister Personality, huh?"

"Lieutenant, I wanted to deck him more than anybody I ever met."

"For what it's worth, and strictly off the record—I would've helped you. But it's his job, and like you he's got to do it the best he can."

"I know, but that doesn't make it any easier," she said.

"At risk of making it even less easy, I've got a couple of last questions myself," Guerra said. "We're going over Jordan's old cases now, but it would save us a lot of time if you knew of anyone your partner put away who'd hold a grudge, maybe want to do something about it later on."

"I don't know. I don't think so, but he'd been working in another division for a long time before he got transferred to my precinct. It's possible, I suppose, but I wouldn't know where to start."

"What about now? Were you two working on anything that might make someone want to get rid of either or both of you?"

"No. We were transferred to Juvie a few weeks ago, and most of that time's been spent talking to kids, looking into some local suicides."

"Yeah, I'd heard something about that. Any chance these suicides were more than that? Maybe somebody was afraid you'd find out something you shouldn't?"

The question stopped her. "I don't think so," she said. "Our homicide people looked over everything pretty carefully. They came up blank."

Guerra closed his notebook. "All right, that'll do for now. If I have any further questions, I'll call you." He started toward the door.

"Lieutenant?" He stopped. "So what's the verdict?"

"My report will be in—"

"Please. I just want to know for myself."

He saw the look in her eyes, and understood. "Off the record, we're listing this as a homicide. A guy wants to kill himself, there's lots of easier ways to do it. Many of the injuries can't be accounted for by the fall. And the rest . . . well, you know about that part. We're as sure as we can be that someone, or more likely several people, were responsible. My guess is that somebody followed him from the bar, managed to get him onto that street, and then attacked him, suffocated him, and threw him over the retaining wall. Given everything in the coroner's report, you'd probably need at least two big guys to do it.

"So obviously, the first thing you look for is a personal connection. A motivation. Maybe a drug deal gone wrong, bad debts, whatever. Problem is, if that doesn't pan out—and from what you've told us it looks like it won't—then you're stuck with something a lot nastier and harder to pin down. A random killing. Maybe a gang, maybe a cult, maybe just a couple of psychos out there prowling the streets. In which case you also have to start worrying about who they're going to attack next."

He rubbed the back of his neck. "It's an ugly set of possibilities." He opened the door, held it for her. "You coming?"

She glanced toward the violated bedroom. "In a little while, Lieutenant. If you don't mind, I'd like to . . . clean up, before his family gets here."

"The regulations—"

"Please."

He hesitated. "All right," he said, "just be sure you lock up afterward and put the ribbons back up outside."

When he was gone, she walked back into the bedroom and began to put things back the way Jordy had left them.

Homicide, Guerra had said.

Murder. Cold-blooded. Ruthless. Sick.

Bastards, she thought, the rage building up. Her hands shook as she straightened and tucked and filed.

Whatever it took, however long it took, she would find them.

Then she would hurt them.

2

Carlyn Martino put away the groceries, then walked upstairs. The door to Chris's room was ajar, and she could hear the radio playing. She knocked at the door. "Chris?"

"Yeah?" His voice was small in the room.

She opened the door. Chris lay in bed, still in his pajamas, his face pale. "Hi, Mom."

"Chris, why didn't you *tell* me you were sick?" She sat down on the bedside, placed her palm against his forehead. "I could've gotten something for you. How do you feel?"

"Okay, just a cold, that's all."

"You sure? We can take you to the doctor if you're nauseous or—"

"No," Chris said, too quickly. "I'm okay, I'm just tired."

She touched his hands. They were cool but dry, not clammy. "You want me to bring you something to eat?"

"Maybe later."

"All right," she said, and patted his leg. "But if you change your mind, just—"

She stopped.

Her hand had brushed Chris's feet, which she could feel beneath the thin sheet. They were cold, even through the fabric.

"Chris?"

"It's nothing, Mom."

"Let me see."

He pulled back the sheet. His feet were paler than the rest of him, and when she touched them, they were cold, as though he'd been walking up to his ankles in ice water.

"This isn't good," she said. "Is there any tingling? Can you feel your toes all right?"

"They're fine, Mom. Really."

"How long have they been like this?"

"Not long. They're better than they were."

Carlyn tapped her fingers on the sheet. "I'm giving you a couple of hours. If they're not better by then, we're taking you in to see a doctor."

"All right."

238

She stood, and pulled the sheets back over his feet. "I'll bring you some tea in a minute," she said. "And that window gets closed right now. The last thing you need in here is a draft."

She crossed to the window and glanced out.

Below was a twenty-foot square patch where the grass, green and lush just the other day, had turned black and died. Even from here, the ground had an unwholesome look. "When did this happen to the grass?"

"Beats me," he said. "It was like that when I woke up this morning."

"Probably have to have the whole area replanted. I wonder what could have done it?"

"I don't know . . ." Chris said. "Maybe some tea would be a good idea."

Carlyn turned. "Okay. One crisis at a time, then." She headed downstairs, hearing Chris get out of bed and walk to the bathroom behind her. She'd check on him when she brought back the tea. If he wasn't better soon, she would definitely take him to a doctor.

Chris fought the nausea that threatened to clog his throat, and closed the bathroom door. He ran hot water into the tub until it stood three inches high. Then, gritting his teeth, he lowered his feet into it. Needles lanced up his legs. It felt as though his feet had been asleep for hours, and were only now waking up—but the sensation was magnified a hundredfold. If he timed it right, he would be able to warm his feet and get back into bed in time for his mother to check them again, finding them warmer than before.

Maybe this time, the warmth would even last for more than ten minutes. But he didn't hold out much hope.

3

Roger's watch had stopped days ago, and he'd thrown it away. It wasn't needed. He knew it was night without having to go topside. He could feel it.

They felt it, too.

It was going to be glorious.

He clutched the yearbook to his chest and walked forward. The tunnel walls seemed almost luminous. From the shadows he could hear a whisper of voices, a murmuring chorus of encouragement. *Yes, this is the time. Now it all begins.* It was a sound like distant thunder, a tickle of foreign thoughts, heard more with the mind than with the ears.

What do you want? they asked.

And he thought back, To hurt them.

What do you want? they repeated.

I want it all.

And still they were not satisfied. *What do you want?*

I—

What do you want?

What do you WANT?

He stopped. And he knew. There in the darkness, surrounded by the shadow chorus, he told them. Two words. That was all.

The voices murmured back, *Yes.*

His heart swelled with that one word.

Yes.

That was to be the culmination of the process which, once begun, could not be stopped. He didn't need Chris. He was ready. What he had to do, he could do just as well alone.

She came from the shadows, and drew close to him. Pale and beautiful and terrible, her eyes caught the sheen from the walls and threw it back, red. Her fingertips stroked his cheek, and where they touched they left fire that burned cold through to the bone. *It was time,* she whispered, her lips brushing his face, her voice joining the hushed chorus, *it is time and we are here and it is fire and we are here and it is thunder and we are here and it is time, time, time . . .*

Then she slipped away, and he let himself be borne forward by the momentum of their whispers, drawn into the light that was deeper than the darkness. They moved out of the shadows, and they touched him, and their long fingers probed in through pore and mouth and breath. They took what they needed, took what he needed to give them, took the fire that would fall and the thunder that would come and they took the hate, they took all of it. He was one with them, seeing through them as they felt through him, each feeding, each taking, each giving, the murmur louder and ever louder, until he thought the earth itself must split and the force of their communion explode into the world with fire and storm wind.

His spirit wavered under their touch, but held fast, fueled by his desire. He *was* strong enough. He *was* perfect. In that moment he was one with them.

And he was everywhere.

4

Gary Stavros climbed up the side of the school fence as far as he could go before reaching the chickenwire, and grabbed for the tree branch above. He snagged it and pulled himself up, careful to wait until his foot was on the top brace of the fence before slowly bringing his leg over the chickenwire to the other side. He balanced there a moment, steadying himself with the branch, before bringing his other leg over, then jumped the remaining distance to the parking lot.

He landed feet first, hard enough to rattle his teeth. He grinned. With school having closed so suddenly, he was willing to bet that the woodshop hadn't been locked up the way it usually was for an extended holiday. He knew the chickenwire would be no problem. It'd been put up last year after a lot of equipment had been stolen, to discourage any future attempts. Trying to carry off heavy equipment became difficult when you were dancing over razors.

But he wasn't here to steal.

This was strictly payback. Bad enough to get a D-minus in shop. But to get it from that greaser, Ortiz, was too much.

He'd been laughed at for weeks afterwards. Who the hell *ever* got a D-minus in shop but a moron? You had to be some kind of first-class idiot not to know how to cut a piece of wood. The only reason he'd taken the class in the first place was because he'd figured it'd be an easy A. Most shop teachers didn't care if you showed up or not, as long as you didn't get in their way, you were guaranteed a C at least. If you actually *made* something, you got an A.

But Ortiz had an *attitude* from day one. Wanted him there every day. In his seat. Making a progress report, turning out the work—who needed that kind of shit?

That's what he'd told Ortiz.

That's when Ortiz told him to shape up or get out.

That's when Gary called him a greaser.

And that's when Gary got a D-minus.

Well, fuck him. Gary worked his way to the shop window. The latch never really held in the best of conditions; he doubted anyone had even thought to buttress it when school had shut down. Gripping the frame, he jammed it upward. On the third shove the lock popped and the window slid open. He crawled inside, and turned on one of the small worklights, angling it so it couldn't be seen from outside.

All this new equipment. After the old stuff had been ripped off, Ortiz managed to pick up some new equipment at cost. Some of it had hardly been used. Even so, everything was coated with a patina of sawdust and filings. The smell of pine and metal shavings was strong, and made his nose itch.

He worked his way across the nearly dark room until he found a good, thick length of pipe and a pair of work gloves.

He started with the lathe. He brought the pipe up over his shoulder and swung like a major-leaguer, smashing the bit, the handle, knocking off switches and controls. Glass shattered and crunched under his feet. He swung around, brought the pipe down on the power saw, punching out the blade. He dented the brace, knocked off the adjusting knobs, smashed the gauge . . .

He stopped to catch his breath.

It was then that he noticed the sound for the first time. A low whine.

He turned. The band saw had started whirring behind him, the thin strip of metal rotating faster and faster in its narrow slot.

Must've kicked a switch or something, he decided, and edged toward it. The band saw was one of the few pieces of equipment that made him nervous. It was the biggest thing in the shop, nearly five feet tall to accommodate the circle of steel that spun at who-even-*knew* how many revolutions per minute.

He could hear it alternately speeding and slowing as he drew nearer, the sound moving through the shop like a wave. He was almost to the OFF switch when the band saw came loose with a clang of metal against metal that made the machine ring like a bell struck by a massive fist.

It's come off its track! Gary thought, and dived for the ground. The saw blade whipped once more and smashed into the side of the narrow slot. The blade shattered, spewing out pieces and ribbons of metal like shrapnel. They whizzed past his ear and slammed into the cabinets, embedding themselves in the hard wood.

242

Gary covered his head, barely in time, as a piece of blade ricocheted off the machine and sliced into the back of his hand. He cried out, bunching into a fetal position. More shards rocketed past, one embedding itself in his calf, another in his forearm.

The sound of shattering metal stopped, even though the machine, deprived of ammunition, continued to whine.

Fighting the pain, he sat up and stripped off his jacket. The shards in his forearm and hand were not big, but they had sunk into the flesh, saw teeth holding on like barbs on a fishing hook. He took hold of the piece in his arm and pulled, wriggling it back and forth until it came loose, bits of flesh clinging to the teeth. Blood flowed in a neat trickle down his arm.

Next came the piece in his hand. His fingers were shaking from the pain and the fear. *Shit, it's gonna get infected, I know it.*

The final piece, in his calf, was the largest of the three, and he jiggled it for nearly a minute before working it free. He threw the piece across the floor, feeling sick. He didn't care about finishing the job, didn't care about Ortiz, didn't care about anything except getting out.

He staggered over to the window and eased himself out, pain lancing up from his leg as he pulled it after him. He reached the parking lot and walked as quickly as he could back to the fence. He paused a moment to catch his breath, then forced himself to take hold of the fence and, despite the pain, began slowly pulling himself up the side. He could feel the blood from his hand running warmly down the arm of his shirt. *Just let me get out of here, I swear I'll never do anything like this again.*

He stopped just short of the top of the fence and grabbed for the branch overhead, this time forced to use his other hand. He missed twice, then finally connected. Wincing against the pain that spasmed up his body, he pulled himself up until he was again standing on one side of the brace. *Just a little more,* he thought and, very carefully, swung his injured leg out over the chickenwire atop the fence and down, onto the other side of the brace, so he was again straddling the sharp wires—

—as something fell out of the tree branches above him, two somethings, black and small, and he couldn't see them, saw only a blur of motion, and they plunged past, each grabbing hold of one of his ankles and together pulled in opposite directions.

NO! Then his footing slipped, and they pulled again, and he fell spread-eagled onto the chickenwire that stretched between his legs.

5

Red Circle.

6

Patricia Alberts measured out the apple juice into Jeff's bottle, trying to shut out the sound of the cries coming from his crib. She wondered what God-given instinct enabled babies to find exactly the right frequency that could drive a person to within half an inch of homicide.

She capped the bottle and brought it to Jeff. He quieted down as soon as his lips found the nipple.

Patricia went back to the television and tried to find something worth watching. When she was pregnant, it seemed all she could bring herself to watch were sitcoms. Now she could hardly stand to look at one. It reminded her too much of that terrible summer. It had been incredibly hot, and that had made the pregnancy all the more unbearable. She'd had to leave school in mid-semester because of the kid, and her friends had done all they could to keep her informed on school gossip—as well as all the parties they went to, the boys they were dating, the evenings spent getting high and not having to worry about things like diet and bloating and throwing up every morning promptly at eight.

Oh, they had been quite understanding, and she'd wanted to strangle the lot of them.

She glanced at the clock. Lee would be getting home soon, which meant another argument. He hadn't gotten the promotion he'd been hoping for at Sears, and that didn't do much for his temperament. When they'd met, he'd been the star of the track team, and she'd considered herself lucky to have him, to see the looks in all the other girls' eyes when they went down the hall together.

Except then she'd gotten pregnant.

244

And being a track star didn't mean much in the outside world. So he went to a job he hated, and came home to a family he hadn't wanted, and wore his letter-jacket until she thought it would disintegrate.

It'll get better, she thought, without really believing it, but thinking it anyway because that was the only way to get through the days and nights.

She flipped channels, the faces of news anchors and commercial actors flashing past, static punctuating each image as she held down the SCAN button, past one channel after another—

"Remember me?"

She stopped.

What the hell?

She backed up, trying to figure out which channel she'd been scanning when she'd seen it. But it was gone now. It had been just a flicker of an image, but it had looked for all the world like that nerk Roger Whatshislastname, the four-eyed weasel who'd actually had the gall to ask her out once, right in front of everybody she knew. As if she'd be seen *dead* with someone like that. So she'd hit him. She hadn't intended to hit him. It just happened, reflexively, and he ducked, seemed actually afraid of her, and then the others were yelling at her to hit him again, and—

She smiled. It was the first and only time she'd ever actually beat up a guy. They'd all called her slugger for days thereafter.

Those were the days, she thought, and glanced back at the set. It couldn't have been him; must've been someone who looked like him. After all, the picture tube didn't explode.

As Jeff's sucking noises got louder, she got up and went to the crib. "All right, let's see how you're doing."

She screamed.

Inside the bottle, a rat floated dead in the apple juice, eyes rolled up in its head almost as though looking at her, claws tucked up against its chest. Jeff was giggling, unaware of it, or the small mites floating with it. The rat bobbed back in the bottle until it hit the other end, and rolled over and around, tail following head in a macabre ballet . . .

Red Circle.

8

Michael Estrada pulled the beer up from its concealed place between his legs and waited for the light to turn green. He gunned the engine impatiently. He had plans for the night. First the party at Emilio's, then back to Lisa's place for a little action if her parents weren't home. He took a pull at the beer, and looked up as Horseface walked by in front of his car. Obst.

"Hey! Horseface!" Michael yelled, honking the horn.

But Horseface was already staring at him, and when their eyes met, Obst smiled. Waved.

Michael gave him the finger. Who the hell did he think he was, acting like they were buddies? "Screw you," he yelled.

The light turned green.

Michael shot forward into the intersection, only there were cars there, and he saw that, impossibly, the light was *not* green, it was red, and there was no time to do anything as a horn wailed and the semi-truck roared into the intersection, wheels burning rubber, trying to stop, but there wasn't enough time, and the last thing Michael felt was the crunch of his ribcage being crushed against the door, the sickening crack of his head as it rammed the windshield.

The last thing he saw as his life ebbed out of his chest was Horseface standing next to the car in the crowd of onlookers.

Horseface was smiling.

9

Red Circle.

10

He was bored. Paul Geyer walked down Hollywood Boulevard, barely paying attention to the storefronts and theaters he passed. Nothing was the same anymore, not since Steve had died. *Stupid. Plain, dirt stupid.* The rest of the bunch had drifted apart afterward, without Steve to pull them together.

Stupid. Plain, dirt stupid.

He flicked his cigarette into the street, and watched it roll into the gutter. He needed to stop thinking; he needed to get *high.* So far, he hadn't spotted any of the usual dealers, but they would turn up. The night was still early.

He walked on past Las Palmas Boulevard, and the Army-Navy Surplus Store. A bunch of punks in mohawks and green hair stood out front, faces pale even in the night, dancing to the music bleeding over from the electronics store next door. *Assholes,* Paul thought.

He continued down Hollywood toward Wilcox, checking down the intersecting streets for anyone looking to do some business. He licked his lips. A little smoke, a little coke, that was what he needed to get through the night.

Just past Wilcox, he paused. Down the street, a car slowed, then stopped in front of an apartment building. Two black guys came out of the alley beside the building. Negotiations were made quickly with the guy in the car, money was handed out in exchange for a small white baggie, and the car drove away. The two guys stepped quickly back into the alley.

Bingo, Paul thought, and started toward the alley. He could see them leaning up against a wall, smoking.

"Yeah?" one of them said. His voice sounded Jamaican.

"Just doing a little business," Paul said. He took a tentative step into the alley, not wanting to be seen from the street, but not wanting to be beyond the safe glow of the lights, either.

One of them held out a handful of crack vials. "Twenny bucks each, mon. Good shit. Uncut."

"Twenty? C'mon." That was nearly twice the going rate. He took a step back.

"Whoa, okay, look, fifteen. Tellin' you, mon, totally uncut. Fifteen. Last offer. You don' like it, you kiss my ass. Won't get better shit anywhere."

"Fifteen, huh?" Paul shrugged. "Okay." He reached into his back pocket for his wallet. "Give me two."

The dealer held out the pair of vials.

Paul flopped open the wallet; something gold fell out and clattered to the street at his feet.

A badge. Police badge. L.A.P.D.

"Fucking *shit!*" one of the dealers yelled. "Get the son of a bitch!"

"Wait—"

Too late. They threw him up against the wall. "Who you think you're messing with, asshole?" one of them yelled.

Then something sharp plunged between his ribs. Jerked upwards. Twisted. Came out and plunged in again. Paul cried out. Red strobed behind his eyes. Twice more the knife sank into his gut.

"Move!" one of the attackers yelled, and they disappeared into the darkness.

Paul slumped to the ground. *They stuck me.* He put his hand to his stomach, and felt skin move under his touch. *Bad, oh god, it's bad.* He tried to crawl back into the light, but it was far away, too far away, and his legs kept sliding out from under him.

"Help," he cried, but his voice was small in his ears, his lungs refusing to power it. "Help . . ."

A shadow appeared beside him. He looked up.

Obst.

"Help," Paul said, clutching at Obst's leg. "Help, get—get an ambulance!"

But Obst only reached down, picked up the badge, and put it in his pocket.

Then he unzipped his pants and, smiling, urinated on him.

As, Paul distantly remembered, Steve had forced Obst to do that long-ago afternoon.

"Fuck you," Obst said.

Then the world tilted, and Paul fell into the beckoning darkness.

11

Red Circles.

12

David Anderson.
Red Circle.
Victoria Bendel.
Red Circle.
Enrique Fortuno.
Red Circle.
Thomas Nagy.
Red Circle.

27

The telephone screamed. Gene pulled himself across the bed, hardly awake, fumbling with the phone. "Yeah?"

It was Susan. "Have you seen the news?"

"No . . . I was sleeping . . ." He looked at the bedside clock: 7:32 A.M. With school out for two more days, he'd slept late.

"Turn on the TV. Channel Four."

"Wait," Gene said, sitting up, "how're you doing?"

A sigh. "I don't know anymore. Sometimes it seems like the whole world has gone nuts. Watch the news, you'll understand. I'll talk to you later."

Gene pulled on his robe and staggered into the living room, where he turned on the news. The anchor was finishing up a story on a recall vote in the San Fernando Valley.

Then: "Updating our main story this morning, Los Angeles Police Chief Darryl Gates held a press conference a little while ago, apparently attempting to put to rest many of the rumors circulating regarding last night's string of teenage deaths, most of them in the Inglewood/Lennox area."

Gene felt his skin go cold.

"According to the Chief's statement, at this time there appears to be no gang connection in any of the deaths, though it seems one may have been drug related."

The anchor continued over videotape of the aftermath of the carnage: a wrecked automobile, lit by red flares against the night, a police officer guiding traffic around the scene; a body shrouded with a blanket at the base of a high building. "Six teenagers were killed and two hospitalized in serious condition last night in separate incidents throughout southwest L.A. Police are still investigating possible causes or links in the incidents. Despite the fact that all of the victims are teenagers, the police are maintaining thus far that there is no indication that the events are tied in to the 'wilding' that has terrorized many metropolitan cities over the last two years.

"We will continue to update this story as we learn more details. Meanwhile, a seventeen-year-old mother was arrested last night on charges of child abuse and neglect. Officials released a statement saying that a rat had been found in the infant's bottle. The mother had apparently fled the apartment and was later located at—"

Gene switched off the set. He was aware of the phone ringing somewhere behind him, but he didn't reach for it. He felt ill. *How many of them did I know? How many were in my class last week?*

What's going on?

2

"Look, Susan, give me a break. Strictly by the regs, you've got another twenty-four hours of desk duty before I can put you out on the streets." Captain Phillips took a drag on his cigarette. He looked as if he hadn't slept much the previous night. The first news about the kids had started coming in around eleven P.M.

"I'm not asking to be assigned to homicide," Susan said. "But we've got something major going on here, and I've been on the case since day one. I've got all the files, I've talked to all the people—"

"They're not related. All this shit that's coming down—they're just isolated events."

"How can you be so sure? I ran a check. Every single one of the dead kids was between sixteen and eighteen years old, and that includes the ones Jordy and I started investigating a couple weeks ago. I'm just asking you to look at the figures. Ten kids dead in less than a month.

Every one of them attending the same school. Plus another three from a couple of other schools, and that teacher who killed himself last week.

"If there were some kind of gang-banging going on, maybe you could write it off. That we understand. But these are middle-class kids. That many deaths, in the same school, the same age range—the odds against it are astronomical. I don't know what it means any more than you do, but Jesus Christ, *something* sure as hell is happening. We're looking at what could turn into a major crisis. When the press starts putting this stuff together—and they will, bet on it—they're going to start asking a lot of questions. And it'll help to defuse the situation if there were some kind of continuity in the investigation. At least it'd *look* like we've got it covered until we *do* get it covered."

Phillips chewed his cigarette. "All right. Check in with Lieutenant Manning. He's heading up the investigation. Give them whatever you've got that can help. Unofficially, I think you're right. Superficially, these things look like individual accidents, but my gut tells me there's no way you could have this many fatal accidents in this amount of time unless there are drugs or gangs involved. Since we've got neither, there's got to be some other connection. If you can help figure out what it is, go for it."

He threw his pencil on his desk. "Kids. This could be worse than the fucking Zodiac killer."

"Thanks," Susan said, and started for the door. "I appreciate it. I really want to see this through. Jordy'd want me to finish what we started."

"I know," Phillips said. "Just be careful, all right? And stay clear of whatever nailed your partner."

"I will," Susan said.

3

Gene came down the stairs of his apartment, putting on his jacket. He wanted to see Susan, needed to know how she was doing. He figured she wouldn't have more than a few minutes to spare, but he wanted her to know that he was there if she needed him.

As he crossed the parking lot, his neighbor appeared, garbage sack in hand.

"You hear about those kids on the news?" he asked.

Gene nodded. "Tragic. Senseless."

"Yeah, but it seems that's what you've got to expect with kids nowadays. If they're not killing somebody else, they're killing themselves." He threw the sack into the dumpster. "By the way, somebody came by for you yesterday, but you weren't home."

Gene stopped beside his car. "Who?"

"A kid. About five-foot-three or so, dark brown hair, wearing a windbreaker. Said his name was Chris, I think."

"What did he want?"

"Didn't say, but he seemed real anxious to talk to you. Said it was important. Then he just left."

"Okay, thanks," Gene said, and climbed into the car. There were only two Chrises in his classes, and only the Martino boy matched the description. Question is, why was he coming to see Gene—unless it had something to do with Roger.

He debated whether to go directly to the station and talk to Susan, or stop off first and see Chris. Remembering that Roger had dropped out of sight about the same time all hell started breaking out, he started the car and drove east. He figured he could remember the way to Chris's place, even without the address.

4

Chris knew something was wrong as soon as his mother came in with the newspaper; her face gave away her concern. After she left for work, he dug the newspaper out of the trash.

The faces that stared up at him from the front page of the *Herald Examiner* were the same faces he had seen in Roger's yearbook.

Except unlike the yearbook photos, these weren't circled in red.

Chris sat down at the kitchen table and read the accompanying article. Until this moment, he had tried to convince himself that Roger's actions had been more theatrical than real, more threat than action. But now . . .

His gaze moved irresistibly back toward the grainy, black-and-white photos.

All those red circles, too many for coincidence.

There were only two possibilities:

1) Roger knew what was going to happen to them, or

2) Roger *made* something happen to them.

Much as he wanted to believe the first possibility, bad as it was, he could no longer deny his suspicion that the second was the right one.

Roger was out of control, and had to be stopped.

Yeah? Chris thought. Who's gonna do it, smart guy? You? Remember what happened the other night. Remember the blouse. Remember the threat.

That was the part that stopped him. He could live with the danger to himself. But his mother was something else.

So to protect your mom you'll let everybody else go to hell, is that it, Chris?

He didn't know.

Yes, you do. You're going to sit here and do nothing and put the blame on Mom because it's cleaner than the truth—he doesn't give a damn about Mom, but if you take a stand against him you know it's YOU he'll try to nail, it's YOUR picture that'll show up one morning in the *Herald*.

It was true. He *was* afraid.

The sudden ringing of the doorbell startled him. He walked to the door, half-expecting to see Roger outside, grinning, holding up a newspaper. *Made the papers, Chris. Big time!*

But instead it was Mr. Edwards. "Hi, Chris. I hear you came to see me yesterday."

Chris felt his stomach lurch. "No, I—I don't think so."

"Are you sure? It sounded a lot like you."

"No," Chris said, and he knew his face was flushing. He had never been a good liar. "Must've been someone else. Sorry."

Mr. Edwards studied him for a moment. "All right. How are things with you?"

"Okay. Fine." Chris shifted nervously from foot to foot. Why didn't he go away?

"You sure?"

"Yeah."

Liar.

"I'll see you in class, then, Chris," Mr. Edwards said. "Whenever that is. Take care."

He turned and headed down the sidewalk. Chris closed the door and leaned against it, his heart pounding.

He closed his eyes, tight, until they teared. *Let this all be a dream, I can't deal with this anymore, I don't know what to do.*

Before he could let himself think about what he was doing, Chris raced across the lawn. "Mr. Edwards!"

"Yes?"

Chris folded his hands into fists and stuffed them up under his arms to keep them from trembling. "I know where he is. I know where Roger is." He felt, distantly, that his face was wet. "I'll tell you everything, I swear, the whole thing, but you got to promise you won't let anything happen to my mom, that's all, just promise me."

Mr. Edwards put a hand on his shoulder. "I promise. We won't let anything happen to your mom."

"Okay," Chris said, wiping at his face. There was a painful lump in his throat. "Okay."

And now it starts.

28

When Susan had joined them after a fast call to the police station, Chris began with the lemon writing, and their first message; he told them of the beatings given them by Steve, the incident in the girls' locker room, Roger dropping out, the argument with Huntington, the argument with Roger's dad, Roger's descent into his Keep, and now the threat to Chris's mom, the pictures in Roger's yearbook, and the pictures in the newspaper.

They listened in silence. Finally, Edwards stood up. "Can you give us a minute alone, Chris?"

"Sure," he said, and wandered into the living room. He tried to listen through the door, but they spoke too softly to be overheard.

But he didn't have to hear what they were saying. *They don't believe me.*

After a moment, Edwards invited Chris back in. Susan was standing by the window. She studied his face as he walked in, and Chris couldn't tell if she was angry at him or just trying to size him up. Either way, her gaze made him uncomfortable.

"Have a seat," she said, her tone not unfriendly. "Now, Chris, I'm going to tell you a few things, and I don't want you to get upset."

"You don't believe me, right?"

"I believe that *you* believe it," she said, "so no one is dismissing anything you've said. Right now, you've got a lot of facts and a lot of feelings and a lot of suspicions floating around in your head, and there's nothing wrong with that. My job is to separate the facts from the feelings. And my first reaction is that you've been driving yourself crazy with guilt about things you're not responsible for.

"Let me give you an example. When I was your age, I had a falling out with my mother. Now when you're in an argument, you say a lot of things you don't mean. I said a bunch of them. And at one point, I said, 'I hate you, I wish you were dead.' And I stormed out. Well, two days later, she was in a car accident. She wasn't killed, thank god, but she was pretty banged up. I spent the next two years blaming myself for what happened, as though by saying what I did, I *made* it happen. I didn't. It was synchronicity."

"What about all the rest of it, the lemon writing, the yearbook, all that?"

"I think Roger was playing with you. Or maybe for reasons of his own he's created the fantasy that he is responsible, and convinced you along the way. It's pretty easy to fake the things you describe. You said yourself you only got a quick look at the yearbook—can you be sure every one of the kids you saw in the paper was circled in red?"

"No."

"And do you know for *certain* what those circles may have meant?"

"No."

"All right, then. So all I'm saying is, let's wait until we have all the facts before we start making assumptions. And the first, best way for us to do that is to find Roger and talk to him. If he's in trouble, we'll see to it he gets all the help he needs."

"You bringing that other cop with you? Your partner?"

Her gaze faltered. "I'm afraid not."

"Too bad," Chris said. "You're going to need him."

2

It seemed they had no sooner climbed into Susan's squad car than they were pulling up to the corner of the vacant lot. *Just like going to the dentist,* Chris thought. *You always get there faster than you should.*

"This way," Chris said, and led them across the lot. Now that

the weather had cleared, it was hot; the sun beat down on the surrounding buildings and piles of cinderblocks. He stopped in front of
the open hole that led down to the maintenance tunnels, and Roger's
Keep. "This is it."

"You're sure?" Susan said.

"It's the only one around," Chris said, and with a deep breath
started toward the entrance—

"Wait," Susan said. "I'll go in first."

"I know the way," Chris said.

"That's all right. I'll figure it out." She pulled a flashlight off her
belt, and sat down on the concrete lip of the entrance. She edged
down, and gradually disappeared into the darkness.

Chris glanced at Mr. Edwards. "I hate this. I really hate this."

"I know what you mean," Mr. Edwards said.

"No, you don't," Chris said.

After a moment, her voice came up out of the darkness. "All clear.
Come on down."

Before Mr. Edwards could move, Chris scooted to the edge of
the hole and followed her, trying not to notice that his hands were
shaking on the rungs. When he reached bottom, he turned, and saw
nothing. There were no magazines, no cartons of food, no chairs, no
candy wrappers, no clothes.

No yearbook.

No Roger.

"Is this where he was?" Susan asked.

Chris nodded, numbly. "Right here, I swear."

She shone the flashlight down the intersecting tunnel. "Let's take
a look then."

She stepped under a low-hanging pipe and into the next tunnel.
Chris followed, then Mr. Edwards. This was the tunnel where Chris
had seen Roger whispering to the shadows, but now the shadows were
nothing more malevolent than the absence of light, there was no cot,
and nothing moved in the glow of the flashlight.

They reached the end of the tunnel, which ribboned off into
others that looked as though they hadn't been used in years, then
circled back toward the main room. The place was clean, but still it
felt somehow unwholesome. He couldn't shake the sense that at any
moment he might turn a corner, and there Roger would be. Chris
could almost feel his presence, almost touch him—

But Roger wasn't here, was he?

They stepped back into the main room, and there was an awkward moment. "I guess he must've moved on," Susan said, and Chris heard doubt in her voice.

"I guess so," Chris said.

"Do you have any idea where else he might be?" Mr. Edwards said.

"No. Look, he *was* here. I'm not making it up!"

"No one's accusing you of making anything up," Susan said. "But you have to admit it's . . . difficult. This place doesn't look like it's been used in years."

"I know," Chris said, despairing. "I don't understand."

"There's not much more to see. If he was here, he's gone now, so either way we're back to square one." Susan sniffed, and coughed the air out. "Let's get out of here. This place smells awful."

She climbed out first, the others following.

But he was here, Chris thought. *I know it.*

Question was, how to prove it?

Damn, he thought. *Damn, damn, damn.*

There was something he was missing.

Something . . .

3

From the journal of Roger Obst:

I am we and we are you and you have been looking for me for me for so long so long goodbye farewell it doesn't matter nothing matters unless I can see you but you are among us but not of us and the Word is made Flesh but the flesh is weak nothing matters nothing matters in the end He said it He said that there will be nothing left, and in the end there is just the darkness and Jesus said He loved everyone but there are some even Jesus does not love and John 3:1 lied where am I do you feel it it's not in my thoughts it's real and it's here and you're real and I know they hate but to hate is to fall but is that not better than being crucified listen listen there is no love there is no hate there is only me and there is only you listen listen

He has betrayed us and he has betrayed you and he is us and he is not-us and he could not see us because we could see him see him know him and he does not belong you belong I belong we belong and for the rest there will be fire and darkness and it is almost time it is almost time it is almost

4

The ride back to Chris's house had been nearly silent the whole way. When they dropped him off, Mr. Edwards's only comment had been that they would be "in touch."

Loose translation: *Get lost.*

Chris paced the room, furious with them and with himself. In a way, he couldn't blame them for not believing him, not after finding the Keep deserted. It was as though Roger had never been there.

But he *had* been there. Chris tried to work it through. There was no way Roger could have known Chris was going to lead the others there. Chris didn't know it himself until Mr. Edwards arrived at his door. There had been less than an hour between that and the moment they'd arrived at the lot. Not enough time for Roger to clear everything out. Whatever he could do, whatever he might have become, Roger was not omniscient.

Okay, so working from that assumption, when we got there, why didn't we see—

He stopped.

They hadn't seen anything, true.

But perhaps that was because Roger didn't *want* them to see anything.

Chris tried to remember exactly what it was Roger had said, tried to visualize the moment they had stood in the girls' locker room, unseen by everyone; *they'll only see us if they* decide *to see us.* Or if Roger *let* them decide to see him.

Something cold uncoiled in Chris's chest.

He could have been there the whole time! He probably was there the whole time, and we just didn't see him because he didn't want us to see him, or anything that belonged to him!

The possibility unnerved Chris. Had Roger stood there in the darkness and studied them, eyes hard and glittering with hate at Chris's betrayal?

If so—why hadn't he done anything about it?

<hr>

260

Maybe he's saving it up for later, Chris thought. Or maybe there were too many of us. Everyone else who's been hurt was alone when it happened. Maybe he can't deal with more than one person at a time.

He found the thought comforting. It meant at least the possibility of a vulnerability that could be exploited in the future. But it did little to change the present situation. He knew that he'd have an even tougher job persuading Susan and Mr. Edwards to go back with him a second time. Finding solid evidence was the only way they would believe him.

Terrific, Chris thought, already knowing what all this was leading up to.

He would have to go back. Alone.

5

Susan pulled up in front of Gene's apartment. "Sure you can't come up for a minute?" he asked.

"Sorry, no. I've got to get back to the station."

"You sound pissed."

"I am. I don't like it when someone runs a number on me."

"I don't think he was," Gene said.

"Come on."

"No, really. I was watching his face the whole time. He looked absolutely bewildered when Roger wasn't there."

"You're saying you *believe* him?"

He hesitated. "I'm not sure what I believe. But I think that Chris was telling us what he thought was the truth."

"Maybe, but I wouldn't bet the rent on it," she said. "Gotta go, love."

He kissed her. It felt strange to be kissing a cop in the front seat of a squad car, but he decided he liked it. "Take care. If there's anything I can do—"

"I know," she said. "Thanks."

He watched her car pull away. Chris's frightened story still rang in his ears.

It couldn't be true, he thought. *Could it?*

No, it couldn't.

Because if it were, then they were all in danger.

6

Roger tried to sleep. A mistake. He had barely closed his eyes when the voices called to him from the dark places, murmured to him from the shadows. Summoning.

Tired, Roger thought, *I'm so tired, I just want to sleep, just leave me alone.*

But they weren't going to leave him alone. They knew he didn't really *want* to be left alone. Not being alone anymore was the whole point, wasn't it?

What do you want?

What do you want?

He knew he had to go. The final moment was almost at hand. What he started had to be finished.

He pulled himself erect. The shadows rushed to the spot where his feet touched the cold floor of the tunnel, embracing them and covering him and carrying him forward.

For the last time, she came to him, out of the shadows, they *all* came, and they touched him and called to him and wept with joy for him, and in that moment he loved them with a white-hot purity. They clutched his hand to their breasts as he passed, just for a moment, their breasts cool and pale and where he touched them they took the warmth from his fingers for their own, and they sighed, and he gave it gladly, for it was the one thing he had to give. Then they were gone, swallowed by darkness, and the only sound that reached him was their joyous sobbing.

The process was almost finished.

As they carried him forward, he watched the ceiling move past him overhead. *Almost finished*, he thought, *almost finished, almost finished, almost finished.*

This was to be the grand finale, he could sense it; the one moment he had been born for. Soon he would achieve the goal he had so long sought after, though he had never given voice to his desire.

But it had known, hadn't it? It had known, and felt, and offered it without question or hesitation. He felt weak, drained, but that, too, was part of the process, wasn't it? What right did he have to complain, after it had done so much for him?

I am you and you are me and we are together together together.

What right did he have to be selfish? To complain?

None.

The shadows carried him until he was just below the entrance. If he twisted his head just so, he could see the night sky overhead. He felt as though he lay on an open field, exposed beneath the stars.

Except the field he lay in had eyes. And moved of its own accord. And whispered into his ears.

He arched his back so he could see them. Waiting. Patient. Accepting. The embodiment of love. They could do nothing until he gave the sign. He could sense their eagerness pulsing in his own veins.

What right did he have to be selfish in the face of such love?

He closed his eyes, and called their names, and they descended upon him, enfolding him like a womb carved from shadows.

He gave them what they needed.

They took from him what he needed to give.

And they overflowed the entrance like an artery deep in the earth exploding up, and into, and beyond, carried by the nightwinds.

At long last, it was *time*.

7

It was almost nine o'clock by the time Chris got off the bus and started down the street toward the lot. He was halfway there when a sudden wind kicked up. Grit flew into his face, and he held up a hand to shield his eyes. In that moment, although he could not be sure, it looked as though something vast and dark rose up from the lot and launched itself into the night sky. But because everything was dark-on-dark, he couldn't make out details. The street was momentarily shadowed as something went between him and the quarter moon overhead.

A cloud, Chris decided, and pressed on.

The closer he got to the entrance to the Keep, the slower he walked. There was a terrible smell in the air that even the brisk breeze of a moment earlier had failed to scrub away, fetid and stale and acrid, like rotting meat. By the time he reached the hole, it was almost too powerful to stand. But he knelt and shone the penlight he'd brought from home down into the opening. He could see nothing.

Quit screwing around, you're going to have to go down there, might as well get to it.

This time, he found it difficult to get his feet positioned on the ladder; they kept sliding off the rung. He reached down with one hand and gingerly felt along the side of the concrete hole. It came back moist, and slick, his fingers covered in a thick, grey fluid that reminded him of the stuff snails trailed behind them when they moved.

Still he levered himself over the side, trying to avoid slipping on the stuff. Despite his efforts, his hands and feet were covered with gunk by the time he reached bottom.

Chris switched on the penlight.

Everything was there, exactly the way it had been before: the high seat, the magazines, the food containers . . .

the yearbook.

He hurried across the floor and picked it up. It shifted awkwardly in his hand, as though something had been crammed inside. *Look at it later*, he thought. He swept the light in a circle, half-expecting to see Roger come out of the shadows.

But this time the place felt truly abandoned. Maybe he's left for real this time, Chris wondered, but if so, then why leave all his stuff behind? Unless he went away for just a while, he thought, in which case, why leave everything out in the open?

Maybe he's not worried anymore about being caught. Maybe he doesn't care.

Chris backed up, reaching behind him for the first rung of the steps. He stuck the penlight and the yearbook in his jacket, and started climbing. He reached the top and stumbled out of the hole. *I did it*, he thought. *I did it, I did it, I did it!*

He pulled out the yearbook. Whatever had been stuffed into the middle of the book fell, glittering, to the dirt. Chris stooped to pick it up.

It was a policeman's badge, the letters L.A.P.D. smeared with peanut butter. *Better give this to Susan, too*, Chris thought. It might mean something.

He paused long enough to open the yearbook and leaf through it, needing to convince himself that the red circles and X's had been there, that he hadn't just imagined them. Once he showed them to Susan and Mr. Edwards, they'd have to believe him. There had been ten circles, and ten kids had been—

Chris stopped, frozen by what he saw in the yearbook.

There were more than ten circles; more than twenty.

Every picture on one page was circled in red.

Every picture on the next page was circled.

Every picture on *every* page was circled in red.

He flipped through it, a feeling of dread squeezing the breath out of his chest. *It can't be, oh jeez, no, it can't be.*

Then, suddenly, the lights in the lot went out, all at once.

Chris snapped the yearbook closed. The darkness closed in like a living thing, so thick that he could barely see his hand.

The streetlamps that moments before had thrown light over the fence had also gone black.

As had the neon signs, the stoplights, and the lights in buildings and offices.

Blackout.

8

Susan was less than a quarter-mile from Gene's house when the lights went out. Instantly, the traffic halted.

Great, she thought, tapping impatiently on the wheel, *some jerk with a backhoe hit another power line.* She rested her elbow on the open window and looked up past the line of cars.

From here, she should be able to see a good part of the skyline, but it was completely dark. She'd assumed the power interruption was local, covering only a few blocks. But if it was anything more wide-spread . . . She remembered reports of the New York blackout of two decades earlier. Looting, assaults, stores sitting vulnerable without alarms, impossible traffic.

She craned her head out the window, but the streets and buildings were dark for as far as she could see. Weren't they supposed to put in safeguards to make sure this kind of thing could never happen again? she thought. Your utility company—love 'em or burn 'em to the ground.

There was the sound of a crash from somewhere ahead. She could just make out two cars, a Volvo and a Toyota, joined at the front bumper in the middle of the intersection. More cars joined the chorus of horns. She considered lending a hand, but she had changed into her civvies back at the station. Besides, she could hear sirens closing in on the intersection; other units would be there in a minute.

To her right, she noticed an alley barely wide enough for her car to fit through. If she were lucky, it would take her out on a less-crowded street.

She turned into the alley. It was strewn with garbage and old newspapers, the smell of alcohol and stale urine strong between the enclosing walls. She rolled up the windows and drove slowly forward. Halfway down the block, she stopped in front of a dumpster that sat off to one side; it jutted far enough into the alley that there wasn't enough room for her to squeeze past.

Terrific, she thought, and got out of the car. The floor of the alley was slippery, and the smell was even worse this close to the dumpster. She rapped against the rusted metal side. Half-full, she guessed. Should be able to push it back.

Something moved in the alley.

She froze. Listened. There was not one sound, but many, a whisper of movement against asphalt, as though the night had sighed. She strained into the dark but could see nothing.

"You shouldn't go into somebody's home without asking permission."

She spun around at the sound of the voice, coming from a spot somewhere behind her. A young voice, strained and intense. She caught a flash of movement in the moonlight: a figure, quick and feral, his skin so pale it was almost translucent. "Not nice," he said, "not nice at all." Then he disappeared into the shadows.

The sound of movement returned, louder now, a rustling of unseen shapes all around her.

Susan backed toward the car. She could see nothing—but she had the awful sense of being stalked, watched. She was no more than a foot from the car when another sound came: the whisper of escaping air. There were deep tears in the sides of the tires.

She ducked into the car and snared the revolver she had laid on the passenger seat, holding it in both hands. "Police," she said, her voice firm. "Come on out of there."

They did.

They boiled up from the sewers that carried away refuse from the alley, surged up from the shadows, dropped from boarded-up windows and hit the ground with a roll and clatter. Brown and black and hard and shiny, they moved forward in a mass that swelled toward her like a solid wave.

She got off six shots in six seconds, emptying the chambers, blowing momentary holes in the mass that sealed up instants later as others moved up to fill the gaps.

She worked her way to the trunk where she kept additional clips, aware that now the sound was also coming from behind her, blocking the only hope she had of escape: the alley mouth that led back to the street.

They were nearly to the front of the car when she reached the trunk and popped the lid. She grabbed the clips even knowing they would do no good.

She could hear them now, on the hood of the car. Scrabbling across. In another second they would be on her.

She saw the pool cue.

Thirty-seven times stronger than steel ... withstands the hardest break shot without vibrating ... graphite molding ... one hundred percent straight ...

She snatched it out of the trunk just as the first one dived at her. She connected with a solid *crack* that rattled her to her marrow. It slammed into the wall, fell to the ground, and righted itself, moving slower now.

She glanced to the alley mouth. *Seventy feet*, she estimated. She stuck the revolver in the back of her belt and hefted the pool cue.

Go!

She ran, swinging the cue wildly in front of her as they launched themselves at her, swung and connected, swung and connected, fifty feet, and they snatched at her clothes, hung on until she lashed out with the butt of the cue, and they fell and surged forth again, clawing at her, thirty feet, snatching at her legs, and she ran, and for every one she hit another slashed at her face, her hands, and blood ran down her arms, the cuts not deep, not yet, but painful, but she didn't let go of the stick, wouldn't let go, twenty feet, staggered forward, and they were everywhere, and she was yelling now, incoherent, a sound born of fury and madness and pain and ten feet and they flew at her face and they would not have her five feet they would not have her they would not have her—

"*Damn you!*" she screamed and lunged out of the alley mouth into the street, staggering out—

—and into the path of a van that rushed forward out of nowhere. She dived out of the way as the van raced by, never slowing. Still clutching the pool cue as she spun around to face the alley mouth, she automatically snatched the revolver from her belt.

Nothing followed. She gulped air, straining to see into the darkness, but there was nothing there, nothing there at all.

Is this what happened to Jordan? she thought. *Would they have gotten me in there? Or did they want to drive me out into the street, in front of a car, they'd probably think it was suicide or something god oh god what* were *they, what—*

"Freeze!"

A cop stood silhouetted against the light of the passing cars, both hands wrapped around a revolver. "Drop it!"

She realized how she must look, disheveled, a pool cue in one hand and a revolver in the other. "It's—it's okay," she said. "I'm a cop."

"*Drop it,*" he said again. Of course there would be no way for him to believe her. She set the gun and the pool cue down on the sidewalk and assumed the position. He edged forward and kicked the gun away. "Cop, huh?"

"My shield's in my jacket pocket," she said.

He reached in and withdrew the slim leather pouch. Flipped it open. "No shit," he said. Then he noticed the blood on her arms. "What happened?"

"I'm not sure," she said. "Somebody jumped me back in the alley. I think he got away." There was little point in trying to tell him what had actually happened; she wasn't entirely sure herself.

He stepped back. "Whole damn town's going crazy. Blacked out all over the place. You need an ambulance?"

"You got a first aid kit?"

"Sure."

"That'll do. And I need a ride. My car's all busted up."

"I'll see what I can do," he said.

She waited until he was gone, and then glanced back into the alley, shivering. Only now, when she was out of immediate danger, did the impact of what had happened begin to take its toll. *What were they? What the hell's going on?*

Then she remembered the kid.

You shouldn't go into somebody's home without asking permission.

His name swam up out of the darkness, and she began to suspect that she should have believed Chris after all.

9

His father was pissed off at him, but that was nothing new. David Anderson knew music and writing, not gas heaters, and would just be in the way. Besides, it would only be a matter of time before they reopened school; he was determined to put in as much time practicing as possible. Working by flashlight—another damn power failure—he backed up the portable tape deck and got it recording as he tried some more chords on the guitar, humming through the lyrics he hadn't worked out yet.

He stopped the recorder. Backed it up again. Hit PLAY. But there was no guitar sound on the tape, only his voice, barely audible, talking rather than singing. Puzzled, he turned up the volume, straining to catch the words.

Get out, get out of the house, put down the guitar, for Christ's sake, run, oh god, run, get out of there, get out of there!

Then he noticed the smell of gas, too late, as something down-stairs exploded, and the floor rocked beneath him, and there was fire everywhere, everywhere.

10

"Can I come use your bathroom?"

Susan stood unsteadily in the doorway. Blood was caked on her face and arms, and her blouse was torn.

Gene stepped aside. "Jesus, what happened? Are you all right?"

She nodded without slowing. "Just give me a minute."

He followed her through the candle-lit apartment to the bath-room, where she stripped off the torn blouse and washed the dried blood off her skin. "You got a shirt I can borrow?"

He pulled a checked work shirt off a hanger and handed it to her. "Are you sure you're okay? I can call an ambulance—"

"No. They're needed out there. I'm all right." She glanced up at him, and her gaze wavered. "I'm just—I'm just real glad to be here."

She came to him, and he held her until she stopped shaking. Starting slowly, she told him what had happened. Her injuries made compelling evidence. He could feel her shiver through the thick shirt.

Finally, she kissed him, then pulled away. Ran a hand through her hair. "I need a phone. And some coffee. Badly."

"You've got it."

It was ten minutes later when she hung up and accepted the cup of coffee. "Thanks."

"Be glad it's a gas stove," he said, "or we'd be out of luck. So, how bad is it out there?"

"Bad," she said. "When you're in a city, you like to think you're invulnerable, but the fact is, any city has four major soft spots—food, water, electricity, and traffic. Cut off any of them, and you're screwed. . . .

"About a year ago, an expert on terrorism gave a talk to the department. He said all you'd have to do to bring Los Angeles to a stop would be to cut off the power, and cut off access on five, maybe six major streets that lead to the freeway. Traffic backs up, gridlock sets in, and suddenly ambulances can't get where they're supposed to, fires burn and nobody can do anything about it."

"That's what's happening now?"

"And then some," Susan said. "The lines at the station are flooded with calls for help. Had to use the private line to my own desk to get someone to answer. They'd tried to reach me at home. They're calling up everyone on emergency duty, trying to restore some order out there. Good luck."

"What about you?" he asked, but before she could answer, there was a knock at the door. Susan already had her revolver beside her.

"Check it out," she whispered, "but be careful. Even if it isn't more of those things, it might be trouble. There's looting all over the place."

Gene walked to the door. "Who is it?"

"It's me." Chris. "I've got to see you!"

Gene opened the door, and Chris rushed in, his face covered with dirt and sweat. "I got it," he said, talking very fast, "I got it, I got the proof, you got to help me, I got the proof now."

"Okay, okay, take it easy," Gene said.

"Are you all right?" Susan asked.

"It's bad out there," he said, his eyes wide and scared. "I got on a bus, but two guys got on and held up the driver, it was nuts, and I dived out the back window, but I think they stabbed him, I'm not sure. And the cars, it's—"

"It's all right, you're here now, you're safe."

"Maybe. Maybe not." He took a parcel from under his arm. "Here. See for yourself."

Susan opened it; Gene peered over her shoulder at the pages. Each one of the student photos had been circled in red. "I thought you said only the victims were circled."

"I did. Don't you get it? He's after *everybody* now! The whole damn school! You've got to stop him! Here, look!"

He grabbed the yearbook, and flipped to the front. The first four photos had X's through the red circles: Jim Abinetti, Cathy Alvarez, Lupita Amador, Mark Anda—

Then suddenly, as they watched, a red X appeared in the middle of the circle over David Anderson.

"Shit!" Susan said. She threw the yearbook down on the sofa.

"You saw it, didn't you?" Chris said. His voice cracked. "Another one, right? Another X. Every time he hits somebody, an X appears. He's going alphabetically!"

Susan knelt down in front of him. "Where is he, Chris?"

"I don't know—"

"Is he where you showed us before?"

"*I don't know!* Maybe. He wasn't there when I went by before, maybe he's back now! But you've got to stop him, you've got to do something!"

"We will. Did you find anything else when you were there? Anything that could help us?"

He dug in his shirt pocket, came up with the badge. "Just this."

He handed it to her.

She said nothing. Closed her hand over it. Walked off a pace.

"What is it?" Gene asked.

Her voice was unsteady. "Jordy. This was Jordy's. They never found his shield. Gene, *they never found his shield.*"

She choked back tears, and when she turned again to Chris, her voice was firm, and cold with determination. "We need to get back to the tunnel. We were only there once, and I'm not sure I could find it at night, let alone during a blackout. Do you think you can lead us back there?"

He didn't waver. "Yeah. But I want you to call my mom first, make sure she's okay. Tell her I'm with you, and that I'm all right."

"Done," Susan said. "Gene, can we take your car?"

"Sure, but remember, the streets are practically solid cars out there."

"Then we'll drive on the fucking sidewalk, I don't care. This son of a bitch killed Jordy, and I swear to God, Gene, I'm going to nail his head to the wall."

She stalked out of the room, her lip trembling.

"What's your phone number, Chris?" he asked.

Chris told him, and Gene dialed. As the line rang at the other end, he glanced at the yearbook, drawn to the next face in the alphabetical row of photos. A girl.

11

Mary Aposhian waited upstairs while her father went down into the basement to find the candles and flashlights. He didn't come out for a long time. When she finally followed him, to see what was taking him so long, she heard nothing except a sigh of motion as the darkness uncoiled and hurled itself at her.

Red Circle.

12

The suburban streets around Gene's apartment were quiet. In the windows they could see silhouettes of neighbors visible against candle light and lanterns. *Waiting for someone to give them permission to go back to their lives,* Susan thought.

Chris was in the back, Gene driving. She loaded her revolver. She'd talked the cop who found her into retrieving the extra clips and a few other items from her car, one of which was back in its sleek leather case on the back seat.

They drove past storefronts with stoved-in doors and shattered display windows, past bonfires burning in garbage bins and trash scattered all over the street. Electronics stores, department stores, supermarkets, record stores, all lay gutted alongside the road. They passed a Sav-On pharmacy, of which little remained but the walls. The front had been completely demolished in the rush of looters and addicts to get what was inside.

How long would the blackout last? Susan wondered. The dispatcher had said the utility crews were working as fast as they could, but a lot of the major power lines had been totally disconnected. *Just got a call a little while ago, and they said some of the cables looked as though they'd been chewed through,* he'd said. *Jesus, that must've been some kinda rat!*

Susan doubted it was a rat; had, in fact, a pretty good idea what had chewed through those lines.

The question was, why?

Maybe he wants so much havoc, so much chaos, that nobody'll notice what's happening with the kids until it's too late.

On the other hand, maybe he's enjoying this.

"Hey!" Gene said.

Someone dashed out of a store, caught momentarily in the headlights. He carried a small portable TV, still sporting a bright yellow price tag, and glared at them with the disdain one shows a potential competitor for the few spoils left thus far unclaimed.

"Pretty brazen, huh?" Gene said.

"Why not? Who's going to stop him?"

Chris sat forward from the back seat. "Right up ahead, then right again."

"Got it," Gene said, and turned onto another street.

It was deserted, no pedestrians, no looters, no cars.

"Hold it!" Susan said.

Gene stopped. "What's wrong?"

"I don't like the looks of it. There ought to be cars around."

Gene drummed his fingers on the wheel. "You want to double back? We can find another way."

Susan chewed her lip. It *didn't* look right. But doubling back would cost them time. "Okay, give it a try. But slow. And if I yell, punch it."

"Okay." Gene guided the car forward.

They were just past the middle of the block when suddenly there were voices all around them, screaming. Gang members ran out of the surrounding buildings, armed with chains and baseball bats, charging the car—

"Hit it!" Susan yelled.

Gene floored the gas pedal.

A truck backed out of an alley in front of them, to block the way out.

"The sidewalk! Go on!"

Gene whipped the wheel to the left and shot up on the sidewalk, barely getting past the pickup before it could cut off their escape. He glanced up at the rearview mirror. The looters squeezed past the truck and ran after them, throwing bricks and lead pipes. Gene didn't take his foot off the accelerator until they were two blocks away.

Susan switched on the radio. ". . . with looting still reported in the Fairfax district, East Los Angeles, Inglewood, and much of the south side as the blackout now enters its third hour. Police spokesmen are calling this the worst breakout of rioting since the Miami outbreak last year. First aid centers and temporary shelters have been set up at the following locations—in the Palladium in Hollywood, in the Inglewood Civic Auditorium . . ."

Susan felt cold. *All this in three hours*, she thought, and glanced back at Chris. "How many pictures with X's on them now?"

He opened the book again, and sucked his breath. "Seven. He's into the B's now."

"Damn," Susan said. "Gene—"

"I know, I know," Gene said, and jammed down the accelerator.

Five minutes later, they arrived at the lot. Gene reached to switch off the engine when Susan put a hand on his. "No," she said.

"I'm going with you."

"I said no, and I meant it. You've got to keep the car moving. I don't know what we're going to find down there, but we may need to make a fast exit, and it won't do us a bit of good if the car gets stripped."

"I don't like it."

"I'm not real big on it either, but it's the only way." She touched his cheek. "Keep circling the block until we come out, and if we come on the run, get ready to floor it."

She climbed out of the car, Chris following.

"Okay, let's do it," she said.

13

The Keep was deserted, but this time the debris was exactly as Chris had seen it earlier. The wet substance on the walls had dried, leaving a powdery grey-white film behind.

They searched the intersecting tunnel thoroughly, but found nothing.

"He's not here," Chris said at last, disheartened.

"How can you be sure? We thought that earlier, too."

"No. He's gone. You can almost feel the difference."

"Okay, then where to next?"

"I don't know."

"Damn it, Chris, think!"

"I'm trying!"

She slammed a fist into the wall. *"You're not trying hard enough!"*

"So what do you want me to do?"

"I don't know!" She was shaking with anger and frustration. "All I know is every five minutes another X shows up in that damn yearbook. All I know is that that son of a bitch had something to do with my partner being killed, and I want a piece of him for that!"

She stopped, breathing hard, her hands balled into fists. "I'm sorry," she said. "You're doing the best you can. And I appreciate it. I appreciate the risk you're taking. It's just . . . maddening, that's all."

"I know."

She straightened. "All right. Let's get out of this place. You can't think down here, it smells like a morgue."

They headed up the steps. Chris reached the top, pulled himself up on the surface—and someone grabbed him. He was hauled roughly aside, a huge hand clamped over his mouth. He struggled, but it did no good. Susan's head appeared at the lip of the hole. "Chris?"

Someone grabbed her by the hair, yanked her forward. "C'mon out of the hole, bitch! C'mon!"

Two others came out of the shadows. There were four men now. "Sonuvabitch," the one holding Chris said. "You were right!" He looked at Susan. "What were y'doing down there, huh? Playing house with the kid?"

Susan said nothing. The man holding her hair yanked it. "He's talking to you, bitch! Whatsamatter, you only good with boys? Huh? Give you what a man's got, that'll fix your ass good."

Susan shot her head back, straight into the man's face. It hit with an ominous *crack*, then a whuff of escaping air as she slammed an elbow into his gut. He went down hard, and the others started toward her, but in an instant she'd reached behind her back, and the revolver was in her hands.

"Freeze! Police!" she said.

"Shit!" one of them said. "It's a goddamned setup! We're screwed!"

"Let go of the boy!" she said. The man on the ground behind her writhed in pain, his hands cradling his face.

The man holding Chris hesitated. Glanced to the others. "I don't hear no sirens. Do you? I think she's shittin' us. There's no backup. And I still see three of us and one of her. And I got the kid."

Susan cocked the revolver, pointed it past Chris at the man. "I said let him go."

The other two circled toward her on either side.

"Screw you," he said.

Suddenly the man on the ground kicked her behind the leg. She cried out and fell to one knee, the gun still in her hands.

"Get her!" someone yelled.

Then wood exploded behind them, and there was a rush of motion as Gene's car plowed through the fence bordering the lot and crashed toward the nearest of the two men, hitting him head-on. He screamed and went over into the darkness.

"Clear out!" the other yelled, and ran.

"Hey!" Susan called.

The man holding Chris turned.

There was a tremendous blast. Chris thought he'd never heard anything as loud, and suddenly he was free, and the man tumbled to the ground behind him. Chris turned, everything slow, slow, and the man had a hole in the side of his cheek and another, much larger, in the back of his head, and there was blood streaming onto the dirt—

"Chris! Come on!"

Susan pulled him toward the car, practically throwing him into the back. "Go!" she yelled; Gene hit the gas and the car shot forward.

The lot receded back into the night as they bounced over the curb and onto the street.

"Everybody okay?" Gene asked when they had reached a safe distance.

"Pull over," Susan said.

276

"But—"

"Pull over! Now!"

He slammed on the brakes. Susan lurched from the car, managed to get a few feet away, then fell to one knee, throwing up on the sidewalk.

Chris looked at Gene, found him pale and sweating behind the wheel.

I'm going to pass out, Chris thought, as from far away, feeling the world tilt all around him. He fought to hold on. After a moment, he risked a glance to where Susan still knelt beside the road. She was dry-heaving now, nothing left inside her to release. Then she forced herself to her feet and walked unsteadily back to the car.

"You okay?" Gene said.

She avoided his gaze. "Five years," she said, her voice hoarse. "Five years on the force, I never had to shoot anybody before."

"We can rest here a few minutes, if you want."

"No," Susan said, "just . . . give me a second, that's all. I'll be okay." Her face was pale in the moonlight. "So what the hell took you so long, anyway?"

"I was making another circle back. Didn't see what was happening until a couple seconds before I got there." He looked back over the seat. "How about you, Christoph? You okay?"

"I'm—" He glanced up sharply. "Why did you call me that?"

"I thought that's what you preferred. It's what your mother called you when I spoke to her from the apartment."

The horror struck Chris like a knife through his heart, cold and hard and sharp. "Ohmygod, ohmygod—"

"Chris?"

"Christoph! That's what *it* called me! My mom calls me Chris! That's what—oh god—he's at my house! Don't you understand? HE'S AT MY HOUSE! HE'S GOT MY MOM! *HE'S GOT MY MOM!*"

"Jesus!" Susan said. "Hit it!"

Gene launched the car forward.

He's gonna kill her, Chris thought, *and it's my fault, it's my fault, how could I be such an idiot, oh god, please don't let her get killed because of me, please God . . .*

And then another horror struck him: *Who was Gene talking to? Her? Or it?*

What if we're too late?

14

Chris frowned. The street didn't look right. Every house was silent, inner darkness throwing back and renewing the night. Only in his house was there a flickering light.

Maybe they heard about the rioting on the radio and they're keeping low, Chris thought. *And maybe . . .*

He didn't want to think about it.

In the dim car light, he risked another glance inside the yearbook. Four more X's in four more red circles.

"Okay, this is it," Gene whispered, killing the engine.

"Let's take this slow," Susan said. They stepped out on the curb. "Get the stick out."

Gene reached into the back seat and pulled out the pool cue. "You think this'll do any good?"

"It helped me once, might again. If this goes down anything like what I saw before, it's a hell of a lot more use than bullets. I'll hold on to the gun for anything larger."

Anything larger, Chris thought. "You mean Roger?"

"I killed a man for the first time tonight, and if I can avoid doing it again, I will. I'd like to find some other way to handle this." She straightened. "You better stay here for now, Chris."

"Why? You let me go with you before."

"This is different."

"But—" Then he stopped, and in her face he saw her reasoning. *She's afraid I'll see my mom dead and freak out.* "My mom's alive," he said, very firmly. "She's alive and I'm going with you, unless you want to handcuff me to the car."

She glanced over at Gene. "Okay. Break the stick, Gene."

He unscrewed the cue stick, and gave Chris the upper half. She was right; it wasn't much. But at least it had a solid heft to it. Moonlight glinted off the brass ferrule at his end of the stick, and he could just see the word SAW engraved there.

Appropriate, Chris thought.

Susan checked the chambers in her revolver, then snapped it shut. "Okay," she said.

They started toward the house, Susan leading, the gun pointed straight up, pressed tight to her shoulder. Gene followed, then Chris. She paused in front of the porch, staying low, then ran quickly up the two steps to the front door. She stopped, back flush against the wall beside the door. She held the gun in both hands, grip tightening and relaxing, tightening and relaxing.

A signal, and Gene came at the door, fast, and kicked it open. He dived out of the way, and she took his place in the doorway, sighting—

Nothing.

Silence.

Darkness.

She moved back beside the doorway and waved them forward. Gene came up next to her, Chris just behind.

"Stay together, but not too close," she whispered. "For god's sake, don't get separated once we're inside."

She took a step into the house, then stopped. Listened. Moved forward another pace. Whatever light there was upstairs must have been in closed rooms. The downstairs was pitch black. Chris could only barely distinguish Gene and Susan in front of him.

A floorboard creaked upstairs.

Chris heard the brush of cloth as Susan reached for the flashlight at her belt. She switched it on, illuminating a sea of bright silver pinpoints that swam in the darkness all around them.

"Ohmygod," Susan said.

She recognized them first.

Razor blades.

They were in everything, in the floorboards another few feet in front of them, in the walls, the ceiling, the chairs, the sofa, hundreds and hundreds of them, sparkling in the glow of the flashlight, embedded in wood and cloth and plaster, the blades glittering all around them in uneven rows. The windows were boarded up, the wooden planks covered with razor blades.

Then: a sudden blur of movement.

"Watch out!" Chris yelled.

Susan cried out as something struck her hand and bit. The flashlight flew across the room and shattered against the wall.

"Get back!" Susan said. "Hurry!"

Too late.

The door slammed shut behind them.

Something skittered past them on the floor.

Gene fought the lock. "Won't move," he said.

They stood in the dark, knowing what was embedded in the floor all around them, and did not move.

A voice came from somewhere above and in front of them. "Hello, Chris."

Chris froze. "Roger."

"You told." This time the voice came from the other side of the room. *He's moving so we can't get a fix on him.* "I warned you not to do that. I warned you."

"Where's my mom?" Silence. "Damn it, Roger, where's my mom?"

A long pause, then from a nowhere spot near the top of the stairs: "Up here. With me."

A mouth pressed against his ear. "Keep him talking," Susan whispered. He could feel more than see her trying to pick her way forward, maneuvering around the blades.

"Look, Roger, let her go, okay? I admit it, I told, but she didn't do anything. If you're pissed off at somebody, be pissed off at me. Just leave her out of it."

"Warned you," Roger called, and the shadows on the other side of the room echoed back, "warned you."

Then silence.

"Roger?"

Silence.

"Roger? Where are you?"

"Here," he whispered. "Most of me, anyway. The rest of me is . . . elsewhere. Little pieces of me, everywhere." The voice bounced back and forth in the room. "Another one of them just got it, Chris. I can feel it, see it. And *I'm* doing it, Chris. Not the OtherSyde. Me. It just showed me how, helped me. It's like a superconductor, and I'm the power source. Everybody always tried to make me think I was weak, but I'm not! This is me, Chris! This is ME! And I can do anything I want!"

The house shook, not with one jolt, but with a rattle, as though hundreds of things in the house shifted all at once. He could hear movement in the walls, on the ceiling, upstairs—

—*behind him.*

Chris licked his lips.

"It's wonderful, Chris," Roger said from another part of the room. "I can hurt anyone, just the way they hurt me, and it can't be traced back. All I do is . . . *touch* them. And they do something stupid. They fall downstairs, or they get into a car accident, or they forget to turn off the gas." His voice dropped. "Or you get them to climb out on something high, and fall, like your friend, the cop. He told, too. And look what happened to him."

Chris listened for a response from Susan, but she remained silent. Moving forward.

"They don't leave a trace, but the Eaters are real. Oh, yes, very real. Aren't they, Mr. Edwards?"

Chris reached out to Gene. "No," he whispered, "don't touch me. They're all over me."

"They sting, don't they?" Roger said. "And they'll keep on stinging you and stinging you and stinging you. Unless you want to try to shake them off. Come on, run! Maybe they'll fall off."

Gene didn't move, though Chris could hear him moaning. *If he panics, he'll run right into the razors.* Abruptly, the sound stopped.

"Your friend the cop took a lot of bites before he finally fell. Good cop. But I finally shut his mouth. Shut his mouth and filled it good, showed him what I thought, showed him—"

"*Bastard!*" Susan yelled. She fired at the source of the voice.

Three muzzle-flashes illuminated the room like strobes. Roger moved fast, impossibly fast, first here, then over there, and even in the rapid-fire glimpses he was terrible to look at, pale, feral, his eyes wide in the darkness, his body thinner, as though he had been somehow *stretched.* Susan fired a fourth time, and again he was gone; there was only the gunshot and, frozen in the light of the muzzle-flash, something small and gleaming and hard that threw itself at Susan.

Then it was dark again.

She screamed.

Chris heard the gun clatter to the floor a few feet ahead of him.

Chris felt madness clawing behind his eyes. "Stop it!" he yelled, straining to see. "Stop it, stop it, stop it, STOP IT!"

Silence.

"Why should I?" A pause. "If you were my friend, I might think about it. But you're not. You're just like them."

"But I am your friend! Hell, I'm your *only* friend."

"Liar!"

Chris edged forward, trying to feel along the floor with his foot.

"Okay, look, I admit I screwed up when those guys jumped us. I was afraid. But they're gone now, right? You paid them back. Why are you doing all this?"

"You wouldn't understand."

"So make me understand." His sneaker caught on a razor stuck in the floor, which almost cut through to his foot.

This time the voice came from the same place as it had a moment before. "If I could make you understand, would you come with me?"

"With you where?"

"Where I'm going. I think you'd like it there. You'd understand then. They like you. They always said they liked you."

"Who's—"

Chris cried out.

A razor sliced through his sneaker and into the soft tissue between his toes. His crouched instinctively, and his knee grazed another razor. He cried out again.

"Chris?" Roger said.

Chris moaned, trying to fight down panic. He hadn't heard a sound from Gene or Susan since the shots. But he couldn't think about that now, couldn't afford it.

Pushing the pain away, he reached across the floor, fingers dancing across blades. It had to be there somewhere . . .

"Chris? You all right?"

"I'm cut," Chris said. *Where was Roger?*

"I'm sorry," Roger said. "I'm sorry it had to go this way. But if you'll listen, maybe there's still a chance."

Chris reached as far forward as he could. *C'mon, c'mon!*

At last his hands found something cold and hard.

"I never *wanted* to hurt you, Chris. You know that, don't you?"

The revolver. His hands closed on it, shaking violently. "Yeah, I know."

He stood. Slowly. As a form moved through the darkness, and he could feel more than see the approach, a pale luster against the absolute dark. A hint of yellowed eyes, so large. "I mean, you're still my friend, right?"

Chris tried to answer, but the words didn't come.

"Chris? Are you my friend?"

"Yes, Roger," Chris said, his voice barely audible. "I'm your friend. I'll always be your friend."

He pulled the trigger.

The gun erupted in his hands, almost knocking him over. He glimpsed Roger's face for the flicker of a second it was illuminated by the flash, directly in front of him. In his eyes was surprise, and pain, and madness. Then the darkness rushed in.

Roger screamed.

It rose higher and higher, ending finally not in a moan or silence but in a crash of glass from somewhere upstairs.

"Mom!" Chris cried, and suddenly the lights went on.

He saw at last where he was standing, in the middle of the floor, razors extending away in every direction. He turned at the sound of gagging. Gene was on one knee on the floor behind him, coughing up something brown and viscous that seemed to move for a moment before dissolving into the wood. Susan struggled to reach him, tearing at one of the things that still clung to her face, half-dissolved, its surface like rotting meat. She ripped it off and sucked in air.

"Is he okay?" Chris asked.

She stood behind Gene, reached her arms around his stomach, and pulled in, sharply. Gene coughed more of the brown matter out onto the floor. Chris could hear air going in now as well as coming out.

"I think so," Susan said, ignoring the blood coming from bites on her own hands and face. "Go on, we're okay, check on your mom."

Chris ran for the stairs, ignoring the pain that lanced up from his foot. He took the steps two at a time until he reached the second floor. "Mom?" Her door at the far end of the hall was closed. "Mom!"

He threw open the door. The room was a shambles, the curtains torn, the bedsheets ripped, every glass and mirror in the room shattered. She wasn't there. "Mom?"

Something moved inside the closet.

He opened it just a crack, enough to let the light in.

Dressed in her robe, his mother sat cross-legged on the floor, staring downward, eyes fixed and unwavering. Both arms were wrapped tightly around her shoulders, and she rocked slowly back and forth.

He knelt in front of her, touched her shoulder.

She looked up, slowly, as though pulling herself from someplace far away. Gradually her gaze fixed on him. ". . . Chris?"

Then she fell forward, embracing him, sobbing, and Chris held her, feeling tears on his own cheeks as well.

15

Susan stood by the door, watching as the paramedics carried Chris's mother and Gene toward the ambulance. Even with the lights back on again, it had been difficult to turn up an ambulance not already in use, but the request had been expedited by informing the dispatcher that she was a cop, that these people were crucial to an investigation, and that if he didn't have an ambulance there within six minutes she'd have his ass in a sling for the rest of his natural life.

The ambulance had gotten there in five.

She stood aside as they were loaded inside the back. Gene was at last breathing regularly, though his throat was still raw. They had tried to get her, too, the same way they'd gotten Gene and Jordy. But she had clamped her mouth shut, tried to pull them off her face whenever they got a grip. She shuddered at the recollection of those bony, pointed claws, scratching at her lips, which were now sore and bloodied. Chris's mother didn't seem to remember anything of what had happened. The paramedics figured it was probably shock. That made her one of the lucky ones.

Could've been worse. A hell of a lot worse.

It wasn't over yet. Not entirely.

Roger was still out there, and there was no telling if he was dying, dead, or merely wounded, waiting to strike back.

Chris limped in from the other room. The medics had bandaged his foot and given him a tetanus shot. Susan had wanted him patched up. She needed him to finish the job.

"How's the foot?" she asked.

"I'll live," he said, and winced. "Did you call the police?"

"Second call I made. I checked the last red X in that book and sent them to the homes of the next five kids on the list, figuring that he might've started something but didn't have the chance to finish it before you nailed him."

"You think it'll do any good?"

"Yes. I just called back, and they said they've already found a couple of the kids hurt, but still alive. Another half hour, and it would've been different. At least there's only a handful of them, and we've got a chance to help them."

"Is that why you didn't call it in earlier? Because there were too many of them?"

She sighed. "There was no way they could protect every single kid in the book. By the time they got to any of them, the next one would be in danger, and they'd never catch up. Now that's changed. What we've got to do now is make sure it doesn't change back."

She took his arm. "You up for a little traveling?"

"Why? Where to?"

"You tell me. Roger's gone. My bet is he won't go back to his— well, his *place*, since we know where that is. He's not here. So he must be somewhere else. Is there anyplace else he'd go, where he'd feel safe? Another hideout?"

Chris shook his head, then stiffened slightly, as if remembering something.

"You got an idea?"

"No," he said after a moment. "I don't know where he'd go." He winced. "This bandage is killing me. Let me go adjust it real fast, okay?"

"All right. And while you're at it, keep thinking. If there's any place else we can check, let's do it, and fast."

"Gotcha," Chris said, and disappeared into the back of the house.

Susan stepped to the door and watched the ambulance pull away, running lights and sirens. Gene and Chris's mother would be okay. Thank god for that.

Then she headed toward the back bathroom. The door was locked. She knocked. "C'mon, Chris, we gotta go."

No answer.

"Chris?" She tried the door again.

Great, she thought. *NOW what?* She backed up a few paces, then kicked the door beneath the knob. The door flew back.

Chris was gone.

The window stood open, a light breeze rustling the curtains.

"Damn," Susan said. "*Damn it.*"

He *did* know something after all.

16

With the lights back on, the streets looked almost normal, except for the broken shop windows, the debris, and the roving squad cars. Even a few buses were back on the street.

Chris caught one of them, and got off a block from the school.

The blackout had not been kind to it.

The façade of the main building was covered with eggs and toilet paper, and some of the windows had been broken. He squeezed through an opening in the chain-link fence and headed for the gym.

If Roger was still alive, he would be there.

Is there anyplace else he'd go, where he'd feel safe? Susan had asked. *Another hideout?* And he'd remembered the times they'd stayed in the gym after school had let out, to give Steve and the Dumbass Deathsquad time to get bored waiting for them to show.

So long ago, Chris thought.

He tried the rusted back door they had used to get in and out; it pulled free with a racket. When he let go of the knob, Chris looked at his hand. There was blood on it.

Old blood.

He stepped inside, closing the door after him, and was swallowed again into darkness.

You're crazy, he thought. *You're out of your fucking mind to come here alone. He could as easily kill you as look at you.*

Maybe.

But he had seen it through this far. If he were lucky, Roger's influence had ended when he was shot. The lights coming on, and the attacks stopping, were indications of that. He hadn't wanted to do what he did to Roger. He owed it to Roger to try and make up for it, to try and help, one last time.

And let him help you right into a grave.

He stifled the voice in his head and moved on through the storage room into the gymnasium.

He found the light switch and brought the dimmers up slowly.

A single light came up gradually in the middle of the gym. The walls bled off into a darkness that stepped down the opened bleachers into center court.

Roger sat on the floor, huddled back against the bleachers, arms wrapped around his midsection. His pale eyes squinted against the light. "Too bright . . ."

Chris brought the light down. "Better?"

Roger nodded. A soft moan escaped his lips.

Chris stepped across the gym, his footsteps echoing, and sat beside Roger. Roger's eyes were closed, and he rocked back and forth.

It reminded Chris of the way he'd found his mother, and for a moment he felt a flash of anger, but it didn't last.

Roger was bleeding, though what was coming out didn't look right. It looked like blood after it had started drying, after the life had been leached from it. Pale, almost powdery.

"I knew you'd come," Roger said, and shuddered with pain.

"I'm sorry," Chris said.

"It's okay," Roger said, and exhaled sharply. Chris couldn't tell if it was a gasp of pain or a stifled laugh. "They—they said it was part of the process. They just—didn't tell me it would hurt so much."

"I can get an ambulance—"

"No. Too . . . late for that. I can feel it inside. Everything's all . . . soft. Feels like it could just slip away if I close my eyes . . ."

Chris looked toward the banners strung across the ceiling, tears stinging his eyes. "Damn it," he said, *"why?"*

"Told you . . . you wouldn't understand." Another shudder.

"Understand what?"

Roger's eyes were wide, golden, melting. "It asked me . . . what I wanted. What I wanted more than anything else in the world. I thought . . . I thought it was to get even. I thought it was getting back at . . . at the creeps. But that wasn't it. Wasn't it at all . . . ."

His head lolled slightly to one side.

"Roger!"

He straightened, as though coming out of a long slumber. "Cold. It's cold in here, isn't it, Chris?"

The room was stifling. "Yeah," Chris said, softly. "It's cold."

"I wanted to *belong*, Chris. That's all. Just . . . *belong* somewhere. It said, it said it could do that. But I had to show them . . . show them I was perfect. Had to show them I belonged."

He reached out, and put a hand on Chris's leg. It felt light, like a dry branch. "I'm not the first," he whispered. "It told me all their names. Oh, you'd know them, Chris. You'd know all of them. They proved they could do it. Proved . . . they belonged. Don't you understand? *That's how it grows.* It . . . it's like a skin graft. It looks for a perfect match, and then, at the end . . ."

He shuddered. Chris reached to him, but couldn't bring himself to touch the pale skin.

"Thought . . . I'd have a little more time. I guess I was wrong.

287

Don't . . . don't feel bad for me. They said"—another tremor—"they said it would have to happen like this for me to finish, to prove, to prove . . ."

He hesitated. "If anyone had to do it, I'm . . . I'm glad it was you. Better than a . . . stranger."

Then he doubled over, eyes clenched tight in pain.

"Roger?"

The voice came out barely a whisper. "You'd better go now. They're here. And you . . . you don't belong."

Chris could hear them. He'd been vaguely aware of another sound building for a while, and now he saw them. Forms, shadows shifting beneath the bleachers, peering out at them. Waiting.

Chris stood.

"Go," Roger whispered. "Hurry."

Chris looked down at Roger, now suddenly so small, broken, and in his eyes he saw a flicker of the Roger he had known.

"I'll miss you," Chris said, no longer bothering to conceal the tears.

"Ditto," Roger said. "Egg-zactly."

Chris hurried toward the door, aware of the shadows pressing in around him, never looking back.

Roger watched Chris go. He *was* a good friend.

But now he had more. So many more.

They came down to welcome him, to embrace him. He struggled to his knees and held his hands out to them, letting the last of the blood flow freely. And he saw that the faces that had been forming so slowly, so carefully, were now at last complete.

They were his face, multiplied a hundred, a thousand times.

They whispered to him, and they praised, and they pressed in around him until they were all he could see, and they touched him, and he offered himself up to their love, to their embrace.

I love you, he thought at them, weeping, and they took his tears away, and touched his mind, and murmured their love in return.

Perfect, they called him. *Perfect.*

Roger smiled, and closed his eyes.

And belonged.

EPILOGUE

By the end of the week, the mess resulting from the blackout had been cleared up. The controversy would not die down for a long time, though. Chris followed the news as much as he could. It had turned into a major scandal. Utility companies were brought before the city council and asked to explain how such a thing could be allowed to happen, what had gone wrong with their safeguards, on and on and on.

The utility people had no answers, because there were none to give. None that would make any sense, anyway.

Worst of all was the list of casualties. Over a dozen people injured in the rioting. Two fatal heart attacks. Countless auto accidents. Two deaths due to the failure of vital medical equipment.

Ten high school students dead.

Three more badly injured.

All of them from Lennox High.

The school was still in a state of mourning. It opened special classes to help students work through their grief. Dan Rather gave a whole five minutes to the story on the "CBS Evening News." *Where did the system fail?* he asked. *What can we learn from this tragic incident to prevent it ever from happening again?*

What indeed? Chris thought.

The deaths that occurred before the blackout also made the news, but no one ever put the two together. A couple of local newspapers ran stories commenting only on the fact that for one reason or another, juvenile suicides always seemed to come in groups.

And wasn't *that* an interesting statistic? Chris wondered.

At least his mother was recovering. She remembered almost nothing from that night—for the best, Chris decided. Otherwise there would be too many questions, all nearly impossible to answer. The doctors said she could go back to work in a few days.

Susan came by a day after it ended and asked for the yearbook, the notes, everything. She told him the police had found a notebook in Roger's Keep. He'd asked if they were going to release the full story. She hadn't answered him. After that she never came by again. Last he'd heard, she was putting together statistics on other suicides around the country, and the thought made him even more curious about what else she'd found in Roger's Keep.

He had a feeling it would never be over for her.

He was sure she didn't believe him about Roger. When he'd taken her to the gym, there had been nothing there. They never found a trace of Roger.

He didn't blame her for not believing him, but it was unfortunate.

He wondered what was in the notebook.

He wondered if they would ever tell him what they found.

He doubted it.

Mr. Edwards came back to class after a few days sick leave. Since then, he seemed determined to treat Chris as though he were made of crystal. Eventually he'd have to talk to Gene, and ask him to stop before the other kids noticed.

It wouldn't be easy, though.

Gene never talked about what happened. Not even when they were alone.

Never.

And maybe he was right.

That's how it grows, Roger had said in his final moments in the gym. Since that night, Chris had repeatedly run the scene through his head, trying to unravel that statement. He knew from what he'd studied that everything evolved—people, animals, insects.

He wondered sometimes if the OtherSyde was evolving. And if so, into what?

Put it out of your mind, Chris thought, and tried to concentrate on his homework.

He guessed he had made the transition back to normal better than either Edwards or Susan. Maybe it was because he had seen it all from the inside. Maybe it was because he had been able to make his peace with Roger. Maybe—

Get back to work, he thought, and glanced down at the assignment sheet.

NAME THREE CONTEMPORARIES OF POPE INNOCENT III AND DEFINE THEIR RELATIONSHIPS.

He wrote, KING JOHN OF ENGLAND, PHILIP AUGUSTUS OF FRANCE, FREDERICK II OF GERMANY.

His mother entered the dining room and sat at the other end of the table. She said nothing. These days she seemed constantly preoccupied, as though trying to form a thought that didn't quite seem to fit right in her head.

She was doing that even now, looking past his head to a spot on the wall, drumming her fingers on the table.

Chris went back to his homework.

Tap. Pause. Tap. Tap tap-tap.

He glanced up sharply. His mother was rapping just one finger on the table, her face vacant.

Tap-tap-tap. Tap-tap. Tap-pause-tap-tap.

He recognized it, and automatically began to decode.

Hello, Christoph.

He dropped his pencil.

We required a place to stay. Just for a little while. We thought you wouldn't mind.

"Get away from her," Chris said. "Leave her alone."

Already done. Too bad. You could have been perfect.

A pause. *You're no fun anymore.*

Then: *Going now.*

"Going . . . where?" Chris asked. "And who are you? Who's 'we?' "

Silence for a moment. Then: *Going to and fro in the earth, and walking up and down in it.*

Then a longer pause, and in the moment just before his mother looked up, freed at last from its influence, came the reply:

Roger says hello.

2

At eleven-seventeen P.M., on a side street in an industrial section of south Chicago, a pay phone rang.

There was no one there to answer it.

It continued ringing.

It rang until seven thirty-five A.M., when the receiver was lifted by a man in a hurry, a man who wanted nothing more than to call his office and tell them why he was going to be late.

He pressed the receiver to his ear.

And heard a sound like distant thunder, growing close.

The first handwritten signs began appearing on telephone poles and construction barriers in Kankakee three days later.